Haunt Me

An Immortal Vices and Virtues Novel

Amanda Pillar

Maatkare Books

Haunt Me

Amanda Pillar

Published by Maatkare Books Copyright © 2022 Amanda Pillar

Immortal Vices and Virtues universe Copyright © 2022 Kel Carpenter LLC.

Edited by: Analisa Denny and Pete Kempshall

Proofread by: Dominique Laura

Cover design by Yocla Designs

Photography by Lindee Robinson

Models featured: David and Kailey

In loving memory of Saxon. The best cat that ever catted. And the most patient cat in the world. I miss you more than words can say. Thank you for choosing me as your mom.

"*Death must be so beautiful. To lie in the soft brown earth, with the grasses waving above one's head, and listen to silence. To have no yesterday, and no to-morrow. To forget time, to forget life, to be at peace.*"— Oscar Wilde

CHAPTER I

SABRINA

Fourteen months earlier...

W hy did she think pretending to be human was a good idea? It sucked. Which was a damned shame, because all Sabrina Fhearchair had ever wanted, was to be 'normal'.

She blamed the media for it. It had been romanticized in those old-school movies she'd watched. In the books she'd read. They hadn't focused on the nitty-gritty of what it meant to have a human life, and none of the representations had shown what it was like to live in a world where magic ruled. Still...she thought it would have been better than this, that she would have been treated better—

"You!" a woman yelled from two tables over. "Come here!"

—and, that's exactly what she meant.

Sabrina sighed. The customer whose order she was already taking, a shifter, rolled his eyes, and she glanced over at the shouting lady who was seated—alone—in a six-person booth.

Great. She was taking up space someone else could be using. Saying that, the lunch hour at the House and Gem Inn wasn't exactly busy.

The woman jabbed a finger in Sabrina's direction. "You."

"One ribeye, rare, and a pint of pale ale," Sabrina repeated back to the shifter. "Was that all?"

"Yep," he said, tapping his tanned fingers on the table. He wore a silver ring that boasted a banded green-and-purple stone. Fluorite. "If I were you, I'd get your ass over there. Witches don't like to be ignored."

"Thanks." She gave him a quick smile—not too friendly, not too fake—and tucked her notepad into her apron, then headed over to the shouter. Sabrina tried to keep her interactions with the supernaturals around her as brief as possible. She had to be careful; one swipe of an enraged shifter's paw, or one bite from a careless vampire, was enough to kill her. And if she died here...

Better not to think about that.

Death was too close, as it was.

Hopefully the witch wasn't annoyed at her. She'd heard plenty of stories about curses gone wrong. She did *not* need an incurable form of genital warts, or something even worse.

"Hi ma'am, how can I help you today?" Sabrina tried to mix the right amount of chirpiness with servitude. She kept her uneasiness out of her voice and off her face.

Never show weakness.

"You can sit down." The woman scowled. She had long brown hair that was partly tied back with a bandana, and blue eyes so pale they appeared gray. They were lined with kohl and thick mascara, offset by red lips that Sabrina thought might be natural in color. The witch looked to be in her thirties, but she could be a hundred years old. The air around her buzzed and shimmered a little, making Sabrina's skin tingle.

She'd always been able to 'see' magic, but magic that had been used, not magical *people*. *She must be pretty powerful...*

The woman's clothes were well-made, and she had a kind of boho chic look about her. A dark-red scarf patterned with silver thread was draped over a navy blouse, which billowed in a breeze that didn't exist. She was playing with a deck of tarot cards.

Not a good sign.

"Thank you for the invitation, but I have a couple orders I need to hand over. What can I get you?" Sabrina tried her server's smile again.

"The cards have a few things you need to know," the woman said, ignoring the comment entirely.

Sabrina's gaze flicked down to the tarot deck. "I can't afford to pay you."

Hopefully that would dissuade her. Nothing in this world came for free, especially magic. And Sabrina didn't particularly want to know anything about her future. She could already predict it, and she didn't need it all laid out for her, removing any hope she might develop.

Those pale eyes—wolf eyes on a witch's face—turned hard. "Sit down."

Sabrina glanced toward the bartender, who was also the shift manager; he gave her a subtle nod, which Sabrina took as consent. Nibbling on her lip, she sat, clasping her hands together on top of the shiny wooden tabletop.

Beware witches bearing fortunes.

Everybody else around her seemed to be working hard at pretending they weren't listening in. Great. She had an audience.

The witch flicked her fingers, and a web of pale blue-gray light formed around them. The sounds of the pub died down. "This is between you and me. They don't need to hear anything."

An anti-listening spell.

And done so effortlessly... Sabrina could only ever dream of buying magic like this. "I really can't afford to pay you."

The witch smirked. "I know. Think of this as me practicing my tarot reading skills."

Both of Sabrina's eyebrows rose. "You need practice?"

"No."

The witch began dealing the cards in a complicated pattern. Sabrina now understood why she wanted the bigger table. As the witch leaned forward, her necklace slithered into view: an emerald pendant dangled on the end of a rose-gold chain, engraved with the House of Earth and Emerald's symbol.

Sabrina swallowed.

Earth and Emerald was a powerful House, mostly because they were popular. People liked their rules—or lack of them.

She really could not risk annoying this woman.

Sabrina watched, a queasy feeling taking root in her stomach when the Death card appeared fairly early in the sequence. There were swords, cups and pentacles, and a tower that appeared to be on fire. She had no idea what any of it meant. She'd never bothered to learn much about omen reading—it wasn't part of her family's skillset.

The witch's mouth thinned. "Hmm." She finished the pattern, then swept up the cards, and started again. This deal's layout was smaller, less intricate than the first, and this time Death was the second card. It wasn't like Sabrina needed to understand the complexities of a tarot deck to get that—the grim reaper holding a scythe was a pretty universal symbol.

But the witch didn't leave it there. She picked up these cards too, then did one final deal.

Just one card.

Death.

"Death often means new beginnings," the woman said, her pale eyes serious. "But in your case, it just means you're going to die."

"Unsurprising," Sabrina replied, before her brain could tell her mouth to keep quiet.

The witch's lips thinned slightly. "But for you…death isn't what you are expecting."

"Who says I am expecting anything?"

Probably better not to argue with a witch. But Sabrina often spoke before she thought—her father had lamented that all of her life.

The woman rolled her eyes. "I see a man in your future." She studied the backs of the cards, face grim. "Several, actually."

Sabrina snorted on a chuckle, quickly covering her mouth with her hands. Like she hadn't heard that line before when it came to fortune tellers and women's futures.

"You laugh, but it's less cliché than you think. The men in your future…they are all tied to your death."

Sabrina's hands lowered. "What do you mean?"

The witch frowned. "I can only tell you what the cards say."

Sabrina looked down at the pile of tarot cards, at the intricate filigree pattern of leaves on their backs. At the single Death card, still face up. "They speak?"

The woman chuckled, then tapped the side of her head. "In a way."

"These dark handsome men, will one of them be the love of my life?" Sabrina asked. She knew the answer: negative. She wouldn't have time to fall in love. But it didn't hurt to check.

"Who said they were handsome?" The witch picked up the Death card, turning it over in her fingers. "Beware smiling men who knock on your door."

"Thanks, I think." Sabrina stood.

The woman wrapped the tarot cards in crimson silk. "For you, death will be the beginning. You're destined for big things. Remember me when you start achieving them."

"Right." Sabrina tucked her hands into her apron's pockets. "Big things. Me."

Now I know she's pulling my leg.

Sabrina was only destined to do one thing: die.

She knew it.

The witch knew it.

Her family knew it.

The sounds of the pub suddenly roared back to life, the spelled web dissipating as if blown away. Laughter, the clinking of cutlery and glasses, and the sound of chatter rose to meet her as she stepped away from the booth.

"Sabrina!" the bartender hollered.

"I have to go," Sabrina said. "Thank you for your time."

The witch stared at Sabrina through thick lashes. "Oh, and I'd hurry up and finish packing, if I was you."

CHAPTER 2

SABRINA

Three days later...

For the last few days, Sabrina had been walking on eggshells, terrified she'd open the door to find some creepy smiling guy hovering there, ready to lead her to her death. She hadn't been able to cope with the constant stress of it all.

She was going home.

Tonight.

Reaching down, Sabrina grabbed her suitcase, the handle too cool in her shaky palm. She threw the empty luggage onto the bed, the lid popping open, almost like it was yawning at her in boredom. Mocking her.

Get a grip. It's just a bag.

The worn leather had once been the color of blood, but it was scuffed and scratched now, and had taken on a pinkish hue. It had had a tough life these past five years, dragged all over the UK.

Worth it.

The taste of freedom—no matter how much it had actually sucked—had been heady.

Everything she owned, aside from the clothes on her back and her necklace, was on the bed. Her hand rose to her throat and clutched at the amulet that hung there. Everyone in the family had one. Well, everyone who had the potential to inherit the family's magic, anyway. It had one branch at the top, which bent down into four metal prongs. And between the bottom curve of the arch and the innermost two prongs, was a full moon engraved with a crescent, joining everything together. She had no idea where the symbol had come from or what it meant, but she'd had it since she turned ten years old.

She grabbed one of the three piles of clothes and dumped it inside the suitcase. She didn't bother folding anything. She would just be pulling them back out again in a day or two, anyway.

It was kind of galling to be doing this. Five years. She'd *only* lasted five years.

She had desperately wanted to get away from the craziness that was her family; away from the drama and the politics. She'd wanted a life free from magic—well, as free as she could get, considering her apartment was built over a powerful ley line—and just to *live* a little. Because her family had a secret, a big one, and she hadn't wanted to be a part of it.

She shoved the last two piles of clothes in the case, placing her sketch book on top. She ran a finger over the decorated cover. She'd wanted to study art, had lived and breathed that dream for more years than she could count. It was what had driven her to leave the clan in the first place. Even in this world, artists were desired, but apparently humans like her didn't have the finer sensibilities required to become an *artiste*. They couldn't see in extra spectrums like vampires or shifters, so their understanding of color was too limited. They didn't have a flair for the extraordinary like the fae or gods, and they didn't have the purity of vision like an angel.

All in all, Sabrina just wasn't…*enough.*

She rubbed her wrist. All her bones ached, not just her wrist, but that hurt the worst today. Tomorrow it might be her knee, or a rib. It was hard to say. Her head pounded, too, and her once nimble fingers were cold and clumsy as she zipped up the suitcase.

She didn't know how much longer she would survive; sure, she'd won a few battles, but cancer was winning the war. The doctors and shaman she'd seen last month had certainly been surprised by her continued existence. And that witch—

Best not to think about that fortune teller.

Ye cannae truly escape.

Uncle Max had said that the day she'd left the clan. She'd chuckled, because she hadn't believed him. Sabrina had thought she was free.

She'd been wrong.

Wrong about so many things.

"You're going to die…" the witch had said.

Yeah.

It hadn't been a newsflash. Everyone died. But Sabrina was going to die a little sooner than she'd planned.

I'm not ready, she thought, dragging her suitcase off the side of the single bed and onto the carpeted floor. A plume of dust rose to her knees, before drifting back to the ground. The clock had been ticking for her ever since she turned twenty-five. That was two years ago. Sabrina should have already undergone the rite of passage that was destined for all the potentials in her family line.

She'd learned the hard way why that was the deadline: the body started to fail after that. Her aches and pains and near constant headache were just symptoms of a bigger problem. Turn twenty-five and the genetic time-bomb starts counting down. Go home. Die by your own hand in the right place, and if you got lucky…

Well, she had to hope she'd get lucky.

Sabrina jumped as three sharp raps sounded at the door.

What the—?

Nobody was meant to know where she lived.

And, well, she didn't have any friends. Plus, her uncle, Max, who was meant to meet her at the Edinburgh train station, didn't know where she lived. He had no idea she was in London. And she'd already paid the landlord, so he shouldn't be bothering her…

She sidled up to the door, listening for a moment. *I wish this had a peephole.* But the apartment complex where she'd been living was cheap, and cheap didn't come with any extra security measures you didn't pay for yourself.

Three more strikes against the wood. "Sabrina!"

How—?

Her heart rose into her throat before her brain kicked in. She knew that voice.

She opened the door.

Colin stood on the other side, a fake smile plastered on his face. He rested one arm against the doorjamb as he leaned forward, towering over her. She wasn't a short woman, but he was six foot three, maybe six foot four. His long brown hair hung over his forehead, above eyes the same blue as hers. His looks were something he'd used to his advantage growing up.

Such a bonny lad, they'd said. *So sweet to the eye.*

But Colin had been Sabrina's *least* favorite cousin. And she had a *lot* of cousins. His semi-perfect face hid something cold inside; he viewed people as if they were chess pieces on the game board of life, and he was the queen. Everyone else was a pawn. There was no king, bishop or rook. Just him at the top. Great if you wanted a strategic mind that was solely focused on winning. Not particularly good for anyone else around him.

"You going to ask me inside?" he said. "Or you just going to stare at me some more?"

Sabrina took a step back and swung her hand inwards.

He dropped his arm from the jamb, and strode inside, his mouth lifting in a sneer as he looked around her apartment. It was a small studio, with a bench that pretended to be a kitchenette, and a tiny bathroom through a connecting door. And it looked like it was last cleaned about a century ago. The only things that weren't dust-covered were the bed and the bathroom—she didn't use anything else.

Colin wore jeans and a plaid shirt, with a knife strapped to his belt. He also had a gun holstered under his arm, but most everyone had a weapon of some kind on them. She didn't go anywhere without her switchblade.

How did he find me?

"How's things been?" he asked, breaking her train of thought. "You've certainly been living your best life." He smirked at her suitcase, before running a finger over the layer of dust on the so-called kitchenette's counter.

"Yeah," Sabrina said, swallowing her unease and faking a bright smile. "Long time no see."

"So, how did art school go?" His smirk made her jaw clench.

She crossed her arms over her chest. "It went."

"The grass wasnae greener on the other side, was it?" He rocked back on his heels.

"Do you see any grass here?" she asked. She ran a hand over her red hair. She was already annoyed, and they'd barely spoken. Time to change the topic. "How is everyone going, back home?"

Yeah, it was lame. The type of general chitchat you made when you didn't really know what to talk about. But part of Sabrina *needed* to hear how the family was. She hadn't spoken to them in five years, apart from the brief 'I'm coming home' note she'd sent weeks ago and then regretted. She'd been considering backing out until the witch had read her future.

Colin's fingers closed around the hilt of his knife. The shiny and yellowed handle looked like it was made from bone. She couldn't tell what kind: there were plenty of magic-born monsters that lurked in the shadows of the Highlands. It had most likely belonged to a kelpie, since they had tried conquering Loch Muick—her family's ancestral area—two hundred years ago. The clear, fresh water had been a strong lure, especially since Loch Ness had already been claimed.

"I bring some bad news about the family." Colin winced, but the expression was about as sincere as her efforts to clean the apartment.

"What happened?"

Maybe he'd hunted her down to tell her there was no clan to go back to. Nausea churned in her gut. *Please, no.*

But magic was capricious…

"There's been a lot of deaths in the family lately." Colin stepped forward.

Sabrina held her ground, more through confusion than determination. *Dead? Who's dead?*

People weren't meant to die in her family. Well, not permanently, anyway. Only those who didn't have the potential, or who hadn't made the rite of passage, were at risk.

Colin leaned forward slightly. "Well, Penny died during a hunt four and a half years ago. A misplaced arrow to the back. Then cousin Peter fell off his horse—you know how much of an avid rider he was. They were both twenty-four years old. Total accidents."

If they hadn't made the rite…

Sadness threatened to choke her. They hadn't even made it to the doomed age.

"They *died*-died?" she asked.

"Yes. Cousin Bernard was next—a mere eighteen years old when his brakes failed, and his car smashed into a tree. His sister, Bertha, was with him when it happened. And Stewart, well, he died on his twenty-fifth birthday. He tripped over carrying scissors. On his way to the rite." Colin was smiling now.

"Wait—what?"

Tripped over? Holding scissors?

Then it all fell into place.

Every one of her dead cousins had been next in line for the chieftain, ahead of Colin.

"It was quite…tragic."

Her heart beat a funny rhythm, and her hand formed into a fist. Only her uncles and father were left to stand between Colin and the clan chief role. And they'd made the transition, so they were a lot harder to kill.

More like impossible to kill.

"Tragic," Sabrina said, gritting the words out. "But fortunate, for you."

Colin moved on, until they were barely an arm's length apart. "And you. You're next, after me."

"And about another dozen after me."

"But they're wee teenagers. Grandpa would never pick one of them." His pale aquamarine eyes glowed. "I deserve to be the next clan chief, even Grandpa said so. Yet I'm the one stuck waiting in the wings. Well, not anymore."

"You killed them," Sabrina whispered. Her left hand slid down to her jeans pocket, where her switchblade was stashed.

"Yeah, I arranged a few 'accidents'." He used his free hand to make air quotes. "Oh yeah. And your dad…well, I may have arranged something special for him."

A sharp, burning pain erupted in her stomach.

She looked down.

He'd stabbed her.

She grabbed Colin's hand, shock making her clumsy.

"I really wish I could've claimed credit for that one," he said casually, while he turned the knife in her gut.

She screamed so loud her eardrums should have burst, and kept screaming while the pain spiraled out from the wound, speeding through her until it was all she could feel. Until she couldn't think beyond it.

He let go of the blade and stepped back. Sabrina wobbled, and the world went black for a moment.

She woke with the side of her face pressed against the dirty carpet, a film of dust resting over her body. Her stomach still hurt like the devil, and her body was awash in sticky blood. Her fingers were going numb, as were her feet. The taste of iron was rich in her mouth.

Colin squatted next to her, smiling like he was strolling around the loch with her, not watching her bleed to death.

"What did you do to my dad?" she whispered.

"Always thinking of others first," he sneered. "It's why the family was so shocked you upped and left. They could-nae believe it. Perfect Sabrina, running away. Aren't you worried about the knife in your gut?"

"Are you going to take me to a healer?"

"No."

"Then why worry about the inevitable?" Sabrina rolled onto her back and hissed as her vision swam with black dots. She wanted to fight, to get away, but her already weakened body was no match for the injury he had in-flicted.

He sighed, like she'd just sucked the fun right out of the situation. *Because me dying is a fucking thing to enjoy.* "I had your dad kidnapped and sent through a portal to rot on the other side. He has no paperwork, no allegiance to a House on this side—he has no way back. The clan think he's on the run from one of the Houses for murdering one of their witches. They think he's a godsdamned hero."

"Let me guess," she managed. "You killed the witch."

"Bingo. You aren't as dumb as you look."

"How did no one guess you did it all? All the heirs dying?"

"I had the witch cast a spell before I killed her. They think *she* murdered Bernard, Bertha, and Stewart. But it needed proximity to work. And you weren't there, so…"

So, she would have asked a lot of uncomfortable questions. Her left hand weakly grasped the bone hilt.

"I wouldnae take that out," he warned.

"Why not?"

"You'll die quicker."

Funny, how she hadn't realized a gut wound took so long to kill a person. But from the look in Colin's eyes, he'd known. And he'd wanted her to suffer.

"I ken that you're technically not in front of me in the queue for the title, but I didnae want Grandpa to decide you could jump ahead. He always had a soft spot for you. But you've been living as a human for such a long time. And being human, you're quite a target for rogues. It's with great sadness that I have to bring your body home. I'll even manage to shed a tear, I think. At your funeral."

Sabrina's right hand rose to clutch at the amulet around her neck. Dying here was not a good idea. There wasn't a node of magic like at the loch, so she had no idea if she was going to survive this or not. No one else had ever done so before. But there were ley lines running underneath her apartment, each one a conduit of pure magic. There was a reason why she'd picked the place, even if she hadn't liked magic. It had felt like home.

Sabrina hadn't done the ritual and she wasn't in the correct location. But she was dying, and she wasn't going to make it back to the clan to do it right.

The least she could do was die on her own terms.

Maybe that would mean something.

Grabbing the knife in her left hand, fingers clenched around the amulet in her right, she pulled the blade out from her stomach, teeth gritted against the pain as she did so. One heartbeat. Two heartbeats.

She reached for the ley line, fingers and chest burning as her soul touched the magic. *I will survive. I will survive.*

"What are you doing?" Colin shouted.

No more heartbeats.

Pain flooded her.

She closed her eyes, exhaling one last time.

Everything went dark.

I'm dead.

…But why am I thinking?

Opening her eyes, she took in the scene: Colin leaning over her body, prying her fingers away from the amulet, cursing.

It hadn't worked.

Then why am I—?

She looked down at her hands. They were transparent. Like they should be. "Hah!" she yelled. "I made it! Shove that in your fat gob and chew on it!"

Then it clicked. Her body shouldn't exist. He shouldn't be leaning over *anything.*

Phantoms…we don't leave a physical body behind when we shift into our spirit form.

Her stomach dropped as understanding kicked in.

"Hey," she shouted, waving a hand in front of his face. "I'm here!"

But he couldn't see her, or he was doing a bang-up job of pretending not to.

She flung out a hand and it passed straight through him. He didn't even flinch.

Her jubilation turned to bitter ashes. She hadn't made the transition, after all. Her desperate grasp at the ley line hadn't worked.

She wasn't a phantom.

She was dead.

Dead.

Sabrina Fhearchair was a godsdamned ghost.

CHAPTER 3

KIERAN

Around two-ish months ago...

Torture was boring.

Kieran wheeled a stainless-steel trolley into the dungeon room, whistling a jaunty tune as he did so. The trolley was covered in an assortment of knives, pins, graters, and other kinds of bits and bobs he should know the names of, but didn't.

The hurty thing.
The ouchie-maker.

They were the names he used—and it seemed to inspire more terror into his…clients. After all, Kieran Aspen had seen his unfair share of torture, done to him, *and* done to others. You couldn't take it too seriously or you'd go mad.

At least, that's how he dealt with it all. His step-uncle, Elias, king of the House of Blood and Beryl, said it was an unhealthy coping mechanism, but Kieran didn't really care. It wasn't like he'd gotten onboard the whole 'wellness' train.

I don't think a therapist can fix what's wrong with me.

It was a fundamental problem. It was in his genes. His origins.

The rattle of chains brought him back to the present. The room was about ten feet by twelve feet in size. It had stone walls that were once a pale beige, but that were now stained to become an indeterminate brown. The room stunk of shit, piss and vomit, despite having been cleaned a year or so ago. None of which seemed to belong to the newest resident, who was chained to the wall. The manacles were made of an iron alloy, enriched with metals from each portal world and so many spells they made his spidey senses tingle. There wasn't a magical race alive that could break free of them.

Adora, Kieran's shifter accomplice for this introductory 'session', stepped into the room behind him and closed the door. She wore black like him, arms covered in a long-sleeved shirt and her toned legs in tight-fitting jeans.

Kieran found black was better to hide the bloodstains. Plus, it made him look *fantastic*.

Adora's eyes were a warm brown, contrasting with her multihued blue-green hair, but the prisoner wasn't looking at the beautiful shifter. No, his gaze was locked on Kieran and the toys spread across the tray in front of him. Then he looked at Kieran's face, and his distaste showed for a moment, before vanishing in a wince of pain.

"Like what you're looking at?" Kieran asked.

"Not really," the man rasped, his voice a thick Scottish brogue. "Ye are a bit too skinny for my tastes."

Skinny?

Kieran's muscles had muscles, and they were insulted.

"Hmph. At least I'm not a blood nut."

"A *what*?" Adora blurted.

Kieran sighed and waved a hand at the prisoner. "A ginger."

"But why did you—never mind." The shifter shook her head, teal-colored hair swaying with the movement. "I don't think I want to know."

But the human's reaction—that distaste—was back.

That's what happens when you're half-death fae and also half-vampire. And a torturer by trade. You get hated on for existing.

He patted his bicep. The man had just used the skinny insult as a substitute for his true dislike.

And it wasn't like that was the worst thing he'd ever been called, anyway.

Abomination. That's what his mother's race called him when they thought he couldn't hear. *Mutt.* That's what his sperm donor's used. Too bad that 'mutt' was probably the worse insult.

Yeah, people had issues with his origin story. Vampire-fae hybrids were not meant to exist. Ever.

Yay for me.

Hybrid or not, he was still an information specialist, AKA torturer, answerable only to his step-uncle.

At first, Kieran had kind of enjoyed the role—being a death fae and having a taste for blood had made him a teeny tiny bit feral. But now boredom and anger had made him realize he was worth more than the role he played.

Plus, I'm wasting my looks on a dungeon-bound audience.

Torture had become routine. Stab someone a little, break their bones, pull some fingernails out, smash a few kneecaps, pluck out an eyeball or two, insert thing where things shouldn't be…You know, the usual.

And it was dull.

D.U.L.L.

His lack of enthusiasm had been noticed by Ysabeau, Elias' second-in-command, who'd assigned him other duties, mostly intimidation and retrievals. Kieran didn't mind that so much. He didn't like most people, so keeping his interactions minimal—aside from scaring the fuck out of them—was fine by him.

Even fun sometimes.

This prisoner had been gifted to King Elias from the House of Sea and Serpentine. Apparently, the human should've died a hundred times over, based on the previous torture they'd been dealt. He'd been sent to the House of Blood and Beryl because Sea and Serpentine wanted to know if there was anything 'unusual' about his blood.

And if the House of Blood and Beryl was renowned for anything other than being fucking crazy, it was their understanding of blood. The vampires in the House had some interesting gifts, the Laskaris line being no exception.

"What's your name?" Adora asked the prisoner, breaking Kieran's meandering train of thought.

The redhead spat on the ground.

"Yeah, yeah," Kieran said under his breath. "You'll tell me everything you know, if only I'd stop."

"Ye havenae started yet." The man's voice was raspy, like he'd screamed so much his vocal cords had been permanently damaged.

"Haven't I?" Kieran tapped the side of his head. "Maybe the mind games have already begun."

The human's hazel eyes narrowed. His dark auburn hair had a handful of silver threads, while his jawline was whiskered blood-red. He looked barely thirty. It would take a long time before Kieran looked like that—if ever.

Adora stepped forward and, with a quick jerk of her hand, snapped one of the human's fingers. When she sliced off another, the man barely even grunted in pain.

Kieran hadn't realized she'd been carrying a knife. "What the fuck?!"

He'd had had his fingers broken a few times *and* had bamboo under his fingernails. It fucking stung. For this *human* to have very little reaction...

He's stronger than I thought.

The shifter checked her watch, and then tossed the severed finger up and down in the air like it was a gods-damned ball or something. "You talk too much."

"We're *supposed* to get him to TALK." He slashed a hand through the air. "This is *an interrogation.*"

Adora snorted derisively and motioned for him to continue.

Godsdamned hothead.

Kieran turned his attention back to the prisoner—the man's hand seemed to turn a bit...transparent? Then it was solid flesh again, the broken finger no longer bent at an odd angle, and the missing digit... restored.

This man was meant to be a pureblooded human. But he couldn't be. Even Kieran knew it took weeks for a human's body to repair broken bones.

Not seconds.

And they didn't magically grow back missing body parts.

"Uh...did you just see that?" Kieran asked, tilting his head to the side as if that would help this situation make more sense. Newsflash: it didn't.

"See him magically regrow a finger?" Her voice was uncertain.

"Yes."

He was getting a headache.

Kieran approached the prisoner, holding out a knife as he did so. He used the blade to tilt the man's chin up, so he could see the planes of his face better in the flickering light. Kieran ran the sharp edge gently over the prisoner's cheek and blood seeped from the wound. It ran red, a little darker than normal. It maybe even had a slight purplish hue, although that could be a trick of the light. And it smelled a little sweet, a bit like death without the pungent rot.

Looks human. Sounds human. Smells…mostly human.

Isn't human.

The heavy torture the man had received at the previous House had been because he'd murdered a young sea witch (apparently), and been captured and punished for the crime when he'd supposedly been running for a portal. Normally, that would mean being killed, but the man hadn't died, despite Sea and Serpentine's best efforts.

Probably because his bones heal in seconds.

"So, are we going to discuss how your fingers mended all on their own?" Kieran asked.

"Most broken bones heal on their own," the man replied.

Smooth. No lie. Also, not the truth.

Kieran could *feel* Adora's rising irritation.

He was only involved in this interrogation because Elias had wanted him to play referee for Adora. She was a little too handsy with a knife, so Kieran had just recently discovered.

Still holding the blade under the man's chin, Kieran noticed the rust-colored whiskers were fading a little, too.

Fading?

Maybe my eyes are playing tricks on me.

Humans didn't turn semi-transparent; they weren't ghosts—and Kieran had met his fair share of those, unfortunately, it came with the territory. But ghosts didn't linger in this realm for particularly long before they were shepherded off to the afterlife. Some, the death fae ferried across, while other spirits found their way on their own. Most went to the light without help.

"Are humans meant to do that?" Kieran asked.

The man's skin turned a pale shade of gray. "I dinnae know what ye are talking about."

When people lie, they have tells. The better you knew the person, the easier it was to know when they played with the truth. But Kieran didn't need to look for the slight widening of the eyes, or the quirk of a lip. He didn't have to look, simply because the man's hand flickered in and out of sight.

Kieran turned to the shifter. She had a face that stopped men—and women—in the street. The first night he'd seen her, she'd been pursued by one of Blood and Beryl's vampires, only to have said vampire lose an arm over it. But her beauty didn't really do much for Kieran. He wasn't into romantic entanglements. What he found fascinating was that she was also a truth reader of some kind; she could sense the heart of people.

"Anything?" he whispered, close to her, but not close enough to touch.

She shook her head. "I can't see. It's cloudy. Warped. Like seeing images through a veil."

"How is that possible? I thought you could 'see' into someone's mind."

She tossed her hair over her shoulder. "I'm not a mind reader, ass. And I don't know. Maybe a spell or something that's blocking me? It's not infallible."

"Did you see his hand?" Kieran asked her.

She frowned, then turned the full force of her glare on the prisoner. "Did you kill that witch?"

The man gave Kieran a half-smirk, like he was in on the joke. Too bad Kieran didn't know the punch line. "They brought the big guns out for little old me, didnae they? I can tell ye both are the best of the best."

"If only you knew," Kieran muttered.

"Answer the question." Adora leaned forward, menace radiating from her.

"Ye think ye can scare me?" The prisoner laughed, a broken sound.

"He's a tough guy," Adora snarled.

"Well, he was worked over by the House of Sea and Serpentine for a year," Kieran said. "I'm sure that was more effective than drinking concrete."

She scowled at him. "Drinking concrete?"

"Yeah, you know, to harden up."

"You're not helping."

"Aren't I?"

The man's arm grew transparent. The manacle was still in place, like it was securing flesh, but flesh that could not be seen. No, technically Kieran could still *see* the man's arm, but it was a ghostly appendage.

Adora closed the distance between her and the prisoner and poked his arm with her knife.

"What the fuck? Can you stop stabbing him?" Kieran demanded.

"See?"

The blade passed straight through the limb, meeting no resistance.

Kieran frowned. "So, it's not turning invisible…"

"It's gone," she finished.

But…it was still there. He could see it. But she couldn't.

Interesting.

"What *are* you?" Adora demanded.

"None of yer business."

"Uh, that's where you are wrong," Kieran said. "Learning what you are is basically our *only* business here." He put the knife down on the trolley; he'd been holding it a little too long and it made him want to stab someone. "Since you can't seem to die, that means we have plenty of time to work out how you did that."

"I've already made it my top priority." Adora crossed her arms over her chest.

"Look." The man's hazel gaze turned calculating. "Ye give me a wee something, lassie, and I may give ye a wee something in return."

"Did he just proposition you in front of me?" Kieran asked.

Adora growled. "Are you ever serious?"

"Rarely."

"Just because your mother—"

"Come now," Kieran interrupted, picking up a cheese grater. "Let's not bring our parents into this."

"Are ye going to jabber all day or do ye want answers?" The man's arm solidified.

"See, he's now offering to help us," Kieran said. "And you only maimed him a little. I didn't even have to stab him. Talking *works*."

Adora focused on the prisoner. "First, tell me if you killed that witch."

"I didnae."

She turned to Kieran and spoke softly, "He doesn't appear to be lying."

"Yay." He hadn't particularly cared if the prisoner had killed the witch or not. "So, what are you?" he asked the prisoner. "Poltergeist gone wrong? Reanimated corpse?"

"Ye willing to cut me a deal?"

"That was quick. I didn't even get to the climax myself." Kieran sighed.

"I just—what? When did we swap to sex analogies?" Adora demanded.

"About ten seconds ago. You really need to keep up."

She ignored him. It was probably for the best. "Why us? Why didn't you cut a deal with Sea and Serpentine? You were there for over a year." Suspicion laced her words.

It was a fair question.

"Ye could say I was holding a grudge."

"Do go on." Kieran loved a good revenge plot.

"The bitch empress cut my fucking head off. Decapitation tends to make me a wee bit cranky."

Not the answer he was expecting, to be honest, but Kieran nodded sagely. "Totally fair. I'd be pretty upset in that event myself."

"Not. Helping," Adora growled at him.

"What?" Kieran shrugged. "Tell me you would like to get your head cut off."

"That is beside the point."

"I would say that it's *entirely* the point."

The shifter ran a hand over her hair, frustrated. "Why didn't you cut a deal with them *before* they decapitated you?"

"Because they were assholes."

Also fair.

"And we're such friendly people that you're suddenly willing to talk to us?" Adora's eyebrows were nearly in her hairline.

"No. Not at all." He paused. "I made a blood oath to keep what I am secret. But I have a feeling about *him*." The prisoner nodded at Kieran. "He's going to help me."

"Me?" Kieran pointed at himself and laughed.

He was the *last* person this guy should trust.

"What do you want?" Adora demanded.

The prisoner met Kieran's stare, then the shifter's. "For ye to find my daughter."

CHAPTER 4

KIERAN

One month ago

Their prisoner, it turns out, had been keeping secrets from them.

Kieran had spent close to a month tracking down the guy's daughter. She had lived quietly under the radar, so much so that it was like she almost hadn't existed, until suddenly, six-ish years ago, she had enrolled at the Eternal College of the Arts run by the House of Spirit and Sapphire. The prisoner—Douglas, his name was—had clued them in on that, but what he hadn't known was that her time there had been limited. She'd left after a mere two years of study; there'd been a note on her record saying she had been of exceptional talent, but her humanity had held her back. Her teachers hadn't thought she had a future, compared to the other, more physically gifted students.

After that, Kieran had tried the traditional methods of tracking: hacking, interviewing and magic. There was nothing. If she had been working, it was short term, and if she lived anywhere, she hadn't registered her real name.

She had also been careful not to leave a blood trail that could be magicked.

He'd thought he'd tracked her to a small town in Italy at one point, but when he went there, no one remembered a Scottish girl with red hair. Finally, he'd been able to pinpoint her at a pub on Oxford Road, London. Not because of her work as a waitress—there was no official record of that—but because he'd found a mural she'd painted on an external wall.

But she hadn't been back for over a year. Just cut and ran, according to the bartender, not long after a witch from the House of Earth and Emerald had read her fortune.

The bartender unfortunately couldn't recall anything about said witch. And since he belonged to the House of Air and Amethyst, there wasn't much Kieran could do to jog his memory, that wouldn't cause a political incident.

Elias did not appreciate 'incidents'. Not ones that he himself hadn't caused, anyway.

But now was the time of truth: Kieran had found her apartment.

Something about the whole thing felt off, though. It was on the fourth floor, and the whole building reeked of neglect. The blue patterned wallpaper in the hallway was peeling, and the once-pale carpet had turned an unpleasant brown color. Kieran could practically smell the decay and desperation that permeated the place.

He knocked on apartment forty-two's door and waited. It had scratch marks on it, like something had once tried to claw its way in. He wondered what the other side looked like.

He knocked again. Someone was home—he could sense a heartbeat.

"I can hear you!" Kieran called. *Not creepy at all.*

Eventually, a series of heavy footsteps ended with the door being opened the barest crack.

"Who are you?" A single amber eye glared out from the narrow space between door and jamb, the voice full of suspicion.

Nobody you want to meet, Kieran wanted to say, because he wasn't above a bit of drama, especially if it was true. Instead, he said, "I'm looking for Sabrina Fhearchair."

"Don't know her." The occupant went to shut the door, but Kieran wedged his boot in the gap. The door slammed into his foot, and he bit back a wince. That had broken a bone or two, which would heal within minutes—the benefit of being what he was—but that meant the guy on the other side of the thin timber panel was *strong*. From the smell of things, he was a werewolf. They got territorial, fast, so better not to destroy anything the shifter considered his and avoid being turned into a punching bag.

Not that Kieran *would* be a punching bag; he was one hell of a fighter, even if he said so himself. But it was the principle of the thing.

Kieran held out his right hand and flipped the guy the bird. He wasn't being a jerk—well, he kind of was—rather the ring on his middle finger had the House of Blood and Beryl's crest on it. "Official business."

The werewolf inhaled sharply, before swinging the door inward.

"What does the House of Blood and Beryl want?" he growled.

He was a little over five and a half feet in height, with shaggy blonde hair and piercing amber eyes. The lack of height suggested one of two things: the guy didn't have tall genes in the family, or he came from a time when people were shorter. With the long-lived races, it could be hard to tell. The only reason it mattered was that old werewolves were even more crotchety than the younger ones. They had a 'bite first, piss on the corpse later' mentality.

"Looking for the previous tenant," Kieran said. He assessed the apartment quickly: bed, tiny bench that attempted to mimic a kitchen, single door leading off to what he presumed was the bathroom. And bare floorboards. Rows of tiny holes in the wood indicated the place had been carpeted previously.

"They 'vanished'." The wolf made little air quotes as he said the last word.

Kieran was about to make a smartass response when he caught it: the faint aroma of blood. Old, dying. *Life's blood.*

And it smelled…delicious.

He swallowed. "You don't seem convinced."

"You can smell it, can't you?" the werewolf asked.

Kieran nodded. *I wish I couldn't.* He'd never smelled something so…arousing before.

"They ripped out the carpet and washed the floors with bleach, but I can still smell it," the werewolf said. "Been getting fainter with each month, though."

Old werewolf, to have senses that strong. Especially since the blood was at least a year old.

Kieran snorted. "Everyone knows you should use hydrogen peroxide instead of bleach to clean up old blood." There were also a few magical solutions as well, which meant the landlord was a cheap bastard.

It took a lot of blood to leave an old scent trail.

Someone had died here.

Which was a shame, because he *really* would have liked to meet the owner of that blood.

The werewolf raised a brow. "You part vampire or something?"

"Or something."

Kieran had pointed ears, so people often just assumed he was fae, if his hair failed to cover them. But a few noticed that he was...*more* than that. His bloodhound nose was a bit of a giveaway, though.

The werewolf rocked back on his heels. "The blood smelled...strange. Not like the typical human. But not like anything else I've come across before."

A little bit like the sweet start of decay? Kieran wanted to ask, but kept his lips sealed. *This* blood didn't smell like that to him, but Douglas' had. And he had no idea why it was different. From the wary look in the werewolf's eyes, it didn't appear the blood smelled as wonderful to him.

"Were there any personal effects left behind?" Kieran asked.

The wolf shook his head. "Place was cleaned out, aside from the blood."

Kieran squatted in the middle of the room, his black trench coat flowing around him in a dark fall of fabric. He took a deep breath, sensing the blood on a level that was beyond scent. He raised two hands, then slapped his palms together, the action drawing magic out from within, power exploding from him in a glimmering web of crimson filaments.

Specks of old blood began to rise into the air. At first, it looked like a small pool of dust had risen near him; asymmetrical, as if a puddle of blood had pooled around a body. There wasn't much splatter, which indicated whoever had been attacked hadn't suffered an arterial wound—those tended to be messy.

The tiny particles slowly coalesced into small bubbles, then eventually into one large, liquid drop. His magic had given it life. Again.

It was like watching some fucked-up science fiction movie effects.

And it was totally awesome.

"Fuck me," the werewolf breathed.

"No thanks." Kieran pulled out a glass vial from his coat pocket and the large drop flowed inside, filling it.

Around an ounce had been restored, and it smelled even better reanimated. His fangs dropped down, and he prodded them with his tongue.

Sabrina Fhearchair…what the hell were you?

She couldn't have been the same species as her father; his blood smelled *nothing* like hers.

"What are you?" the werewolf asked, eyes wide. "I've never seen anyone do that before."

Kieran stood. "And you probably won't again." This blood magic, it was power created from his mixed heritage. He'd never heard of another death fae being able to do it, and vampires didn't have traditional magic, unless they had acquired it. Or were Masters.

The man scanned Kieran's face; trying to assess the threat he presented, he supposed. "Do you need anything else?"

"What's your landlord's number?" Kieran asked.

"Let me get it for you."

He grinned, then patted his pocket, where he had stashed the old blood. "Fantastic."

"Is it enough?" he asked the raven-haired witch.

Dahlia—one of the House of Blood and Beryl's most talented magic-users—glared at him with moonlight eyes, then motioned to the bronze cauldron she had set on the table. "Would I have bothered to set this up if it wasn't?"

"I'll take that as a 'yes', then."

He surveyed the hotel room: two exits, one into the hotel corridor and the other being a balcony. They were on the second floor—mostly because if they had to get out quickly, they would both survive the distance to the ground. Witches weren't as physically hardy as vampires, or fae, as a general rule.

Magic did make up a lot of the difference, though.

The rest of the room—identical to his own—comprised a bed and sofa, with a door off to an adjacent bathroom.

Dahlia dropped some flecks of Himalayan rock salt into the cauldron, then followed it with a bunch of herbs Kieran couldn't identify; he dealt in death, not garden offcuts. She then tipped in ashes of some sort and held out her hand. "The blood."

Reluctantly, he handed over the vial. Her palm was cold to touch. Everything about her was.

She flicked two small drops of the precious liquid onto the rest of the ingredients, then handed the vial back to him. He stashed it in his pocket, breathing through his mouth; anything to stop him from reacting to the scent of Sabrina's blood.

It was a sheer testament to his will power that he hadn't drained the vial dry already.

Dahlia closed her eyes and held her hands out over the bowl, muttering in Latin under her breath. The concoction caught fire with a snap, the flames glowing blue before settling to an unnerving green.

Dahlia then dropped a purple-and-green stone—*not* fluorite—into the flames.

The fire vanished.

"This feels very dramatic," Kieran said dryly.

She glared at him as she fished out the rock, not a mark to be seen on it, despite the fact the mineral had been in the middle of a fire moments ago. "Magic requires focus, not blather."

"Yeah, yeah. You already did the spell."

"It's not finished." Stone in hand, she strode over to the bed, where she had spread a map of the world. The thing was huge, so you could see larger towns as well, not just capital cities. The six portals were marked in red: Ireland, the Himalayas, the Sahara Desert, Portland, the Amazon, the Pacific Ocean…

The witch dropped the mottled rock over the map. But it didn't fall like it should—instead it hovered about four inches above the paper, then zigged and zagged for a few seconds, as if orienting itself. It zoomed to Scotland and lingered over a small loch, where it dropped like, well, a stone.

Dahlia pointed a long finger at the now dormant rock. "There."

They both leaned forward, and Kieran squinted at the tiny print. "Loch Muick?"

"The area is technically under Gold and Garnet's control, but is mostly populated by regular humans—the few that are left," Dahlia said. "If you are going to scout the area out, I'll arrange some cloaking spells."

"Me? What about you? Aren't you going, too?"

She gave a faint shudder. "Gods, no. Why would I do that?"

"I thought you liked the idea of travel. Isn't that what you said, so you could come on this jaunt?"

"I liked the idea of not playing babysitter to the *thing* sitting in the cells. Elias said it was my turn after Adora."

Ouch. Kieran couldn't care less about the prisoner himself, but he had a particular loathing for words like 'it' and 'thing'.

It's a wonder Dahlia can stand working with me.

Very few people could. He was too much of an asshole, and he didn't follow anybody's rules but Elias'. And that was because he owed his king.

"If I find the girl, can you break the blood vow he made?" Kieran asked. They wanted to know what he was, but the human-type individual had sworn a vow not to say or write anything about his origins. And blood vows, well, they turned nasty when broken. Like boiling your blood in your veins, aneurysms—if you were lucky—or rotting from the inside out.

Dahlia sighed and began cleaning away her supplies. "Doubtful. But I have a few ideas of how we can get around it. Vows always have loopholes."

"And what's that?"

She smiled, a slightly alarming expression. "Pictionary."

CHAPTER 5

SABRINA

Present day...

Being a ghost sucked.

That was Sabrina's hot take from the past year.
Zero out of five stars; do not recommend.

She'd drafted the entire negative review in her head, she just didn't have anywhere to post it.

She'd thought that the ghost part of being a phantom would be fun. She'd always been slightly envious of her relatives for that skill, even if she'd been prepared to reject the whole thing. But phantoms could reach out and touch the physical plane; they could swap between being corporeal and incorporeal whenever they felt like it, and she couldn't.

She couldn't touch anything, and her telekinetic ghost skills were rubbish. All she could do was float around. *More like mope around.* Yeah, she had gotten to the sulking stage and she wasn't even going to feel bad about that. Even though Colin hadn't been able to see her when she'd first died, she'd figured that was because he was in his physical state. But she'd stalked her family for days attempting to communicate with them whenever they swapped into their spirit forms, but she'd gotten nothing. Zilch. Zero.

They couldn't see her in *either* form.

As far as she was aware, no one could.

And that was the part that sucked the most.

She'd been living on her own for five years, so she'd thought that she'd known what it was like to be alone, but this wasn't the same at all. Even the day-to-day interaction she'd had as a waitress had resulted in *some* social connection. She'd had people to talk to: the clientele and her co-workers, who she'd been friendly with, even if they hadn't been her friends. It was those daily contacts, those basic things, that you really took for granted until you couldn't do them at all anymore.

Now…now she was surrounded by people, and she'd never been lonelier.

Sad, huh?

She'd thought she wouldn't be able to make it back to the clan on her own, but she shouldn't have worried. Colin had rolled her body up in her comforter, shoved her in the back of his truck, and driven her body home to Loch Muick. She'd been tethered to her corpse, bouncing around like a demented helium balloon against the back of Colin's truck all the way.

It had been one of her less dignified moments.

After he'd arrived home, he'd carried her body ever-so-gently into the main hall of Braemar Castle, the clan's main seat. He'd then fallen to one knee, before dramatically laying her corpse on the floor, right in front

of Grandpa Angus. She'd screamed, screamed so loud she
was surprised the windows hadn't shattered.

She'd then shouted her story—how Colin had murdered
her, how he'd killed all the other cousins—but no one had
heard; no one *saw* her. She'd even forced herself to step
through Grandpa—which was a big no-no when it came
to phantom etiquette—but he hadn't even noticed she was
there.

Instead, she'd had to watch Colin's stellar acting per-
formance. He had even pretended to shed a tear over
the untimely loss of his cousin (*he hadn't lied when he'd
said that*), and explained how it was so *sad* that she had
managed to survive for five years on her own, only to die
just days before she came home.

No one seemed to question the fact that she was recently
killed, her corpse so fresh the blood had only just dried on
her clothes.

In fact, everyone had seemed so willing to see the good
in Colin, that she just couldn't understand it. The witch
he'd killed must have cast one hell of a spell. The only
one who seemed suspicious was Uncle Max, but he kept
a wide berth from his nephew. Sabrina had never really
noticed that before, but Max didn't seem to like Colin,
and he appeared to be the only one.

I'm with you there, buddy.

And so Sabrina had spent the last year on reconnais-
sance. That's what she called it, anyway. Stalking sounded
so lame. She followed Colin everywhere. She'd stopped
trailing him to the bathroom after the fourth time, because
really, it wasn't like he was doing anything she wanted
to see. But other than that, or when he was sleeping, she
stuck to him like spiritual glue. She'd come to learn he was

shady, but clever about it. He planned things meticulously, in ways that no one could catch him. His contingencies had contingencies.

He even had a safe hidden in his room that no one even suspected. And her family could travel through the walls.

His newest project was huge.

He was trying to learn how to kill a phantom.

But it was impossible. Even if you killed the physical body, they just turned into their spirit form and rematerialized whole again. You could behead them, and both parts of the body would just disappear before reforming intact.

Colin had spent a long time compiling all the information he could find. So far, no known metal or substance that could kill them, no spell that could do the job. She'd seen all the data, hovering over Colin's shoulder as she did. He'd told her he'd murdered a young witch, but what he hadn't mentioned while Sabrina had been busy dying, was the witch had been hired by her father to investigate her cousins' untimely demises. Colin had forced her to cast a misdirection spell, then killed her, and blamed her for some of their cousins more suspicious deaths, claiming she'd done it in a fit of unrequited love.

And then he'd framed her father for the witch's death, and in a way that her family thought of her dad as a savior.

It was all rather…tidy, really.

Sabrina couldn't believe how trusting she'd been before death—or BD as she now called it. She'd thought that the family was there for each other through thick and thin, that nothing stood between them. Yeah, okay, there were politics; people jostling for supremacy in the clan, those who aspired to be the next chief or just have a little more power. But Grandpa Angus had been the clan chief for the last two hundred years, and it wasn't like he was going to step down anytime soon. His great-great-grandfather had only abdicated because he'd decided it was time to let the young ones have their turn, just like the previous clan chief had. In fact, their first immortal chief—Great-great-great-great etc. grandfather Fergus was still around, if you could find him. He spent most of his time in his phantom form, haunting the valley in an eye-wateringly colored suit.

Sabrina didn't think that Colin needed to kill Grandpa; the elder just had to step aside. Although, she doubted he would be willing to do that. And Colin wasn't happy to wait. Knowledge of how to kill a phantom meant he could remove his uncles and grandfather from the equation.

But his research indicated there was nothing out there that could kill them, not on this side of a portal, anyway. No one even knew if old age could do it—there were some ancestors that were five hundred years old, but they just seemed to age super-slowly. Great-grandpa Fergus looked about forty and had done for as long as Sabrina could remember.

"What the fuck?"

Sabrina jumped, not that anyone noticed.

She'd been following Colin on autopilot and only just realized they'd ended up in the war room. Well, it wasn't *officially* called that. To be honest, it was just another room in the castle. It had red and gold wallpaper, navy blue carpet and a huge walnut table that had space for twenty seats. It was technically a games room or a dining room, but this was where most of the tactical decisions for the clan were made. It was coated with anti-listening spells, and had extra insulation so sound couldn't travel. And, with Sabrina being the obvious exception, her family could see each other when they were in their phantom form, so spying wasn't possible.

Grandpa, Uncle Max, Uncle Barr, Uncle Clement, Aunt Connie and Colin were all present, a sign that they were going to discuss something serious. They weren't responsible for *all* the decisions regarding the clan; anything to do with the actual happiness of the people, or things that impacted on the day-to-day activities tended to fall to her grandmother and her posse. True, financial decisions were in Uncle Max's domain, but since Gran wasn't here, and Grandpa hated accounting, it was safe to say that this was security related.

And considering how butt-hurt Colin was acting, it was clear he was just learning whatever it was now.

"What do you mean they're coming *here*?" His blue eyes flashed, icy rage emanating from him.

Who is coming here? Whoever it was, it seemed they were enough to put a spanner in his works.

Family members wouldn't get him worked up like this, and the clan either lived here at Braemar, at Balmoral Castle, or in the surrounding lands.

It has to be a stranger. Or strangers.

Colin didn't like outside interference. While he could mess with the clan, threaten them, and kill them, he didn't want anyone else doing the same thing. An attack from the other races would spell a disaster—what he was doing was for the benefit of the clan. At least, that's what he muttered to himself late at night while he was pawing over his data.

Yeah, she couldn't roll her eyes hard enough.

Typical sociopath.

Sabrina sat, hovering as if she was sitting on an invisible stool, and crossed her legs at the knee. She placed her chin in a hand.

"They are sending representatives out to the clan," Grandpa said slowly, as if he were repeating himself for the dozenth time, rather than the first. *Maybe he's already said it eleven times. Not like I was paying attention before.*

She'd been too busy worrying about her own unfortunate existence to pay attention to something that was apparently game-changing.

"Who is?" Sabrina asked. "What did I miss?"

No one answered.

They never did.

"Which Houses are they sending, and why?" Colin demanded, hand curling into a fist on the dark table.

"Oh, oh! Let me guess—" Sabrina began.

"The House of Blood and Beryl, the House of Air and Amethyst, and the House of Spirit and Sapphire," Grandpa said quietly, rage threaded through every word.

They didn't let her guess.

And she didn't think she'd ever seen him so pissed off.

"Why those three?" Aunt Connie asked. She had dark-red hair like Sabrina—well, Sabrina's was inherited from her. A handful of fine, silver threads were the only indicators that she was a day over a hundred.

"It appears they somehow learned about our existence," Uncle Max said. He jabbed his finger at a piece of yellowed paper that sat on the table in front of him, before briefly looking at Colin. "They somehow learned we are immortal."

"How could they learn that?" Uncle Barr ran a hand over his beard. He was technically Sabrina's great-great uncle, but she didn't usually bother with adding 'greats' to titles, not when there were so many family members to remember.

Grandpa slammed his open hand on the table. The sound reverberated around the room; if Sabrina had had a body, it probably would've made her teeth rattle. "We have a leak."

"How?" Colin asked. "We are all blood bound not to say anything."

Sabrina knew that all too well. Although, now she didn't have a body—and no blood to enforce the vow—she was probably no longer tied by it. Not that she had anyone to tell.

If only I did…

"A powerful witch might be able to break that vow," Aunt Connie murmured, fingers playing with her amulet.

Uncle Barr shook his head. "Everyone is accounted for. And aside from Sabrina, no one has left for any length of time."

Hearing her name sent a strange shock through her body, like electricity had jolted through her spine. *Wow, I guess this means I've been feeling forgotten.* After she'd died, and Colin had brought her body back, the clan had mourned and buried her, then continued on like she hadn't existed.

Uncle Max glowered. "Sabrina wouldnae have broken her vow."

"Damn straight, I wouldn't."

"She was weak," Colin said. The accusation hurt, more than she thought it would. Because it was true. She *had* been weak; weak of body, since she had been dying, and weak of mind, since she'd been ready to give up. *Way to make your opinion known. Assface.* "And she clearly ran with bad crowds."

"Like you can talk, you piece of shit," Sabrina growled. It felt good to say it, to hear her own voice.

But Grandpa shook his head. "Douglas."

Sabrina froze.

"He isn't on Earth," Aunt Connie said. "He went through a portal."

Dad.

She stared at Colin, to see if there was any body language at all that gave him away, but nothing. The man was stone cold.

"We dinnae have proof he went through," Uncle Barr said.

"So, where has he been for the past year and a half? In hiding? There's nowhere on this world he can go where Sea and Serpentine wouldn't look for him. If they had him, they would have come for us long before now," Colin said.

Sabrina sang, "And the Oscar goes to…"

Meanwhile, her mind was racing. *You seem pretty convinced Dad went through.* And that he wasn't coming back.

"He was on the run for killing that sea witch. The note he left said as much. I doubt he'd be foolish enough to return to Earth." Colin crossed his arms over his chest, like he'd somehow won the argument using the fictitious note as his evidence.

Grandpa slashed a hand through the air. "We will learn if Douglas betrayed us. And if he did, then he will suffer for it, if he hasnae already. But first we must make sure these people leave."

"Father," Uncle Max said, holding up the parchment, "they willnae leave until we join a House."

"We *must* remain autonomous."

"Dinnae all magical beings have to belong to a House?" Uncle Barr asked.

"Technically, no," Max replied. "But a large group of true immortals…"

"We cannae die," Grandpa growled. "Let them come."

"Not all of us have made the transition," Aunt Connie said. And she should know, her twin daughters were only seven years old. If they died now, they died-died, or became ghosts like Sabrina.

Funny, that I haven't met any other ghosts here.

So maybe they just…died.

She'd looked for Peter, Penny, Bernard, Bertha and Stewart among the castle's grounds. They'd been murdered like she had, but they hadn't seemed to make the transition to ghosthood. *Maybe they hadn't reached for the node like I did the ley lines.*

"We can always make more of us," Colin said. "The loss may be worth it."

"Ye were but a bairn when the Houses warred last time," Uncle Max said. "There will be nothing left of Loch Muick if they come."

"Careful," Sabrina said, wagging a finger. "You're showing your true colors there, Cousin."

"Ye are talking about *bairns*." Aunt Connie glared at her cousin, at Grandpa. "Are ye willing to watch the little ones die for yer pride?"

"My *pride?* Dinnae think to tell me what to do—"

Uncle Barr cut Grandpa off. "We should meet them, listen to what they have to offer, then make the decision.

If we can negotiate a deal that would benefit the clan, then it may be worth it."

"There willnae be a benefit worthwhile—"

"Ye dinnae know that," Uncle Max said. "All it would take is for a new portal to open up in Scotland for us to be fucked. Ye ken what happens when new portals open—the country they open up in becomes a war zone. Look what happened to Portland. We may survive, but the *family* willnae. Having the protection of a House may save us."

"The likelihood of that is small," Colin argued.

"We live on a node of magic—where do ye think all those portals come from?" Uncle Max asked. "They're attracted to magic."

"If we lose the node," Aunt Connie said, "then we willnae survive."

"Fine." Grandpa frowned. "We meet them. We listen. Then we decide."

"But," Sabrina said into the quiet, as if she were a narrator and this was a movie, "he was never going to listen."

CHAPTER 6

KIERAN

K ieran hadn't anticipated returning to the highlands of Scotland anytime soon. But here he was; only this time, he wasn't alone.

If the House hadn't wanted to know so badly what Douglas was, Kieran would have just given up a month prior, after he found the blood. The girl was dead, nothing further to add. But the House *did* want the information, so he had found the clan that occupied Loch Muick. From there, he had traced things back to two castles: Braemar, home to the Baron of Invercauld and Omnalprie, and Chief of the Fhearchair clan, and Balmoral, once owned by the former English royal family.

The people he had observed—they weren't quite right. Not in Braemar, not in the castle, and not around the loch. Sure, they looked human, but he would bet his meagre fortune on the fact that many were like Douglas.

Kieran had done his recon under a layer of magical protections—slip in, slip out, with no one the wiser. He'd found a graveyard near Braemar Castle, complete with wrought iron fence, spooky vibe, and lopsided tombstones. It had looked like something out of an old-school horror movie: skeletal trees, the occasional crooked headstone, all topped off with a menacing fog that slowly floated about, like gravity was merely a suggestion, rather than a natural force.

He had searched through the headstones, noting that there were handfuls of older residents interred in the cemetery. About five hundred years ago, it seemed like the aging population had largely vanished from the graveyard. Normally, if these people were just humans, it wouldn't make sense for the old folks to disappear. Not unless they shipped their dead elsewhere, or cremated them and threw their ashes to the wind. Which he doubted. You didn't tend to bury the kids and not the adults.

Eventually, he'd found what he was looking for: Sabrina Aiofe Fhearchair. Her grave had seemed a bit…sad. The tombstone was a simple granite, and the epitaph was 'loving daughter' along with her birth and death dates. No flowers, no essay about her significance, the lack of which was noticeable because most of the others had lines of text.

Nothing to show any sentimentality about her loss. And she'd been dead over a year.

Disappointment had gnawed at him, but not because he had bad news to bring home. No, it was because the owner of the most delicious blood he'd ever smelled was gone. Nothing but bones in the ground.

After that, he'd headed back to the House headquarters in Portland, not bothering to meet up with Dahlia. She was a big girl; she'd find her own way home.

Douglas had been devastated by the news of his daughter's death. In fact, Kieran didn't think he'd seen anyone break so hard before. Not even under torture. It was like the man became a shadow of himself, and that was saying something, since he could turn invisible.

Kieran couldn't say anybody would care that much if *he* died, not even his mother. Oh, she'd miss him, but her life would certainly be easier without him. His stepdad would probably dance a jig on his grave.

Yeah, they had issues.

But he wasn't the only one.

It turns out that the blood oath Douglas had made was as serious as he'd thought. But Dahlia had spent the remainder of her time in England working on finding a loophole, going over the man's vow with a fine-tooth comb. And she'd found it. Which was lucky, because they needed to know what he was.

They only knew what he *wasn't:* a ghost, since ghosts couldn't take on physical form unless they were possessing someone. And Douglas wasn't possessing a body; his manacles would have turned a pale blue if that were the case. Since he could dematerialize in the cuffs—although they did prevent him from escaping—he wasn't a strangely powerful poltergeist or something like that.

And just like Dahlia had proposed before he'd gone to Scotland the first time, they'd played Pictionary, since Douglas couldn't *write* or *say* anything about his species. It had taken Kieran, Adora, Elias and the king's mate, Dannika, to work it out.

A phantom.

Thank fuck for *Phantom of the Opera*, that's all he had to say there. The discovery of a new species—and one that may well be truly immortal—was enough to piss Elias off. Their fearless leader didn't like surprises and he didn't like powerful beings living footloose and fancy free. That way led to chaos: it was why the Houses were established in the first place.

Elias had reluctantly informed the House of Sea and Serpentine, before telling the others. Nobody liked the fact that there were human immortals living under the radar, unchecked and ungoverned.

Douglas couldn't show them how his people had achieved immortality—apparently that was beyond the bounds of his drawing skills, not that Kieran thought the guy would tell them, anyway—but they were certain he had started out human.

The blood sample Kieran had tried didn't tell him much more than what the game of draw-your-species had, either. He'd taste-tested a sample from Douglas, as had Elias and Ysabeau. It was…different. Not bad, not good. It was like cotton candy, tasty but with no substance. It had an iron-y aftertaste; strangely, it didn't taste like it smelled, of sweet decay.

And it was *nothing* like Douglas' daughter's blood.

Of course, he hadn't offered up *that* sample to either Elias or Ysabeau.

Which brought him back to now.

Kieran stood in the cold fall air outside the Invercauld Arms Hotel in Braemar. The small town was picturesque; trees filled with burnt orange and golden leaves, the sky blue and clear, despite the bite of pre-winter. The hotel was located opposite a stone church, which had long since been re-purposed—hard to believe in a single deity, when gods had waltzed through the Himalayan portal a few thousand years ago to leave havoc and mayhem in their wake.

Normally, all six of the Houses would have to come out to do the official meet and greet; the remote nature of the clan, and the fact that they disliked outsiders, however, had made the Houses send a more limited group of ambassadors.

Plus, there were plenty of problems at home right now, anyway. Not to mention coups. *Air and Amethyst, and Fire and Fluorite, I'm looking at you.* Indeed, Air had only sent ambassadors in an attempt to show they had not been weakened by recent events—at least, that's how Kieran saw it.

Even Kieran himself was only here because Elias had decided he needed to be. It wasn't because of his stellar personality, or his ability to act as a diplomat, because he had neither. It was because of his ancestry. Phantoms appeared to be spirit in nature, at least partly, so Kieran could see Douglas when he was incorporeal, whether the man wanted to be seen or not.

Apparently, the others didn't have this ability.

Elias had decided Douglas would continue to remain their involuntary guest, at least until the House issue was sorted. Sea and Serpentine wanted him back, but Elias wasn't playing nice with them. Better to have a hostage than hand over their one advantage.

And there were no plans to return Douglas to the phantoms. The Houses had agreed to keep how they'd learned about the new species on the down-low, for now, hoarding their secrets. Although, surely the phantoms had to suspect it was Douglas who had exposed them: he was taken by Sea and Serpentine over a year ago. But, if they didn't realize he was missing—maybe they thought he had settled elsewhere—they may not realize the Houses had him.

Plus, they might try to incapacitate the phantom if they brought him along, and this wasn't about playing into the phantoms' internal drama. This was about fostering global harmony.

Hah! First time I've ever thought that magnanimously.

As for Douglas, well, he was pissed. Sabrina's death had had a meteoric impact on the man; he seemed to think the clan was somehow responsible for her loss, even if it had just been through the negligence of letting her roam free.

No use fighting over spilled milk—or a dead girl.

There was always plenty of both to go around.

Didn't mean Kieran wasn't slightly disappointed, though.

As he waited for the other House representatives to arrive, he leaned a hip against the Bentley they'd borrowed from the Blood and Beryl embassy. Ysabeau—his diplomatic 'buddy' for the trip—was still inside the car. She was a pureblood vampire, rumored to be two thousand years old. She'd been selected over Dahlia or Adora because Elias wanted them to stay behind and study Douglas.

Plus, Adora just tended to distract people . . . or piss them off. Ysabeau, however, was cold, calculated and vicious. A nice foil to Kieran's feral nature.

She was also one of the few members of the House who could tolerate Kieran. And vice versa. He was too…intense to tolerate most people's bullshit.

Without thinking, he reached inside his jacket and touched the vial of blood hidden there. He kept it tucked close to his chest; his excuse that his magic was what sustained the blood. In reality, he hadn't been able to part with such a delicious-smelling substance.

He had only sampled it once, the tiniest drop. It had been the best thing he'd ever tasted. A simple mantra had revolved through his mind ever since.

You should try it again. Just to see.

His hand closed on the vial and flicked off the lid. The scent that reached him... *damn.* He ran a finger around the rim of the bottle before slipping the lid back on. Then he licked his finger.

Fuck.

It was almost enough to send him to his knees.

He'd never tasted anything so good—like blood berries and honeysuckle, lust and love, lightning and thunder—and this was but a hint of the real thing, wisps left on the rim of a vial. If he was ever able to drink from the source, he would probably die from the pleasure of it all.

Maybe it's a good thing Sabrina's dead.

He didn't like to think what he would do if someone with that blood was left walking around. Of what he would do just to taste it. What he would be capable of to protect it.

Ysabeau tapped on the window of the Bentley before the glass panel lowered with a smooth, electronic hum. Her dark skin glowed, her face framed by dark bangs and a sleek, ebony bob. Her eyes were hidden by a pair of dark sunglasses; even the weak daylight seemed to bother her. "You ready?"

He grunted.

"Kieran—" Her tone held a warning to behave.

"What? I'm ready for this shitshow to begin." He narrowed his eyes. "You aren't going to give me a list, are you?"

The last time he'd been given a list by high-ranking members of Blood and Beryl had ended with Elias almost attacking him. It was not a fond memory.

"No." Ysabeau made a breathy sound, which he interpreted as a chuckle and/or snort. "Air are here."

He rubbed his thumb over his lips and glanced down the road, which was empty of even a pigeon. Then the sound of a motor reached him, followed thirty seconds later by a car.

Remind me never to try sneaking up on her.

With hearing like that, living in a communal house must be a bitch. No wonder she kept separate apartments whenever she could.

"They are supposedly bringing a fae and a siren," she said, head tilting slightly as she poked at the tablet on her lap.

"Do we know what kind of fae?"

Ysabeau tapped the screen. "No."

It would probably be an elemental magic user. Death fae like him were rare, and tended to congregate in the House of Gold and Garnet—the one place where you could get almost anything you wanted, as long as you were willing to pay the price.

As for the siren, well, he hadn't really crossed paths with one before. Rumor had it they could force people to obey their spoken commands, or hypnotize them into forgetting their own names.

"How do you know it's Air?" he asked as the car approached.

The corner of Ysabeau's lip rose slightly. "Because Spirit wouldn't bother with a car."

Sure enough, by the time Air pulled up, a small, temporary portal had appeared to the side of Glenshee Road.

The assholes from Air and Amethyst still hadn't emerged by the time the Spirit and Sapphire ambassadors had come through the portal. Ysabeau had elegantly exited the Bentley to stand next to him, all poise and lethal grace in a business suit and pumps. She made him look like a thug. Which was cool. People wouldn't give him shit, then.

Within seconds, the Spirit and Sapphire representatives strode toward them. Kieran almost did a double take—one of the diplomats was a human. Well, *appeared* human. She had pink hair, sun-kissed skin and a look that said not to fuck with her.

"Hmm. Clever," Ysabeau murmured. "Send someone who looks human to make the phantoms feel more at ease."

The remaining Spirit and Sapphire representative was a shifter; some kind of cat, from the way they moved. Long-limbed and lithe, his skin was so dark it had a blue shimmer in the weak sunlight, while his green eyes were flat, hard.

He has seen some shit.

Finally, the Air and Amethyst representatives left their car. Kieran clenched his jaw at the sight of the fae—an air user, but not just any air user. This was the Moonlight Wraith's former left-hand woman, Feyre. She could form tornadoes and send you flying every which way to Sunday. And while he hadn't known the species of her companion, he recognized her face. She was Oleander

Price—an assassin who pretended to be a courtier. All smiles and glitter, until the knife slid between your ribs.

Kieran much preferred the more direct way.

Stab, then talk.

"Hi, I'm Sky Serpell." The human-seeming woman from Spirit and Sapphire held out a hand to Ysabeau, who glanced at it like it was poison.

She didn't believe in playing with her food.

Kieran shook it, so she wasn't left hanging. A rare act of kindness, but he was *trying* to be diplomatic. "I'm Kieran Aspen, this is Ysabeau St. Clare. House of Blood and Beryl."

"I'm Clint Leopald," the shifter drawled with a twang reminiscent of the deep south of America. No hand offered there.

"And we are Feyre and Lady Oleander Price," the Wraith's pet courtier said. She had glittering pale hair, wide-set crystal blue eyes and plump lips that should have given him fantasies. Instead, they made him want to check where his weapons were.

"Lovely to meet you," Sky said, her voice calm and sure.

Oleander's mouth quirked in a facsimile of a smile. "I'm sure it is."

I'm not sure how I'm going to make it through the next couple weeks, if this is anything to go by.

Kieran didn't play well with others, but he would suck it up, do the nice-nice, and bring back a report to Elias. He had no intention of making friends, though.

Friendships were for fools, and they certainly weren't made between Houses.

This was going to be a fucking nightmare.

CHAPTER 7

SABRINA

T he main hall of Braemar Castle was usually filled
with people; it was where her young cousins and
the townspeople went to school, where people gossiped
and hung out. It was the heart of the clan, one that beat
with laughter and pulsed with love and energy.

Today, it was empty except for the head of the clan and
his closest advisors. That roughly equated to about a dozen
people, but even then, the room felt cavernous.

The polished floorboards gleamed a dark mahogany,
and the burgundy walls boasted family portraits—their
ancestors' disapproval was almost palpable.

Maybe they should have taken them down.

Her gaze roamed over the paintings: there, right in the
middle, was an image of Great-grandpa Fergus. It looked
as if it had been painted yesterday—if yesterday he'd been
wearing a costume designed to look like fifteenth-century
formal wear. And there was Grandpa Angus as well, at the
far end. His portrait had been painted more than a hundred
years ago, but the man had barely aged a day.

"Fucking heathens, the lot of ye!" a disgruntled voice yelled. And there he was—her elusive great-great-great-great and so on grandfather, rumored to be one of the first to achieve immortality in their clan. He was in his spirit form rather than corporeal, but it didn't seem to affect the volume of his tirade. "Ye fools tell the Houses we exist, and ye cannae wear even a suit to meet them?"

"Grandfather," Grandpa Angus said slowly, as if talking to a toddler, "I am not about to… pander to these…'people'." He really wasn't: Angus was wearing jeans and a flannel shirt, like he had just stepped in from the fields. He looked barely thirty, not a strand of gray to be seen in his chestnut hair.

None of her relatives had dressed up for the occasion, she realized, except for Great-grandpa, but he always looked like that, since he never took physical form anymore. He had slicked-back, carrot-colored hair, cold gray eyes, and a purple suit with tartan tie. Sure, the suit clashed horribly with his hair and tie, but there was a sense of style to it, even if it made her eyes want to bleed.

And I don't even really have eyes.

Grandpa Angus, meanwhile, sat on a 'throne'; a large wooden dining chair that had been repurposed for the event, with Granny Kim standing next to him. She wore denim overalls and a peach-colored shirt with one too many frills to ever be fashionable. Her dark hair was swept up in a messy bun, where a few curls had escaped to frame her face.

Great-grandpa Fergus floated around the room, hands clasped behind his back, face set in a scowl. On either side of her grandparents were some of Sabrina's uncles and aunts, each in casual wear, and Colin. Colin was the fanciest. He wore black jeans and a pale blue top, the latter carefully designed to highlight his eye color. She'd heard him muttering to himself when he picked it out.

Vain, much?

All of their amulets were hidden under clothing.

Sabrina, well, she was still in the clothes she'd worn the day she died.

The House of Air and Amethyst, the House of Blood and Beryl, and the House of Spirit and Sapphire…

Sabrina had met plenty of people who belonged to the Houses, simply because she'd met lots of supernatural creatures after leaving the clan. But she'd never met anybody that was a high-ranking official from one of the Houses. She was so keen to see these newcomers she'd thought about traveling to the edge of her range and spying on them when they entered Braemar's grounds. But she was too invested in watching her relatives' reactions to actually leave.

From what she'd overheard, none of the kings or queens or councilors or whatever they called themselves, were attending this particular meet and greet. The head of just one House, apparently, would be chosen to meet Grandpa, leader to leader, once an alliance was formed.

That had only made her grandpa angrier. He didn't want to deal with lackeys, he said. It was disrespectful and a waste of time. Sabrina, however, didn't think it would be a good thing for Grandpa to meet with one of the leaders, only to insult them to their face.

Because he would insult them, of that she had no doubt.

Better he had some time to cool off.

Colin's phone beeped and he glanced down at the screen. "They're here."

"It's about time," Grandpa muttered, then squared his shoulders. She could hear his jaw grinding from her position next to Colin.

Because they're so late.

In fact, they were kind of early. Which was a good thing—for her. She was *dying* to meet them.

Hah. Aren't I funny?

"It's only been two days since we got the letter saying they were coming," Connie murmured to her brother.

Two days.

Colin and the others had been scrambling around like headless chickens for forty-eight hours straight. It had totally ruined Sabrina's routine. She wasn't able to do her nightly recon on the rest of the family because Colin had mostly stayed awake, and she hadn't wanted to leave his side. He was hatching a new plan, and she wanted to know what it was.

Colin was *pissed* that the Houses knew about the clan.

"Well," Sabrina said to Colin, while she took a seat on an invisible chair. "If you hadn't gone and murdered that witch from the House of Sea and Serpentine, this wouldn't be happening. So, really, this is all your fault."

If only she could tell Grandpa that.

Her cousin clenched his jaw. Maybe he could *sense* her disdain. She flapped her hands at him, trying to waft over more of that hot, hot contempt.

"And you know what?" Sabrina continued to herself. "Why didn't the House of Sea and Serpentine send an ambassador? Are they doing some sneaky recon or something while these folks distract us?"

She'd have to scout around and check, in the few hours Colin slept.

There *had* been talk of strange tracks left in the soft soil out near the loch, lately.

Footsteps approached, and the large double oak doors were shoved inward by her cousin Sammy. The dark-haired teenager stared wide-eyed into the room for a moment, before turning back and waving his hand toward whoever was out there.

"This is it!" Sabrina said, clapping her hands and bouncing in her seat.

Around her, the others inhaled sharply.

They came in in pairs: two women entered first, their noses tilted upward, as if they were already bored. They wore a combination of silver and purple, and the woman on the right had glittering, pale hair. She was tall, with sharply pointed ears, and *exuded* elegance in a dress that fit her like a glove, highlighting every curve and sweep of her body. *Typical fae.* It made Sabrina feel dowdy, trapped in her jeans and bloodstained knitted sweater.

Not that I have a choice, there.

The other woman had dark green hair and cat-shaped eyes, which glowed with a golden light. She didn't seem like a witch, and she didn't move like a shifter; there were no pointed ears, either. Did her skin have...*scales*? Sabrina had no idea *what* the woman was, but she was dangerous. She'd bet her non-existent savings on it.

Is it wrong their beauty kind of pisses me off?
Probably.

But she was only—sorta—human.

The first pair was followed by a woman who looked human and a man who had the lethal grace of the stalking cat. She was attractive, like most House members, with dark pink hair and tan skin that looked like she spent a lot of time in the outdoors. He was tall, with strokable dark skin and a face that should have been on the cover of one of those old fashion magazines. Sabrina figured he was probably a shifter.

Her attention moved to the final couple and her brain froze.

"Whoa."

He. Was. *Hot*.

Like, the most beautiful guy she had ever seen.

Sabrina blinked, rubbed her eyes, then blinked again. Nope. He didn't get any less sexy.

Fuck.

She was having trouble catching her breath, which was stupid, because she didn't have lungs. *I just want to jump him, ride him until I can't breathe.* Which again was odd, because she didn't have hormones, and so seeing this guy shouldn't be getting her motor running.

I have no motor. Not anymore.

She waved a hand next to her face, as if she could cool heated skin that didn't exist.

But, *damn*. She didn't think she'd ever pictured her ideal man before, but if she had, he would have been it. Shoulder-length black hair was swept back into a low ponytail—no man bun, thank the gods—and he had piercing gray eyes that looked like they could see into your damned soul. His firm jaw was lick-able, and she wanted to nibble his lips, which were plump enough to bite. And he was *built*. Tall, muscular and with long, sexy fingers.

Yummy, with a side of delicious.

It was then she noticed his ears, just visible under the length of his hair—pointed like a fae's.

Damn.

Fae weren't exactly known for liking humans.

Whoa. Hold up. You're dead. Stop trying to picture him as a potential boyfriend. Alive people don't date ghosts.

He couldn't even see her.

Finally, she managed to turn away from him and take in the woman he was with. She was gorgeous, with a sleek bob and dark sunglasses that gave her an Audrey Hepburn *Breakfast at Tiffany's* vibe. But there was an edge to her, a sense of great age. Grandpa Fergus gave her the same feeling, but unlike him, this woman seemed cold, calm, and collected.

And murderous.

Definitely murderous.

The woman gave a slight smirk as she took in the hall and the clan representatives. A hint of fang was visible.

Vampire.

Eeep.

Sabrina had never had much to do with blood suck-ers—she had never been sure if they'd be able to tell some-thing about her blood wasn't quite right, and she hadn't wanted to give away the family's secret, even by accident. But she knew they were dangerous. The House of Blood and Beryl was run by a vampire king; and his reputation was enough to make most people wary of the race.

Drawn like a bee to a delicious honey, Sabrina's gaze tracked back to the fae man. He was studying the family around her. His eyes lingered for a second on Grandpa Fergus, who he probably shouldn't be able to see, before sweeping past to settle on Grandpa Angus.

"Welcome to the Fhearchair clan," Grandpa Angus boomed. His demeanor had changed the moment the doors opened. Gone was the irritated and rude clan chief; instead, a benevolent barely middle-aged man greeted them, a wealthy retiree just enjoying his life.

I didn't know he was such a good actor. Maybe I underestimated him.

The rest of the family all wore pleasant smiles, and seemed utterly relaxed. Gran looked soft and kind and *happy* to see the delegates, and Sabrina hadn't thought she had a fake bone in her body. Even Colin appeared pleased, and he had been seething all morning.

I think I underestimated all of them.

The six representatives came to a stop about ten yards from Grandpa Angus' throne.

"I am Lord Angus Fhearchair, Baron of Invercauld and Omnalprie, and Chief of the Fhearchair clan. This is Lady Kim, and my...brother, Max..." Grandpa Angus could hardly say Max was his son, when they looked barely a decade apart in age.

Sabrina looked back at the guests, at...*him.* Something tightened in her chest as the man's gaze followed the introductions...and lingered on her face when they got as far as Colin.

Did he see me? Or did I imagine it?

She could've sworn he even gave her a little half-smile, which was weird. It made her think she was losing her mind.

I want to touch him. Just a little.

Grandpa Angus finished talking. Sabrina realized he hadn't introduced Great-grandpa Fergus.

Then the male fae spoke into the sudden quiet, his voice recalling warm brandy and cool sheets. "And who is the girl?"

Me! Sabrina straightened up, stunned. *He means me!*

Grandpa Angus's brow furrowed, and he looked around the room, confused. "Which one?"

"Never mind," the stranger muttered. His voice was sexy and rough.

I could listen to him speak all night long.

His vampire companion gave him a sidelong glance, but he just shrugged. And then he looked at Sabrina.

Like, properly *looked*.

If she'd been alive, her breath would've caught in her throat. Instead, a sudden rush of electrical tingles zapped up her body, and she could have sworn that she became more real, more tangible.

Her hand fluttered over her chest, before grabbing her knitted sweater, fingers tangling in the material.

And then her world rocked.

He winked at her.

He. Winked. At. Her.

He sees me.

CHAPTER 8

KIERAN

K ieran's eyes lingered on the gorgeous redhead; she drew his gaze to her like a lodestone. She floated in between two of the phantoms, staring straight back at him, hand tangled in her sweater like she wanted to rip it off and dance topless around the room.

Maybe you're just hoping she'll do that.

Because the girl was stunning, hands down the most beautiful woman he'd ever seen. Her hair was a deep russet, and her eyes a cool aquamarine that shone, even in her near-transparent state. She looked different to the other incorporeal phantom who was hovering in the room; and it wasn't solely due to their fashion statements. The male phantom wore a bright purple suit that was in danger of destroying Kieran's eyesight, whereas the girl wore jeans and a white knitted sweater. One that had a bloodstain over her stomach.

His hands itched at the sight of her injury, but he knew it wasn't a recent one. The other phantom seemed more real, seemed *alive*. Even though purple-clad phantom hadn't been introduced along with all the others, Kieran knew the other phantoms were aware of his presence, their eyes occasionally flickering in his direction.

But the girl…

There had been genuine looks of confusion on the other phantoms' faces when Kieran had asked who she was. They didn't know she was there, he would put good money on that. And no one else in the Houses' welcoming committee seemed to realize she was, either.

Ghost.

She had to be.

Too bad Douglas hadn't been able to give me a photo before.

But Kieran didn't need a picture to tell him this woman was likely the recently dead Sabrina Fhearchair. Her jaw-line had similarities to Douglas, and her hair was clearly akin to her aunt's and the eye-watering 'invisible' phantom.

And…Kieran just knew, in his gut. The blood from earlier still a faint taste on his tongue…he *knew.*

She was muttering to herself, too quiet for him to make out across the distance.

Then the fae's introduction cut through his musing. Her voice was chilly enough that he expected frost to form around her. "I am Feyre, from the House of Air and Amethyst."

The phantoms didn't look impressed. He wondered if they realized this woman had been playing politics and doling out death longer than most of them had been alive.

I am not going to sleep well knowing the Air and Amethyst ambassadors are here.

Then again, it was going to be hard to sleep knowing the phantoms could spy on him whenever they felt like it, and he had to pretend he didn't know.

"I am Lady Oleander Price. House of Air and Amethyst." The siren's voice was ethereal, so beautiful it almost made his ears ache.

He didn't like it.

This was a woman who'd slit his throat while offering him *hor d'oeuvres* with her other hand. He could easily see how her voice could lull people into a false sense of security. And how it could kill with the right intention.

The others also introduced themselves, but he ignored them, focused on the female ghost. She was approaching him.

Ysabeau gave him a jab in the ribs with her elbow.

It hurt.

"I'm Kieran Aspen, House of Blood and Beryl." He used his mother's maiden name, even though she had taken on the Laskaris surname after formally mating Kieran's stepfather.

The girl was standing right in front of him now, so close his body felt a tingle of electricity, his nerve endings coming alive and the little hairs on his arms rising.

"You're so delicious, I wish I could bite you," the ghost whispered in his ear. If she'd been alive, her body heat and scent would be making him harder than a rock. As it was, her presence was making things a bit uncomfortable.

Fuck, he wanted to reply, *I'd let you bite me if you could.* She was that hot.

And that was saying something, because he didn't do sex. Not because it wasn't fun—it was—but it just always ended up being too complicated. He didn't like dealing with people and emotions.

I'd much rather torture someone than comfort a crying person.

He tried not to look at Sabrina, because he didn't want people thinking he could see someone who wasn't in the room. There were two reasons for his caution: one, he doubted anyone but him could see her; and two, he didn't want anyone to suspect that he could.

But ignoring her was hard.

"Hrm. You can see me but can't hear me, is that it?" She strode around to stand next to his right arm.

What is she doing?

No.

Now was not the time to worry about the ghost. He had to stay focused.

Focus.

The phantoms.

Right.

Not the ghost who was now running her hand up and down his bicep, leaving ghostbumps—uh, goosebumps—in her wake.

He took a deep breath and exhaled slowly, tuning out the delightful ghost running her hand over his pec, leaving tingles in her wake—but it wasn't a true touch; no, it was insubstantial and left him craving more.

He instead tried to concentrate on what Lord Whatever and his family were saying. Clearly, these phantoms did *not* want Kieran or the others here.

At all.

Oh, their convivial smiles were excellent, they really excelled at pretending welcome, but the incorporeal phantom was muttering to himself about intruders, and crap about how 'this wouldnae have happened in my day'. A slight pinch around the clan chief's mouth indicated that he was annoyed at his relative's antics, but he obviously wasn't going to do anything about it.

Nobody else was meant to see—or *hear*—it.

The other phantoms wore varying expressions of irritation, curiousness, and reluctance, all coated in sugary welcome. The male on the end though—the one with eyes similar to Sabrina's—he was just flat-out cold. Analytical. He gave off a preparing-to-slit-your-throat-in-your-sleep vibe.

It reminded him a bit of Ysabeau, to be fair.

He's dangerous.

The ghost's hand was sliding down his stomach now.

He swallowed, his throat suddenly dry.

Totally not how I thought this meet-and-greet was going to go.

"I know you can see me. Do I have to feel you up, before you'll acknowledge me?" Sabrina asked, hand sliding lower and lower.

Fuck.

He did *not* want to sport a boner in public. Because what she was doing…it was scorching his brain cells. Flaming.

Get a hold of yourself. She's dead. *You can't fuck a ghost.*

But…if he could work out how to, he wouldn't have to worry about her getting attached—

He darted a glance at her and then back to the front, trying to tell her he could see her, but he couldn't play right now. She paused her hand's downward sweep.

He nodded, just the teensiest bit.

"Ohhh. Okay." She pulled her hand away, and the loss of contact almost made him want to grab her hand and shove it back, but that was neither possible nor smart. "Are we playing some kind of pantomime game, except you just make small movements and I have to guess what you mean?"

It's not like you could feel her properly, anyway. Just a tingle. But it had been a good tingle.

A *very good* tingle.
Better than no tingle.
You. Are. An. Idiot.

"It is a pleasure to have ye all here," Lord Angus, Baron of Whatever, said, interrupting Kieran's internal dilemma. Titles didn't mean much to Kieran, not unless it was 'king' or 'queen', and you were a ruler of a House. *Or a god.* It was never wise to piss off a deity by using the wrong name.

"I would assume so," Feyre the fae said.

Angus frowned but didn't bite back.

"We will be serving tea and cake soon," the woman next to the clan chief said, ignoring Feyre's barb. She smiled, broad and wide, but it was as fake as Kieran's love for his stepfather. If she had a knife in her hand, Kieran was sure she'd be thinking about burying it in the fae woman's chest.

"That's my grandmother," Sabrina said, almost casually. She sat on that invisible chair again, this time right next to him. "She doesn't appreciate smart mouths or cussing."

Noted.

"For now," the grandmother continued, "I will have Samuel show ye to yer rooms. Ye can get settled in, and then join us a wee bit later."

"Sammy is my cousin," Sabrina said. "The one who let you in here. He's a good kid. Don't try and mess him up."

Kieran lifted an eyebrow.

"You're from the House of Blood and Beryl. You fuck things up, then fuck things up some more later." Sabrina sniffed.

He tried not to look offended.

Sure, Kieran had tortured hundreds—if not thousands—of people before, but he didn't target kids. Mostly because Elias didn't believe in torturing kids, but that wasn't the point.

He hadn't done it.

And he wasn't about to start now.

Ysabeau tilted her head ever-so-slightly in acknowledgement and turned to Kieran, while the people from Spirit and Sapphire were nodding. "You ready?"

"Yes."

"Oh goody!" Sabrina clapped her hands. "I'll get you all to myself soon."

His heartbeat kicked up a notch and Ysabeau shot him a curious stare. He fought the urge to rub his chest. Being alone with this ghost, whose touch sent his body into electrical overdrive, it would be agony. But the best kind.

Keep calm and pretend everything is fine.

Sabrina tugged on his arm. "Let's go, let's go! The asses from Air and Amethyst will beat you out the door, otherwise."

Do not smile. Do not smile.

He strode for the door, Ysabeau close on his heels. They met the fae and the siren at the open entryway and Kieran gave them a cool smile. "Beauty first." He then swept out before them.

"Well, that's the first time a male has complimented himself over me," the fae said, giving him a creepy smile, almost like she was hitting on him.

"The mirror doesn't lie," he replied. Ysabeau shot him a scathing look.

Show no weakness.

"Hmm. Aspen, you said?" Feyre tapped one plump lip with a finger. "Nephew to King Elias?"

He nodded. He hadn't introduced himself with a title because he technically didn't have one and he wasn't a blood relative of the king. But if Air had done their research properly, they would have known who he was long before he stepped foot in the castle.

Mind games.

He hated them. Unless he was behind them.

The fae smiled, like a wolf exposing its teeth. "Please, do go ahead, I would be more than happy to admire the...view."

She *was* hitting on him.

Great.

"Hands off, fae. I saw him first!" Sabrina shouted, making him jump a little in surprise. And pain: she'd yelled it right next to his ear.

He turned to tell her how she'd nearly deafened him, but words failed him at the sight of the redheaded ghost clawing the air, like...well, a crazy—but very sexy—house cat.

He wasn't sure what to think of that. But he wanted to laugh.

Kieran wasn't the laughing type.

He started walking.

"Kieran," Ysabeau hissed. "We're meant to play nice."

"Treat 'em mean and all." Kieran shrugged.

"I don't think this is the right place—"

"Hello!" said the phantom boy. "My name is Samuel, but feel free to call me Sammy. Nice to meet ye all. Please follow me, and I'll show ye to yer rooms." The dark-haired lad was nothing but appalling enthusiasm, layered in a thick accent.

"What a pleasure," the siren said, oozing predator vibes. Her golden eyes swept over the boy's lanky frame.

Ew.

Sirens lure human males to their deaths…

Kieran would have to keep an eye on the lad, make sure the siren didn't kill him before the two weeks were up. If she succeeded, it would turn this entire thing into even more of a nightmare.

Why me? Why did I get this gig?

Oh yeah. *Because you were sick of torturing people.*

Remind me never to complain to Ysabeau ever again.

"He's actually happy you're here," Sabrina said, her expression sad. She was watching Samuel chatter happily to the Spirit and Sapphire representatives as he led the group through the labyrinthine castle. "The younger ones, they don't mind the idea of change."

And you? He wanted to ask. But didn't.

"Mr. Aspen."

Kieran jumped, just a little. "Present."

The others chuckled, and the youth turned an interesting shade of red. "Your room."

"Thanks." He nodded at Ysabeau, and then opened the door to his suite. He stepped inside, closing the door before anyone else could try and sneak a look inside. He didn't want the others to have a lock for teleportation, in case one of them had the ability.

"Well, uh, okay then. Follow me!" Samuel's cheery voice was muffled, but still discernible, through the thick wooden door. Footsteps indicated the others we moving on, but they hadn't got far before the shifter, Clint Leopald, had his name called.

Kieran's room looked like something out of a tourist brochure. A huge wooden four-poster bed took central position, covered in thick swathes of green material printed with a gold pattern. The walls were wallpapered in gold to match, and the carpet was a deep forest green. A desk was positioned under a window that overlooked an autumnal courtyard, and a sofa stood against the far wall, next to a door that led to a bathroom—or so he assumed.

It was a little…much, for his tastes.

"Finally," Sabrina said, drawing him back to his ghost problem.

Or solution.

He had yet to decide which one it was.

"Finally?" he mouthed, still not game to voice anything yet, humor sparking inside of him at the way her mouth dropped.

But her surprise was short-lived. Something wicked flared to life in her eyes, and she lay back on his bed. "We're all alone."

CHAPTER 9

SABRINA

F uck.

He was even hotter in private. That shouldn't be a thing, considering he was still fully dressed—*what a shame*—but it was. Yeah, she'd gotten right up in his business in the hall, trying to breathe in his scent with a nose that didn't exist. But that had been different. She'd been trying to get a reaction out of him; a moth drawn to a dangerous flame, unable to look away, *wanting* to get burned. It had been a game. Here in his room, for the split second he'd actually focused on her, it had been better than sex.

It was insane how hot it was to be heard. To be *seen*.

She'd been dead over a year now, with nobody knowing she existed. She'd talked to herself, talked to paintings, talked to her cousins, talked to her fingernails, to the mice, to the birds… Yeah, okay, she'd talked to pretty much everything she could. And no one—or nothing—had ever acknowledged her. It would have been pretty scary if the paintings had started communicating with her, but hell, she would have taken anything at that point. It was like she didn't exist, even when she was clearly real.

At least to her.

And now, apparently to *him*.

Kieran Aspen.

Member of the House of Blood and Beryl. *Nephew* to the friggen *king*.

"So, what does being nephew to the King of Blood Rage get you?" she asked, genuinely curious.

He ignored her.

Ignored her.

In fact, his gaze swept right by her *like she wasn't there,* and he began studying the room, as if trying to pry apart its secrets.

Pain lodged itself right about where her heart would have been, had she still been flesh. *Why is he ignoring me again?*

And why am I so fucking pathetic?

That was the real question here.

Look at her. Acting like a needy-ass ghost, lying all over the guy's bed like a creeper. She was as bad as that fae woman, all leer and lust.

Sabrina sat up.

Show some self-respect, girl. He's alive and you're dead. Stop trying to fuck him—which, hello, impossible—and start trying to work out how he can help you.

There.

That was better.

Too bad the voice in her head had kind of sounded like Colin. She would normally think that was a crime against nature, but in this situation, *Be More Like Colin* was probably not a bad thing. She needed to be canny, and to work the odds so the game was in her favor.

In short, she needed assistance.

And Kieran Aspen was the guy who was going to give it to her.

He'd emptied the drawers in the dresser and was now going through the knick knacks around the room like he was searching for something.

"Your clothes are in your suitcase," she called out, "which is by the door."

Again, he didn't acknowledge her.

As she watched, he withdrew a tiny camera from its hiding place in a vase full of fake flowers—sunflowers, of all things.

Huh.

He threw it on the bed next to her, the cable connected to it bigger than the tiny lens. She pulled her legs up onto the bed and sat cross-legged, waiting. The whole search took around twenty minutes, but he found three cameras, including one in his adjoining bathroom—*ew*. He threw them all on the bed next to her; she reached out to touch one, but her hand passed through it.

So, my family planned on spying on the ambassadors. Did they think the guests wouldn't check for cameras?

Wait. How many cameras are there over the castle? She'd never checked. Then again, in all her forays, she'd never seen anyone setting up spy equipment in the first place.

Kieran dug out a candle from his suitcase, along with a cloth-wrapped bundle. He unwrapped the swathed object to reveal a piece of dark-gray crystal. *Smoky quartz?* She'd never been very good at identifying minerals. She knew the gems for the Houses and that was about it.

It wasn't like she had a lot to do with witchcraft.

Beware smiling men who knock on doors.

Yeah, look how that had worked out for her.

She really should have taken that premonition to heart.

The fae set the crystal up on the tallboy and chanted a few words in a language Sabrina didn't recognize. A golden glow burst through the room, making white dots dance in front of her vision. Then her whole body vibrated in an unsettling, teeth-chattering way, before going back to normal.

She didn't *have* teeth to chatter.

What the hell was that?

"What did you do?"

He straightened up and turned to look at her. "Anti-bugging spell, followed by an anti-listening spell."

Fuck.

There it was again, that whole attention-on-me-thing that got her hot and bothered. Well, bothered, at any rate.

"Couldn't you have done that before you found the cameras?" *In other words, why did you ignore me?*

Wow. So she was back to being pathetic.

You need to grow a spine.

Easier said than done, when one didn't actually *have any bones.*

"And have them think I was talking to someone who wasn't here?" His voice was deep, dark, and made her incorporeal form shiver. "The cameras were only one form of spy technology they used."

Wait. No shivering. Just business.

Her family had used magic on the ambassadors?

They had actually lowered their standards enough to purchase magic? Aside from the warding spells around each castle and the loch?

Turns out she didn't know as much as she thought she had about the inner workings of her family.

"All right. Good point."

"They are the only points I like to make." He grinned, but it was more menacing than happy. Which made her want to lick him.

I really need to get a hobby.

"So…" She waved a hand in the air, unsure how to ask what she so desperately wanted to know.

"How come I can see you?"

Could he read her mind? Or was she that obvious?

He lifted an antique Edwardian chair, which had been shoved over near the small desk, like it weighed no more than a feather. Those things were *heavy*. She'd learned that as a kid, playing in the castle.

Fae strength. Making furniture removal easy since the sixteen hundreds.

He dumped the chair near the foot of the bed, and sat down, legs spread, elbows resting on his knees. He was right opposite her, so close she could reach out and touch him. Well, pass through him. Same deal, but different.

Sabrina nodded. "Yeah, that."

He spread his hands out, palms up. "I'm a death fae."

She frowned. "Doesn't that mean you kill people with a touch?"

"Each death fae is different. Some kill with a touch, others with a kiss, some secrete poison. And some, like me, see ghosts."

She had a feeling he could do a whole lot more than that, considering his menacing aura, but she could understand him keeping his cards close to his hot, muscular chest…

"Can anyone else see you?" he asked.

She thought about lying, but figured it wouldn't serve her best interests. She shook her head. "How did you know I was a ghost and not a…" It seemed even death hadn't altered her aversion to talking to strangers about her species.

"Phantom?"

She winced. She couldn't help it, hearing that word on an outsider's lips… "Yeah, that."

She rubbed a hand down her arm, nervous for some reason. Jittery.

"Well, you're wearing a bloodstained top and you're translucent…"

"But if you know what my family is…"

"They look different to me."

How? Why? In what way?

But she had a feeling that if she asked, he wouldn't answer. He'd be fool to give away his secrets so easily, and she didn't think he was a fool. Way too sexy for his own good, but not stupid.

His gray eyes turned serious. "What's your name?"

Right.

They hadn't done the whole introduction thing yet.

Funny, how she felt like she already *knew* him. Kieran Aspen. Nephew to the Blood and Beryl King. Handsome as sin, if sin were a person. Secretive. Intelligent.

She only realized she hadn't replied when his fingers began tapping on his knee.

"It's Sabrina." She held out a hand.

"Nice to meet you." He smirked, and fuck, it was deli-cious. He then pretended to shake her hand, and it made her whole being zing. They couldn't touch properly, but his palm didn't just sweep through her. "Normally I get introduced to folks before they try to grope me."

She pulled her hand back, needing to stop her thoughts from short-circuiting due to the not-contact. "I'm dead. Social etiquette doesn't apply to me."

He chuckled, just a little, and looked kind of surprised that he had. Like he wasn't used to laughing.

You and me both, buddy.

Being dead wasn't exactly a barrel of giggles.

His mirth died and he clasped his hands together. "So, who murdered you?" His expression was serious, gaze intense.

Wow.

That question was a punch to the carotid.

"Who said I was murdered?"

One dark eyebrow rose. "The bloodstain on your jumper. Unless you happened to have stabbed yourself in the gut?"

"How is that evidence of a stab wound?" Her hands balled into fists to stop herself touching the stain.

She didn't know why she was denying it. *I mean, the urban legend says ghosts are made through murder or misdeeds.* But she'd never met another ghost, so she couldn't actually say that was true. Sabrina wasn't even sure why *she* was a ghost.

She *thought* it was because she'd reached for the ley lines when she was dying, but it could easily just be because she was part-phantom. Her father had sired her after his transition, and her mother had been human. So, Sabrina had been told, anyway. But that didn't explain why her murdered cousins hadn't taken up ghosthood—most of them had been born after one or both of their parents had become immortal.

"A wound on your stomach that leaves that much blood is most likely a stab wound. Unless you knifed someone else, and just wiped the blood on yourself?" He made it sound like something any reasonable person would do.

Like, where else would you wipe the blood?

"No, I didn't get to stab anybody else." She really, really wished she had, though.

"Shame. It's always nice to stab the people who hurt you."

"*Always* nice?"

"If you don't tolerate it when people hurt you, people don't hurt you. If they punch you, you break their arm. If they insult your outfit or pick on your hair color, you stab them a little. If they say you're too skinny, and insult your muscles, you mentally torture them. Tit-for-tat. People stop trying to hurt you after that."

"What's wrong with my hair?" She poked at her pony-tail. It had been like that since she'd died.

His eyes narrowed. "*That* is your takeaway from what I just said?"

"Stab, stab, stab." She jabbed a hand through the air, pretending to stab it. "People look at you, stab 'em."

He sat back in his chair. "Close enough."

Sabrina laughed, surprising herself. This guy was a psycho. But he was *her* psycho.

Wait. No, he wasn't *her* anything.

"You're not gonna answer my question?" he asked.

"What question? Did I stab someone?"

"Your family tried to film my junk; you could at least give me the courtesy of telling me who murdered you."

She fiddled with the hem of her sweater. "It's kind of a personal question, you know?"

Sabrina had no idea why she wasn't willing to tell him. Why she just didn't blurt out that it was Colin, that he was responsible for killing her and all her cousins. Well, not *all* her cousins—she still had plenty—but some of them. The ones that mattered in terms of succession, anyway.

Here was her chance to tell someone, *anyone*, the truth. And she wasn't jumping on it.

What the fuck is wrong with me?

"Well, when you feel ready to tell me, just let me know. I'm here." Then he muttered, "Not like I'm allowed to be anywhere else."

CHAPTER 10

KIERAN

K ieran stood and returned the Edwardian chair to near the window. It was heavy, so he could at least use it to block the door if he needed to. Although, the phantoms could probably just mist through the walls of the room, so a bit pointless there.

His current guest certainly wouldn't be hampered by the barrier.

Her presence didn't bother him though, which for him was a *huge* deal. He didn't discriminate, he often told Elias—he tended to hate everyone equally. It's why he hadn't had a problem with being the in-house torturer, until it got boring.

"You didn't want to come?" Sabrina asked. Her voice had the musical lilt of the highlands, but her accent wasn't as strong as the others he'd met so far. Her time away from the family must have changed her speech.

"I'm not a politician or a diplomat." He turned and met her pale blue gaze. It was intense, the way she stared at him, like he was the most vital thing in her world. He knew it wasn't because of any romantic interest—it was because she was able to talk to him. To be heard.

It was a pretty amazing feeling, that.

He'd learned that the hard way, after being imprisoned by his sperm donor for four years.

Better not to think about that.

Bastard was dead, anyway. Not much he could do from the grave. Especially because there wasn't one.

I hope you enjoy your ashes floating in the deepest part of the ocean.

Yeah, it was totally against death fae custom to cremate the dead, pulverize the bones, and then have them sunk all over the Mariana Trench. But Kieran had held a grudge. As had his mother and her husband, but he hadn't really done it for them; he'd done it for *him.*

Oh, his mother said she didn't regret having him. Never him, she said. But she had been mid-transition to becoming a vampire when she was raped—looking like a corpse for all intents and purposes—and had then been held captive until Kieran was born. His sperm donor had used magic to keep Kieran in her womb, since her body had wanted to reject him—mid-transition vampires were not meant to get pregnant.

I wasn't even born alive.

No, Kieran had come out dead, but there'd been witches and fae at his birth, and he'd come out the other side of it all breathing. His sperm donor had thought it would make Kieran the most powerful death fae ever born—one with vampire blood running through his veins. And maybe it had. He'd never bothered to compare himself to any other. But once his mother had recovered from the birth, she'd grabbed him and ran.

His stepfather, Edward, had found them, taken them to safety—even though he'd made it clear he'd tried to get his mother to leave her child behind.

He had hated Kieran because of what he represented: his mother's rape and capture and subsequent pariah status. Which Kieran understood, but it didn't mean he had to tolerate the guy's crap.

"Uh, hello?"

A shiver rushed through his arm and straight to his cock.

What the—?

He focused.

Sabrina.

Right.

The sexy ghost was standing in front of him, frowning, one hand pressed against his bicep, leaving no pressure, but lots of electrical tingles. "Hellllooooooo."

Fuck. How come her touch was able to make his body come alive?

Because you're a screwed-up death fae who wants to fuck a ghost.

"Uhh, yes?" His sperm donor had been into necrophilia—Kieran wasn't liking the idea that he might have inherited a similar personality trait.

At least he wouldn't fuck a corpse.

"You zoned out then."

He ran a hand over his head, suddenly feeling a bit awkward. "Yeah, it happens."

She moved her hand away and shot him a sidelong glance. "Someone's coming."

"Right. Thanks." He took a step forward then stopped. "When we're not in this room, I can't talk to you."

"Oh, so you wanna hide us?"

"Hide *us*?" He frowned.

She quickly looked away. "Yeah, our, ah, interactions. That's what I meant."

Right. *She wasn't implying you're a couple, idiot.*

"Yeah," he said. "That's kind of the point."

"No, no. It's fine, I understand. You don't want everybody to know that you can see dead people."

"Correct." He chuckled. Why was she so amusing? Why did he *like* her?

"But I'll still talk to you," she said, and waggled her eyebrows.

He did not understand the waggle.

"Fine. But no groping." He held up a finger.

"I'm a ghost, what does it matter if I grope? It's not like you can feel it anyway."

Yes, yes he could feel it. Not in the traditional sense. But he liked it. Way too much. But he couldn't—wouldn't—admit to that. "Ever heard of consent?"

She winced. "Fine. But you're the one missing out."

Didn't he know it.

There was a knock on the door, and Kieran could hear the impatience in it.

He opened it to find Ysabeau on the other side. She looked irritated—the corner of her mouth had twitched upward. That was about as visibly pissed off as she got, unless she was ripping your spine out of your stomach.

She tended to demonstrate her emotions physically.

Show, don't tell.

"What took you so long?" Ysabeau demanded.

"You don't want to ask that."

"I already did."

"Then I'll rephrase: you don't want to know the answer to that."

She huffed, flicked a glance at his groin and turned on her heel, the motion so smooth it took a moment for his brain to register she'd done it. Kieran hurried out, locking the door behind him and muttering the words to a spell he'd brought along. If anyone tried to bust into his room, they'd be in for a nasty surprise.

The hallway was ornately decorated with gold-striped wallpaper highlighted against a maroon background, and they were the only two living people in the area. Sabrina came to a stop next to him.

"So where do we go now?" he asked.

Ysabeau tilted her head ever-so-slightly and sniffed. "This way."

Her senses were far beyond his, and he had awesome senses. She was about as powerful as you could get, without reaching Master status: the top of the top, when it came to vampires. But Kieran wasn't an ordinary vampire, so it wasn't like his genetics played by regular rules. Ysabeau couldn't scent blood the way he could, despite her age and species.

As they reached an intersection in the corridors, he realized this place was a maze.

"You're just going to follow her?" Sabrina asked as she trailed after them.

He lifted one shoulder in response. This was going to get difficult. He wasn't able to reply without Ysabeau asking uncomfortable questions, the main one being why he didn't want to share the fact he could see Sabrina. And why Sabrina existed. He was going to have to work out how he could reply using body language, while looking like he *wasn't* using body language.

Elias wouldn't be happy if he screwed this up.

"She's pretty hot," Sabrina said. "And scary. Scary hot?"

Kieran glanced at her, since Ysabeau's back was to them.

She shrugged. "I mean, I've got eyes in my head. I can see who's good looking and who's not. And she's amazing. Like, ten out of ten. But I also get the vibe that she would slit my throat if she knew I was here. I mean, it wouldn't really matter, considering I'm already dead, but I really do have a problem with knives and stuff. You can get why." She waved a hand at her stained sweater.

Kieran bit back a laugh. He'd already chuckled today, which was weird, and he wasn't willing to investigate it further. His emotions were bottled up for a reason, and he preferred to keep it that way.

"Are you sure you know where you're going?" Kieran asked Ysabeau as they seemed to turn down the same hallway for the second time. The hairs on the back of his neck were prickling, and he kept his eyes focused forward.

"We're not alone anymore," Sabrina murmured.

No shit, he wanted to reply.

Ysabeau's pale eyes narrowed. "My nose normally never steers me wrong. But this place is a labyrinth, and the scents are crossed over and over. I was following the trail of the young boy that showed us to our rooms."

Kieran gave a little cough. "He's probably been all over the castle a dozen times today."

Ysabeau sighed. "True."

"How about we—"

"This way." Ysabeau backtracked to the last corridor they were in, and Kieran was finally able to see the spy.

It was no one he'd seen before. Female, looked to be mid-twenties, with long black hair and a pretty face, wearing jeans and a tank top. She had a leather thong around her throat, but the end of the necklace was hidden under the tank. Totally not weather appropriate and also very forgettable.

"That's cousin Charlotte," Sabrina said. "She looks sweet, but she has a thing for guns. And knives. Don't piss her off."

He wasn't sure whether he appreciated the intel or not. Guns weren't much of a threat, and he doubted she'd be able to best him in a knife fight.

He was harder to kill than the regular vampire.

They stopped at a junction in the corridors, where Ysabeau was clearly trying to sort out the scent trails. Kieran felt the phantom stalker drift closer to them, and he realized she was studying Ysabeau with far more interest than himself.

After a couple of seconds, he felt a tingle on his rib cage. "You need to turn left there." Sabrina pointed.

He raised an eyebrow and she looked at him back, almost daring him to not follow her advice.

"I think we turn left here," Kieran said.

Ysabeau paused and looked at him; the phantom's gaze still drawn to the vampire. "Are you sure?"

"No, but I don't want to stand here like an idiot."

If looks could kill—

"Fine."

If only she realized they had an audience of not just one, but *two* invisible people.

They turned left.

"Now right," Sabrina said.

He turned right. And left. And right. Then, suddenly, they were in a dining hall.

What the hell?

Whoever had designed this place was either brilliant, or a total imbecile. So hard to navigate that your enemies would get lost before they ever found you, but then the people who lived here would also have trouble finding their way around.

That's if you relied on doors...

True. If walls weren't exactly an issue to you... you could just ghost directly through and end up wherever you wanted.

How long have these people been living like this?

That was a question they hadn't bothered to ask Douglas, but it was something he was definitely going to ask Sabrina, when he got her alone again.

Why are you looking forward to that?

Better not to answer that.

"There ye are!" The woman who had said there'd be food later—Sabrina's grandmother—stood there grinning at Kieran and Ysabeau like they were mischievous scamps. "We were worried ye got lost."

She was a fantastic actor, except for the fact that her eyes were stone cold.

The phantom who had been following them nodded at her, and then disappeared back out the doorway.

"We took the scenic route," Kieran said and returned the smile, the expression feeling awkward. But if this woman wanted to pretend they were welcome, he was going to pretend he enjoyed being here.

Funnily enough, it wasn't exactly a lie. Mostly because of a particular ghost, who was staring at their host with confusion stamped on her face.

The woman grabbed Kieran's arm and dragged him forward. He fought not to shove the contact away; he didn't like to be touched, not unless it was by someone he knew. "Come now, ye must be starved. Ye do eat, right?"

"Of course," Ysabeau said and smiled as well, a shark baring her teeth. "And we're simply starving."

CHAPTER 11

SABRINA

The grandfather clock in the corner of the dining room chimed, and Sabrina startled. This was the longest she had ever been away from Colin since she'd died, except when he was asleep, and she'd barely felt the time passing. Which was unusual, considering she'd constantly felt time slipping through fingers over the last year.

Her asshole cousin had just entered the room in his invisible form—he'd been following the glittering fae and the siren from the House of Air and Amethyst—so she could keep an eye on him now, at least. The people from the House of Spirit and Sapphire were already here; the shifter had been demolishing half the food on the sideboard over the last fifteen minutes.

Sabrina wondered what she was going to do in the longer term: stick around Kieran, or follow her nemesis?

For the first time, she was conflicted. Here, she had somebody who could see her, listen to her, interact with her. But Colin was hatching a plan, she couldn't just leave him to his evil devices—not an exaggeration—with which he could, and eventually would, cause havoc. What if he learned how to kill a phantom, and she wasn't around to stop it? Well, morally oppose it. Shout loudly about it, at any rate.

Now Kieran was here, he might be able to help her put an end to things. She could tell *someone* what Colin was planning. About what he'd done to her cousins; about what he'd done to *her*.

You assume Kieran Aspen is trustworthy.

And she had no idea if he was. Not really.

Her gut said he was, but she could just be thinking with her groin.

Kieran didn't know her or owe her family anything. He didn't have to help; he didn't have to even talk to her. He could've pretended she didn't exist, and he would have been within his rights. She had no idea why he was communicating with her; for all she knew, this could be some plan to get information about the family...

She was looking for conspiracies everywhere.

Following Colin around had done that to her—made her suspicious of everyone's motives. Although, *everyone* had an agenda, and she'd do well to remember it. It was the one honest thing she'd learned by her cousin's side.

But if she told Kieran about Colin...

It would mean betraying everyone.

Betray? No.

Help? Yes.

But the clan may not see it that way. Grandpa Angus wouldn't. Trying to help the family by giving away their secrets? Yeah, Grandpa Angus would *not* be happy with her. In fact, she had a feeling he would try to kill her for it, even though she was already dead.

Because you never give away the clan's secrets.
Ever.

"I'm going to do some recon," she said. "Be back soon."

Kieran's expression barely changed as he talked to the vampire woman, but his eyebrow lifted ever-so-slightly. She took that as affirmation he'd heard her.

As she turned to leave, she stopped, then spun around. "You should try the cakes. Grandma is an excellent baker. She once studied under a Michelin-starred chef."

There.

Now she could leave.

You don't need to be telling him how delicious Granny's cakes are. They were a prized family legend, he'd find out for himself. *But if I am nice to him, then hopefully he will begin to trust me.*

Yeah. She'd done it as a tactical thing, not because she thought he'd enjoy the delicious treats. Or that it would make her grandmother secretly happy.

"Where are you going?" the female vampire asked.

Kieran's deep voice answered, "To try a cake."

"Are you sure there won't be any poison in them?" That came from one of the House of Air and Amethyst ambassadors: Oleander Price, the green-haired siren.

Sabrina froze.

What. Did. She. Just. Say?

"Did you just accuse my Granny of poisoning you?" Sabrina demanded, hands on hips, fury rushing through her, making her form shimmer.

Kieran's face went strangely blank.

Ysabeau blinked. "Do you think that question is wise, given our current environment?"

"My question is wise *because* of our 'current environm ent.'" The siren rolled her eyes.

"Do you think my family are idiots?" Sabrina demand-ed.

"No one would be that stupid," Kieran said, his voice low and smooth.

Sabrina's form solidified. She wasn't sure if he was in-sulting her, her family, or the siren.

Maybe all three?

Feyre flicked her silvery hair over a shoulder and shot the siren a glare. But the green-haired woman kept talk-ing, despite the nonverbal warning. "It's happened before. Kings and queens have died from such carelessness with their food."

"Just cos you're literally named after a poison—" Sabrina muttered.

"You would know, wouldn't you?" The chill voice had them all turning to the speaker: Sky Serpell, the hu-man-appearing Spirit and Sapphire woman. She held a plate filled with teacake, and the shifter behind her also had a mouthful of something. He chewed quickly.

"What's that supposed to mean?"

Sky smiled coolly. "You've been a member of both Air and Amethyst and Gold and Garnet. You would have seen and heard a lot during your tenure."

There was an insult in there, Sabrina thought, not that she understood exactly what it was.

"Gold and Garnet was just a temporary…accommoda-tion," Oleander said. And from the venom in her gaze, she wished it had never been brought up.

Granny better not have poisoned the food. It really was a stupid thing to do. Sabrina had no doubt some of her family had wanted to hatch a plan like this, but Sabrina knew Connie at least would have thought it through. As would have Uncle Max. And her Granny Kim was nothing if not logical.

Sure, they could kill this round of ambassadors, but then they'd have an army descend on their doorstep soon after. The phantoms who had made the transition wouldn't die, but, as Aunt Connie had said, there *were* people—kids—who could die, and stay dead.

"Now, how about some cake?" Kieran said, voice kind of…upbeat, like he was trying to pep everyone up. He strode over to the sideboard and helped himself to a huge slice of Dundee cake and four scones, heaped with jam and cream. She had no idea how he fit it all on the plate.

She floated over to where her grandmother and Aunt Connie stood, their faces wearing strained smiles of welcome.

"That one has a good appetite," Granny Kim said, with grudging approval. She'd always admired a man with appetite.

"Nice shoulders," Aunt Connie replied.

"What do his shoulders have to do with anything?"

"What does his appetite have to do with anything?"

They were getting along as well as ever, Sabrina realized. She couldn't remember if they were sisters or not, but they certainly fought like it.

"Did you hear?" Colin whispered suddenly. He had appeared between Connie and Granny, but she had the feeling he was still meant to be 'invisible'. Except that he—and the others—never were, not to Sabrina. She could see them in whatever form they took.

"Hear what?" Connie asked.

"They accused us of poisoning the food." Colin looked pissed, but then that wasn't a new expression for the ass.

"Angus wanted to," Granny murmured, hopefully too quiet for anyone else to hear.

Sabrina had no idea what their guest's senses were like, but there was an old vampire and a shifter, so at least one of them probably had exceptional hearing.

"He didnae, right?" Connie asked, watching as Kieran took a huge mouthful of scone. Somehow—by some miraculous fate—he didn't end up with a moustache of jam and cream. She had no idea how he managed that.

He even eats sexily.

Which had her mind turning toward him eating other things…

Aunt Connie and Granny Kim took a deep breath as he chewed, drawing her attention away from her interesting thoughts. Kieran looked over at Sabrina, tongue flicking out to lick a tiny crumb from the edge of his mouth. "These are delicious. What are they?"

Her whole form *burned.*

I never thought I'd envy a crumb.

But there it was.

"Scones with jam and cream," Aunt Connie said with a smile.

"I think this is one of the best things that has ever been in my mouth."

Sabrina coughed. "Phrasing."

His eyes flicked over at her.

She sighed. "That's cos you've never tasted me."

His eyes widened ever-so-slightly, and she realized he could still hear her.

Fuck.

Apparently ghosts feel embarrassment. Yay. If she could have dissolved into a puddle of ectoplasm, she would have.

"Wait until ye try the Dundee cake," Granny said, striding forward and pointing at the huge slice on his plate.

One of his eyebrows rose. "Named after Crocodile Dundee?"

"What? No." She shook her head, confusion warring with amusement. "This cake was made for Mary, Queen of Scots, in the sixteenth century—"

"It's *how* old?" He held the plate away from himself, studying the slice like it was some decay-defying culinary miracle.

Granny Kim and Connie laughed. Like, genuinely laughed.

And one by one, he charms them all.
Colin scoffed.

Well, most of them.

As long as he doesn't develop any feelings for them…

Granny and Connie might be hundreds of years old, but they looked to be barely in their thirties. Not that they would ever be interested in an outsider. Connie had been married. And Granny…well, she hadn't settled down yet.

"I baked it yesterday," Granny said. "Legend has it Queen Mary didnae like cherries, which were in traditional fruit cake recipes. So, her cook at the time came up with this—the Dundee cake. It is a proud Scottish tradition."

"But why is it called Dundee?"

"It was made in a place called Dundee," Ysabeau said, her voice dry. She plucked a single dried almond flake from his plate and ate it.

"Right." He scowled at her.

The vampire lifted one shoulder in reply.

Sabrina didn't like how any of this was going.

You're jealous.

Well, Kieran was the only person she could talk to. And while he was busy eating cake and being flirted with by her aunt and grandmother—*ewww*—it meant he wasn't paying attention to *her*.

Wow. Entitled, much?

Sabrina sighed. She had issues.

Colin left the room, only to reenter it a few moments later dressed in jeans and a different shirt, carrying a black glass and a decanter full of thick, red liquid. He strode up to Ysabeau. "One of the family donated this earlier," Colin said. "Would you like some?"

Ysabeau studied the bottle, her nostrils delicately flaring as she sniffed. "Thank you."

Colin smiled and poured, showing absolutely zero qualms about serving a vampire blood from his own family member.

Then again, he had no problem spilling my blood, did he?

His voice was slightly husky as he said, "I hope it meets your...needs."

Sabrina scrunched her face up. Gross. She would have puked a little in her mouth if she'd...well, you know.

"It is acceptable." Ysabeau seemed to meet Colin's gaze, but it was hard to read her expression, considering the sunglasses.

The lack of response seemed to make her cousin more...intense.

He probably wants to win over someone powerful.

Because Ysabeau was old—she had to be, given she could track people via scent in a house like Braemar Castle. Vampires got stronger with age, until they peaked, unless they were born a Master. Ysabeau wasn't a Master, at least Sabrina didn't think she was, but vampires had been created by the portals opening, so she could be as old as the Himalayan portal, and that had opened thousands of years ago.

Probably better I don't know how old she is.
Sabrina had a feeling it was safer that way.

CHAPTER 12

KIERAN

The tall, blue-eyed phantom from the hall was trying to flirt with Ysabeau. He would never succeed—not because he wasn't handsome or charming, but because Ysabeau didn't engage with menu items. Plus, she was already in a...situation.

One Kieran did *not* understand. But he didn't have to deal with her boy toy, so he didn't care.

The scent of blood reached him, and it smelled...boring. *Huh.* Kieran wondered if it came from a phantom or a human; it didn't have the sickly-sweet odor of decay that Douglas' had, and it didn't smell anything like Sabrina's. *Nothing smells like Sabrina's.* He assumed it was a human donor, or pre-phantom. Because there were kids and teenagers in the castle that didn't appear to be phantoms yet. And he hadn't seen any incorporeal phantoms that looked younger than their mid-twenties.

So maybe they're made?

It was something Douglas hadn't been able to draw, not that he would have, given the choice, Kieran thought. And it was the most crucial piece of information they lacked.

How did someone become a phantom?

And was the process restricted to humans, or could a vampire become one, too?

Sabrina was back at his side. She touched his forearm as he picked up his cake, distracting him from taking another bite. The tingle spread throughout his body again, this time even stronger than ever. Thankfully his dick didn't respond. Appearing to get a hard-on over a piece of cake would be embarrassing.

"I think my grandmother likes you," Sabrina said. Her voice was quiet—whispery, almost. He flicked a glance at her, but she wasn't watching him. No, her gaze was locked on the blue-eyed phantom talking to Ysabeau.

Kieran shoved the cake into his mouth before he could say something to her. *Fuck.* This is almost as delicious as Sabrina's blood.

Her head whipped toward him. "My blood?"

She was looking at him, *really* looking at him. "Did you just say this cake was tastier than my blood?"

Shit.

No.

He *hadn't* said that out loud.

Then…

He shook his head ever-so-slightly.

She frowned. "I swear you said this cake was almost as good as my blood." Her eyes narrowed. "Where would you have tasted my blood before?"

I didn't say anything, he thought to himself.

"You didn't say it, but I definitely heard it."

They stared at each other.

What the fuck was happening right now?

"Lord Kieran, ye appear a bit bamboozled. The cake that good?" One of the phantoms—Connie, he thought her name was—looked a mixture of suspicious and amused.

"I'm no lord. And this cake is just taking me to another place." He grinned. The expression didn't reach his eyes, but they seemed to take it at face value.

Sabrina pressed her hand against his arm again. "Can you hear me?" she asked, but her luscious mouth hadn't moved.

Was she able to hear his thoughts? Was he hearing hers?

He blinked. *"Yes."*

Fuck.

"Fancy that." She gave him an evil look.

They *could* read each other's mind. It appeared limited to when they were touching, but he wasn't sure it would stay that way. He'd never heard of that happening before, not unless the ghost had had telepathic abilities *before* they'd died. And telepathy wasn't something that Douglas appeared to have possessed.

It was an ability some Masters had, but it wasn't common. He had no idea about death fae—maybe they *could* telepathically communicate with ghosts. But he'd met a few spirits before and they hadn't ever triggered the power in him. Then again, he hadn't drunk their blood posthumously, or had them touch him.

She was grinning, but he could *feel* her inner turmoil. She stepped away from him, breaking the connection. He almost sagged with relief. Because inside...inside he was also freaking the fuck out.

Kieran didn't *like* the idea that someone was privy to his thoughts. They had always been the one thing that belonged to him and no one else. Sure, there were telepaths out there, but he had never had to deal with one, and his mind was shielded by magic.

Wait.

My mind is shielded by magic.

His thumb spun the House ring around his middle finger. He had had the spell done on the beryl stone in the ring—crystals held magic for decades, if not centuries, if done right—and he had paid a small fortune for it. He had never wanted to risk his mind being pried open, not after he became a confidante of Elias.

Plus, he had plenty of his own secrets.

So how was Sabrina able to read his thoughts?

Why could he hear hers?

What the fuck was happening?

Too many questions. Not enough answers.

It had to be tied to her blood. He had tasted it twice now, and aside from it being delicious, maybe it hid something else? Something he didn't want to think about in too much detail, considering Sabrina's state of life. Or lack thereof.

"So, can you hear everything that I'm thinking?" she asked, drawing him out of the quagmire of his thoughts.

"I don't know, I don't know what you're thinking right now." Kieran thought back at her. He noticed she wasn't touching him anymore, either.

She frowned, then rubbed a finger over her lower lip. Had she heard him? He looked down at the cake, trying to convince himself he had to pay attention to anything but her. She was a distraction he couldn't afford.

Oh, he was still registering everything in the room: Colin was trying to chat up Ysabeau; Air and Amethyst had finally started eating from the sideboard, although

Feyre and Oleander had pinched expressions despite the food being pretty amazing. Maybe their faces looked like that *because* it was so good.

The Spirit and Sapphire ambassadors were just finishing off the last crumbs on their plates. Clan members hovered around the edges of the room, some attempting to engage in polite chit-chat with Spirit and Sapphire but leaving the Air and Amethyst ambassadors well alone. *Smart move.*

In other words, the whole thing was awkward as fuck.

This is not the place for me.

No, he didn't have the ability to charm. Too bad he couldn't solve the problem with a little torture or a brick to the head.

"So…do you normally have telepathy?" Sabrina asked aloud.

Kieran ran a hand over the back of his neck. "*No. But it means I can reply to you, without having to look like I'm having some kind of seizure.*"

She chuckled. "Well, it's pretty weird, but I'm okay with it."

Okay. So, she didn't need to touch him to hear him. That progressed fast.

And how easily she accepted the extraordinary. His mind was still reeling from the development.

"*I will need to concentrate on what people are saying here as well,*" he thought at her. Her eyes narrowed. "*But yes, it's good we can talk.*"

Funny how that didn't sound as awkward as it felt. But he liked her *and* found her amusing.

Which was just as mind-blowing as the telepathy; because he didn't like anyone.

"So, what was this about my blood?" she asked, casually leaning as if against an invisible wall.

Kieran winced, but smoothed his expression before anybody noticed it. At least, he hoped no one saw it.

"How about we discuss that later?" he asked her. He wasn't really up to having that chat right now.

The doors to the room slammed open, framing the girl who had shadowed them in the open space. Her black hair was a wild nimbus around her head, and her eyes glowed with rage. Twin swords were sheathed behind her back, and a gun was holstered on each hip.

She hadn't been wearing that outfit when incorporeal. She looked ready to commit murder.

Then she threw something small and green at the clan chief, rage burning on her face. "Sammy's *dead*! Someone killed him!"

CHAPTER 13

SABRINA

N o.

No. No. No.

Sabrina turned and rushed out the room, anguish driving her. It didn't take her long to find Sammy, almost like she willed herself to his side. Her cousin was in his room, lying on his bed, lifeless. His blue lips were open in surprise, and his shirt half-unbuttoned, like he'd been in the middle of undressing or changing clothes. The eighteen-year-old's skin was pale, and his eyes wide.

She reached down and touched his foot, wondering if he had made the transition, despite his age.

He shouldn't have a body if he turned full phantom.

But he could be a ghost…

"Are you there?" she asked, hoping desperately for an answer. She looked around, searching. She saw everything you'd expect from a teenage boy's room: double bed with bland-colored sheets, posters of his favorite musicians on the walls, a giant TV propped up next to the doorway against the wall, a gaming console with crystal connection, and a glass tank with snake inmate jammed in the far corner.

But no spirits. No ghosts.

He was just…gone.

Sammy had been one of the younger cousins; she had never spent a lot of time with him when she'd been alive. He would have been around twelve or thirteen when she left the clan, and she hadn't had much time for kids back then. She had been too consumed by her dreams, too distracted.

But he had always seemed full of life, a generally optimistic kid. Kind. Sort of like she used to be, before she left and the real world had given her a rude awakening and a death that she hadn't expected.

He was one of Uncle Barr's many, *many* kids—that man had never been able to keep to one woman or one family—Sabrina had never really had much time for her uncle. She didn't like how he would abandon one family to start a new one. He claimed it was because he was still looking for his mate, but she didn't even know if phantoms *had* one. Other supernatural creatures did, but the clan weren't exactly like the others.

Sammy will never find a mate. He will never laugh again. Or dream. Or play. He was dead. His potential lost. Seeing him here, it broke her heart clean in two.

Tears spilled from her eyes, over her cheeks, before vanishing into nothingness when they dripped from her face.

His black hair curled over one cheekbone, his pale skin in stark contrast. His rib cage was prominent, the skin defining each particular bone. He looked thinner than he had when alive, and she didn't know if it was how death looked on a person, or if it was a result of whatever had killed him. There were no bruises, or scratches, or signs that he had struggled against an attacker.

"How did you die?" she asked herself.

Aside from his body, there was nothing else in the room that hinted as to what had happened. No overturned furniture, no stray clothing from another person marring the bed or the floor. The TV was on, some anime show running in the background.

Could he have had a heart attack? Or had the cancer struck early?

No.

Nothing was ever that simple.

Footsteps pounded down the hallway and the door slammed open, the wood banging off the wall as Grandpa Angus shoved through the entryway. Colin was right behind him, with Uncle Max also attempting to jam his way into the room, but Grandpa had come to a stop just inside, leaving Colin blocking the doorway.

Grandpa Angus took in the room, his eyes lingering on Sammy. Then his shoulders drooped, and he took the few steps toward the foot of the bed, walking right through her as he did so. It was a strange sensation, like all her nerve endings had come alive, but instead of it being pleasurable like it was with Kieran, it was painful.

She did *not* want a repeat of that, so she moved to the top of the bed, sitting on the mattress next to Sammy's head. Funny, how she had managed to avoid being walked through since she'd died. Maybe because she hadn't wanted concrete proof that they had no idea she existed.

It doesn't matter. Kieran can see me.

That had changed a lot of things for her.

"What the fuck happened?" Grandpa Angus demanded after a minute of total silence.

Uncle Max shoved past Colin. He reached out, feeling for a pulse on Sammy's neck. Her cousin was clearly dead, but Uncle Max checked anyway. He was that kind of guy. Thorough.

Max shook his head.

Sabrina tried to smooth away the lock of hair that had fallen across Sammy's cheekbone, but her fingers passed through the tress.

If only I'd been paying more attention…

Oh, so you could have stopped this?

Honestly, what could she have done, even if she had seen it happening right in front of her? Rushed to Kieran? Would he have even believed her?

Sammy's death wasn't on her.

So why the hell did it feel like it was her fault?

"I found this," Cousin Charlotte said, her eyes wild. She thrust a little green leaf forward toward Grandpa Angus. Sabrina didn't recognize what type of plant it belonged to. Her grandpa took it in a fist, crushing it. Rage was stamped on every line of his body.

"What is it?" Connie asked.

Granny had also arrived now, and the room was jam-packed full of people. Sammy wouldn't have liked it.

Then again, Sammy wouldn't have liked being dead, either.

Granny Kim pried Grandpa Angus' fingers apart and took the leaf. She studied it, her face turning eerily calm. "It's oleander."

Someone snorted from outside the room.

Sabrina tried to look over the sea of family members, to the people hanging around outside the door, but it was difficult to make out who was there. She *knew* Kieran was present, not needing to see him, although with his broad shoulders he towered over everyone else, aside from the male shifter.

"Did you think we wouldnae know?" Colin spun, pointing a finger at someone in the hallway.

"Oh, pluh-ease," one of the Air and Amethyst ambassadors said, exasperation plain. "You honestly think I would be that stupid?"

"Well, you thought we would be stupid enough to poison your food," Colin snapped back.

"You are hillbillies from the middle of *nowhere*. We are from the House of Air and Amethyst. You honestly think I would leave a piece of oleander behind at a crime scene, just because my name is Oleander?"

"Your species are known as man killers!" Colin shouted, as if infuriated.

But he *wasn't* angry. Sabrina had been around him so much in the past year that she could tell this was all a show. Had he known Sammy was dead? Or was he just trying to make everyone suspect Lady Oleander so the Air and Amethyst ambassadors would be forced to leave?

The timing of this is not coincidental...

And while Sabrina thought Feyre and Oleander were pretentious bitches, she also recognized they were *dangerous* pretentious bitches. Plus, she agreed with Oleander; the woman would never be so obvious.

It could be a fake though, her mind whispered. Leave such an obvious clue because no one would think she could be stupid enough to plant a, uh, plant on her victim. It would divert suspicion onto someone else.

You have watched too many crime shows.

Colin liked them, so she'd seen a *lot*.

"I'm a siren. Yes, I might have a taste for men, but I didn't even get a *chance* with young Samuel here." The crowd had thinned, and Sabrina could see the woman's face. She was pouting. Pouting, as if she had been the one who was ripped off, not the poor kid dead on his bed.

I will never understand the Houses. Or the creatures that populate them.

But looking around at her family…how could they just stand around talking, when one of their own was lying dead right in front of them? Were they so desensitized to death that they didn't care there was a corpse right here? One that had left stains on the bedding?

It must smell horrible.

At least she couldn't detect that. That was one small mercy.

"You should have a witch examine the body," Kieran said from the hallway.

"Allow another one of yer people here?" Grandpa Angus said, incredulous.

"We could ask for someone from a different House," Ysabeau said.

Grandpa glared. "We will get a doctor to examine the body."

"Because a doctor will be able to determine cause of death if there has been magical foul play," Kieran said. "Or would you prefer not to know the whole truth?"

Wow, Sabrina thought. He had just challenged her grandpa of trying to sweep the death under the rug and assign blame, all while sounding entirely reasonable.

"Fine," Grandpa Angus said through gritted teeth. "Get us a witch."

Sky spoke, "Great. Let me make a phone call."

Why did that feel like more of a threat than a good thing?

CHAPTER 14

KIERAN

K ieran stood next to the shifter at the back of the small crowd that had formed outside Samuel's bedroom. The hallway was packed, and the dark walls seemed to close in on them as they waited. Clint was even taller than Kieran, which made the guy at least six feet seven inches or so, and they could see over everyone's heads and into the room. Ysabeau, who stood next to him, would be using her heightened senses to spy on what was happening.

It's what he'd do.

A small group of family members, including the clan chief, were gathered at the foot of the bed. Sabrina hovered over the comforter, near Sammy's head, her face a mask of pain. He could see the diamond shimmer of tears on her pale cheeks. It made him want to kill someone or something. Or make her laugh.

It was complicated.

What the fuck happened?

The oleander leaf was tacky, he had to admit, which irritated him, because he had to agree with the siren. If she had sucked the life out of that boy, she wouldn't have been stupid enough to leave a calling card behind. Not when she was playing ambassador to a bunch of people who wanted her dead.

Kieran didn't like her, but he didn't think she was an idiot.

This was a setup.

But he didn't know who the setup was for. Would the phantoms really have killed one of their own and staged it like this, just to make the ambassadors leave? Or had one of the ambassadors left the leaf, for who-knows-what reason?

To frame one of the other Houses.

That seemed likely.

The Houses were always at odds with each other. It could be a minor thing, like a petty argument over who had the most powerful witch on their books, or all-out blood warfare because your king mated a shifter from another House, who was the mate to the heir of said other House...

Wait.

Not the issue at hand.

But it was a possibility. One of the stronger ones.

The phantoms killing the poor boy to try and cause a war seemed unlikely. Especially when they seemed so incredibly insular and protective of their own.

Kieran should offer to taste the boy's blood, to see if there was any kind of poison or drug present. He could also detect if magic had been used; if it had infiltrated the bloodstream, anyway. But he didn't want the phantoms to know much about his abilities.

"I'll be back soon," Sky said. She kept apart, her arms crossed over her chest, like she didn't want to bump into anyone or touch anything, then stepped down the hallway and pulled out a cell phone.

Interesting.

The shifter sniffed the air, like he was trying to detect any unusual scents. Considering they weren't familiar with what was considered *normal* around here, Kieran wasn't sure how useful that would be.

"Could the boy have died naturally?" Ysabeau asked into the sudden quiet.

The clan chief turned to glare at them. "He's a boy in the prime of his life, why would he die?"

"Well, that's the question, isn't it?" Ysabeau murmured.

"I still want a human doctor to look at him as well," Angus said, ignoring Ysabeau's comment.

"Of course," Lady Oleander said.

"Clearly, someone is trying to set up the House of Air and Amethyst," Feyre said, her voice as sharp as a blade. "We didn't do anything, and we won't stand to be accused. I think it's best that we learn what—or who—killed this boy as soon as possible. Wouldn't everybody agree?"

"Agreed," said Kim, provider of cakes. Kieran wasn't sure if she was the clan chief's wife or sister or aunt, but Sabrina called her granny, so she must've been a matriarch of some kind.

"Nobody is to touch the body, until the witch and the doctor arrive. Is that clear?" Kieran said, stepping forward.

One benefit about his previous career, he knew who would be coming with the witch: representatives from the Portal Watch: supernaturals sent from all Houses to guard the portals around the world. To be accepted was an honor, but the position was dangerous, with the guards fighting off monster incursions, as well as conducting investigations if there was even an inkling that any of the portals were involved. Considering the House ambassadors didn't have a motive, he had no doubt Sky's message would come across that way.

The phantoms scowled at him, but Sabrina couldn't seem to look away from the dead boy. He wanted her to, which was a bad sign.

"Who are ye to tell us how to treat our dead?" Angus demanded.

"We need this to be dealt with clearly and logically," Kieran said slowly, trying to be polite but probably sounding condescending. "The crime scene, if that's what this is, must not be tampered with. We need to have a guard outside this door until the doctor and the witch arrive. It should include one of the ambassadors, and one of the phantoms." Kieran smiled, an empty, magnanimous expression. "We can't prevent any of you from accessing the room in your incorporeal form. We just have to trust you won't interfere with anything."

The clan chief's eyes narrowed with rage. "Are ye saying my people cannae be trusted?"

"Clearly," Oleander said, her gold eyes turning molten as her voice whipped through the hallway and room.

Kieran winced. Fuck. That had made his skull ring.

Kieran had done his unfair share of murder over the years, but even he would have been annoyed if someone had accused him of killing a kid. There were some lines you didn't cross, and child killing was one of them.

The bastard blue-eyed phantom next to him clenched his teeth, his jaw visibly tightening. "You dinnae get a say in how we do things here."

"He has a point," said another phantom—Max, Kieran thought his name was, but Sabrina had been distracting him during the introductions. "We need to preserve this room and everything within it. That way, when the witch comes, she can inspect to make sure there were no spells used."

"Fine," the clan chief grunted. He rubbed one of his ears, as if it hurt. "We willnae enter the room, in our physical forms or otherwise. Max, ye stand first watch."

"I will also take first watch." That was from the shifter, Clint. He flicked a glance at Kieran and murmured, "I'll see what I can smell."

Kieran nodded. He wanted Sabrina to come with him, tell him what she'd seen, since she had been one of the first on the scene. She had disappeared from the hall within a blink of the eye after Charlotte's dramatic entry. It worried him.

But it would have to wait.

He didn't like how that made him feel: edgy, angsty. Like he needed to see her just to assure himself she was fine, when she was about as far from fine as you could get.

I wonder if the boy became a ghost?

Because he didn't appear to have become a phantom. And considering how angry the chief was, he doubted they could make the boy transition posthumously.

"So, he was not a phantom?" Ysabeau asked as the family exited Sammy's room.

Angus glared at the vampire. "That is none of yer concern."

"That is *exactly* our concern," Kieran said. "In fact, you could say it's the *entire* reason we are here."

Angus came to a stop in front of Kieran. "Ye have no business being here. Look what's happened because of it."

"And you have no business hiding an entire town of supernatural creatures here." Ysabeau raised her voice.

"A whole race of un-killable half-ghost humans is something that belongs in a House." Wow. That had been a mouthful. But it was the truth: without the Houses, there'd be chaos. Pure chaos. And the world needed a semblance of order.

"The Houses are only here to talk because they cannae kill us," growled the blue-eyed phantom—Colin.

"I'd start acting grateful for that," Feyre chipped in, nose in the air. "We're here to negotiate. Normally you'd all just be carrion."

Brutal. But true.

"The Houses will take this boy's death seriously," Ysabeau said.

"The Houses did this!" Angus shouted, the mask of genial lord well and truly discarded.

Oleander Price tossed her green hair over her shoulder. "That has yet to be proven."

"Dinnae worry, the evidence is there," Colin said. "It's only a matter of time."

Kieran studied the blue-eyed man. Then he nodded, more to himself than anyone else. "Then we wait. The truth always comes out in the end."

CHAPTER 15

SABRINA

Sabrina ran a ghostly finger over Sammy's forehead one last time. Just earlier today he had been so excited, so full of life. And within twelve hours of the House ambassadors arriving, he was dead.

Sadness warred with anger within her, but she didn't know who to direct it at. Had one of the Houses murdered her cousin? Had it been Colin?

Or had Sammy died of natural causes?

She didn't know the answer to any of those questions. And it ate at her.

Because if her younger cousins weren't safe, then no one in her family was. The clan protected the clan—phantom and human members alike. Well, except for Colin. But Sammy wasn't in line to inherit the chieftain role: at least six of Uncle Barr's children were ahead of him in the queue, and none of them had been harmed. So why Sammy?

Plus, Colin was now next in line. He hadn't even needed to kill Sabrina to secure that. He'd just wanted to.

Maybe he'd just wanted to hurt Sammy, too.

So, what did it all mean?

Nothing.

It means nothing.

And that was probably why it hurt the most. If Sammy had been killed, it had been for nothing. No gain to the clan. No gain to the Houses, aside from enraging her family. Just a loss that couldn't be replaced.

Why didn't you grab the ley lines like I did? she wondered. The magic node was right near here, and it was full of so much power it had made her giddy when she'd gone near it before her death. The grove where the node was accessed was only fifteen miles from here.

So even though he wasn't twenty-five, he should have been able to make the transition, at least to ghosthood, like she had.

Maybe he just didn't think to reach out.

Maybe he hadn't been able to sense them, like she could. To be fair, she had no idea if any of her relatives could; it wasn't something she'd noticed until after she'd left the clan, because here the node's magic was *everywhere*, a constant presence. It was only after she'd been away from it had she realized how persistent it had been.

I just thought everyone could.

But since there were no other ghosts, maybe she was alone in that.

There was obviously something different about her family, at least genetically. Tumors had begun growing in her body shortly before she turned twenty-four, like they had been pre-programmed, starting like clockwork.

Maybe the node has a type of radiation that interacts with us; it either kills you, or turns you. It was a theory she hadn't thought about in too much detail because it made her confront the degradation of her body, the mutant cells running through her system.

She'd been lucky to survive past twenty-five really, but that had only been because she'd used a magic form of chemotherapy to prolong her life. She'd been dying anyway, however, which is why she'd decided to go home. To make the transition she never thought she wanted.

Truth be told, if she'd had a normal life expectancy, if she'd known she was going to live to be eighty or a hundred or even one-hundred and twenty, she wouldn't have bothered to return.

One life lived, that would have been enough for her.

But only twenty-seven years...

No, that hadn't been enough.

And Sammy had only been eighteen.

The door clicked shut, leaving Sabrina alone in the room with her cousin. No one was meant to come in here, but she wasn't sure the family would abide by that. Uncle Barr hadn't been one of those who rushed to the room, and once he heard, she doubted even Grandpa Angus would be able to prevent him from seeing his boy.

And she couldn't blame him for that, even if it would weaken the clan's position in this situation.

A form shimmered through the door.

It was Charlotte.

The dark-haired woman dropped down on her knees, lowering her chin to her chest. She was in her phantom form, dressed in the same clothes she'd died in. Gone were her swords and weapons—they would have dropped to the floor when she'd ditched her physical body. It was the one part of phantom-hood that matched Sabrina's ghostliness; you appeared in what you wore when you died. Only for them, when they took physical form again, they were naked as the day they were born. There were a lot of random clothes piles scattered over the castle as a result.

Charlotte reached out a hand, leaving it to hover over Sammy's foot, not quite touching it. She looked up, tears running down her cheeks. "I'm so sorry, Sammy. I'm sorry I wasn't there in time."

Sabrina lurched forward on the bed, coming to a stop near Sammy's feet. "What do you mean? Did you see something?"

Charlotte hiccupped and wiped the tears from her face. She stood, her expression turning hard. "I'll find out who—and what—did this to you. And I'll avenge you. You have my word, Sammy. You didn't deserve this death. Whoever did it will pay."

Then she misted through the door and was gone.

Sabrina turned and took in the room one more time, thinking about that interaction. Charlotte was from one of the side branches of the family; a Muick rather than a Fhearchair. She wasn't in line for the clan chief role, and couldn't be even if she wanted to, because of her father. It was quite the scandal, even if no one talked about it anymore. She was more than twenty years older than Sabrina, so they hadn't had much to do with each other growing up. She'd been a brittle youth, and she had turned into a hard woman. But she wasn't a fool.

This is a giant mess.

"I'm sorry, Sammy. I'll be back," Sabrina said, and left the room, feeling hollow and sad.

Uncle Max was stationed outside the door, standing straight and tall, glaring down the hallway like he would stare away any intruder. Had he seen Charlotte? Or had she managed to sneak by him?

Some of her relatives could turn totally incorporeal, so that no one—not even another phantom—could see them. It wasn't a common ability, and Sabrina hadn't known Charlotte possessed it, but she may have kept that to herself. Colin had it. As did Grandpa Angus, Great-grandpa Fergus, and a few others. But it was a closely guarded secret: normally phantoms could see other phantoms, no matter their form. This was the accepted norm.

Sabrina had only learned about it because of her stalking Colin.

Turns out she could see them in whatever form they chose, no matter how invisible to everyone else they were. It was one of the few advantages she had. Like seeing magic.

The shifter sniffed the air. "One of your kind was just here. They may have gone in the room."

Sabrina came to a stop. The shifter could *smell* them? Even when they weren't physically here? That was something she'd never even considered.

Uncle Max stiffened. "I didnae see anyone."

"Right." The shifter's green eyes narrowed.

"I *didnae*."

The Spirit and Sapphire ambassador shrugged. "Let's just hope if they did go inside, they didn't fuck anything up. You do realize that if this goes sideways, you guys suffer?"

Max leaned back against the wall. "Aren't we suffering already?"

The shifter turned to him and chuckled. "If you think this is bad, you ain't got *any* idea what you're really in for."

Sabrina bit her lip.

Great.

I need to find Kieran.

He'd know what to do. At least, she hoped he would.

She hurried through the castle to his chambers, cutting through rooms on the way. She ignored the angry whispers, the half-naked relatives, the arguments. She misted through the door into his room, coming to a stop just inside. Ysabeau was there, the beautifully dangerous vampire standing opposite Kieran, who was sitting in the Edwardian chair near the window.

Damn. He looks even hotter.

Funny how she was still able to register that, despite how she felt inside.

"This is going to turn into a nightmare, I guarantee it," Ysabeau said, her tone exasperated.

His gaze focused on Sabrina near the door, before turning back to the vampire. "You think it hasn't already?"

Ysabeau shrugged one shoulder. "Murder always complicates things."

Wow. Guess dead teenagers weren't a big deal to the vampire, then. Sabrina rubbed her sweater, right over the bloodstain.

"You don't think the House of Air and Amethyst actually had something to with it?" Kieran asked. "Price was eyeing off that boy earlier."

"Murder is as easy to those two as breathing, but they aren't stupid. They didn't survive the Moonlight Wraith being dethroned and re-throned without having some basic intelligence. This is a setup."

"Could you smell anything?"

"No. The place is riddled with the phantom scents. It would be like picking a needle out of a haystack."

"So, you couldn't scent if one of the other ambassadors was there? Or any other creature?"

Ysabeau shook her head. "No. But I wasn't allowed in the room."

"Are you going to call Elias about this? Or should I?" Kieran rubbed his palms over his thighs. Sabrina felt a pang of jealously, wishing it was her hands, or her legs. Either way.

I just want to touch him.

And she was desperate to know what it would feel like for his hands to stroke over her skin.

Now is not the time.

No.

And seriously, what was wrong with her? Her cousin lay dead on the other side of the castle, and she was here, lusting over a fae. *At least I know he didn't do it.* He'd been with her the whole time.

Everyone else…they were all suspects.

But Sabrina was going to find out who did it.

And somehow—somehow—she was going to make them pay.

CHAPTER 16

KIERAN

"I'll make the call to our fearless leader, then," Kieran said to Ysabeau.

"Good. I'm not keen to deliver this news to him. I'm sure he is going to be absolutely thrilled." Her mouth twitched at the corner, like she wanted to smile.

"Careful," Kieran grinned. "Sarcasm suits you. You wouldn't want to engage in it too often."

"Maybe you're rubbing off on me."

"Eww. Phrasing."

And there went their rare moment of accord. He was excellent at ruining these kinds of things. One might even say he did it deliberately.

Sabrina choked on a cough. He decided not to dignify that with a look.

"Get out of here while I make the phone call," he said.

"I was going to anyway," Ysabeau replied. "I'm going to scout around the castle, see if I can notice anything out of the ordinary."

"You mean like a whole castle full of people who can turn incorporeal at the drop of a hat?" Kieran asked.

"Not fair," Sabrina muttered.

"Like that." Ysabeau turned toward the door. Sabrina shuffled to the side, to give her room to move by, not that Ysabeau realized she needed it. The vampire looked back over her shoulder. "I just hope we don't all end up being murdered in our sleep."

He quirked an eyebrow. "That presumes some of us need to sleep."

"Touché." Ysabeau said and closed the door behind her.

Kieran leaned back in his chair and looked at Sabrina. She moved closer, stopping near the bed, where she sat down. Funny how, when there was furniture in a room, she naturally gravitated toward it. But she didn't *need* these things to sit. He had seen her sit on—and lean against—air.

Strange how some behaviors survived even death.

"Who do you think did it?" Sabrina asked, sadness cloaking her.

"Fucked if I know," Kieran replied, leaning his head back against the wall. He fished his cell from his pocket, and dialed Elias' number.

The king answered after six rings. "You only just got there. Why the fuck are you calling me already?"

"Nice to speak to you, too," Kieran replied.

"I am in the middle of something and you're meant to be busy."

"Love you too, Uncle."

"Quit being an asshole and out with it."

Kieran tapped the video call option and waited. Elias accepted. His hair was ruffled, and his lips were a bit swollen. He had scratches on his bare shoulders. Kieran smirked. "Oh yeah, you've been 'busy' all right."

"You haven't quit being an asshole."

"Hard to, when that's your default nature."

"Is that Kieran?" a sleepy voice asked off screen. Elias' mate.

Tenderness coated the king's reply, "Yes."

Danni shuffled in the background. "Tell him he owes me fifteen vials."

"Fuck off," Kieran replied.

Elias' voice dropped to a growl. "Kieran—"

"Fine. She cheated though—"

"That is not what I meant," Elias said.

"Right."

"You guys are crazy," Sabrina muttered.

She was one to talk.

"We are at Castle Braemar. But a teenage kid has been murdered."

Elias straightened, his mouth growing taut. "By who? He wasn't a phantom?"

"Guess not. And that's the million-dollar question, isn't it?"

"What's the plan?"

Sabrina crossed her arms over her chest. "Find the killer."

"A witch and a doctor are coming here to examine the body and look for any clues," Kieran replied.

"Anything out of the ordinary at the scene?" Danni asked, appearing on the screen as she laid her head against Elias' shoulder. Her silvery hair shone like trapped moonlight.

"An oleander leaf."

Elias' eyes narrowed. "Isn't one of Air and Amethyst's top assassins called Oleander?"

"Yes, and she's here."

Danni shook her head. "Too obvious. Air likes daggers to the back; they don't leave blatant clues behind."

"Exactly my line of thinking." Kieran actually liked Danni—far more than he did her sister, Adora. He wouldn't admit it on record, though. She was good for his uncle, and he respected Elias more than anyone on the planet.

"Should I send Dahlia or Seraphina?" Elias asked.

"Spirit and Sapphire said they would organize the witch."

Elias shoved dark hair back from his forehead. "Of course, they did."

"Where are they finding a doctor?" Danni asked.

"Phantoms said they would cover it."

"Hmmm."

"Exactly."

"What's that supposed to mean?" Sabrina demanded.

"*It means that if your family is responsible for this, they will hire someone who has their best interests at heart and may not present the full picture.*"

"Same could be said of the witch."

"*Exactly.*"

"Well, keep me informed, Kieran," Elias ordered. "This isn't looking like a great start, is it?"

"No, my liege. It is not." He ended the call.

"He was just a kid." Sabrina ran a hand over her forehead. Kieran want to reach out, to touch her hand, pull her close and comfort her. Anything to make the pain on her face go away.

You're in way over your head, buddy.

Didn't he know it.

"To be fair, I wouldn't have thought someone from the Houses would have done it. Sure, Price made eyes at the boy earlier, but she's not stupid. She's the Moonlight Wraith's left-hand woman. She would've lured him to her side. Then, once your people picked a House, she would've convinced him to join Air and Amethyst, so he was no longer within your reach. And then, after a year or two, he would have been dead. Provided he never became a phantom, of course." He rubbed his cheek. "Then again, she might have *preferred* it if he had been a phantom."

Sabrina looked at him. "What do you mean?"

"From what I understand about sirens, they don't just feed from someone once. They like to have their prey fall madly in love with them. They destroy their sense of self, their sense of purpose, until all they know is the siren. They get their prey to a point where they will literally do *anything* for them. It's about obsession, as much as it is about feeding. Sirens usually keep their prey alive for years. They don't rush."

"So, what does being a phantom have to do with it?"

"She could kill him over and over again and he would come back to life. A perpetual food supply, fueled by obsession."

"So, you're saying you don't think it was her."

"That's exactly what I'm saying. And the oleander leaf? That's just crude. She has more style than that." He hated to admit that, but it was true.

"It was a bit too obvious," Sabrina said, shaking her head. "But who else could have done it? I don't think my family would have."

"What do they have to gain from it?" he asked.

She narrowed aquamarine eyes. "What do you mean?"

"That's what I'd ask myself: what do they have to gain from it? Unless you have a serial killer hiding here, most people kill because it gains them something. Not just for funsies."

Silently, she chewed on her bottom lip.

Fuck. He wished those lips were flesh. The things he would do with them...

Holy hells, get a grip on yourself.
Wait. That wasn't helpful either.

Stop thinking with your dick.
There, that was better.

"*I just can't believe he's gone; I should have saved him.*" Sabrina's thoughts reached him.

"You wouldn't have been able to save him, unless you have telekinesis. That's assuming he didn't die of natural causes."

Her gaze sharpened on him, like using their telepathy had reminded her of something. "How did you taste my blood?"

"I don't really have time to go into it now," he replied.

"Why not?" She swung one knee up onto the bed, leaving her other leg hanging down.

Of course, she had to be the persistent type.

"It's a bit of a story."

"I have time." She waved a hand.

"I—"

Someone banged on the door. Loudly.

Saved by the bell, he thought. Or the door knock.

He got up and opened it. Kim stood on the other side, her previously welcome smile gone. "The doctor will be here in three days."

He wondered why she'd come to tell him, when any other ambassador would have been just as easy. And three days wasn't exactly great, either. Bodies could do a lot in three days.

Maybe they knew that and were delaying things deliberately.

Which assumes they killed the boy.

For some reason, that didn't sit right with him.

Sabrina came up to his side, studying her grandmother.

"Has the witch arrived?" he asked, realizing he'd been thinking a little too long.

Kim pressed her lips into a thin line. "Not yet."

"I'll let the others know. But if Spirit and Sapphire are arranging it, they'll be able to portal here within the day."

"They won't be able to portal into the castle." Kim said, shaking her head. "We have wards."

"Well, we better go see about arranging a welcoming party."

So, they had invested in some heavy-duty magic then. Seems they liked the Houses and witches when it came to providing their protection, just not enough to join forces with them.

How had they gone undetected so long?

He walked out the door, waiting for Sabrina to follow before re-activating the anti-intrusion spells. He had no idea if they would work against her, but he didn't want to risk hurting her in case they did.

You big softie.

"Ye do realize we do not want to join a House," Kim said as she watched him finish the spell.

He glanced around the hallway—they were completely alone, aside from Sabrina, who Kim couldn't see. She'd chosen to do this without an audience. Why? What was in it for her? Why the honesty?

"We had gathered that, yes," Kieran said, uncomfortable. Why hadn't she gone to Ysabeau? That's what the other vampire was here for.

"Sammy's death has complicated things."

"Oh yeah, we see that."

"It won't end without more bloodshed," Kim warned him. He wondered why she even bothered. Could she actually be on the Houses' side? Or did she just like him because he'd eaten some of her cake?

Kieran flashed her a toothy grin, but nothing about his expression spoke of mirth. "Let's just hope it isn't yours or my blood spilled, then, shall we?"

CHAPTER 17

SABRINA

S abrina didn't know why Granny had decided to warn
Kieran, but she was kind of glad she had. It showed
her family weren't complete bigots, hating everyone just
because they weren't part of the clan. Although, it could
be some fancy trick, getting Kieran on their side, so he
would help them, rather than pursue his own agenda.

Wow, she thought, *I am suspicious of everybody*. It might
be time to drop her new motto—'Be more like Colin'—because it clearly wasn't doing anything for her ability to
trust people.

But then again, who could she *really* trust?

Colin had been able to murder six of her relatives, without anybody even guessing he was responsible. No, he'd
managed to pin that largely on the dead sea witch, with
the others appearing to be 'accidents'. Sure, Uncle Max
seemed to think there was something up with Colin, but
he was the only one.

Kieran and Granny started walking down the hallway.
"Where is the closest a witch can portal to?" Kieran asked.

Granny frowned. "Probably at the end of the drive. We had the entire castle grounds warded."

"Maybe that's why I can't go beyond the grounds," Sabrina said to Kieran.

"*Interesting, I thought it was because you were tied to your body. But maybe there's more going on here than we realized,*" he thought back at her.

"How do you know my body is here?" Sabrina asked.

Instead of answering, he said, "Let's go find Sky."

Granny withdrew her phone from her pocket, before tapping rapidly at the screen. It pinged a few seconds later and she nodded to herself. "She's at the front door."

"You have her phone number?"

"No. I have John's number."

"Who's John?"

"The phantom who is assigned to her."

That wasn't unnecessarily confusing at all.

He started walking. "Great, let's go."

"Kieran, my body? And my blood?" Sabrina trailed after them.

"*I'll answer your questions when I am not trying to have two conversations at once.*"

She drew back. Ouch.

He glanced at her. "*I didn't mean that the way it sounded.*"

"No, no, you're right. I'm bothering you." She sped up, floating to the entry hall ahead of them, cutting through rooms on the way.

Since most people didn't bother to stick to the walkways when in their phantom forms, there was an unofficial rule in the castle that you kept out of people's bedrooms. Before the rule had been put into place, there'd been plenty of embarrassing moments, mostly involving nakedness. At least two of Uncle Barr's indiscretions had been discovered that way.

Since she'd died, however, Sabrina had never bothered to follow the rule. Privacy was for the living, and she didn't exactly care if she saw dangly bits anymore. Sure, she drew the line at watching Colin take a shit, but anybody would do the same.

She reached the black-and-white tiled entryway well ahead of Kieran and Granny. Sky stood in the foyer near an antique side table, a long coat buttoned up to her chin, her pink hair piled up in a messy ponytail. Her arms were crossed over her chest, and her hands tucked under her armpits, like she was freezing.

Charlotte was also in the foyer, and she was trying to convince John he had somewhere else to be. Clearly, she'd decided to take on his post. Their other cousin shook his head but agreed to leave after Charlotte whispered something to him. Sabrina had no idea what the exchange was; but it was effective, since John hightailed it out of there.

Charlotte had re-dressed in her black tank top and jeans, with her swords strapped to her back once again, but she'd discarded the guns. Sabrina had no idea what the temperate was—but either Sky really felt the cold, or Charlotte's rage was enough to keep her warm. Her cousin's blue eyes were cold as she watched the Spirit and Sapphire ambassador, her face drawn. *She's way over-armed to be dealing with this ambassador.*

Sky didn't look strong enough to hurt a fly.

Sabrina wasn't sure Charlotte should be on active duty. After seeing her in the room…

She should be given time to grieve.

They all should.

"Are they Yoshihara swords?" Sky asked. She had an Australian accent, Sabrina realized. The woman hadn't really talked enough for her to pick it up before.

Who's a what-now? Sabrina wondered.

Charlotte straightened, turning her pale eyes on the woman. "Yes."

"Of the Bizen or Sōshū tradition?" Sky's gaze ran over the two hilts, like she was memorizing them.

"Clearly, it's the Bizen-den," Ysabeau said, gliding into the hallway, wearing a black turtleneck, pants and dark sunglasses. She was technically walking, but it was so smooth, so predatory, there was no real way to describe it other than gliding.

Charlotte turned on her heel, trying to keep the vampire and the Spirit and Sapphire ambassador both in her line of sight, although she mostly had eyes for the beautiful vampire. "How can you tell from just the hilt?"

Ysabeau shrugged. "I lived in Bizen during the Heian period."

"Wasn't that over a thousand years ago?" Charlotte asked, eyes going wide.

"Give or take."

That still didn't answer the question of just how old Ysabeau actually was, but it meant she was older than Grandpa Fergus. And he was barely sane.

"My supervisor said Odin and Lady Gabriella would talk to the other House leaders and arrange for a witch to arrive," Sky said. "I received notification that one was ready to portal here."

Odin and Lady Gabriella. A god and an archangel, the elected rulers of Spirit and Sapphire. Sabrina shuddered.

She never wanted to meet anyone who had that much power at their fingertips.

Kieran and Granny Kim strode down the staircase. It was a grand thing, the staircase, all polished timber and red carpet. It split into two branches at the top, leading into two of the four wings of the castle. She'd slid down the banister more times than she could count as a kid.

Dressed in a black leather jacket and dark jeans that molded to his thighs, the death fae was mouthwatering. She licked her lips absently.

No wonder Granny picked him over the others.

Sure, the shifter was hot, but Kieran was next level.

"We can meet her at the end of the driveway," Granny said. She looked calm and collected, as if she had just partaken in a leisurely afternoon stroll instead of preparing to have a witch land on their doorstep.

She should have been an actress.

Kieran took in Ysabeau's presence, along with Charlotte's and Sky's. *"You ran off,"* he thought to her.

Sabrina flicked some invisible lint from her sweater. "You were busy."

One of the servants appeared and handed Granny her gloves. "Let's go."

"I thought you were scoping the castle?" Kieran asked Ysabeau as the four of them exited the castle. He spoke quietly, but Sabrina was hovering next to Ysabeau. Damned if she was going to walk next to Kieran.

Because he is going to be so upset by your absence.

Shut up.

"I was about to head outside when I saw Sky and the sword maiden at the door," Ysabeau replied.

Kieran raised an eyebrow. "Sword maiden? Don't you mean shield maiden?"

Strange way to refer to Charlotte.

"Tomayto, tomahto."

"That is high praise from you."

She turned her dark-sunglasses stare on him. "Who said it was praise?"

"Right."

Why are you even mad at him? Sabrina wondered, ignoring their banter. *Because he didn't want to answer your questions then and there?*

Yeah. Fine. She was being a bit of a brat.

But he had tasted her blood—or at least, he *thought* he'd tasted her blood. And he knew she was buried at Braemar.

So, *how* did he know that? And *why*?

She was going to stay mad until she had her answers.

The small group walked through the paved courtyard that surrounded the castle and separated it from the turreted curtain wall. Granny led the way through the wall and past the yett, to the tree-lined drive. The sky was a clear cerulean blue overhead, barely a cloud scudding across the expanse. The white gravel crunched underfoot, and birdsong flowed through the grounds. Autumn leaves floated gently to the earth on a slight breeze, and the world seemed bright, fresh. New.

It's beautiful.

Too bad she hadn't really appreciated it more when she was alive. Nowadays she was usually deep inside the castle, spying on Colin or her other relatives. But it was nice to take a deep breath—even though she couldn't smell squat—and enjoy nature.

The magic is stronger out here, she realized. Somehow, the castle walls dampened the feel of the node.

They soon reached the end of the driveway. Sky pulled out her cell and snapped a few pictures of the location, before tapping on her screen rapidly. "This will give her something to lock onto."

A few minutes later, the air shimmered, and Sabrina's form began to vibrate in response. She clenched her fists as the sensation became almost unbearable.

"What's wrong?" Kieran demanded.

"Nothing."

"Don't you—"

A glowing oval appeared in the sky, just above the gravel path. In the center of the circle were the dark stone walls of somewhere not here, lit by flickering firelight. A woman stepped through, dragging an enormous suitcase behind her. The portal vanished, and Sabrina let out a sigh of relief.

Everything was back to normal.

But her feeling of respite was short lived.

Because Sabrina *knew* this witch. The long brown hair was now worn in a combination of braids and loose strands, with metal beads, feathers and gems intertwined among them, but those pale, pale blue eyes were the same, as was the kohl and thick mascara. She wore a maxi dress under a denim jacket, about three scarves, and black leather boots. The air around her buzzed.

"Beware smiling men who knock on your door."

Gee. Thanks for that warning.

If only she'd slammed the door in Colin's face.

Sky nodded at the witch. "Tamsin Redthorne. Thank you for coming at such short notice."

"Yes, it's wonderful ye could help so quickly," Granny echoed, but she had taken a step back from the witch, as if bothered by the woman.

Tamsin glanced around at the small group, waving a bloodstained hand through the air, as if in greeting. Her eyes lingered near where Sabrina hovered, but not directly on her. "Oh, the pleasure is all mine."

CHAPTER 18

KIERAN

K ieran had heard of Tamsin Redthorne. She was renowned across the Houses as the best precognitive this side of a portal, aside from Blood and Beryl's own Dahlia.

Most fortune tellers, he thought, tended to be hacks. Sure, they could read *a* future, but it was never certain. It was in a state of flux, because people in the present constantly changed their minds, and every little decision they made altered the direction of the future.

But rumor had it that Tamsin Redthorne was able to see past all the 'what ifs' to pinpoint the most likely outcome. Elias had been after her to join the House of Blood and Beryl for the past decade. She'd simply told him that when she left the House of Earth and Emerald, it would be for diamonds. Whatever the hell that meant.

Either way, if she read your fortune, and it didn't look good, it probably wasn't going to *be* good.

And she was here, right now.

Kieran didn't like it.

He knew enough about his past to know his future probably wasn't going to be great, and he was okay with that. But he didn't need to hear about the details *before* they were going to happen.

There was also the fact he didn't like how the witch was looking at Sabrina. Well, in Sabrina's general direction. Her dark-rimmed eyes weren't staring *exactly* at Sabrina, because his ghost was about two feet over from where she was looking, but she definitely seemed to sense Sabrina's existence. That was the first time anyone other than himself had reacted to her.

His teeth ground.

Jealous much?

No. He wasn't the jealous type. He didn't get jealous of people because he didn't *like* people. Plus, it was silly to get annoyed that someone other than himself could see ghosts. You either could, or you couldn't.

Yeah, keep telling yourself that.

Great.

He *was* jealous. Damn it.

You just like how Sabrina looks at you. Like you're the best thing in her world, because you can see her. Be a friend to her.

Yeah, that's it, *a friend*. He had never even slightly lusted after her. Never.

You are a fool.

He'd take that one on the chin. Because it was nothing but a fool's dream, thinking he and Sabrina might one day get to do the naughty. She was *dead*. And unless she possessed the body of a living person...

Well, that had a whole host of other associated problems.

And he was ignoring the real issue: Tamsin Redthorne was meant to be one of the most powerful witches alive, and if she could see Sabrina, then his time with the ghost would be limited. Because Sabrina had been starved for conversation, for contact—of course, she would want to speak to someone other than just him. Someone who possessed social skills. Someone who didn't accidentally insult her.

You should just apologize.

I tried that already.

Then he'd have to be honest. Well, more honest than he had been.

She's dead. It's not like she can go and tell Elias you spilled House secrets. Who else would she tell?

Tamsin.

Right.

This was giving him a headache. He fought the urge to rub his forehead.

"Spirit and Sapphire didn't have a witch they wanted to send?" Ysabeau asked dryly, eyeing Tamsin like she was nothing more than an amusement. Maybe when you were a zillion years old, that's all a fortune teller was to you.

Tamsin smiled, the beads chinking in her hair as she tilted her head to study the vampire. "I just go where I'm told to. Not my fault I'm famous across all the Houses."

"So, ye are not another Spirit and Sapphire representative?" Lady Kim asked.

"She is one of the world's leading soothsayers," Sky said, her voice cool and efficient. "But she is from Earth and Emerald."

"Is there really such a thing as a 'world-leading sooth-sayer'?" Tamsin muttered. "I mean, it's so easy to get the details wrong. And for people to ignore your advice. Nobody likes hearing bad news. Even when it's offered for free." She glanced in Sabrina's direction.

Kieran frowned. "Mistakes happen." He'd wanted to say 'people are idiots', but decided that he should keep that one behind his teeth.

"You aren't wrong," Sabrina said.

Shit, had he said that out loud?

She tapped the side of her head, indicating it was their telepathic bond that had given her that gem.

Frustration gnawed within him. How much could she hear? How could he control it?

Even though he *liked* Sabrina, he wasn't happy that she had an access-all-areas pass into his brain. It wasn't a nice place. She shouldn't visit without warning him. He had to tidy up the cobwebs, metaphorically bury the bodies. That kind of thing.

Sabrina sidled closer to him, until she was obscured behind his back.

"*Are you hiding from her?*" he asked.

"Hiding?" Sabrina shook her head, and he could feel the movement against his back, tingles going back and forth. It did uncomfortable things to his heart rate and groin. "Why would I need to hide from her?"

That was non-answer if ever he heard one. "*Cos she can sense you?*"

"Focus on the conversation at hand," the ghost said, tone tart. "I didn't think you could do two conversations at once."

Ouch.

Too bad he liked it when she was sassy. He wanted to see more of that side of her.

You just want to see more of her.
Better not to focus on that.

Gravel crunched in the background, and they all turned to look toward the castle. Chief Angus was approaching from the yett, the blue-eyed dick, and a tall man with dark auburn hair following close on his heels. The latter had an expression that twisted between rage and pain—Kieran could see some of Sammy in the man's features.

His father?

"Oooh, I've always liked Scottish men." Tamsin waved a hand next to her face, like she was trying to cool herself off. "There's just something so appealing about the accent. Do you think they wear kilts very often?"

"Not appropriate timing, Tamsin," Sky murmured quietly.

"Oh yes, sorry." She dropped her hand, and four bracelets dropped down over her slender wrist. "This was all so last month for me."

Kieran's headache was getting worse.

"Last month?" Charlotte asked, and he could hear her jaw grinding from where he stood. "You mean you saw Sammy die and did nothing to stop it?" The phantom took a step toward the witch.

Tamsin stared at her, before pursing her lips and flicking a glance at Ysabeau. "I did. And I also saw that if it were not him, it would be someone else. Every future led to a death. Every single one. So, either he died, or someone else did. I can't stop every death." She paused. "Some are inevitable."

"So, ye saw who did it?" Angus demanded, having reached them. "Why stand about blathering then? Let us find them!"

Tamsin shook her head. "Your wards hide a lot of information. They were well built."

She knew, Kieran suddenly realized. She'd known about phantoms for a while, and she hadn't told anyone. Why? What had been her end goal?

"So, is the human doctor here yet?" Tamsin asked, grabbing the handle of her suitcase.

"Not for three days," Kieran replied.

"Well, I had better go place a stasis spell on the room. And ward it so naughty little phantoms can't sneak in, hmm?" She stared at Charlotte as she said this.

Charlotte straightened, thrusting her chin out.

Kieran blinked and turned his head slightly. *"She broke into the room?"*

"Yeah, I was going to tell you, but I didn't." Sabrina shrugged, visible just in the periphery of his vision.

"Did she touch anything?"

"No. She knelt on the ground at Sammy's feet and swore to avenge him."

Shit. That was just what they needed. *"Blood oath swore?"*

"No. Does that matter?"

"Yes."

"Well, I didn't see any blood."

"Good."

"A stasis spell?" Kim asked, drawing Kieran's attention back to the others.

"Yes, it will keep the room as is until the doctor arrives," Tamsin said. "Time will stand still. That way, no magical signatures will fade, and the body won't...decompose."

That kind of magic was expensive. And taxing.

Earth and Emerald really had sent the best of the best for this.

They must want the phantoms in their House.

They hadn't been selected as one of the three Houses to send envoys to the phantoms, so they were playing their own game.

Kieran and Ysabeau were going to have to up the ante; Elias wanted the phantoms to join his House, too. Spies who couldn't be tracked? That was a 'hell yes' from his king and his queen.

The auburn-haired man's mouth thinned. "That is my son yer talking about."

"I am very sorry for your loss," Tamsin replied, and she appeared to be sincere.

"Shall we?" Angus held out his arm, suddenly all gentlemanly and gallant.

Tamsin took it, dragging her suitcase with her free hand. "We shall."

CHAPTER 19

SABRINA

Sabrina had never heard the name Tamsin Redthorne before, but she got the feeling from everyone's reaction she was kind of A Big Deal. And that Sabrina had been very lucky—or unlucky, as the case may be—that the witch had read her tarot for free, back in the House and Gem Inn.

"Beware smiling men who knock on your door."

It was too bad she couldn't have just said, "Colin is going to murder you. Maybe you should get out of town ASAP."

That would've been a hell of a lot more useful.

Plus, Sabrina had been leery of Colin anyway. Always had been, deep inside. On some instinctive level, she'd always known he was a damned serial killer.

Now, the person who had predicted Sabrina's doom was walking arm-in-arm with her grandfather toward the turreted curtain wall of Castle Braemar. Her grandfather. Walking next to a witch. Right in front of the ancestral home of the phantoms. Sabrina was surprised

Great-grandpa Fergus wasn't sweeping down from the sky above, shouting obscenities.

Who else is she going to warn-but-not-warn-properly?

Or was the witch on a type of death-foreseeing holiday, since half of the people living here were immortal?

Yeah, Sabrina had a bit of a bone to pick.

Too bad Tamsin couldn't truly see her. Sure, she'd been looking in Sabrina's vague direction earlier, but she could've just been staring off into the distance.

I don't think I want her to see me, though, Sabrina thought. If this witch was as powerful as everyone seemed to think, it was probably better her attention was turned elsewhere.

What if she can give you your body back?

Necromancy?

No.

From the little Sabrina had heard, that kind of magic was heavily frowned upon, so even if Tamsin was powerful enough to do it, it didn't mean she *would*. And what kind of a price would she demand for restoring the dead? She'd already given Sabrina one freebie; the next time she probably wasn't going to be so generous.

The group walked toward the castle, following Tamsin and Grandpa Angus. He seemed to be telling the witch about the architectural history of the building. "The castle was originally constructed in 1628, by the Earl of Mar…"

Fan-fucking-tastic.

Sabrina moved closer to Kieran, finding reassurance and a strange sense of safety by his side. It wasn't that anything could hurt her, there was just something about him that made her feel secure. Especially with the witch who had predicted her death nearby.

Her grandfather was still talking. "The curtain wall is actually in a star-shape, with six points—"

"It is made from granite, yes?" Tamsin asked.

"Aye, lass. Coated in harl."

"Good for protection and positivity. I had heard this was one of the most haunted castles in Scotland," Tamsin said with a laugh. "I guess I know why."

Grandpa Angus' smile grew forced. "Indeed."

"Oh, don't worry." Tamsin patted his arm, as if consoling him. "There is no possible future where your people would have stayed secret forever. It was always going to come out."

Great.

That was just what her grandfather wanted to hear, Sabrina bet. But at least it made her feel better about their current circumstances. It was fate that had led the Houses to the castle's door.

Not her father.

They made it through the curtain wall and to the large red, double doors without any incidents. Inside, they came face-to-face with the two ambassadors from Air and Amethyst. Both wore jackets, as if they had been about to step outside into the fresh, autumnal air.

Feyre's sparkling hair was swept into a fancy updo, and her pointed ears had been decorated with silver-studded amethysts. She looked beautiful, as always. The fae turned her lip up slightly at the sight of Tamsin, arm-in-arm with Grandpa Angus. Lady Oleander, however, inclined her head ever-so-slightly, as if bowing to the witch. She then placed both her hands in her pockets and smirked.

"Who do we have here? Is it the great Tamsin Redthorne?" Feyre said, drawling her words.

"I don't know about great," Tamsin said. "Widely known, perhaps? Either way, Councilor Hekate asked me to provide some assistance. And I am always more than happy to help a grieving family move forward. Death is such an inevitable—but terrible—consequence of life. Well, to most of us." She nodded at Grandpa Angus and withdrew her arm from his. "Now, while I normally relish a little social bickering, I need to get the stasis spell up and running. It's taking up a fair bit of room in my suitcase, and it's heavy."

Sabrina's mouth dropped.

She wasn't sure which part surprised her: the vague condolences the witch had shown for Sammy; the way she managed to handle Feyre's attitude with ease; or the fact she'd made it appear like everyone had failed her for making the poor witch drag her own suitcase up the drive.

"Would you like me to carry the suitcase for you?" Ysabeau offered, all mock graciousness.

Kieran stiffened ever-so-slightly. "*She thinks of witches as food. I'm surprised she's offering help.*"

"Ysabeau thinks witches are food?" Sabrina asked.

"*Ysabeau views everyone as either food, or not food. There isn't much distinction between them. The fact that she's being polite to Tamsin means that she actually respects her.*"

The tone of his voice implied that this was a miracle, indeed.

"Are you classified as food?" she asked. *I mean, there are definitely parts of him I want to bite. And lick—*

"*No,*" he answered, derailing her interesting—but rather pointless—train of thought. "*I bite back.*"

"Ysabeau, it's always a pleasure," Tamsin said, giving the vampire a smile. "Thank you for the kind offer."

Ysabeau's mouth quirked ever-so-slightly as she picked up the suitcase, like it weighed nothing.

"*I can do that too*," Kieran thought.

Sabrina patted his arm. "I'm sure you could bench-press it, while saving orphans from a fire."

He chuckled mentally, the sound warming places inside of her that she didn't know still existed.

Ysabeau strode toward the staircase. "Are you coming?"

The group hurried after her. It took about five minutes of fast walking to reach Sammy's room on the fourth floor. None of them seemed out of breath, not even Tamsin, who was probably the frailest of the group. If she'd still been alive, Sabrina would have been bent over at the waist gasping for air, at the pace they'd set and with all those stairs.

Tamsin took the purple suitcase from Ysabeau and laid it on its side. Its wheels spun uselessly for a few seconds before coming to a stop. The witch's fingers danced over the combination lock so quickly that Sabrina couldn't register the numbers before Tamsin unlocked it and re-scrambled the code. She unzipped the bag, and Feyre, Kieran and Ysabeau recoiled a little, their nostrils flaring.

Something inside must have smelled bad.

Tamsin pointed to a packet of fluorescent yellow powder in a Ziploc baggy. "That would be the powdered dragon urine. Has a bit of a stench, doesn't it?"

Maybe it was a good thing Sabrina couldn't smell anymore.

Tamsin withdrew a large bronze bowl, an armful of bags and a bunch of what looked like horsehair. "I need to go inside to set the warding spell and the stasis spell. Do you consent to this?"

Uncle Barr stepped forward, his blue eyes locked on Sammy's door. Tears welled up. "Ye aren't to touch him."

"I don't need to."

"Can I come with ye? Just to see him?" Uncle Barr asked.

They all looked at Grandpa Angus. The clan chief lowered his head, and clapped Uncle Barr on the shoulder. "I'm sorry, but not today."

"He's my *son*."

"And we need to know what happened." Grandpa Angus nodded at Tamsin. "Go ahead."

The witch strode inside the door and carefully placed the bowl, hair and bags inside the room. Then she came back and grabbed some more items out of the suitcase. One glass jar seemed to have desiccated frog legs inside it, while another had what looked like snot.

Magic is gross.

Tamsin then picked up a ten-pound bag of salt that had been stashed in the case and, heading back inside, poured it all around the edges of the room, and on the windowsill. By the time she came back to the door, the bag was almost empty.

"I need a phantom's blood."

"What?" Grandpa Angus stepped back, as did Colin and Uncle Barr. Only Charlotte held her ground, her mouth locked in a grim line.

"If I am to ward this against phantoms, I need their blood."

"What about the others?" Colin waved a hand at the ambassadors.

Asshole always has to be in the thick of things. At least it meant she could keep tabs on him, while still being near Kieran.

Tamsin placed her hands on her hips. "Most warding spells have been designed to incorporate all known species. This," she pulled a plastic baggy from one of her dress' pockets, "has concentrated blood from every known supernatural creature on the planet. Even gods. But guess what it doesn't have?"

Everyone was silent.

Her pale gaze locked on Colin. "I said, 'Guess'."

"Phantoms."

She clapped. "Phantoms. Because until a few days ago, the Houses didn't know you all existed. Now, I need some blood." She held out her empty hand.

Grandpa Angus sighed and stepped forward. "Ye can use mine."

"Excellent." A pin had appeared in Tamsin's other hand, and the little baggy had vanished. "Now, let's get started."

CHAPTER 20

KIERAN

T he witch spent a good two hours in Samuel's room. After she collected blood from the clan chief, she converted it into a dried form right before their eyes—which was interesting, because Kieran hadn't realized witches could do that almost as easily as he could. Sure, she needed a spell and Kieran just needed to *want* it, but same end result. She added the powdered blood to her baggy and then returned to the room, leaving the door open.

Tamsin rolled up the white-and-red patterned rug that had covered most of the floor and dumped it in a corner, then began using the polished wooden floor as a giant chalkboard. Kieran had sidled closer to the doorway to inspect her work—as had the Air and Amethyst ambassadors. She was drawing a series of lines, circles and stars that connected with each other, as well as a ton of runes, most of which he had no clue about, besides recognizing some as being fae in origin. It was a complex spell, one she was weaving with confidence and ease.

The level of skill…

He didn't know a lot about witch hierarchical structures, but he knew there were maidens, mothers and crones. Your status didn't depend on your reproductive ability; some witches were crones before they ever had children, some were mothers before they ever had sex.

But Tamsin *had* to be a crone. A very young-looking, childless, crone.

The witch had to shush them at least six times, because the phantoms got bored and started talking. The fae and siren kept quiet, however, understanding the complexity of the spell. Ysabeau just leaned against the wall, staring at Charlotte for some unknown reason.

Interestingly, Sabrina didn't try to enter Sammy's room. He wasn't sure if it was because the ward prevented her—she did have phantom blood in her. Well, sort of—or if it was because she was avoiding the witch. He'd caught her trying to hide behind his body more times than he could count since the witch had arrived, and wasn't sure why. He'd have thought she would have liked a second person to talk to.

Sabrina had certainly been keen to talk to me.

But maybe she wanted someone that wasn't so grumpy or feral.

Although I have been acting pretty tame the last twenty-four hours.

Being on his best behavior was an uncomfortable sensation.

A bright burst of white light exploded from Sammy's room, blinding in its intensity. Kieran rubbed his eyes until the spots stopped dancing in front of his vision. *Hello, instant headache.* It was like a hot metal prong had been stabbed into each eyeball.

When the light finally dissipated, he glanced around frantically.

There.

Sabrina.

She was still alive—or, present, as it were.

She was blinking quickly but seemed otherwise fine. The activation of the stasis spell hadn't affected her.

Relief shuddered through him.

He chose not to think about his reaction.

The two Air and Amethyst ambassadors were in the same spot as before, on the opposite side of the open doorway. Ysabeau was adjusting her sunglasses, and the three phantoms were glaring at Sammy's room, while blinking rapidly, trying to pretend like their eyes weren't shooting stabbing pains directly into their brain.

Tamsin emerged from the chamber, dusting off her hands as the door clicked shut behind her. "The spells have been done, and the warding is complete. No one will be able to access this room until the doctor arrives, and the only person who can break the warding is me."

"What do ye mean?" Angus asked.

"Exactly what I said. So, if something happens to me and you want to get in there, you're shit out of luck." Tamsin squatted down on the hallway runner, and flipped the suitcase lid closed, before zipping it up.

"What about the stasis spell? What happens to that if you were to die in the next three days?" Colin asked.

"Showing your hand there, Cousin," Sabrina muttered from behind his shoulder.

"What do you mean by that?" Kieran asked her telepathically.

"Nothing."

"*Liar.*" But his voice was silky, smooth.

Tamsin stood. "The stasis spell will last until I break the ward. So, if I were to die before the good doctor arrives, this room will survive long after the castle rots around it."

"Best for you not to die, then," Kieran said.

"Yes, I would say so." Tamsin's gaze lingered on Colin.

The phantoms nodded, clearly getting the message. Kieran didn't think they understood the true implications of what she *wasn't* saying. Tamsin was able to stop *time itself* within the room. For an indefinite period. Not just three days, but potentially, forever. The kind of power required for such a spell…and she had managed to do it in two hours…

That was next level. Even for a crone.

"Now," Tamsin smiled, clapping her hands together. "Can someone show me to my room? I'm covered in horsehair and chalk, and I don't really want to have to stay like this."

There wasn't a single hair on her dress, although her fingertips were covered in white powder, and bloodstains were still visible on her right hand, under the chalk.

Angus offered to lead the way, even picking up her suitcase. Tamsin followed, her dark-rimmed eyes flashing with something like amusement. Before she turned the corner at the end of the hall, she glanced toward where Sabrina had been hovering seconds ago. Then they were gone.

Their group idled in front of Sammy's room. What was Kieran meant to do now? They had two and a half more days until the doctor arrived, and well, things weren't exactly peachy-keen.

It would be so much easier if he could just torture the answers out of everyone. Who would've thought he would miss the good old days? Simpler times, when he just ripped a few fingernails out, and people started talking. Most of the stuff they said was irrelevant and a waste of his time, but at least the conversation flowed, you know? It wasn't like he had to try too hard at all, and he certainly didn't have to use a filter, like he did here. After a while, all he had to do was look threateningly at them, and they spilled every thought on their mind.

He didn't even have to break out the hurty thing or the ouchie-maker.

Someone swore in Gaelic. One of the phantoms had tried to enter the room—the kid's dad. He jumped back, rubbing his nose.

"Have a bit of a kick to it?" Kieran asked, fighting amusement. The guy's kid was inside, dead. It wasn't a good look to laugh at the grieving father's encounter with a ward.

Even though it kind of was.

"Are you laughing?" Sabrina demanded.

"Uhh, no." Kieran looked around the room.

She stood in front of him. "You were trying not to laugh. I saw it."

"Why were you hiding from the witch?"

"Don't try and change the subject."

"I already did."

"Why were you laughing?"

He gave a tiny shrug. *"It's funny when someone walks into a ward they already know is there."*

"Sammy is his *son*."

"I gathered."

"And you still found it funny?"

"*I was trying* not *to laugh.*"

"You're a psycho." She crossed her arms over her chest and jutted her chin out. Man, she looked sexy, all disapproving and exasperation.

"*And you are only just working this out now?*"

"Here's a hint," Oleander said, looking at the phantoms. "Don't touch the ward."

The auburn-haired phantom glared at her. "Thanks for the warning."

The siren nodded, ever-so-slightly. "That aside, I wanted to tell you that I am truly sorry for your loss." And the thing was, she sounded sincere.

The two Air and Amethyst ambassadors turned and left the hallway.

"How do we know it will really keep you out?" Charlotte demanded. "This could be a ruse."

Ysabeau sighed. "Really?"

The vampire then walked up to the ward and touched it with a single finger. The air shimmered, a blue opaque wall appearing in front of the doorway, tiny sparks flying from where Ysabeau held her finger on the ward. After several seconds—*this woman has brass ovaries*—she pulled her hand away.

The smell of burned meat rose in the air.

Charlotte gagged, as did Sammy's father.

Ysabeau eyed them, then sucked on her finger for a moment. When she pulled it away, it was healed. "Not a ruse."

CHAPTER 21

SABRINA

S abrina still desperately wanted to know what Kieran had meant about tasting her blood, and how he knew she was buried on the property. The latter was probably an educated guess, but the former…he was acting like they hadn't been total strangers when they met.

But that would have to wait. She also needed to know more about the ambassadors and their plans.

Priorities. Her wants, versus the clan's *needs*. And most importantly, she needed to know if any of the Houses were responsible for Sammy's death.

The only thing she could say for certain was that Kieran wasn't guilty. She had been with him at the likely time of the death.

She looked at Colin. Her cousin was staring at Sammy's door, a frown on his face.

Was he annoyed that he had been magically barred from the room?

Did you have something to do with Sammy's death?

She had ruled it out before, simply because there was no direct gain for Colin, aside from creating turmoil with the House ambassadors. But that wasn't a politically savvy move, and Colin was savvy.

It would be foolish of him to kill a Fhearchair, because the investigation would open their secrets to intense scrutiny. Although, it wasn't like they needed to hide what they were anymore.

Clearly Tamsin knew what they were. *Everyone* here knew what they were. But they didn't seem to know how a phantom was made—did they even have to reveal that to join a House?

"I'm going to follow the Air and Amethyst ambassadors," Sabrina told Kieran.

"Why?" he asked, mind to mind.

"Isn't it obvious? I want to see what they know. And they won't know I'm watching them."

He quirked an eyebrow. *"I'd prefer it if you stayed with me."*

Why? Because he was worried about her? She was dead. It wasn't like anything bad could happen to her. "Even though you won't answer my questions?"

"Now isn't the time."

"Then I'll touch base with you later."

He cursed.

Sabrina floated over to Feyre and Lady Oleander, who had just turned at the end of the hallway. She glanced back, unable to help herself; Kieran had stepped away from the door, Ysabeau coming to stand by his side automatically. They were an imposing pair, the two of them. Her with that Audrey Hepburn elegance, and him with his long hair, chiseled jaw and biteable muscles.

She wanted to peel the leather jacket from his body; rip the jeans from his legs.

Those two better not have banged before.
That was an unpleasant intrusive thought.

Don't even go there, she told herself. *He can't exactly bang you like you are now, so why are you even jealous?*
And there was the naked truth: she wanted her body back. She *wanted* to be flesh and blood. She *wanted* to be able to climb on Kieran like he was her own personal exercise bike, and ride him until they were both comatose from pleasure. She just damned well *wanted.*

She was sick of being dead. Of being ignored, of being alone.

But she had to save herself. No one else was going to.

You could ask Tamsin…
How? Through Kieran?

"Think of something else," Sabrina said to herself. Anything else.

Tamsin made her itchy, which was a pain in the ass, because she couldn't scratch. The witch had looked in her direction one too many times for comfort, like she knew Sabrina was around, but didn't know exactly *where.*

And well, once burned, twice shy.

But, if the witch could tell her how to get her body back, it'd be worth it.

You're nothing but bones in the ground.
But was she?

Oh, she knew she was buried. She'd seen her gravestone. She'd gone to her own funeral. But had Colin kept a souvenir or three? It wouldn't be the first time.

Sure, she'd spent far too many hours stalking him, but she hadn't watched him twenty-four-seven at first. He *could* have done something like that. Correction: he *would* have done something like that.

And Kieran said he had tasted her blood, when she'd never let anyone drink from her before…

Why would a death fae want to drink blood? She thought that was exclusively a vampire thing, but maybe she didn't know as much about the supernatural species as she thought. To be fair, her knowledge was pretty sketchy.

Lady Oleander and Feyre remained silent until they entered one of their rooms. Sabrina didn't know whose—it wasn't like they'd put names on the door. It was more feminine than the one assigned to Kieran, with blue-and-gold papered walls, and a four-poster bed swathed in sheer, gold-colored fabric.

All the guest rooms had different names: the Rose Room, the Blue Room, the Green Room. Terribly inventive. It was how her grandmother had organized the castle for cleaning and rostering. This was the Sea Room.

Mermaids surrounded by sea foam, scuttled ships surrounded by kraken tentacles, and sunset landscape paintings were the primary decorations. A fresco decorated the ceiling, the splashes of worn color highlighting a variety of sea creatures and monsters.

Sabrina had spent hours upon hours studying the paintings in each room as a teenager. She'd particularly loved the kraken painting; the dusky colors, the way the light penetrated the clouds to shine on the water and dying ship.

Oleander looked at Feyre, who immediately held her hands over her ears. The siren let out a single screech, the sound wobbling the glass in the window, and causing the gold-framed mirror to vibrate against the wall. Decorative vases trembled across the room.

Sabrina rubbed her ears, even though she caught only part of the sound. *So glad I don't have eardrums right now.* They would have burst.

Feyre waved a hand, and an arc of small glass fragments floated toward her. "They replaced the cameras."

Sabrina's jaw dropped. The siren had made that sound to specifically break the glass on the spy cams?

The fae and siren spent the next five minutes searching through the room, just as thorough as Kieran had been. Feyre dumped the cameras into her gold-colored trashcan, which she then placed in the hall outside. She shut the door with a click, and muttered something in the native fae tongue. The air pressure in the room seemed to change.

Anti-listening spell?

"That boy dying is problematic," Feyre said finally. She unwound a silk scarf from her slender neck, before throwing it on the bed. It slithered over the comforter and onto the floor. The fae waved her hand, and the scarf rose into the air, before floating to the middle of the mattress, away from the edge.

Lady Oleander rolled her eyes. "That's putting it mildly."

Gee, I'm sorry Sammy's death is so inconvenient.

What a pair of bitches.

"They think you murdered the boy," Feyre said. "Makes it difficult to woo them to join Air and Amethyst now, doesn't it?"

"I didn't kill him." Lady Oleander sat on a chair, kicking her feet up on the elegant desk that had been placed under an arched window. "And I couldn't see any obvious signs of murder." The warm light filtering through the window caught on her hair, turning it the shade of blue-green grass.

Sabrina's fingers itched for a paintbrush. She tried to memorize the hue.

"He could've been stabbed from behind," Feyre said, removing her jacket. "He was lying on his back, it would've hidden the wound."

"I didn't smell any blood."

"You and your shark sense for blood."

"Look, I don't know why you're still annoyed at me. I wasn't the one who asked Volker if we could go on this mission."

"He needed someone he trusted."

"But we'd only just got back from Gold and Garnet. We should have stayed there to help him," the siren insisted.

"We *are* helping him. If we can get these...people...to join the House, it would be a huge win. Securing a true immortal? Imagine the power that would give us." Feyre sat on the edge of the bed. "And I'm not annoyed at you. I just am frustrated by the situation. At us having to pretend."

The siren's yellow eyes narrowed. "Pretend what?"

"That we aren't together."

Oleander stood and stepped closer to the fae woman. "The Moonlight Wraith is right. If anyone knew of our relationship, they'd use it against us."

"We're *mates*."

Feyre's voice broke a little on the last word.

Sabrina gasped in shock.

She would never have guessed—not in a million years—that the fae and the siren were together. The fae had been flirting with Kieran earlier, and the siren had made eyes at Sammy, and well, they'd just seemed like they were fair-weather friends. The kind you had during an event or a school semester or whatever, but when it ended, you both went your separate ways and that was that. No hard feelings.

All an act.

Feyre reached out a hand, tugging the siren closer to her. Oleander sighed as she drew nearer.

"Okay, I'm out." Sabrina backed out through the room, the vision of the two of them kissing burned on the back of her eyelids.

Even though she had more in common with a Grade A stalker than she'd like to admit, she wasn't going to spy on people in their private moments. Not when they were clearly unable to announce their union to the wider world.

And well, she thought she had what she needed: she doubted they'd killed Sammy.

But if not them…then who?

It was time to go do some recon with the Spirit and Sapphire ambassadors.

CHAPTER 22

KIERAN

K ieran was *not* thinking about Sabrina at all.

Not at all.

"Where the fuck is she?" he muttered under his breath, while he served himself another slice of Dundee cake. They were back in the dining room, trying to play nice with their hosts.

"What was that?" Ysabeau was nearby and heard. He couldn't see her expression behind the sunglasses, so he shrugged at her.

You should probably tell her there is a ghost here, as well as the phantoms.

She was Elias' second-in-command; he *really* should have filled her in about Sabrina by now. But he didn't want to, because then he would have to admit he could speak to the ghost telepathically—hello, new ability—and that he had kept the vial of her blood on hand. That he'd tasted it without permission, twice.

And he'd do it again, if he had the chance.

Ysabeau would see Sabrina as nothing more than a tool, and Kieran didn't want to involve her in all of that. The ghost had enough shit on her plate, considering she was dead and all.

"Did you notice any unusual scents around the boy's room?" Ysabeau asked as she sipped on a fresh cup of blood.

His fangs ached, but he didn't want what she was drinking—no, he wanted some of the glorious stuff tucked in the pocket of his jacket. Being half-fae, he didn't have to feed as much as the average vampire, and he had used that as his excuse for not drinking. That, and he didn't think his hosts realized *what* he was.

"No. But there was a lot of salt." He frowned, thinking about it. "Did you smell anything?"

"No. Just the salt. Almost like brine water."

"Strange." He shoveled the last piece of Dundee cake into his mouth.

Her fingers tapped on the glass. "Isn't it?"

Clint, the shifter from Spirit and Sapphire, strode into the room, his lanky frame eating up the distance between the door and the buffet table. He helped himself to such a huge mound of food it was in danger of collapsing, then walked over to the two of them.

"Evening," he said, nodding at them both, then started eating.

"Where's your friend?" Kieran asked.

"Doing stuff."

That was about as detailed an answer as Kieran would have provided, had the shoe been on the other foot.

Is Sabrina following her? He'd have to drill—uh, ask—the ghost later.

"You're a cat shifter?" Ysabeau asked.

"Jaguar."

The feline with the strongest bite-force in the wild, only beaten by crocodiles, alligators and hippos. Yeah, Kieran watched the occasional wildlife documentary. And hippos were the assholes of the fucking animal kingdom. He could respect that. "What sharp teeth you have." Kieran smirked.

The shifter snorted. "This ain't *Little Red Riding Hood*."

"You'd be more useful if you were a wolf," Ysabeau said.

Clint scrunched his nose. "No need to get all rude."

"A jaguar's sense of smell isn't as good as a wolf's." The vampire took another sip of blood, like she hadn't just insulted the entire cat-shifter population.

Clint finished eating, his eyes glinting as he looked at her. "I didn't think you'd need a wolf, considering who you are."

"I don't know what you mean."

Kieran bit back a snort. He ignored the look he could *feel* Ysabeau giving him behind her glasses. There were betting pools in the other Houses on how old she was. Old vampires tended to be powerful vampires, although that wasn't always the case. But it definitely was in hers, and everyone else knew it.

"So, why did you need my nose?" the shifter asked Ysabeau, clearly deciding to play along with whatever game she was orchestrating.

"I didn't smell any of us in the boy's room, only salt. Which could be because the witch dumped a ten-pound bag of it over the room, but there were no new scents. Just family—or what I assume was family. Which means one of two things." She raised an eyebrow ever-so-slightly, the arch just visible over the rim of her glasses.

"Either the killer lives here, or whoever did it can mask their scent," Kieran murmured.

Ysabeau tilted the dark glass of blood at him. He tried not to look offended. *She may as well have done a slow clap.* That drink tilt was a salute to him finally catching up.

"You're accusing *us*?" Charlotte demanded.

Kieran spun towards her. The woman seemed to have just materialized out of thin air, but he would have seen her if she had been lurking in her phantom state. She must have caught the end of the conversation as she entered the room, and he'd been too busy being insulted to notice.

Eyes on the prize.

Or in this case, the corporeal immortal.

Yeah, it didn't have the same ring to it.

"I'm not saying anyone from here did it," Ysabeau replied, even though she kind of *was* accusing the family of doing it. Her voice was cool and calm, like they were talking about the weather and not a murder. "But there's no trace of a stranger in the castle, at least one that I or the shifter can detect. So, as I said, it means one of two things."

"You assume I didn't notice anything," Clint said.

They all stared at him.

"I caught the scent of salt water, like the sea." He pulled out his cell.

Who are you texting?

This was why he needed Sabrina here. She could have spied over his shoulder and reported the information to him. They made a great team, that way.

You are not a team. She is dead. You are a dick. Not compatible.

"How does one hide their scent from a shifter?" Charlotte asked.

"Need to take notes?" Ysabeau murmured, her voice cool poison. She was taunting the phantom.

Correction—she was taunting the *blood bag*, as she would call it.

It was unusual behavior for the vampire. She usually kept her insults for her friends.

"Magic," Kieran said, deciding to intervene. "Or good old survivalist tactics. Someone who has worked around shifters a lot would know you can mask your scent using practical things."

Charlotte's eyes narrowed.

Maybe you shouldn't have been so helpful.

She had taken the kid's death as a personal insult. He couldn't say he was happy the boy was dead, either, but he wasn't about to start a vendetta over it.

That's because he's not on your give-a-shit-about list.

Kieran probably *would* go all 'tales of enrampagement', if someone had come after Elias or his mother. As for his stepfather and death fae family, though? Nope. He couldn't give a flying fuck. The last time he'd seen his paternal cousins, he'd told them to go kill themselves for the benefit of society.

"How do we find out if the killer masked their scent or not?" Charlotte asked.

Clint put his plate down on a side table, nothing left but crumbs scattered on its surface. "I'll check the hall again, see if I can find anything. Then we can go for a run."

Charlotte leaned forward. "Go for a run?"

"Yeah," Clint replied, "we will check the perimeter of the property—run the boundary. See if we can sense anything."

"*We?* Who is 'we'?" Charlotte asked.

"Me and the hulk over here," the shifter replied.

Kieran rubbed his chin. "You think we would be able to detect anything outside the castle?" Maybe work out where the killer had come from, if they'd been an outsider...

"I don't know how good your nose is, but it can't hurt to try," Clint said. "Or I can go with Ysabeau. We can't trust anyone to go on their own."

"What about your House buddy?" Kieran asked.

"Why so interested in her whereabouts?" The shifter's eyes gleamed.

"She just seems to be keeping to herself, and right now, that may not be a good look." Kieran didn't really care about the human-seeming Sky, but he knew Blood and Beryl had a cordial—but distant—relationship with Spirit and Sapphire. Maybe this would help.

"I'll let her know." But the shifter didn't type anything on the phone still in his hand.

When Ysabeau didn't volunteer for the recon mission, Kieran said, "I'll go."

He could do with the exercise; it would help him burn off his excess energy. He was getting angsty from desire for a damned ghost. And he wasn't going to be fucking anything other than his hand, at the rate her resurrection was going.

Wow, way to be honest with yourself.

Yeah well, honesty was apparently the theme of the day. And the day sucked.

CHAPTER 23

SABRINA

After leaving the Air and Amethyst ambassadors to get it on, Sabrina had initially decided to follow the shifter from the House of Spirit and Sapphire. After all, if she managed to get a body and climb all over Kieran like she wanted, she would prefer not to have an audience.

Call me a prude, but I want him all to myself.
Every. Damn. Inch.

Her form shivered a little. She'd never wanted—no *needed*—to feel someone touch her as much as she wanted Kieran to.

She stalked the shifter for a while until he had headed to the communal dining room; Sabrina had glimpsed Kieran through the doorway, standing next to Ysabeau, who drank from a smoke-colored glass. If he was there to watch Clint, then Sabrina didn't need to be there too, even though she wanted nothing more than to spend time by his side, being *heard*. Feeling *seen*.

But this wasn't just about her. Sammy was *dead*. They had to find answers, and splitting up was the quickest way to do it.

Plus, she wanted to prove that she could get good intel on her own. That she wasn't just dead weight.

Hah! You're fricken hilarious.

It wasn't like she *had* to prove anything to him though—she doubted he even cared that much. But if she was useful...

Maybe he'd help her then, in her quest to become a real girl.

You are so not Pinocchio.

No, but there *were* one or two similarities. Maybe just one.

Whatever.

Either way, she wasn't about to follow the shifter into the dining room where he could be watched by Kieran, so that had left her with Sky, the other representative from the House of Spirit and Sapphire.

She tracked down the pink-haired ambassador through Granny Kim's room chart: it had been posted on the kitchen wall, next to the chore roster, so it hadn't taken particularly good sleuthing skills.

It wouldn't have been that easy if you didn't know how the castle worked.

Sabrina took a deep breath—she didn't know why—and floated through the wall into the Green Room. Her whole body buzzed, like she'd jammed a knife into a power socket. Nothing else happened, but if she'd had real hair, it would have been standing on end, no doubt.

The room boasted green walls, green floors, and a green-painted ceiling, no less. The ceiling fresco featured a bright red apple falling from a lusciously verdant tree. She hadn't been in this room for years, and she could remember why now.

It hurt her artist's abilities.

Abilities she'd thought she'd buried with her body.

She'd always wanted to repaint this room, and Grandpa Angus had always refused. He'd never really given her a reason why, aside from some long-dead human queen having stayed in it at one time.

We own Balmoral Castle and that was once possessed by British royalty.

Then again, she'd never been allowed to redecorate there, either.

Sky sat in a delicate chair that matched the nearby writing table, a laptop open before her. Unaware of Sabrina's presence, Sky tapped rapidly on the keyboard.

The window in front of her overlooked the courtyard, and one of the sharply pointed curtain walls. On the desk, next to the computer, a gold candle burned on a clear crystal base. There was no heated pool of wax at the base of the wick, even though it appeared to burn merrily. The dull glow emanating from the flame was a purplish color. Magic.

It has to be.

A side effect of a warding or anti-listening spell, like Kieran had. Why else would a candle burn, but not burn? And glow purple?

That buzzing feeling was a ward.

Each one of the ambassadors appeared to have come with a huge arsenal of spells and magic that Sabrina could only dream of purchasing. *The kind of resources that took…*

Just how important were these ambassadors to their Houses?

Kieran was King Elias' nephew, and Ysabeau was the king's second-in-command, but Sabrina didn't know much about the other Houses' representatives.

Moving closer, she studied the woman. Sky's long pink hair was tied back in a no-nonsense braid, paired with a plain white tank top and simple jeans. She looked competent, efficient, and from the empty knife sheath strapped to her thigh, deadly.

She might not be as human as she looks.

It was always hard to tell. Even though Sabrina had once desperately longed to be human, she had always known even the most human-looking person could be a monster on the inside. Magic had a way of warping things to leave no trace.

Just look at her family.

A bunch of immortals, who had no issue nurturing a damned psychopath.

Sabrina floated next to the woman, peering over her shoulder like the Peeping Tom she was. Sky didn't sense her, remaining focused on annotating pictures of Braemar Castle.

Sabrina bit her lip as she stared at the images flicking by on the laptop screen, almost faster than she could track.

"Why are you photographing our house?"

But the photos weren't of the castle itself—no, they appeared to be more about its contents. The Spirit and Sapphire ambassador rapidly typed notes about a Greek vase that had been decorating one of the main halls for almost forever, and then flicked to another image, only to populate new notes about a suit of armor that Sabrina used to climb on—without permission—as a kid.

Why were they important? The notes didn't say anything obvious like 'SUIT OF ARMOR WORN BY HERCULES'. Rather, each had a date, maker, and potential provenance—whatever that was. Like she was cataloguing artefacts for an antique trade or something.

Why was this woman interested in them and nothing else?

It might have made more sense if she was trying to photograph the phantoms or other clan members clandestinely, but there wasn't a person to be seen in the pictures. It was like the people—the whole reason the ambassadors were there—were secondary to her.

"Are you going to steal from us?" Sabrina asked.

There was no answer, but Sky started ever-so-slightly. For a moment, Sabrina froze, then she realized it wasn't in response to her query; a cellphone had started to vibrate on the table, next to the candle.

Sky stabbed a finger at the phone, stopping the vibration. A message box popped up on the screen, with the sender labelled, 'Sexy Shifter'.

Clint?

I mean, he is *sexy.* Just not as sexy as her fae. But…it could literally be any other shifter. Sabrina hadn't ever really met an unattractive one.

Sky flicked the screen and the message opened, with Sexy Shifter having sent 'GETTING FOOD'.

It's Clint.

Why else would some random shifter send her that message, when she was clearly on a mission?

*Sexy Shifter…*Were these two an item, like Lady Oleander and Feyre?

While gossip-worthy, this was not what she was looking for.

'SAVE SOME FOR ME', Sky typed back, then placed her cell on the table. She turned her hand over, closing and opening her fist as she did so. Her skin shimmered with magic as a dagger appeared from thin air, resting on her palm.

Whoa.

Sky grinned and tucked the weapon into the empty sheath on her thigh.

She could summon weapons?

"What *are* you?" Sabrina asked.

The cell rang, cutting into the silence of the room. The ringtone was an old song called *Toxic* by Britney Spears.

Not what I would have pictured.

But then none of her guesses would be even remotely accurate, given this woman appeared to be full of surprises.

The caller ID said REGINALD REYES. Whoever that was.

"Hello?" Sky's voice was smooth and efficient as she answered the cell, leaving her phone on the desk and talking into the speaker.

"Report."

"Good afternoon, Reginald."

"Report your status."

"Redthorne has arrived and placed the room in stasis. We are waiting on a human doctor to determine cause of death." She rolled her eyes at the latter, like it was a waste of time.

"I thought they couldn't die."

"Apparently their teenagers are not death-immune." She tapped a finger against the desk.

"Interesting. Like vampires."

"Vampires hit a second puberty in their twenties, so it's possible."

They did? That was news to her.

"How old was the boy?"

"Late teens."

"Any idea on who the killer is?"

"None." Sky shook her head, even though the video feature was off.

"You would increase the House's appeal with the phantoms if you were able to find the killer."

"Clint is working on it as we speak."

"You should use some of your other abilities—"

"Did you need anything further?" Sky interrupted, voice cool and calm, even though she seemed slightly irritated.

"Have you found anything else of note?"

Sky flicked back through the photographs, coming to stop on an antique painting of Sir George killing the dragon, his hair a flaming red, contrasting against the muddy green scales of the dragon. "No."

"Fine. Report back tomorrow morning."

The call cut off.

"Yes, sir. You're welcome, sir," Sky muttered.

Sabrina moved away from her, frowning. So, if she *had* killed Sammy, she wasn't admitting it to her superiors in the House of Spirit and Sapphire. They either didn't know, or she'd done it of her own volition. Sabrina shook her head. Sky just didn't seem like the kind of person who would do that.

It left her back at square one.

Sabrina winced.

Now it was time to go see a witch about a boy.

CHAPTER 24

SABRINA

"I know you're there, Sabrina." Tamsin's voice made Sabrina freeze, stuck halfway through a wall. It wasn't exactly a...comfortable feeling.

"Can you hear me?" Sabrina asked. Then, realizing that there was nothing actually stopping her from entering the room, she continued through the wall until she had fully emerged.

Ugh. It had really been a rather unpleasant sensation, and the ward she'd no doubt passed through added to it.

Tamsin's room—the Sun Room—was the least fancy of all the guest rooms and it had no doubt been assigned to her as an unexpected guest. But Sabrina had the feeling if they'd known she was coming, the witch would have probably been given better accommodation. Because despite Colin thinking that killing witches was an acceptable hobby, Sabrina's family had used their services in the past. Witches were one of the few magical species the phantoms had a use for.

Funny how Grandpa and the others hadn't wanted the ambassadors to come, but they'd given them all nice rooms and a feast to eat.

Then again, when the Houses controlled the world, you'd be an idiot to insult their representatives, no matter how much you might want to.

The Sun Room was decorated in hues of yellow and the colors of sunset. It was quite pretty, with the four-poster bed taking up most of the floor space in the middle of the room, and a mahogany wardrobe in the far corner. It had a small writing desk tucked under the window, like most of the rooms, and an adjoining bathroom that had been a later addition. As a teenager, Sabrina had had to clean this room more times than she cared to admit. While the family had housekeepers—humans from the village—everyone was expected to pitch in and do their part.

"I assume you just replied to me, but alas, I cannot hear you." Tamsin stood at the foot of the bed, suitcase open at her feet. Her brown hair was tied back from her face, and her dark-rimmed eyes were intense as she searched through the luggage.

There was no sign of Grandpa, so she assumed he'd been gone for a while.

"Wait, you *can't* hear or see me?" Sabrina floated closer.

Tamsin withdrew a dark purple velvet box from the depths of the suitcase. She straightened and looked around the room, before settling her gaze on a spot about two feet from Sabrina's form. The witch popped open the box's lid to reveal a silk-wrapped bundle inside.

Sabrina did not like the look of this.

"I can't hear or see the dead," Tamsin said as she began to unfold the silk. "But I can feel spirits. It's why the House of Spirit and Sapphire have tried to recruit me so often. They believe I can look into a person's soul."

"Can you?"

There was a pause, then, "I assume you just asked if I can. Not in the way you're probably thinking, no."

A dark blue filigree design became visible section by section as Tamsin unwrapped the bundle.

The witch had pulled out her damned *tarot deck.*

"Nope. No. Nup. We aren't doing this again." Sabrina moved toward the door. She was not going to play this game, not again. Look what had happened to her the last time.

"Sabrina, are you okay? I can feel…fear?" Kieran's dark voice wove into her mind, and she felt a moment of pure calm at the sound. Then shock.

He could hear her when they weren't physically close.

"Yeah, I'm fine." That classic line women used when they were *not* fine, but the men in their lives were too gullible to read into it.

He's not the man in your life.
Yet.

"You sure?" She swore she could feel him frowning.

"Yeah. I will fill you in later."

"I'll be waiting." Then his telepathic presence was gone, and she was alone again, with this crazy powerful witch who was about to ruin her life. For the second time.

"Now, before you disappear in a huff, I just want to say that you had to die." The witch's expression was serious, although she was totally addressing the wrong spot.

"Gee, thanks. I really am glad being murdered was on the top of my list of things-to-do." She didn't know why she was being all pouty—she'd been dying anyway.

Yeah, but I probably would have become a phantom, not a damned ghost.

The witch spoke again. "But I can help you."

"I'm *dead*."

Even though Sabrina had hoped for a solution to her life-deprived state, she hadn't been sure there was one available, or if her wish was all just smoke and dreams.

Tasmin shuffled the tarot deck, and Sabrina was unable to look away from the cards, from the magic she could feel welling around the witch's hands.

The witch withdrew a single tarot card, stared at it, then turned it around for Sabrina to see.

Death.

That damned fucking grim reaper and his stupid fucking horse.

She would be glad if she never saw that ridiculous card again.

"This is what's called a Higher Arcana card. As I said last time, Death does not always mean death."

"But you said it *did* mean death for me."

She kept speaking, unable to hear Sabrina's protest. "Death is your future. And your past. And your present. You are a unique being."

"Oh, yay. Aren't I lucky? Doomed to be a ghost forever." Sabrina crossed her arms over her chest. This wasn't the help she had hoped for.

Tamsin set the single Death card on the comforter. "You're destined for great things. Difficult things. And dark things. Your life, if you were to get it back, won't be what you think."

"What's that supposed to mean?" She uncrossed her arms and leaned forward. "Wait—if I get my life back?"

The witch drew another card and made a humming sound in her throat. She placed it next to Death, upright. It showed a man, stepping off a cliff edge into darkness, trailed by a dog. The man held a satchel in one hand.

The card had the words 'The Fool' written at the bottom.

"I'm a fool?" Sabrina demanded.

I mean, I'm certainly not the same person I was when I was alive, but if anything, I'd say I'm smarter. She wasn't burdened with optimism anymore, that was for sure.

"Unlimited potential," Tamsin murmured. "The beginning of a new journey." She looked up, her pale wolf eyes sweeping the room, Sabrina's entire body tingling as the witch's gaze moved past her.

It was strange, the way her form responded to Tamsin's presence, like the woman had so much magic that Sabrina's ghost body couldn't help but react to it. But it was different to how she felt with Kieran—with him, she almost felt...alive. Whole again.

She desperately wanted that to be the case.

The witch trailed a finger over The Fool card. "It's time. I will help you get your body back. I just need a few things first."

"Oh yeah? Like what?"

"I don't need to see or hear you to sense your skepticism." Tamsin laughed, the sound like bells. It was strange—Sabrina hadn't thought the witch could make such a musical sound. She had no idea why she'd thought that; witches no doubt had to sing and chant and stuff to do magic.

"Your blood, your body…and that death fae."

CHAPTER 25

KIERAN

K ieran and Clint had gone back to their rooms to gear up, before meeting again in the foyer. Kieran had been walking around practically naked when it came to weapons, but that was just to be polite. Hell, he *was* a weapon. But now he was leaving the castle, he didn't feel the need to pretend he wasn't about to murder anything that looked at him funny.

Ysabeau had muttered something about blood and scents, and had disappeared as soon as he'd gone to his room. He'd ask her what she'd meant later.

The female phantom, Charlotte, was waiting for them at the bottom of the stairs, already armed to the teeth. Her expression was grim but determined, red mouth pressed in a thin line.

He kind of liked her. She'd be a good fit at Blood and Beryl.

Maybe I'm getting soft.

Or maybe he just respected a woman who looked like she wanted to rip someone's head off.

"Do you think you can keep up?" Clint asked Charlotte.

If looks could kill, the shifter would have been a pelt on the phantom's bedroom floor. "Yes."

This will be a good test, Kieran thought, to assess the phantoms' endurance. Because cat shifters, they were fast. And Kieran...well, he was faster.

Generally, that's not something to be proud about.
It entirely depended on the context.

"I mean," Clint said, and hooked a thumb in Kieran's direction, "I'm not even sure if he will be able to keep up with me."

Kieran rolled his eyes. Being the nephew of the King of Blood and Beryl, he normally didn't show his abilities. It was assumed he had *some* kind of potential; but as he wasn't the blood descendent of Elias, people tended to think less of him. And if they knew he was a halfbreed...

People tended to not think much of him at all. Most thought he'd been born *before* his mother had made the transition to vampire, and thought he was half-human at best, rather than half-vampire.

Those in Blood and Beryl knew better—but they thought he was more vampire than fae.

He didn't get to test his abilities very often, but today, he would. He'd sensed the slight surprise in the shifter that he'd volunteered for this rather than Ysabeau, who everyone probably expected to participate.

She was old. She was fast. She was deadly.

But Kieran was, too.

He'd been a torturer and intelligence agent for Elias because that had been the best role for him within the House of Blood and Beryl. It was one where he could do what he had to, without coming into too much contact with Elias. The separation had existed, not because he didn't like his uncle—Kieran respected the hell out of him—but because people might start to work out that Kieran wasn't the average vampire.

And it was more obvious when compared to a Master, like Elias.

Kieran's birth father had spent a lot of time, magic, and resources on ensuring he made it into this world and lived, because Kieran's death fae powers didn't just exist alongside his vampire abilities, they had merged. Become one. And he'd become more powerful because of it.

Too bad Daddy-dearest hadn't realized that torture and abuse wouldn't lead to Kieran developing any respect or familial loyalty. Instead, Kieran had killed him for it. Deader than dead.

Even Sabrina had more life than his biological father.

His ghost…Her blood was a warm presence against his chest, and he wanted nothing more than to sip from it and watch her. Touch her. *Feel* her.

None of that was going to happen, though.

You need to burn off this…whatever it is.

Yeah, he did. And this little run was going to do him some good. If he'd been the one-night-stand kind of guy, he would have tried to fuck her out his system with another woman, but it would be pointless. He'd have been thinking about her the whole time, anyway.

As Charlotte broke her death stare at Clint, a sudden spike of panic slammed into the back of Kieran's brain. Anxiety speared through his system, increasing his heart rate and sending his pulse into overdrive.

What the fuck?

He hadn't felt anything remotely like this since he'd killed his father.

Taking a deep breath, he realized it wasn't coming from *inside* his brain, it was coming from somewhere else.

Sabrina?

Reaching out telepathically, he found the ghost's mind; surprisingly, it was easier than he'd thought it would be. It was right there, though, nestled close to his, like distance wasn't really a thing.

Maybe being dead meant her mind wasn't blocked by flesh and thus made it easier to find?

"Sabrina, are you okay? I can feel…fear?" he asked, not sure how to initiate a conversation when she wasn't in front of him. But it seemed to work without any real effort on his part.

"Yeah, I'm fine."

Well, the words and tone did *not* match the feeling that had sent his brain into overdrive. But…she had calmed down, almost as soon as he spoke to her, the sense of clawing panic receded.

What on earth could make a ghost freak out like that?

What had she found?

Who was she talking to?

"You sure?" He needed to make sure she really was okay, and not just lying to get him to back off.

"Yeah. I will fill you in later."

Well, that was a dismissal if he'd ever heard one. He wanted to abandon the run, to chase her down, but he got the distinct impression she wouldn't appreciate it. And he'd just look like a crazy-ass fool to Charlotte and the shifter; one minute he was part of their mission and the next he was walking away.

He just sent back, *"I'll be waiting."*

A sense of calm satisfaction reached him, and he disconnected the link. Well, the active link. Apparently, he was still able to sense her emotions—at least really strong ones—even if they weren't directly communicating.

"Shall we go?" Charlotte demanded, and Kieran realized he had probably been quiet a little too long.

"Lead the way." He swept out a hand.

She shot him a look and strode out the front door.

He and Clint followed.

The air outside was cool and crisp, the edge of winter beginning to be felt. The phantom marched to the yett and through the doorway like she was on a personal warpath. And she probably was.

Once outside the castle's curtain wall, they paused. The cemetery was only about a hundred yards up the road, and the driveway meandered into the distance toward town.

"Which way?" Clint asked.

The phantom spun in a slow circle. "I don't know. How did you want to do this?"

"How much land do you have?" Kieran asked.

"A lot."

He and Clint could probably cover a decent amount of territory, and quickly, but even they had limits.

"Are there any major landmarks around here?"

"There's the town," Charlotte replied.

"Do the townspeople know about the phantoms?" Kieran asked.

She glowered at them both. "Yes, most of them. A lot of them have relatives who are phantoms."

"Could one of them have done it?" the shifter asked.

"Unlikely. They're either pure human, or they're phantom."

Unlikely. But not impossible.

"Is there anywhere else someone might visit to scope out the lay of the land?"

"The River Dee is behind us, and Loch Muick is to the south," Charlotte said. "Water is a good way to hide your tracks. We used to have issues with kelpies in the past, but we hunted them out of our territory."

Kelpies.

Not something Kieran had ever had much to do with, especially since they tended to stay close to rivers and waterbodies, making them members of Sea and Serpentine, even if they were a freshwater species.

"Let's go to Loch Muick," Clint said. "It is fresh or saltwater?"

"Fresh."

Clint nodded. "We can go overland and use our noses, and then track back via a different route. What's the distance?"

Charlotte frowned. "Around seventeen miles."

Kieran shoved his hands in his pockets. "A nice easy run."

"Will barely scratch the itch," Clint agreed, something like amusement turning his gaze gem-bright. The shifter started jogging.

Kieran nodded at Charlotte. "Try not to fall too far behind."

Then he started to *run*.

CHAPTER 26

SABRINA

S abrina hovered over the Edwardian chair in the corner of Kieran's room as she waited for him to return.

Her time with Tamsin had been…enlightening.

At last, the door opened with a slight creak, and Kieran stood framed in the wooden jamb. He was backlit, glowing like an angel come to save her from murder and monotony. Behind him, Clint walked past in the hallway, his skin glistening with sweat.

He looked delicious. But nowhere near as delicious as her fae.

"You're a fucking Master vampire!" The shifter yelled, jabbing a finger in Kieran's direction.

Sabrina frowned. Kieran wasn't a vampire, he was a fae. He would have told her if he was a vampire, right?

Right?

"No fae I've met can run that fast," Clint continued, out of breath and pissed. "I'd heard rumors, but hadn't believed you were half-vampire."

Kieran spun around, leaning a nonchalant elbow on the door frame. "I'm clearly not 'half' anything." He sniggered a little, which Clint did not seem to appreciate.

"Whatever." The shifter wiped sweat from his forehead, looking disgusted. "I demand a rematch."

"Oh, quit your bitching," Charlotte snapped, coming into view. Her face was pink and she was sweaty. "He made both of us eat his dust."

Did he now?

Phantoms were quick in their non-corporeal state. Had he managed to beat Charlotte even after she'd shifted forms?

"I'm going now," Kieran said and shut the door on them.

Sabrina giggled at Clint's expression as he was shut out, then stopped when the fae—vampire?—turned to look at her.

His pale gray gaze roved over her incorporeal body, like he couldn't get enough of her. And Sabrina, well, she couldn't get enough of *him*. His dark hair was swept back from his forehead, and his skin was slick with a slight sheen.

"Did you get all sweaty, too?" she asked, voice almost a purr, as she stood.

He moved closer to her, all intensity and heat. "I got caught in a light shower."

She bit her lip, imagining him in a real shower, not a rainstorm. Fuck. Either image was hot. But the shower was her pick, if she got to choose.

"I didn't know rain could elicit that kind of response." He raised an eyebrow, but his voice had dropped an octave.

A small bead of moisture gathered at the base of his throat and then dripped lower. She wanted to lick it. Lick *him*. "You look good wet."

There, she said it.

"Yeah. I do."

She laughed, surprised at the delight in the sound. How long had it been since she had truly been happy?

Too long.

"So, what was that about you being a Master vampire? You're fae, aren't you?"

Then again, he *was* Elias' nephew. By marriage.

"You heard that, did you?" The intensity in his gaze didn't waver, but he also didn't seem happy she'd found out about his little secret.

"I hear lots of things."

"I went for a run with a shifter." He smirked. "He had trouble keeping up."

"*Are* you a vampire?"

"Half."

"And half-death fae." He'd told her he was one when they'd first met. Or had that been a lie?

"Yeah."

"So, you're not a Master vampire?"

He ran his hands over thighs, wiping off droplets of water that had gathered on the material.

Her eyes slowly climbed back up over his body, taking in every square inch of deliciousness.

"Do you want the honest answer or the general answer I give people?" His voice was magnetic, capturing her, begging her to take the easy road.

She was dead.

Roads didn't mean much to her anymore.

"The real answer."

"Yeah, I'm a Master-level vampire." But he didn't look proud of his status.

"Why do you hide it?"

He sighed. "It's a pain in the ass. People expect big things of you, and I hate meeting people's expectations. In fact, I actively avoid doing so."

"It's hard to be in demand."

He winced.

She bit her lip. "I didn't mean it like that."

"Like what?"

"Like I'm jealous."

"Are you?"

"Jealous?" She rubbed the bloodstain on her sweater. "A little. I would love to have someone expect something of me."

Kieran reached out a hand, as if to touch her face. "I'm sorry."

"For what? You didn't kill me." Frustration welled up inside her. No, he didn't kill her. Her murderer was walking around the castle right this minute, probably planning on killing some other poor, unsuspecting relative.

"Who did?"

"Uh, uh." She waved a finger at him. "You have far too many secrets to be asking me mine."

"I do?" He crossed his arms over his chest, his muscles bulging with the movement.

Mmmm.

No. You have to concentrate.

On his muscles?

No!

Her stupid non-existent hormones were getting the better of her.

Wait, what was she—oh, right. "So, did you find anything when you went on your race?"

"It wasn't a race. It just turned into one."

She stared at him.

"We found some strange scents around the loch, but they are inconclusive."

"What do you mean by 'inconclusive'?"

"There's a scent there, something I've never encountered before, and neither has Clint. We don't know what it is, and we found a couple of footprints that didn't really match anything we've ever seen, either. Not humanoid, but no monster or animal I've encountered. And it all smelled like salt, but the loch's water is fresh."

"Strange."

"Do you have a history of creatures hanging around the loch?"

She frowned. "No. Kelpies tried to invade once—we're 'human', so it didn't matter if they killed us or not. But none since Grandpa slaughtered them and put up the wards."

"We took some photos of the footprints. Maybe someone will have a better idea."

She sure as hell hoped so. Monsters? At the loch?

"Do you think it's related to Sammy's death?" she asked. She didn't believe in coincidences, not anymore. But what would some weird creature want with them?

"I have no idea. I'm not into the law enforcement side of the Houses."

"Okay. Then that brings me to my next question." She leaned forward, so they were barely separated. If she had a body, she'd be able to feel the heat emanating from him.

"Which is?" His pupils expanded, the gray of his eyes disappearing in a tide of black.

"How have you tasted my blood before?"

Damn it.

Wait. That hadn't been her thought. That had been his.

He's not happy you asked.

No. But he had to know it was coming.

"Let's just say I was asked to look into your death, and I came across your apartment."

Her whole being came alive with something like excitement or dread. Or maybe a bit of both. "Who asked you to look into it?"

"I can't say."

"Can't or won't?"

"Both." His mouth pressed into a thin line.

Even though he was shutting her down, it made her want to smile. She wasn't sure why. But he…amused her. Even when he was cranky. "Show me."

"What?"

"Show me the blood."

"Why do you think I have it on me?"

She crossed her arms, mimicking his body language.

"Fine." He reached into his jacket pocket and withdrew a small vial. It glittered like crystal, and inside a crimson liquid moved languidly.

She swallowed. "That's my blood?"

"It is."

"But…I died a year ago."

"Yes, I pulled it out of the floor of your former apartment."

Her eyes widened. "*How?*"

She'd bled to death on that floor, alone except for Colin watching her with something akin to joy.

"Magic."

She'd never heard of anything like that before. That was...amazing. He'd brought her blood back to life.

Could he bring me *back to life, too?*

Tamsin had said he was part of the process...

But...seeing her blood in his hand, and sensing the hunger rising within him, she shoved the thought about her resurrection to the back of her mind. His gaze was locked on the blood, and he looked starved.

She bit her lip. "Drink it."

"Sorry?" His hand tightened on the vial.

"I want you to taste it. Now. In front of me."

He swallowed. "I'm not sure—"

She leaned forward, desperate to see his reaction to her blood.

She needed to see him drink it. Drink *her*.

"Do it."

CHAPTER 27

KIERAN

Kieran lowered the crystal vial in his hand slowly, not sure he'd heard her right.

"You want me to drink it?"

He had to be sure. She hadn't donated this blood—it had not been freely given from her vein to his mouth.

His heart pounded in his chest, like he'd run a marathon. Well, he just sort of *had*, but that hadn't made the organ want to burst right out of his chest. No, the roaring in his ears and the sweat that suddenly slicked the back of his neck had nothing to do with exercise.

He wasn't sure he'd be able to handle her blood. It was the most amazing thing he had ever tasted. And even then, he'd had the barest amount. If she was alive—flesh and blood and bone and sinew—he *knew* she'd taste just as amazing.

This…this would be like offering a slice of heaven, while denying him entry to the pearly gates, even though they were right *there* in front of him.

"I'm not sure it's the best idea," he said.

Her tongue darted out, wetting lips that didn't need it. Her eyes flashed, wicked. "But I have exactly one million questions. Why are you keeping my blood on you? Who asked you to find me? How did they even know about me?" She frowned, and he wanted to rub away the crease between her brows, comfort her.

He'd never felt like that about anybody before, especially a dead woman.

Hell, maybe he felt that way *because* she was dead.
She was safe.

She couldn't hurt him because she could never *be* with him.

The ghost tapped her chin with one long, elegant finger. "But you can't tell me the answers to those questions. Let alone the rest. So, let's just deal with the things that we can right now. You've tasted my blood before, and you liked it."

"I did." The memory—was it less than twenty-four hours ago?—was fresh, making his free hand curl into a fist.

He tried to keep his thoughts bottled in his mind, to prevent them from slipping through the ether to her. They were in turmoil, thinking about the taste of her blood, wondering if he had given away too much, not told her enough.

Definitely not told her enough.
But he owed his loyalty to Elias.

He didn't want to risk telling her something she may pass on to someone else.

Even though I really want to.
He'd never had this type of conflict before, even with his mother.

But she'd never posed a risk to Elias, to the House of Blood and Beryl.

Or to him.

Kieran's fingers clenched on the crystal, his mind turning to the glimmering blood within. It would make his body sing, come *alive*. Make his nerve endings raw, and his cock hard.

It would be worth every second, even if she saw how weak it made him. How vulnerable.

But it also made him stronger—his new telepathic ability had only emerged after he'd tried her blood for the second time.

Who knew what would happen this time? Especially as he was going to drink more than he had before.

"You're delaying," she said. "Just do it."

She was right.

He *was* delaying.

But for good reason.

He walked past her, to the chair in the corner of the room. He needed to be sitting for this. Carefully, he lifted the lid on the bottle, inhaling deeply at the first hint of blood. The aroma, it was intense. Lust, sin, blood berries, chocolate and whipped cream, sex, honeysuckle, and everything else delicious. Combine those with the heady, enticing scent that was blood—coppery, iron-rich—and it was indescribable.

The aquamarine of her irises darkened, like watching him was turning her on.

Can ghosts even get turned on?

How much was arousal tied to the body? How much was it tied to the mind?

Because he had been twisted up inside from the moment he'd tasted her blood, from the moment he'd recognized her hovering next to her family. And he was now one heartbeat away from having the most delicious thing in his life descend on his tongue.

He tilted the bottle, using his magic to draw out a tiny drop onto his finger. It was about the size of a small button, leaving enough in the bottle so it could be used—or tasted—again later. With his free hand, he carefully put the lid on, then tucked it back into his jacket pocket. He didn't want anything to happen to the delicate crystal. He wanted to keep it safe.

For him? For her?

He didn't know.

Sabrina leaned closer, until she was barely separated from him. He lifted his finger, sliding it between his lips while locking stares with her.

The taste exploded in his mouth, flooding his body. He wanted to close his eyes, the pleasure was so intense. But he didn't. He met her pale blue stare, letting her see how her blood affected his body, how it affected *him*.

The arousal was instant, his cock getting harder than he ever thought possible. And his heart, well if he thought it was fast before, it was going double time now. His hands clenched the armrest of the chair, like he was on a roller coaster, and he needed to hold tight. It was almost an intense body orgasm, the way she tasted, the way her blood filled his senses, overriding almost everything.

But he still met her stare, her eyes turning smoky with desire.

Imagine if you were drinking straight from her vein.
Fuck.

He couldn't stop his eyes rolling back in his head, or the shudder that wracked him. The idea of drinking straight from her neck, or from her thigh…it was almost too much.

It would be the most exquisite experience of his life.

Even better if he was fucking her when he did so.

He wanted it more than anything.

Opening his eyes, he took in her form. It seemed to have solidified somehow, like she was more real than ever. But when she reached out a hand to touch him, her mouth slightly open, her cheeks flushed the faintest pink, all he felt was that tingle of electricity.

No physical connection.

Goddamn it.

"That looked…intense." Her voice was throaty, sexy.

"It was." He coughed a little.

Her gaze raked over his prone form, coming to rest on the tent in the front of his jeans. He wanted to adjust himself, to show her how hard she made him. But…she was dead. She wouldn't care about his cock, about how he wanted to fuck her, how he wanted to see the head of it disappear between her plump lips.

You are not helping yourself out here, are you?
No.

But he couldn't say that he regretted it, either.

She bit her lip and nodded at his groin. "Do you need to do anything about that?"

And the pressure…it was just building and building in his balls. If she kept looking at him like that, he was going to come all over his pants like a teenage boy.

"I need to have a shower." He stood and hurried into the bathroom, closing the door behind him.

Smooth.

But he was going to jump out of his skin if he didn't do something.

Quickly, he stripped, then climbed into the shower, swearing at the spray of cold water that hit his heated skin like an icy thunderstorm. His cock though, the damn thing didn't care about the cold water, about the fact that one of the phantoms could come spy on him at any second. No, it just wanted Sabrina.

But she was in the next room, and there was nothing she could do to help him out.

Reaching down, he grasped his hard length in one hand, hissing at the feeling of pleasure.

"Mmm. Keep up the show."

He whipped around, surprise having him almost slip over in the shower. "Sabrina!"

"Yes?" Her wild gaze met his, and he could tell she was aroused. That she wanted *him.*

But how?

"What are you doing?" he demanded.

"Watching you jerk off." She floated through the shower glass, coming to stop under the spray. She was so close her energy made his skin tingle painfully, and his cock jumped in his hand. "My blood made you hard."

"As a rock." He should let go; stop what he was doing. End it. But he couldn't. She was staring at him like he was the hottest thing she'd ever seen, and she was so beautiful, it fucking *hurt.*

"I want to see you come." Her hand reached out, touching him, sliding up and down his length, leaving burning tingles in its wake. His hand mimicked hers. She leaned closer, her mouth hovering over his, as if she was going to kiss him.

Gods, he wished she could.

Her lips whispered over his, and he swore he could almost feel it. "I want you to think about drinking my blood while you stroke that beautiful cock."

He wet his lips with his tongue, exhaling in a ragged breath. "That's exactly what I was doing."

Sabrina smiled at him seductively, raising a single eyebrow. "Well, then?" Her eyes darted down, focusing on his movements. "Tell me about it."

Kieran groaned, even more turned on than he had been before. With one hand on the shower wall, he pumped his fist up and down, staring straight at her stunning blue eyes, never losing contact. "You want me to tell you what I'd do to you?"

She nodded, and he grinned as his heartbeat raced. "I'd kiss you until your lips were swollen and you were out of breath. Teasing every inch of you until you couldn't take it anymore."

"I wouldn't complain. I'd let you."

"Then I'd run my tongue over the heated skin on your neck and suck on the flesh. Feel your pulse beat against my mouth while I savored your scent."

"Mmm," she moaned. "No one has ever done that to me before."

"I know. I want to be the first." *The only.*
"And then?"

Pressure built as Kieran's speed picked up, as he squeezed tighter. "I'd kiss the very spot I wanted. Slowly. Thread my fingers into your hair so I could hold you just where I wanted you. And then I'd sink my fangs in, piercing your skin, and I'd fucking drink the sweetest, most delicious, intoxicating blood I've ever had."

His eyes fluttered closed as he hovered on the edge of orgasm. The tightening before release becoming his only focus.

"Look at me when you come," Sabrina said, and his eyes shot open.

The thought of it. The fantasy. Her staring at him with an unexplainable heated gaze. He wanted the real thing. He wanted *her* to want the real thing. Kieran pumped harder. Faster. Sabrina's hand touched his again, grazing over his tip, sending a spark of her ghostly energy through him. Whirling his tongue in his mouth, the lingering taste of her blood became overpowering, and he shattered.

"Fuck," he groaned, the throaty sound reverberating off the walls. He slapped his palm against the wet tile as a shudder racked his body.

"Thank you," she whispered with a wink before floating backward out of the glass door and leaving him by himself.

His mind raced, unsure of how to process what had just happened.

It was dirty, and sexy, and erotic, and he was here for it—it only made him want her more.

He was well and truly fucked now.

CHAPTER 28

SABRINA

S abrina was surprised she hadn't combusted on the spot.

Watching Kieran touch himself after he drank her blood, while listening to him describe drinking it straight from her vein…then experiencing him exploding in ecstasy—it had been empowering, heavy. She didn't think she had ever felt so undone herself, seeing this man reach his own pleasure. She knew in that moment, that if she could get her body back, the first thing she was going to do was jump Kieran and fuck him until they both couldn't walk.

And then she might do it a second time.

And a third.

Something in her very essence, in the core of her being, *wanted* him.

Wanted him more than anything.

But there was only a tiny amount of blood left in that vial, and she needed it. At least, Tamsin had said she needed it, as well as Kieran. Apparently, the blood was required to re-body her, but Kieran was the key.

The creak of the bathroom door opening made Sabrina turn. She'd given Kieran a modicum of privacy after he'd come so hard he'd seen stars. She'd been so wound up herself, she wasn't sure she could have stayed in the room with him and not tried to touch him again. She'd been worried she might accidentally electrocute him, she'd had so much energy burning through her.

His dark hair was slicked back and wet, and his gray gaze was heavy as he took her in, hovering near the end of his bed.

"That was unexpected." His voice was dark and gravelly, like a man who had been well-pleasured.

I did that.

My blood.

Me.

"It looked like you had a good time." She grinned.

Amusement lit his expression, and it turned from intense and sexy, to irresistible, intense and sexy.

"Best fun I've had in a long time." He strode closer to her, until they were barely a breath apart. "If you were alive, we wouldn't be done yet. The things I'd do to you…"

"Let me take you up on that offer when I get my body back."

He frowned. "Dead people generally don't do that. I mean, zombies have a body, and poltergeists can steal one…"

"Have you ever seen a ghost steal a body?"

He shook his head, eyes locked on hers. "No, but I've heard it can happen."

"That's not what I'm planning."

He walked around her—not through her, which he totally could have done—and sat on the edge of his bed. "I'm not following."

"Tamsin told me—"

He held up a hand. "Wait. You spoke to the witch? She can hear and see you?"

"Well...not exactly." Sabrina's hands twisted together. Funny, how when she touched herself, she felt pressure, a firm boundary. No pleasure, no enjoyment in the sensation, but her hand didn't pass through her body, like Kieran's would have if he'd tried to touch her.

"Still not following."

Thank goodness she was semi-transparent; her cheeks couldn't turn bright pink. Funny, the things that embarrassed her, versus the things that didn't. "She can sense I'm around, but she can't see or hear me."

"And she knew it was you?" One of his eyebrows rose so high it nearly touched his hairline.

"Well...we met before."

"Before when?"

Sabrina bit her lip. "The day I died."

"*She* killed you?" His expression went cold in a heartbeat. He turned toward the door, like he was going to march right over to the witch and strangle her for her role in Sabrina's death.

"No!"

He paused, then swiveled back to her. "I think you need to start at the beginning. This is giving me a headache. Or continuing one. I'm not even sure anymore." He rubbed his temples.

I know how we could treat that headache...

No. Now was not the time to think with her ghostly libido, it was time to open the can of worms.

"The day I died, I was working as a waitress in a pub in London. Tamsin was there, in a booth all to herself, reading tarot cards."

The vampire-fae stopped the circular motions on his temples. "I'm not sure I like where this is going."

"She offered to read my tarot for free. I didn't have anything to trade her, no real way to pay for a reading."

"That isn't improving things."

"I refused. She insisted."

"Never a good sign."

She bit back a smile. Hard to believe she could even feel the slightest spark of humor, given the topic. But he did that to her. "Do you need to keep the commentary going? Or do you want me to tell you the story?"

"Sorry." He mimed zipping up his mouth. A few seconds later, his thoughts reached her, *"But you can't stop me thinking."*

She laughed. The gray of his irises heated, until his eyes appeared like pools of desire.

"I could listen to you laugh all day."

And I could watch you touch your beautiful cock all night.

His voice was all heat and sex in her mind. *"I heard that."*

Her cheeks tingled, and she had a feeling that they may have darkened into a ghostly blush. "Every time she laid out a reading, the Death card was there. She said I was going to die soon. I didn't think much of it, because I was already dying."

Kieran frowned, but he didn't say anything, and his thoughts had gone quiet.

She plunged ahead, speaking fast. "I had cancer. An incurable form, from what the healers said. It didn't respond to any treatment, and there was no medicine or spell—that I could afford—that was going to fix me."

"So, you hadn't made the transition to phantom, yet?"

She shook her head. Sabrina wasn't sure she should talk about that; she wasn't sure she even wanted to.

"I knew I needed to come back to the clan, if I was going to have any chance of becoming a phantom, of not dying alone. So, I began packing, thinking Tamsin had prophesized my death and it was earlier than I had anticipated."

He just looked at her, but she could *feel* the questions burning inside him.

"Before I left, someone came to my door. It was my killer."

"Who was it?"

"Not important."

"How is it not important?" Possessive rage glimmered in his gaze.

She swallowed. It was hot. So hot. "Can you promise me you won't storm off and kill the person if I tell you?"

"You mean they're *here*?"

Ooops.

She didn't reply.

"No," he said. "I can't promise you that. Not right now." His eyes fell, focusing on the blood stain on her sweater. "Not when I want you here…with me…and they're the reason you're not."

God. That was an unexpected emotional punch to the jugular. "They brought my body back and buried me here. I think that's why my ghost is tethered to the castle."

"So, it's not just the wards."

She shook her head.

"Interesting." He rubbed his chin, fingers scraping over the faint beard he had begun to grow. "So, Tamsin met you when you were alive, warned you that you were dying, and now has told you that you can get your body back?"

"That about sums it up, yes."

"So, what are we waiting for?"

"A new moon." That was the one thing Tamsin had told her they needed, and it was something that happened when it happened.

Sabrina floated over to the window and looked outside, the night sky soaring overhead. The day had flown. A fat slither of moon rode high in the sky, surrounded by stars. The crescent moon looked like the horns of a bull.

Kieran came up beside her. "Then you have a few days left."

She grinned, excitement shooting through her. "I get to become a real girl again."

She was going to rain hell down on that asshole Colin. And find Sammy's killer.

CHAPTER 29

KIERAN

Three days had passed since Kieran had tasted Sabrina's blood.

Three days he'd spent in clawing withdrawal, pretending that single proper taste hadn't gotten him addicted to her blood. Addicted to *her*. He'd never been the religious type, but he'd been shouting prayers in his mind to any and every god that they would be able to get Sabrina's body back.

Sure, he wanted more of her blood. That was a no-brainer.

But he also wanted more of *her*.

And he wasn't willing to let her go. Let *them* go.

One more day until the new moon. Until they could try to magic her body back to her.

This had better damn well work.

"Focus," Ysabeau hissed at Kieran, her annoyance palpable.

Gripping the arms of his chair, he brought his mind back to the present. They were in a meeting. All six of the ambassadors—plus Tamsin—were seated around a large conference table, with the clan chief, Angus, at one end with his ever-present posse of phantoms. Only one of them was invisible to the other delegates, however—the one with the suit that clashed horribly with his red hair.

Sabrina misted through the wall at that moment, coming to a stop on the other side of the table. She winked at him, and settled down on one of her invisible chairs. Fuck, she was sexy, even in that bland, bloodstained sweater.

"When is the damned doctor going to get here!" Angus slammed a hand onto the wooden surface, the noise thundering through the room. He glared, but none of the House representatives so much as twitched, although a couple of the phantoms jumped.

Sabrina simply looked serene, like she was used to the random outbursts.

"Is he normally like this?" Kieran asked her.

Sabrina shrugged a shoulder. *"More or less."*

She still hadn't told him who'd murdered her. The clan chief was at the top of the list, but she had denied that. His second guess was the smug bastard who had the same aquamarine eyes as her—Colt, or Cliff, or Colin or something. The guy was cold. Colder than he should be.

Kieran should know.

He had the same trait.

But I've never murdered an innocent girl before.
No, the people he'd killed had definitely deserved it.
Most of the time the world was better for it.
"Well?" the clan chief barked.

The woman who had taken to feeding Kieran cake whenever she could, scowled at him. "Today. Later today."

Nobody had been settled since the discovery of the boy's body on the first day. And Kieran couldn't blame them.

He was used to murder and death—it had been his trade for so long he had become immune to the effects of it. But the family—and the clan was one giant family, he'd come to understand from Sabrina—were unused to such things.

And then there were the strange scent tracks Clint and Kieran had been hunting each day.

They still had no idea what was leaving the trails, which seemed to crisscross the phantom's land before vanishing into the River Dee. It was unnerving him. Even Ysabeau had no clue, and she'd been alive long enough to see everything twice over. He had a feeling it was that part that unsettled him the most.

"The stasis spell will hold," Tamsin said into the ensuing quiet. "The castle could collapse around it, and the room would hold. The delay of the doctor is not posing a risk to solving this crime."

The clan chief sniffed, his disdain clearly evident.

Funny, how the man had gone from being genial and welcoming to the witch, to cold and scornful within a matter of days. Maybe he had worked out that Tamsin's loyalty to her House was stronger than the lure of a bag of gold.

"The Moonlight Wraith and the Rebel Queen regret they cannot be here in person to mourn with you," Lady Oleander said, voice smooth as silk and poison. Her yellow eyes surveyed the room, as if assessing for entries, exits and escape routes. Kieran had done that the moment he entered, and he knew Ysabeau had done the same.

They weren't like the phantoms—or Sabrina—who could just mist through the wall if they so desired.

"However, The Moonlight Wraith has sent this message." The siren pulled a tablet out from under the table and played a video of the Air and Amethyst ruler sharing his condolences with the phantoms. The clip ended with a close-up of the fae's face, a man more handsome than he had a right to be. Volker's voice shot through the room, his words clipped and precise. "We will provide all assistance necessary in tracking down the killer. The House of Air and Amethyst does not take this matter lightly."

Angus sneered. "Isn't that the one still cleaning House after he got deposed?"

Ysabeau stiffened ever-so-slightly next to Kieran.

"Oh no, he didn't!" Sabrina said, then clapped her hands over her mouth. Her blue eyes were wide as saucers.

Kieran had to fight the smile that wanted to tilt the corner of his mouth. It wouldn't do for the phantoms or the House of Air and Amethyst to think he was smiling over the clan chief's comments.

"Volker is indeed busy plucking the traitors from his midst," Feyre said, pride in her House and leader evident in every word. "But the House of Air and Amethyst is stronger than ever, and we welcome our new queen, who has added considerable power to our House."

Ah yes.

The new queen.

Blood and Beryl had a new queen, as well: Danni, who had been largely shielded from Kieran due to his 'lack of manners'. Ysabeau knew her better; hell, she knew everything there was to know about the House of Blood and Beryl. The old vampire had been there the day Danni had joined the House.

She was Elias' second for a reason.

But in Volker's case, the fae had disappeared—presumed dead—only to resurface with a mate who was more powerful than she should be. It had helped him regain control of his House, but this time he shared power.

"Odin and Lady Gabriella send their regards," Sky said. "They would like to arrange a time to come and meet with you in person."

A tapping sound reached them, and Clint stood and strode to a window. A midnight black raven sat on the sill, pecking the glass.

The shifter opened the window and the bird hopped inside, cawing.

"Odin can communicate with ravens. When you are ready, you can let the bird know and he will fetch our leader."

The phantoms all shifted uneasily in their chairs.

"Councilor Hekate of the House of Earth and Emerald also extends her condolences," Tamsin said. She wasn't an ambassador, but she had apparently stepped into the role anyway. She withdrew a large, green crystal from beneath one of her many shawls and placed it on the table. She chanted a few words in Latin and a soft glow began to emit from the shiny rock, the light flowing from the crystal to coalesce in a glowing ball above the table. A second later, a woman's face appeared in the ball of magic.

She was beautiful, stunningly so, with skin the color of midnight and eyes a pure white, with no pupil. Hekate was in the most powerful echelon of witches—a crone—and yet she barely looked a day over thirty. No one knew exactly how old she was, but she had been ruling the House of Earth and Emerald for decades.

"Good afternoon." The crone's voice wove through the room, and Kieran swore he tasted music in the air.

"Did you feel that?" Sabrina asked him, expression stunned. So, she'd noticed it, too.

Councilor Hekate's head turned slightly toward the ghost, and Sabrina shrank back.

"I apologize for not being here in person," the witch spoke, as if her slight acknowledgement of Sabrina hadn't happened, "but I hope Tamsin has proven helpful."

"Is this another recording?" the clan chief demanded.

"I assure you, this is no recording." Councilor Hekate smiled. "Tamsin has merely activated a spell using one of two communication crystals."

Angus seemed struck by the woman's unearthly beauty or her power. Or both. His aggravated tone mellowed, "Aye, well, it is a pleasure to meet ye."

"I am sure it is."

Funny, how one of the Air ambassadors had said much the same thing when they'd met mere days ago. Arrogance had its perks. Ysabeau swallowed audibly, but her expression was about as telling as a rock's.

The clan chief seemed unsure how to respond to the statement.

"I would like to offer our continued assistance in finding the cause of your youth's death," Hekate continued. "We take pride in our abilities, hence I personally sent one of our more powerful witches to help." She waved a hand toward Tamsin.

"We do thank ye for the help." The words were grudgingly spoken, but true nonetheless.

The crone tilted her head to the side. "It is worth considering carefully how the phantoms would fit into a House. With Earth and Emerald, we elect our leaders through a democratic voting system, and we respect our peoples' choices. We encourage individuality, and respect privacy."

"What fine words," a new voice drawled.

Kieran's shoulders tensed, and he turned toward the doorway where King Elias stood. He filled the narrow entry, with the witch, Seraphina, half-obscured behind him. His uncle was huge, muscular and intimidating in suit pants and an open-collared shirt. He looked like he was here to murder someone, and if someone wasn't careful, he probably would.

The vampire king strode into the room, Charlotte hot on his heels.

"He appeared in the driveway a couple minutes ago and marched straight into the castle," Charlotte said, looking harried. "No one was able to get close to him."

"Who the hell are ye?" Angus stood, fury emanating from him.

Elias stopped behind Ysabeau and Kieran, placing a hand on his nephew's shoulder, as if telling him to calm down. The thing was, Kieran wasn't upset. He was more impressed than anything.

He flicked a glance at Sabrina, who whistled. *"He's hot."*

Kieran shot her a look, fighting the jealousy that surged through him, making his blood heat. *"He's mated."*

"To you?"

"Ew. No. That's my uncle."

"Then I don't see the problem."

He was getting another headache.

"My name is Elias Laskaris, king of the House of Blood and Beryl. I was informed we were doing meet and greets, and I thought I would drop by and personally offer a welcome from the House of Blood and Beryl."

"Always like to one-up people, don't you, Elias?" Hekate's voice was dry.

"I believe in putting a face to a name."

A non-answer. Politics seemed to involve a lot of those.

The meeting only devolved from there.

CHAPTER 30

SABRINA

K ing Elias was the last thing Sabrina had expected to see in Braemar Castle.

Councilor Hekate had been impressive, and the video message from the Moonlight Wrath had been exciting. But a House leader here, in person?

No, she hadn't thought they'd make the effort. That they even thought the phantoms *worthy* of the effort.

Maybe that's just your insecurities coming out to play there.

Because it seemed like Blood and Beryl *really* wanted the phantoms in their House.

I mean, why not? Invisible spies? I'm surprised that most of the Houses aren't climbing over themselves to win us over.

She would, if she were a House leader.

Yeah, and the odds of that happening are slim to none.

She assumed that Grandpa Angus would pick a House for everyone—but what would happen if some family members didn't want to go to the House he chose? What then?

She bit her lip.

He would be furious.

But there wasn't much he could do, aside from exiling them from the family, and she doubted he'd do that. He'd been frustrated and sad whenever he talked about Sabrina's father leaving. But then, Douglas had been his son, whereas some of the other family members were second, third, and sixth cousins.

It's amazing we even get the choice, really.

If phantoms weren't impossible to kill, the Houses would have just murdered them all and been done with it. It's how they'd handled dangerous supernatural races in the past—that's why her family had been so against revealing themselves to the wider world. It would have meant the vulnerable members of their clan were exposed to risk. But why kill the mortal parts of their family when the immortal would live on to exact vengeance?

Even the clan had paid attention to the Great Sacrifice, and what it meant for the Houses to go to war.

Death. It means death.

King Elias strode out of the meeting room, Ysabeau hot on his heels. Kieran and Sabrina had been loitering in the hallway outside, after Grandpa Angus had kicked everyone out so he could discuss things with the two House leaders. He'd even thrown out the family members, aside from the invisible Great-grandpa Fergus—mostly because he would have had a tantrum at being excluded, and that might have been a little hard to explain.

She was struck again by how different Kieran and Elias looked. They both had dark hair, sure, and they were tall and muscular to the point of unfairness. But Kieran had delicately pointed ears, and there was just something ever-so-slightly feral about her fae-vampire, soon-to-be-lover. Sabrina found it incredibly hot.

But from the outside, you wouldn't know they were uncle and nephew.

"Step-uncle and nephew," Kieran thought at her, pretending he wasn't having a second conversation with her while he greeted his leader-slash-uncle.

"You can talk in there." Colin, who had been stationed at the other end of the hall came forward, pointing at a nearby door.

Sabrina frowned. "Isn't that a broom closet?"

Ysabeau went first, opening the door and stalking inside. She turned in a slow circle and then came out. "Clear."

The four of them—well, technically three—squeezed into the room. It wasn't exactly a tight fit, but there weren't any chairs, and if you swung a cat, you'd hit a wall. And get scratched to death.

She had no idea *why* that was even a saying.

The poor cat.

Kieran tried to discreetly look around the room. *"What cat?"*

"Uh, never mind." She hadn't meant to send that thought.

He's going to think you're nuts.

That's if he didn't already realize it.

"It smells like beeswax and lemon in here," Ysabeau said, almost like she was offended.

As usual, Sabrina couldn't smell anything, but she'd always enjoyed that scent—it had reminded her of the castle, of home.

"I think this might have been a storage closet, which they cleaned out and decided to use for us," Kieran said, acting on her earlier intel.

Intel. What a way to phrase your random musings.

She told her mind to shut the hell up.

She was useful.

She *was*.

"Way to roll out the red carpet," King Elias muttered. "Letting us talk in a cupboard." He shook his head. "I can't stay here for long, but I wanted to see how things were going, and to meet the phantoms myself."

The vampire was compelling; everything about him was. If Kieran hadn't been in the room, Sabrina would have had a hard time trying to look away from the vampire king and his energy, his intensity.

I guess that's what being a king means. You have to command a room.

Even one as tiny as this.

Shame she was a one vampire kind of woman.

"Things are going as well as can be expected," Ysabeau said, the faintest of frowns marring the perfection of her face.

Sabrina had thought it was all going rather terribly, herself.

"If by 'well' you mean somebody getting murdered on our first day here," Kieran said, "with no suspect. *And* there's those mystery tracks. Then sure, everything is going swimmingly."

Ysabeau levelled a look at him that would have skinned lesser folk. "It could be worse."

Kieran shrugged.

Elias clapped his nephew on the shoulder. "Find the source of those tracks and find the killer. Did you learn any more about the girl's death?"

Me? My death?

"She was murdered, but I already knew that," Kieran replied.

"And how did you get that confirmed?" Ysabeau demanded.

He smiled then, smugly. It made her whole body yearn for him. Fuck he was hot. "A little birdy told me."

Yeah, they're definitely talking about me.

How many other murdered girls were hanging around the castle?

A lot.

Well, technically that was correct, but it also wasn't.

"Well, keep me updated if you find out anything more. When the human doctor arrives here later today, I want you to help them in any way you can. Got it?" Elias's voice was clipped and sure.

"Of course." Ysabeau nodded.

The king strode out of the former broom closet and almost straight into a sneering Colin.

"Have a good chat?" her cousin asked.

The Master vampire gave him a narrow stare. "It was enlightening."

Colin crossed his arms over his chest.

Sabrina rolled her eyes. He was trying to have a pissing contest with the *king* of the Blood and Beryl House?

The man was going to lose, if not his life, then a limb or three.

"Colin!" Grandpa Angus' shout echoed across the hall.

Her cousin stepped to the side and then stomped over to their grandfather, who clipped him over the back of the head. "Get yer ass in here." They then disappeared into the meeting room.

A bronze-skinned witch—the one who had arrived with Elias—turned and came over to them. She'd been huddled in conversation with Tamsin, it seemed.

Great, witches colluding. It couldn't be a good sign.

But it is good to see people from the other Houses do get along together.

"Ready to go?" the newcomer witch asked.

The king nodded. He stared at Kieran, as if he could see into the other man's heart. "Be careful."

Then they were striding down the hall and were gone.

Sabrina was left with no answers, only more questions.

Like that's something new.

CHAPTER 31

KIERAN

K ieran should have told Elias the truth, he thought, as he watched his uncle disappear down the hallway, Seraphina at his side.

He should have told his king about Sabrina. About the fact that they had Douglas' daughter right *there*. He should've told him her blood was the most addictive thing that he'd ever tasted. And he definitely should have said something about how he thought her blood had given him a new ability: telepathy.

There were a lot of things he should have told him.

Not just because Elias was his king, but because he was his uncle. He was family.

It was funny how he'd never really truly accepted that connection until now.

But the claps on the shoulder, the way that Elias spoke to him—in this foreign environment it made it very clear he treated him differently to how he treated outsiders, and even his own. Elias acted differently toward him than he did Ysabeau, and she was probably his most trusted friend, aside from Danni.

In fact, Elias had never really seemed to care about the step-title part of being an uncle, or the fact that Kieran was not blood-related to him. He'd been a stern but fair taskmaster growing up, taking more of an interest in him than Kieran's own stepfather had. Mostly because Kieran's stepfather couldn't see past the blind rage his existence triggered.

So, he owed his king and uncle a lot, more than he could probably ever repay.

But he still hadn't admitted the several new truths causing a burning pit of acid to form in his stomach.

Guilt sucked.

He wasn't used to it.

All because of Sabrina.

She makes me crazy.

And not in a bad way. She didn't make him want to pack his bag and clear town, or need to have some precious alone time to get away from her. Which was how he'd historically felt when beginning a relationship with someone. It's part of why he'd boycotted the whole emotional entanglement thing. He just didn't have it in him.

Oh, Kieran was self-aware enough to realize he was probably a sociopath, but he'd been okay with that. Hell, he *still* was okay with it.

But Sabrina made him *feel.*

He wanted to get closer to her, wanted to feel silken skin under his fingertips. He *needed* to taste her mouth, and he absolutely had to experience her blood again. But it wasn't just that. She was loyal. Sneaky. Clever. He loved the sound of her laugh, and the way she said the most random shit that confused the hell out of him.

The ghost wasn't predictable, and that was fan-fuck-ing-tastic as far as he was concerned.

You're falling in love.

Yeah, he probably was.

And it's not something he was going to shy away from, either. Oh, he knew it wasn't a good thing, falling in love with a dead person. It wasn't like they had a future. Or even a present. Unless they got her body back.

But apparently that was on the cards.

Except he was only here for the duration of the meet and greet. Once it was over and the phantoms picked a House—or Houses—then Kieran would be done. Fin-ished.

He'd have to go.

And Sabrina was tied to the castle and its grounds.

If he left, it wasn't even like they could do the long-dis-tance thing, not unless his telepathy could span a conti-nent or two. And what did she even want? She didn't have her body and he had no idea how she even felt about any of it.

Sure, she had been totally into him jerking off in the shower to the taste of her blood. But how long before that got boring?

A love affair with a ghost was doomed for disappoint-ment.

So…he'd made a plan. It was a bit sketchy, but weren't they the best kind of plans?

First: they would get her body back. Do whatever it was Tamsin needed, then Sabrina would be resurrected whole. Second: they'd do whatever it was the phantoms did to become immortal. He knew it had to be some kind of ritual or rite, because they didn't seem to just turn into the living undead. Too bad Douglas *and* Sabrina had been a little reticent to share the details on how the transformation happened exactly. But he'd work it out. Or she'd know and just do it, and all would work out well in the end.

Third…well, he hadn't gotten past step number two.

There was a fair bit of hand-waving involved in the plan, but he had to be flexible, since no one was willing to tell him anything.

She hasn't told you the truth about phantoms. She hasn't even told you who murdered her. Are you sure this is a good idea? What if she doesn't care about you like you do her?

Well, that was an unsettling thought.

You're literally the only person she can talk to. She's lonely. You're the only one who can see her.

Which was mostly true, although Tamsin could tell when the ghost was around. And Councilor Hekate had reacted to Sabrina's comment back in the meeting room. Could her interest simply be lack of options? Maybe, but he didn't think that was it. And if it was…well, he'd deal with it later.

First though, they had to get her body back. Once they did that, he'd come clean to Elias and tell him everything. Because asking for forgiveness was easier than asking for permission.

Tomorrow was the new moon.

"The doctor's here!" Sabrina shouted, right next to his ear. He tried not to flinch at the sound, since they were still in the hall. "And he brought helpers."

"How do you know?" he asked.

She was almost bouncing in excitement. "While you were standing there daydreaming, I did some eavesdropping."

"I do not daydream."

"Woolgathering, then."

He blinked. *"I wasn't anywhere near a sheep."*

Sabrina laughed, and the sound warmed the cold and shadowy corners within his soul. "You're hilarious."

She reached out, as if to grab his arm, so she could drag him wherever she wanted him to go. Instead, her hand passed through him, leaving a tingling sensation. Stronger than before the Shower Incident, but still not enough for actual touch.

"Now, come on!" Her amusement faded, replaced by an urgency he didn't share. "We need to get to Sammy's room."

Right.

They had a killer to find.

CHAPTER 32

SABRINA

The doctor had arrived in the foyer with two other men, one of whom didn't appear to be human. The third—it was questionable, their humanity; they had dark skin and dark brown eyes, and a face almost too handsome to belong to a non-supernatural. The pointed ears on the second tall, lean man kind of gave away that there was another fae in their midst.

Each wore a calm demeanor, like they encountered sirens, witches and vampires every day.

Maybe they did.

"I thought you asked for a human doctor?" Oleander snapped, crossing her arms as she took in the trio. She wore a flowing white dress that spoke of sunny fields and picnics, rather than castles and murder. It highlighted the green tinge of her skin, and the fine sheen of scales that appeared and disappeared, depending on tricks of the light. "Isn't that why we've all been waiting?"

Grandpa Angus glowered at the three men from the foot of the massive staircase. "So did I." He directed his stare toward Granny. She was holding an empty plate, and, when Sabrina glanced at her sexy fae, he was wiping a crumb from the corner of his delectable lips.

It meant Granny Kim liked him, even though he was an outsider.

That will make things easier when I get my body back and we announce our relationship to everyone.

Whoa.

She hadn't just jumped the gun, she'd crossed the metaphorical finish line, too.

You need to take several steps back.

Granny glared right back. "I did ask for a *human doctor.* The others aren't doctors."

Well, damn.

The medical professional—at least, the one Sabrina assumed was the doctor, mostly because he had a stethoscope looped around his neck—was tall, with graying hair and bright blue eyes. He cleared his throat, a little uncomfortable at all the attention. The others didn't so much as flinch at it. They had the hard look of law enforcement.

They have seen some shit, Sabrina thought. Murders, abuse, beatings, the Great Sacrifice… She'd put money on it.

"I am a coroner," the human said, his voice rich with the accent she associated with Edinburgh. Scottish, but different. "A doctor, nothing more. I'm not qualified to tell you who killed someone, just how they died. That's where these two men come in." He waved an arm at his companions. "This is Enforcer Reed, and Enforcer Jones. They have more experience in their pinky fingers than I do, when it comes to hunting…things."

Grandpa Angus puffed his chest out. "I said I wanted humans to deal with this."

"You'll be hard pressed to find pure humans to help you." The fae enforcer crossed his arms, mimicking the siren's body language. He was in plainclothes, but had that kind of pressed and clean look to him that screamed military.

The other one—the one who might, but also might not be, human—added, "I'm here to find out who killed that kid."

Yeah, that's what they all wanted to do.

"Which House do you belong to?" Sky asked, interrupting the interrogation. The Spirit and Sapphire ambassador tended not to draw attention to herself, but everyone was looking at her now. She responded to the looks by flicking her dark pink braid over her shoulder.

The fae enforcer shrugged. "I'm Portal Watch, represented by House of Fire and Fluorite."

"Gold and Garnet." The other enforcer said, tilting his head. So, he *wasn't* human.

Only the doctor was.

In confirmation, the coroner spoke, "And I have no House affiliation. I'm neutrally protected by the Houses for my services."

"Great," Kieran muttered into her mind. *"House of Fire and Fluorite are a bunch of loose cannons."*

"Isn't Blood and Beryl at war with Fluorite?" She used to read the news over Colin's shoulder. There'd been a recent kerfuffle that involved the king and his new queen.

"Eh, not so much. They're just not well-governed at the moment."

Another evasion, but she wasn't going to debate it with him. He could keep his uncle's secrets.

She only wanted to know Kieran's.

"Well?" the doctor demanded in the sudden silence.

"'Well', what?" Grandpa replied.

"Are you going to show me the body?" Impatience laced the man's words.

The clan chief nodded and spun on his heel, marching up the stairs. "This way."

They all looked at each other—even Granny—for a moment, before nodding almost as one and falling in line, like they were in a military precession. Or a funeral march.

It was a grim afternoon.

Tamsin removed the ward surrounding the room, one even Sabrina hadn't tried to breach—it had been too upsetting, seeing Sammy like that—and the doctor and Portal Watchmen peered inside.

The fae male disappeared down the hall as soon as the ward was dropped, only to return shortly after with a large case. He must have left it down in the foyer when they arrived. He opened it, and the trio donned disposable gowns, shoes, masks, gloves, caps and glasses. They weren't messing around.

But it was good to see they were treating the room as if it was an actual crime scene.

She wanted to spy on the medical and crime scene investigation process so bad, but she had things to arrange.

Tomorrow was the new moon.

She wasn't exactly sure what was going to happen: would she become a phantom, or would she return to her human body, the one that had been riddled with cancer?

The unknowns were painful.

But anything was better than being stuck in this half-life. She'd even take being dead-dead over being a ghost, although she *really* wanted to avoid that scenario.

There were a couple of things she needed first, though.

She ran over the list Tamsin had given her: her blood? Check. Kieran? Check. The witch? Check.

But she needed her bones, and her amulet.

Unlike with regular phantoms, her amulet was a simulacrum—when her relatives changed forms, their amulets changed with them. It was the only thing that did. Their clothes simply dropped to the floor, and they appeared in the outfit they'd worn when they'd died.

How did Tamsin know they existed?

It had better be super necessary, Sabrina thought, watching the Portal Watchmen and Tamsin move through Sammy's room. Grandpa Angus loomed in the doorway.

Finding her amulet was going to involve a lot of effort. It wasn't like she could just go and grab it herself. But she had to trust the witch—or, "trust the process" as Tamsin had said.

The thing was, when a pre-phantom died prematurely, the amulet went back to Grandpa Angus, to be handed on to somebody else. At least, that's what had happened the two times somebody had died since she'd been a ghost.

And Sammy, well, they hadn't touched his yet.

She knew where Grandpa Angus stored them—she had spied on him when he'd taken them from her cousin Peter and Bonnie's bodies. But...she wasn't entirely sure that hers was in that pile, or that it hadn't already been handed on to one of the smaller kids when they came of age. Which happened *all the damned time.* When your family was as big as an entire town, there were a lot of children.

But...there was also something she could check first, before she tried to raid Grandpa Angus' collection.

In true serial-killer style, Colin collected keepsakes from his victims. Yep, he was that kind of guy: fucked up. She'd only seen the inside of the safe a handful of times—he'd been too busy hatching his evil plan to pore over his gruesome collection, and it was warded, somehow even against ghosts—but she hadn't noticed her amulet in the little sick shrine he'd built.

That didn't mean it wasn't there.

She'd been too disgusted and horrified by seeing locks of her dead cousins' hair, and a preserved hand from the cousin who had died in a car crash.

So gross.

I should check his room first.

She looked at Kieran, and it was almost painful, he was so gorgeous. Especially now she'd seen the look on his face when he came undone in front of her. She wanted to see it again, and again. From every angle she could.

He was leaning a shoulder against the wall, arms crossed over his chest. His biceps bulged from the position, and it made him even more irresistible, if that was possible. She wanted to lick her way up his throat, while she stroked her hand over those glorious muscles. And she wanted to flick her tongue over the tips of his pointed ears, which were so incredibly sexy.

His eyes flickered to her.

"I can feel you undressing me with your eyes," he said into her mind.

"More like eating you up." She floated closer to him. "And while I could do that all day, I've got to go look for my amulet."

"Amulet?" He straightened a little.

Right. She hadn't told him about that.

"I'll explain later."

"Explain while we walk. I'm coming."

She snorted, then her eyes dropped to his groin. "I wish."

"Hey, my eyes are up here." He wasn't smiling, but a wicked gleam had entered his gaze, and she swore she could *hear* him laughing in his mind.

"Asshole. Fine. Let's go."

CHAPTER 33

KIERAN

Kieran made a noncommittal comment to Ysabeau about having to go check on something in his room, before leaving the hallway. He could feel the others' stares follow him but acted like he could not have cared less.

Which, to be honest, was the truth.

Sure, he wanted to know what the doctors and the two Portal Watchmen found, but he could always find out the details from Ysabeau later. Following Sabrina was more important right now.

Yeah, have fun explaining that to Elias once all this blows over.

If—and that was a big 'if'—they could get Sabrina's body back, he would throw himself on his king's mercy in a heartbeat. But right now…well, he wasn't doing any harm, and it wasn't like he was doing much good standing around in a hallway, either.

"So, what's the deal with this amulet?" he asked.

"It's not something we talk about, because of the blood oath," Sabrina replied. She looked nervous, her eyes darting from side to side, as if somebody was going to over-hear them.

But Tamsin wasn't around, and according to Sabrina, the witch couldn't hear her talk anyway. From what Kieran had gathered, Tamsin did all the talking when the two of them were together.

Councilor Hekate seemed to have *seen* the ghost, mean-while, but she hadn't acknowledged her in any other way. Plus, the Earth and Emerald leader had long departed.

Sabrina needed *her* amulet, which meant she had owned it before she died. *"Were you wearing it when you were murdered?"*

She nodded.

He'd seen chains and strings of leather around most of the phantoms' necks. The ends of the necklaces were never on display, hidden under clothing, but he'd never thought that was significant.

Now it seemed the amulets were more important than that. Intentionally kept under cover, perhaps.

And Sabrina, well, she had a silver necklace around her neck—with the end of it hidden under her bloody sweater.

So, she wore it before she died. And she wasn't a phantom…

So why hadn't she made the transition? Why was she a ghost when everyone else around them was either human or phantom?

"I'm guessing this amulet is tied to you becoming a phantom, then. You know, if it's secret."

She bit her lip as she glided down the hallways. "Sort of."

"That is not an answer."

"It is the best one I am going to give you."

No further explanation, not that he was entitled to one. But, considering he was sneaking through the castle with her—well, not exactly sneaking right this minute, more wandering down the hallways, alone by all appearances. But definitely on his way to do some sneaking—he thought he should be allowed to learn a bit more about what exactly they were doing.

He turned left at the end of the corridor.

She paused, frowning at him. "Why are you going that way?"

"I have to get some things from my room, or did you want your family to see me snooping around?"

She gave him a half-smile, and it went straight to his groin. Fuck. How did she manage to do that? One small glimpse of abashed chagrin, and he was ready to fuck her against a wall.

To be fair, if she had a body, you would be fucking her all over the castle if possible.

And wasn't that a strange thought for him to have—Mr. I-hate-to-be-touched. His sexual liaisons had been brief and infrequent over the years. It came from his trauma, when his father had kidnapped Kieran after he'd hit puberty in the hope he could study him, and potentially make more fae-vampire hybrids. It had broken Kieran's trust of people, to the point where he hated almost everyone equally. It's why he had no problem with torture. Everyone—aside from Elias, Danni, Adora by proxy, his mother, and Ysabeau—were potential enemies.

Sabrina was also on his list of exceptions. Always had been.

But then it was hard for a ghost with limited telekinesis—but unlimited sex appeal—to hurt him. Beyond blue balls, anyway.

They walked in silence until they arrived at his rooms, passing a few phantoms both in their physical and incorporeal forms. He headed inside, Sabrina misting through the door seconds later. He grabbed a few things as she watched, her attention sending tingles along the base of the spine.

For a ghost, she sure packed a sensual punch.

"Are you gonna tell me what those powders and baggies do?" Sabrina asked.

He smirked. "No. You can just see them in action."

"Now that's not fair."

"Want to tell me what the amulet does?"

She crossed her arms over her chest, looking annoyed. It was kind of hot. "I have a blood oath. What's your reason?"

"I'm an asshole."

She chuckled, the sound almost lighting up the room with joy.

It made his heart do a funny little kick.

"Well, I guess I can put honesty into the 'pro' column."

"There's a column? What are the other 'pros'?" He grabbed an amber necklace and slid it over his head. This particular piece of jewelry cost an absolute fortune, and was almost impossible to come by through legitimate means. But it wasn't something Elias had given him to undertake this mission; no, it was something Kieran had stolen from his biological father a long time ago. He had no idea where his sperm donor had acquired it; for all he knew, it came from the other side of a portal.

It was magic, possibly akin to something the phantoms had, except this made him invisible. Completely.

He wore it only in certain risky situations, and it was a prize he had kept secret even from Elias and his mother, as it was the one thing he owned that would allow him to potentially escape any situation.

"So, what's the necklace do?" Sabrina asked.

He looked at her. She looked at him. "It makes me invisible?"

That wasn't meant to be a question.

"Right. Well, I don't know if the person sold it to you was being completely honest, because I still see you."

Well, wasn't that interesting. So, Kieran could see Sabrina when nobody else could. Even people who might be able to normally see ghosts, such as other phantoms, couldn't detect her. And now she could see him when he was meant to be invisible to everybody else, too.

Either both of them had magic that allowed them to detect the invisible innately—which he seriously doubted, since he'd never heard of such a thing before—or they were destined to see each other no matter what.

Something to think about later.

"Are you sure it works?" Sabrina asked as he headed for the door.

Kieran slipped through the doorway, too fast for the eye to follow. Well, too fast for the human eye to follow. If Clint or Ysabeau had been standing there, they probably would have noticed.

He paused in the hallway, near a shiny suit of armor, while one of the phantoms walked by, barely a minute later. The female phantom's gaze scanned the hall, as if doing a survey for the stealthy inhabitants of the area…then she walked straight by him, as if he wasn't there.

"I guess it works then," Sabrina said.

"You sound convinced."

"You're hot. Lila is bi. If she'd seen you, she would have reacted."

Kieran choked a little, and was glad Lila seemed to be out of earshot when he did. The charm didn't make him soundless. That was where his skill came in.

"So where are we going?" he asked.

"To the family wing."

They set off, Kieran careful to keep to the edges of the halls. He didn't want to accidentally bump into one of the residents. Or worse, one of the other ambassadors.

"Would that be to your grandfather's rooms, or somewhere else?" Kieran asked. He wasn't sure where they would keep these phantom amulets, but he assumed it would be somewhere well-guarded and private.

Maybe there was a secret room.

Most castles had secret rooms, right?

"We're going to my cousin Colin's room, first."

That wasn't the answer he was expecting.

She held up a finger. "We can talk about it later."

Far too many staircases later, they came to a stop outside a door, much the same as all the others they'd passed, but Sabrina let out a sigh that said this was the place.

There was something weary in the sound.

He didn't like it.

She misted through the door, and he waited where he was, assuming she was doing some recon to make sure that Colin wasn't in the room. She came back through the door moments later. "Are you coming or not?"

"I was waiting to see if the coast was clear."

"Right, but you're supposedly invisible."

The sass.

He liked it.

"Is the room warded?"

"No, the room isn't," Sabrina said. "Our family is meant to be without secrets. An open book. We allow everyone into our lives."

"Right."

She snorted. "It's only because wards supposedly can't keep phantoms out. At least, not until Tamsin arrived. Now the others know they can."

"Supposedly?"

He opened the door and slipped inside.

It was neat.

Almost too neat.

"Colin managed to find a ward that worked on spirit forms."

The room was arranged with military precision, without a speck of dust to be seen. Sabrina glided straight toward the end of the room, to the bookcase in the far corner. He was going to roll his eyes if the bookcase happened to be a secret doorway. It would be way too cliched.

But she didn't stop there; instead, she took three steps to the left, and pointed to a seemingly random stone in the wall. "Can you press that?"

"Is there magic on it?"

She frowned. "Possibly. Wait." She went to Colin's wardrobe. "There's a glove. He wears this when he opens the safe."

How long had Sabrina been spying on her cousin?

He found the glove and put it on, feeling the slight tingle of magic as he did so. Her eyes widened slightly. "Did you see that?"

"See what?"

"The magic?"

"No. But I felt it."

So, she could see magic. Maybe that explained why he was visible to her, but not to anyone else.

He went back to the wall and pressed the stone she had indicated earlier. He half-expected the bookcase to swing away, but a moment later, on the other side of the room, part of the wall opened, revealing a safe. The electronics were well hidden.

"I thought you said there were no secrets?"

"Mmm. Do you want to know the code?"

He strode over to the safe, noting the digital dial pad. He decided to leave the glove on. *"You've been watching him for a while to be able to work this out."*

"Let's just say I had a personal interest in doing so."

"Care to share the reason?" He had a sneaking suspicion as to why she might have focused on this relative in particular, but he knew she wouldn't confirm it if he'd asked.

Then again, maybe she stalked all of her family and knew all of their dark secrets.

It was all ammunition she could use later.

"Open the safe."

CHAPTER 34

SABRINA

Sabrina had never had the chance to *really* look inside Colin's safe, beyond glancing over his shoulder. He was always furtive, and quick, when opening and closing the safe. He would occasionally bring out items from it to study, but only in the deep of night, and usually for short periods of time.

Seeing the contents laid bare now, it was confronting. A chipped molar tooth here, a lock of coppery hair there, a metal brooch, a serpentine ring, and a whole host of other personal keepsakes he collected, serial-killer style, from his victims. She shouldn't be surprised; he *was* a sociopath. And, well, she had once thought—a long time ago now—that he would have been smart enough to not have keepsakes.

It was stupid to keep clear evidence like this.

But there it was.

Right in front of her.

Proof of her cousins' deaths, and her own.

Her amulet was right near the front.

She didn't know if Colin had taken the amulet from her body before he'd hauled her back to Braemar Castle, or if he'd stolen it from Grandpa Angus after. The exact timeline after her death was a bit fuzzy—mostly because she'd been so surprised and angry at her new undead status.

Kieran frowned. He reached out and pointed at her silvery necklace. *"I'm guessing this is yours?"*

Sabrina nodded, finding it surprisingly hard to speak.

I guess I'm still not over this.

And she doubted she ever would be, truth be told.

"Magic amulet, hey?" He didn't pick it up. Almost like he was waiting for something.

She had no idea what.

"Something like that."

"He has a rather diverse…collection, here. Reminds me a bit of my sperm donor, to be honest."

Sabrina's eyebrows rose. She wasn't sure which part she wanted to ask about first. "Your sperm donor?"

There. Apparently, that was the thing her brain found the most interesting.

Kieran's jaw tightened, and it made her want to touch him, to offer comfort. *"My biological father was disgusting. He had a thing for women; he liked to take them, kill them, fuck them, not exactly in any particular order. He also kept mementos of his 'love affairs' as he called it."*

"That sounds rather…disturbing." If she had skin, it would be crawling.

"He was disgusting, as I said. But he's also dead, so I guess that counts for something." His expression was dark, menacing.

And fuck, he was sexy.

She loved it when he looked like he wanted to rip someone apart with his bare hands.

There is something wrong with you.

She wasn't even going to try and deny it.

They were silent for a moment, as he studied the contents of the safe.

"So, Colin murdered you, huh?" Kieran turned to look at her, speaking aloud. His gray gaze was molten with rage. He was trying to mask the expression, but she could feel his anger burning through their telepathic bond: rage on her behalf, at her life cut short.

It stunned her, the intensity of his emotions.

She'd thought she was the one most affected by...whatever it was between them. But no. He clearly cared about her. For her.

Shit.

She was in way over her head.

"I can count at least another ten objects here. And one of these is a ring with the House emblem of Sea and Serpentine on it. Doesn't he realize these kinds of things can be tracked, with the right spells?"

That ring would belong to the witch whose death had started it all. At least, she assumed that was the case, because how else would the Houses have learned of the phantoms, if they hadn't studied her father?

Wow, that is convoluted.

But it was the only way it could have happened—that she knew of. Unless someone in the family had sold them out, which their blood oath would have prevented from occurring.

"It's why he keeps it in the safe."

At least, that is what she had assumed.

"I thought phantoms were immortal—after a certain age or magical rite, or something." It wasn't a question, but it wasn't quite a statement, either.

She narrowed her eyes. "Who said—"

"Sammy died. That means some of you die before you become immortal."

He was clever, she liked it.

"I only see one House emblem. Were these all phantoms? Or pre-phantoms?"

"They're mostly clan members, ones who died before they made the transition to immortality. I was one of them." Her hand hovered over her amulet—something she had worn ever since she'd turned ten years old, and Grandpa Angus had sensed she had the potential to become a phantom. She didn't know *how* he'd sensed it, just that he had.

"I was about to come home," she continued. "I'd just finished packing my bag when he knocked on my apartment door. I was surprised he'd managed to track me down—I had thought that I'd been successfully living under the radar, so to speak."

Kieran snorted. *"You had been."*

She shot him a look.

"I stalked you for a bit, remember?"

That actually made her chuckle. How did he manage to do that, even when she was reliving the worst time of her life?

"I thought he was there to bring me home," she said. "I guess he did do that, but not in the way that I anticipated."

"Why didn't you tell me it was him? I could've handled him for you." Kieran's voice held undertones of violent, violent things.

"Handled him?" Sabrina asked. "Colin is immortal. There is no known way to kill him. You could beat the crap out of him; you could stab him a dozen times, but he would come back. Phantoms just turn incorporeal when they die, and then re-form whole again. Even decapitation doesn't work—we're the only race on the planet where it doesn't."

"True immortals," he said. *"We suspected as such."*

"I figured it was why your leaders decided to negotiate, rather than just wipe us from existence. Because you can't."

He rubbed his chin with his ungloved hand. *"It really does make your race rather dangerous now, doesn't it?"*

"The best spies and assassins you could look for. Luckily for us, we have been brought up insular and afraid of discovery."

"You escaped."

She rubbed a hand over her belly. "And look where that got me."

"Not for much longer."

Kieran withdrew a little bag of powder from his pocket, flicking a pinch of it into the safe. It glowed bright blue for a second, before returning to normal. He removed the amulet and set a small quartz rock in its place. It gleamed, before morphing into a copy of her necklace.

"What the—?"

"This way he won't know it's gone. At least, not unless he tries to pick it up. Does he handle these much?"

"Every now and then."

"Good."

He closed the safe with the gloved hand and pocketed her amulet. Then he straightened the room, so it didn't look like anyone had been in there. He returned the glove to exactly where he'd found it.

They were just about to leave when the door opened. Kieran froze in place, and Sabrina held her breath, for no apparent reason.

Colin stood in the doorway, framed by the light outside, his face cast in shadow. "I cannae fucking believe it," her cousin muttered.

"Believe it. It wasnae the ambassadors—it was something else." That was Grandpa Angus' voice.

"Something else?" she asked Kieran. He shrugged, the movement quiet.

"But who could it be? Why kill Sammy? He was of no use."

Trust Colin to view people like that.

Peering over the asshole's shoulder, she took in Grandpa Angus' expression: pissed. It seemed to be his permanent mood at the moment.

"I want you to go with Charlotte on the scouting missions. If there is some 'monster' on our land, I want to know about it. Yesterday."

Colin nodded. "Of course, Grandpa."

Suck up.

Colin stepped into the room, but before he shut the door, Kieran moved past him, so fast Sabrina couldn't track him. As the door closed, she saw him on the other side.

Colin frowned and rubbed the back of his forearms.

She walked through the door and watched as Grandpa Angus strode down the hallway, tension in every line of his body.

A monster?

What the hell had they missed?

CHAPTER 35

SABRINA

I t was the new moon.

Sabrina wasn't sure how she felt: nervous, excited, fearful, anxious…desperate. So many emotions all wrapped up into one shivery package. She didn't know how her incorporeal form contained them all. But it did.

Miracles never cease to amaze me.

And tonight, she really needed a miracle.

She'd pray to the gods, but they were capricious at best. She needed all the luck she could get, and then some.

Tonight, I live.

They had everything she needed, well, except for one thing.

"So, we have to go dig up your grave?" Kieran asked. He stood near the door in his room, the black T-shirt he wore under a leather jacket stretched to within an inch of its life as it tried to cover his physique.

She could not wait to graze her fingers over every inch of that torso.

Could. Not. Wait.

"That's what Tamsin said." Her reply was a little late, delayed by her daydreaming about her tongue and his abs. He didn't seem to mind, although he did raise both eyebrows, before biting his bottom lip. Man, Sabrina wished she was his bottom lip.

I hope I didn't think any of that too loud.
It would be embarrassing if he knew how much she wanted him.

"I've never dug *up* a body before," he said. She wondered on the emphasis of 'up'. "Which, considering I'm a death fae, is probably an odd thing to admit."

"Death fae go around digging up corpses a lot?"

"Just my father, to my knowledge."

I shouldn't have asked. "He sounds like a real peach."

"A rotten dead peach, sure."

"Family—if only you could pick them." She gave him a lopsided smile, and something in his expression softened, just slightly.

"Yeah, you didn't win on that front either, did you?"

When it came to her father, she had. And her grandparents and aunts and uncles. But Colin...well, the bastard kind of negated a lot of the good that she'd thought she had.

She realized he was waiting for a reply. "In some ways yes, in others, no."

"I can sympathize with that. You ready?" He shoved away from the wall and pulled the invisibility necklace from the pocket of his jacket. His fingers played with the smooth gemstone as the gold chain slipped through his hands.

A niggling sensation in the back of her mind said Kieran wasn't as blasé as he might sound. After all, this was D-Day. Or Un-death-day, as she liked to think of it.

Tonight, she was going to get her body back, or die trying.

Tamsin had made it clear if it didn't work, if something went wrong...the only thing she had left to lose was her soul. Considering she was a ghost, well, her soul was *literally* the only thing she had left.

She would cease to exist.

But she couldn't keep going like this; centuries upon centuries of being invisible loomed ahead of her. She didn't want to be ignored, tied to a castle she could never leave, forever bound to a family who couldn't care less about her now she was gone. That wasn't being fair to her family, to be sure. But it wasn't as if they missed her like a wound that wouldn't heal: her name barely came up in conversation. They'd moved on, even if she hadn't.

So yeah, she was willing to forego a possible existence of forever, for a chance to be a whole person again. And she had a feeling that was a fair deal.

More than fair.

She just had to hope the cancer that had been ravaging her system would disappear when she woke up. And if not...hopefully when she got her body back, she would have made the transition to phantom. Then the cancer wouldn't matter.

"It would be really good if I could actually talk to Tamsin about this," Kieran said. "Secondhand information can be hard to interpret."

"The information is coming from me. And it's my body, and my ghosthood. Do you think I'd fuck it up?" She was sorely tempted to stomp her foot, but she refrained. Barely.

"I'm not saying you're fucking it up, but witches are tricky. They tell you one thing—but not *all* of the thing. It would be good to hear her word for word and get a feel of what she isn't saying, as much as what she *is*."

Sabrina rubbed her forehead.

She *thought* she understood what he meant. And yeah, she knew that Tamsin was leaving out a bunch of relevant information, but she didn't know what it could be or *why*. In fact, Sabrina didn't even know why Tamsin was willing to help her in the first place, but she wasn't going to look a gift horse in the mouth.

Sure, that could very well end in her downfall, but she doubted Tamsin would've gone to such effort to get rid of one pesky little ghost. She could have just ignored Sabrina's existence and left her to mope around the castle.

There was no need to promise her the world.

"Let's go." Kieran shrugged on a backpack, before slipping the necklace over his head. He then snuck out the door and made his way to the foyer of the castle.

Clint stood near the double doors, sniffing the air. The shifter frowned, but didn't say anything.

"He smells me." Kieran's thoughts pierced her mind, as she spotted Sky coming down the staircase to join Clint.

"We going hunting?" the pink-haired woman asked her fellow Spirit and Sapphire ambassador.

The shifter nodded. "Water monsters, is what the Portal Watch said. They should know."

That's what the current leading theory was. Sabrina had no idea how they'd come to that conclusion—she'd been too busy raiding Colin's safe, and hadn't had time to snoop for all the details. But she would.

"You think Sea and Serpentine are behind this?" Sky asked quietly, as a phantom passed through the foyer on their way through to another part of the house. Her voice was so soft, Sabrina was sure her relative wouldn't have heard the question.

"Empress Asbesta doesn't get involved in the petty affairs of mortals," Clint replied. Then his gaze zeroed in on Kieran's position. He didn't say anything to Sky, however. Instead, he opened the front door, and waited, as if for Kieran to pass by, which he did.

Sabrina followed.

Sky walked through next, unaware of Kieran's and Sabrina's presence.

Kieran's steps were silent on the gravel.

I need to learn how to do that.

"Shall we run?" Sky asked.

"Yes."

The shifter started jogging, but Sabrina could almost feel his stare as he glanced back at Kieran, who was halfway to a storage shed. He was going to grab a shovel and meet her at her gravestone. Sky looked back too, a thoughtful frown on her face, but Clint increased his speed, and the human-seeming woman turned back to focus on their hunt.

I hope you find whoever hurt Sammy.

Because if they didn't, she would.

And she would demand retribution.

But first, first she had to go watch her corpse get dug up. And then, then she'd see what the fates had in store for her.

CHAPTER 36

KIERAN

S abrina's grave was as nondescript as he remembered it.

Small headstone on an otherwise unmarked plot, no flowers.

The gravity-defying fog was floating through the graveyard again, moving in random patterns, as if guided by an inconsistent ethereal hand. The lack of moonlight shrouded everything in darkness, giving the cemetery a slightly menacing feel, like a zombie was about to spring from the earth and demand brains for their effort.

It was way creepier at night than during the day.

The new moon made everything extra unsettling, and, well, death and gloom were kind of meant to be his thing. It wasn't like he hadn't been in a graveyard before—hell, he'd been in *this* cemetery not long ago—or dealt with a dead body. He'd done both quite a fair bit. But this was next level.

Normally, however, he was the one digging the grave, or creating the body to go *in* said grave.

He'd never bothered to dig the body back up afterwards.

That was just gross.

He might be a death fae, but his magic lay in blood and reanimating it, not corpses.

Sabrina had been in her grave for over a year now. He assumed her remains were nothing more than bones, but he couldn't be certain. The type of coffin and soil type had a huge impact on preservation. What if she was partially decayed? How was he meant to move that?

He really hadn't thought this through.

At least I packed a garbage bag, just in case.

"Do you know why we had to do this on the new moon?" Kieran asked. He dropped his backpack on the ground, alongside the machete he'd stolen from the storage shed. He kept hold of the shovel.

"She didn't tell me, just that it had to be. It's not like our conversations involved me asking questions and her answering. It was more Tamsin talked at me, and then I relayed the information to you." Sabrina's mouth quirked a little on the side, like she was sort of amused by it all.

At least someone is.

Kieran wasn't one for second thoughts, but he was beginning to have them.

What if this didn't work?

What was the worst that could happen?

The ghost had been a bit cagey about that, and he had a feeling the answer was something he wasn't going to like. But it was her choice. And if he had to carry half-decayed disgusting remains around, he would.

Sabrina hovered next to the headstone, and it was a statement, even if an unintentional one. Ghost next to grave.

And that sad little epitaph that her family had given her...

He was glad he would get to see her reaction when she was reunited with her 'loving' relatives.

They fucking harbor the man who killed her.
Yeah, he had an issue with it.

Too bad he couldn't rip Colin's face off and make sure he was dead-dead.

I still might rip his face off. Just to try it.
It would certainly make him feel better.

"Do you feel disappointed by your gravestone?"

No, he hadn't really asked that out loud. Or even telepathically.

He hadn't—

"A little. It was a bit of lame effort, wasn't it?"

Then her answer registered. Yeah, he had asked that question out loud.

Great.

You are smooth with a capital SMOO.

"Are you ready to see what's inside?" he asked.

He wasn't sure he was ready, but that didn't really matter. It wasn't his body in the ground.

"I mean, they're just bones, right?" Sabrina leaned forward slightly.

Man, he couldn't wait to see what she looked like out of that depressing cream sweater.

Kieran ran a hand over his hair. "I'm not one hundred percent sure what we're going to find when I open the coffin. It might be bones, or worse." He wasn't sure how graphic he should be. He really should've brought a proper body bag, not just a thin plastic trash liner.

"What do you mean, 'or worse'?"

"Let's just hope it's bones." He tried to give her a reassuring smile.

"I'm not liking your tone."

"Uh, my falsely cheerful tone?"

"That's the one. I much prefer your snide and snarky tone. That's normal. This cheerfulness is slightly scary."

He shrugged. Most people appreciated it when he tried to be kind, or at least polite. He'd even been given a list on how to behave before, so this was his own attempt at being gentle without being prompted. And he'd failed.

But…he wanted to be nice to Sabrina. He didn't want to hurt her feelings; in fact, he didn't want to hurt a single ghostly hair on her head.

Kieran tightened his grip on the shovel, which thankfully, was invisible as long as he was holding it, courtesy of his necklace. But he wasn't going to be able to hide the mound of soil that was going to build up next to the grave as he dug it, or his lonesome backpack and the nearby stolen machete. Hopefully none of the phantoms decided to have a midnight wander through the cemetery.

Time to get digging.

He moved the tip of the shovel so it was over the center of the grave and pressed his foot down. It sunk into the soil about three inches. This was going to take a while.

Sabrina stayed next to the headstone, watching as he excavated shovelful after shovelful of soil. It was a good thing he wasn't human, because digging this grave out on his own would be exhausting. And he had plans if she got her body back.

No, *when* she got her body back.

Thanks to his fae speed and vampire strength, he was able to move the dirt quickly; barely an hour later the shovel thunked on the top of a wooden coffin. He scraped the soil away and frowned at the bare pine box. They hadn't even bothered to get her a *nice* coffin. Just a shitty cheap one.

He'd buried torture victims in better caskets.

"You know, this feels like something out of a bad story," Kieran said, breaking the silence, and hopefully distracting her from realizing her relatives had cheaped out.

"Right? Like there's some kind of zombie or vampire waiting to be resurrected in the coffin?" Sabrina chuckled a little. But then her gaze skittered over the coffin, showing how nervous she really was.

"You do realize that vampires don't have to be buried in a coffin for them to be transformed, right?" It was an urban legend, something humans had believed centuries ago, back when they thought vampires were just a myth. The conversion of a human into a vampire required fewer coffins and more blood and death.

"All right, let's do it." She rubbed her hands together.

He threw the shovel onto the edge of the grave—it was at his shoulder height, so not quite six feet deep—and reached down and undid the clips that held the coffin lid in place. He *could* have just ripped the lid off its hinges, but this required a bit more of a delicate touch.

He stood to the side of the coffin—he'd excavated enough soil around to give him room—and held his breath.

Now or never.

Please be bones, please be bones, please be bones.

He really, really did not want to find a half-decomposed body. He didn't want to have to drag a coffin across the graveyard and then off into the hills. It would be hard to hide the trail, and it would suck.

He opened the lid.

Then he took a half-step back, his foot hitting the wall of the grave. His breath released in a loud whoosh.

"Was not expecting that," Sabrina said.

No. Neither was he.

Sabrina floated next to him, her arm brushing against his, the sensations sending electrical tingles all over his body.

It wasn't bones in the coffin. And, thank the gods, it wasn't a half-decomposed body, either.

No, Sabrina looked exactly as she did the day she died. At least, that's how he thought she would've looked. Long red hair in a ponytail and resting over one shoulder, her cream sweater stained with her death blood, and her jean-clad legs lying limp. Her face was slack with death, her eyes open and staring, while her arms were crossed over her torso.

"They didn't even wash and change you?" he asked, anger rising at the lack of care her family had given her. "There was no preparation at all . . ."

"Apparently not. I don't remember much of the day they buried me. After Colin brought me home, they found a coffin and dumped me straight in the ground. With my dad gone, there was nobody to prepare the death rites. I think they just wanted to move on."

Not how the dead were usually treated in this day and age, but they actually did them a favor.

He tapped the edge of the coffin with his boot. It was wood. Just timber. He moved the lid, closing the coffin before re-opening it. His keen vision cut through the darkness as he studied the grave. "There's no preservation spells on this."

Sabrina scowled. "I don't see any magic, either."

"Do bodies normally stay like this around here?" Sabrina had told him about a magic node that was under Loch Muick. Maybe that influenced corpse preservation?

"I have no idea. I've never dug up any other bodies."

Fair point.

He inhaled deeply and frowned. It didn't even smell. Like, there wasn't the odor of decay he would expect from a year-old corpse. In fact, she looked like she was sleeping, except for the tell-tale signs of death.

"So, this could just be you. Or it could be a thing."

She nibbled on her lip. "Possibly. Hard to say without digging up someone else."

"I've done enough grave digging for one day." For the next century. He might not get so lucky next time. "I'm assuming we now take your body to this node?"

Sabrina nodded and pointed to his backpack. "I guess you didn't need the liner."

He chuckled a little. Her sense of humor was refreshing.

He leaned down and picked Sabrina's body up, holding her fireman-style over his shoulders. The scent of dried blood was suddenly noticeable, and it made his fangs tingle. Fuck. The smell…it was even more delicious in person than from the vial.

You are fucked up.

Yeah, he was. But the fact her blood smelled fresh…well, dried but fresh. Not dead. Not decayed. It meant that they might actually have a shot at this.

Because why had her body preserved, when it should be nothing more than bones?

Could it have been waiting for her to return to it?

"Let's get started."

CHAPTER 37

SABRINA

Tendrils of the magic node's power embraced Sabrina as they approached the grove. The loch was surrounded by steep rocky hills, coated in heather and scrubby vegetation, but on the northern side of the loch, where the forest reached the shore, the woodland was dense and thick. It was easy to get disorientated there, turned around. For centuries, there'd been legends of will o' the wisps and lost travelers about the area.

The cascading branches of an old willow hid the grove's entrance; draping limbs slithered over Kieran as he carried her body beneath. The power made her form sizzle, and she imagined her hair was standing on end. It was invigorating, but also slightly scary.

She hadn't returned to the node's heart since she'd died, but their assumption that if Kieran moved her body, she could travel too, had been right.

Kieran carefully laid her corpse on the grass inside the small woodland clearing, the dark blue-green blades bending under her weight. He dropped his backpack and the machete next to her. The sky above was nothing but pitch blackness, coated in a blanket of twinkling stars. A swirling mist clung to the ground—different to the fog in the cemetery—and it glowed. Just softly, but enough that it was eerie.

Sabrina hadn't ever been here at night.

Her family hadn't forbidden entrance to the glade, but it wasn't encouraged, either. It had been one of Sabrina's favorite hideaways; something about the place spoke to her, called to her. She'd painted the grove a hundred times, only to burn each effort so that she wouldn't get in trouble. She hadn't been able to capture the true essence of the magic-infused site on canvas or paper. It had bothered her, before.

Now it just made sense.

Magic this strong; it wasn't meant to be drawn or captured. It was a force of nature, wild, feral, and just *there*.

The glade was surrounded by dense trees, with an understory of brambles and poison ivy. It was the kind of place you wouldn't know was here, unless you knew it was here. It was the center of the node, the hearthstone, but the node itself was huge, spanning the loch and the surrounding area.

It was a sacred place.

A small cluster of standing stones marked a ring in the center of the grove. They'd always been here, as far as she knew. When she'd been alive, she'd asked people about the circle, trying to understand its properties, how to capture with paint the light they emitted.

Each stone was about hip height, with seven marking the outer boundary, and one squat, midnight black rock in the middle.

They were made from basalt, but they varied in color. Some were Spanish gray, others sienna, with burnt umber, bone and other cream shades intermingled. Fine veins of white quartz crisscrossed some of the stones, while others had dark green olivine inclusions.

When a prospective phantom was ready to undergo the rite, they came to this spot. And they died on the central stone.

"I can smell old blood here," Kieran said, frowning as he looked around the magical locale.

"I'm not surprised," she murmured.

The phantom-to-be would enter the glade after fasting and purifying their body. They would bring a blade of some kind—or poison, it was their choice—and they would sit on the midnight stone, feet on the blue-green grass, gathering their courage. Or saying their goodbyes. Then they would say some magic words—words Sabrina had never been taught—and they would stab themselves in the heart or drink the poison.

They would die.

And then somehow, because of the site's magic and their amulet, they would come back to life.

Not everybody who made the rite was able to transition. If the amulet came loose during the rite, you were dead-dead. And if you weren't strong enough for your body to undergo the transition, then you were also just dead.

The problem was, you never knew if you would be rejected by the magic.

It was always a gamble.

"You need to place my body on the central stone," Sabrina said.

"Not creepy at all." Kieran picked her up and gently lay her on the dark rock. It wasn't a proper altar, not designed to fit a whole person. Her legs dangled over the edge, and her hair glittered like rubies as it fell against the hyper-colored grass. Night lilies began to bloom around her, their purplish flowers emitting a slight glow, reflecting against the glimmering mist.

It was ethereal.

Kieran tapped a hand against his thigh, drawing her attention away from her body. Her corpse. Her weak flesh.

"This place, it has a vibe," he said.

"Sure does."

He looked around, taking in the dense tree line, the open area, standing stones and the gleaming mist. "So, this is what a node of magic feels like. It's kind of annoying."

She didn't feel that way at all. But then, she'd never reacted to things properly. She felt caressed by the magic—welcomed. "My family says the magic node is where a portal may one day open. That they only open on nodes. This node is big and would probably result in one as big as Portland's."

"I've been to the Portland portal. You can walk a small army through it."

"Then this might be even bigger."

And it would destroy her family, and her home, if it ever opened.

The birth of a portal was destructive by nature. The one in Ireland had almost obliterated Giants Causeway, and had become neutral territory since. And with portals becoming No Man's Land ever after, even if her family survived the creation, they would be banished from their ancestral lands.

"So, we have the blood, we have your bones, we have you." Kieran reached into his leather jacket's pocket and withdrew the amulet. "And we have this. What's next?"

Sabrina let out a shaky breath. "Put it around my body's neck, please."

Damn, she really hoped this worked. She wasn't ready to cease to exist, but she needed to try. She needed to *live*.

Kieran bent down on one knee and tied the amulet in place. He then looked up at her. It was strange, watching him half-bent over her physical form. A true out-of-body experience.

"Tamsin said to pour the blood onto the amulet."

Kieran pulled the vial from a different pocket and opened it. His eyes closed as he inhaled, and his jaw clenched tight. "Do I really have to pour it *all*?" He looked at her, his pupils blown out, his body threaded with a tension she could almost taste.

She swallowed.

It was the most magnificent thing she'd ever seen. *He* was the most magnificent thing she'd ever seen. And the lust…gods, if only she could act on it.

Wait—he'd asked her a question. "Yes, all of it."

"Shame." Disappointment flooded the bond between them.

"If this works, I'll let you drink straight from the source."

"Deal." He upended the glass vial, pouring the blood over the shiny metal.

Nothing happened.

"That's it?" He raised an eyebrow.

"I don't know."

Rustling leaves had Kieran jerking to his feet. A heart-beat later, Tamsin emerged from beneath the willow's sweeping canopy, beads clinking in her hair as she moved. She dusted off her arms, like she'd just come in from a day out in the garden. "Sorry I'm late. Had things to do."

"I didn't realize you were joining us," Kieran mumbled.

Sabrina hadn't known the witch was going to, either.

"I've been trying to scry how this all plays out. I think you just need to do the thing."

Sabrina swallowed. "That's not very helpful."

Tamsin turned to Kieran. "What did she say?"

"Something about being helpful."

Not exactly what Sabrina had said, but she wasn't about to quibble.

"When you died, what did you do?" The witch rolled up her sleeves, exposing thin forearms decorated by far too many bracelets.

She shrugged. "I screamed a lot."

Kieran shook his head and said she'd screamed.

The witch rolled her eyes. "You didn't end up a ghost by accident. What did you *do*?"

"He stabbed me in the gut, then he gloated about how long it was going to take for me to die. I didn't want to die on *his* terms, but my own. So, I grabbed hold of my amulet, and then I pulled the knife out."

"You did fucking *what*?" Kieran yelled.

"What did she say?" Tamsin demanded.

He repeated her, word for word this time.

"And then what happened?" the witch asked.

"I dunno. I *reached* for the ley line—there was one running beneath the apartment where I lived. And I touched the magic. It burned. And I just wanted to live so badly…"

Kieran relayed what she'd said.

"It's as I suspected. Reach for the node. Aspen, move her hand so it's touching the amulet. Sabrina, lie inside your body and hold your amulet—or try to. Then reach for the node."

"That's it?" Kieran's hand formed into a fist.

"Say some words if you want. Repeat you want to live. Where there is a will, there's a way." Tamsin looked over her shoulder, back toward the loch. "I will wait outside, give you some…privacy."

Privacy?

The witch disappeared the same way she had arrived.

Do it. Just do it.

"You ready?" Kieran asked. He looked confident, ready to tackle death itself, but she could feel his worry through their bond.

"As I'll ever be."

She glided to her body, and then stepped *into* it. The feeling was unnerving—a little like listening to fingernails on a chalkboard, but instead of noise, it was a sensation. Grinding her teeth together, she slowly lowered into her body, until she sat in the middle of her torso.

"How are you doing? You look uncomfortable."

"It doesn't feel great."

"Stop any time you want to."

"No, I've got this."

Something like pride shone in his gaze.

I can do this.

She lay down.

Fuck. It was like her whole form came alive in tingles and zaps. It *hurt*.

But not as bad as it's going to hurt when you touch the magic.

Last time, she'd wanted to *survive*. Maybe that's where she'd gone wrong. Because she *had* survived, as a ghost. But that wasn't enough for her.

Kieran grabbed her hand, and placed it over the amulet, her ghost arm following the movement, fingers staining red with her reanimated blood. Then she reached out—she couldn't explain how—and touched the node.

Fireworks in her mind.

Power flooded her, running through her essence, burning away her form.

I want to live. I have *to live.*

Pain like she'd never known slammed into her, as her vision filled with white static. Sabrina screamed as every particle of her being reacted to the flood of magic—magic no mortal was meant to touch and walk away from—until it was the only sound she'd ever heard. Her veins ran with lava as lightning shot through her chest, the taste of ozone filling her mouth; her first taste of anything since she'd died. And just when she couldn't take it a single second longer—

She evaporated.

Her ghost form became nothing more than mist and dreams.

I will live! she screamed in defiance of the pain, of the magic, of the buzzing and screams she could still hear. Of the void that had stolen the only body she had—even if it had been nothing more than death and stardust to begin with.

A new wave of agony tore through her, smashing into her, but she rode it, grabbed it with everything she had, until it no longer drowned her in torment.

And then it was over.

CHAPTER 38

KIERAN

K ieran's back bowed as pain unlike he'd ever felt flooded his system. He dropped to his knees next to Sabrina's body, teeth grinding against the assault.

What the fuck was happening?

His hands clenched into fists, his fingernails biting so hard his skin tore. He couldn't focus on *anything* other than the agony. Even breathing hurt. None of the torture his father had put him through compared to this. Every cell in his body screamed.

And then slowly, gradually, the discomfort began to recede.

The pain wasn't coming from *him,* he realized as it dissipated; no, it was coming through the link between him and Sabrina.

If this is what he felt, how much anguish was she in?

Can't let her suffer.

He tried to grab onto the link, tried to pull it back into himself. If Sabrina's suffering was worse than his, then her torment was untold. He couldn't—wouldn't—let her deal with this on her own. He tugged on the psychic link, and the world exploded.

A force of energy blew him back with a sound like a bomb had gone off, his eardrums popping from the change in pressure. His back slammed into one of the standing stones near the edge of the clearing. Something cracked, creating a new wave of pain, but it was minor compared to the burn of acid in his very blood. He opened his eyes, trying to find Sabrina, but the glade was a brilliant white, so bright it blinded him.

The aching stopped.

Rubbing his eyes, he tried to work out up from down, the sky from ground. *Come on, come on,* he thought, opening his eyes. Nothing. Just a bright white glare which prevented him from seeing anything. Strange. He had always assumed a loss of vision would equal darkness, not light.

He pulled himself up onto his hands and knees, his back protesting the movement. *May have broken a vertebra or four.* It would heal. There were some benefits to being a Master vampire. His ears were already repairing themselves—with sound returning quickly: crackling and sizzling, a strange buzzing.

Like the static before a lightning storm.

Kieran crawled forward on one hand and his knees, ignoring the protest from his spine, using his free hand to feel for Sabrina's legs, palm sweeping over prickly grass and delicate lily petals.

Nothing.

He moved forward a few more feet. Then a few more.

Wait.

There.

He trailed his hand up the smooth rock and felt it.
Skin.

Smooth, *warm* skin.

Something clicked inside him at the touch. Re-aligned
his universe.

And he *knew*.

"Am I dead?" Her voice sounded different, less echoey.
Maybe it was his faulty hearing—maybe it was their
new circumstances. He'd never thought it sounded distant before, but now that it was being spoken from
flesh-and-blood lips, it held an earthy quality to it. It had
a little bit of a lilt, and a lot of sexy.

His fingers stroked the skin he'd found—what was that,
an arm, a stomach?

Her scent hit him like another physical blow.

Blood berries, frost, and the slightest hint of honeysuckle. His mouth watered, and his cock hardened painfully,
his body instantly reacting to her presence. To what she
was. To *who* she was to him.

He wanted her—no, *needed* her—more than life itself.

And beneath it all, he could detect the scent of her blood,
which was just as alluring as she was. He hadn't thought
that would be possible; he hadn't thought there could be
anything better out there. But he would crave the taste of
her blood and the scent of her until the day he died.

Mine.

He blinked rapidly, trying to clear his vision, to wash
away the white film that blinded him. He wanted to see
her.

Then he remembered she'd asked him a question. "If
you're dead, I'm dead," Kieran replied. The skin under his

fingertips tautened; she must've moved. His hand dropped away.

"Are you okay?" Sabrina asked as something touched his face, and out of habit, he tried to turn away.

People didn't touch him.

But the contact was electric, compelling. He stilled.

Strong fingers grabbed his chin, holding him in place. He could have broken the hold with ease, but he didn't.

Her voice was breathy. "You're even hotter in person."

Kieran chuckled, he couldn't help himself. "Pfft. I'm always hot."

She laughed, the sound reaching somewhere deep inside him, clicking the broken pieces back together. Then she ran a thumb over his lip, and his cock twitched, aching for her.

"We did it . . ." Her disbelief dried up as joy sparked through their telepathic bond; the feelings stronger now she was alive. Tethered to the physical world again. To each other.

"We did it," he agreed, then swept his tongue out, grazing over the tip of her finger.

She drew in a breath. "I want to kiss you so bad," she murmured.

He swallowed. "I want to fuck you until you can't walk."

Smooth. Prince Charming, right there.

A groan reached his ears, and her hand slid from his jaw to his neck. "The first time I saw you in that hall, all I could think about was climbing you and riding you until I couldn't think straight."

Goddamn it.

He was so hard he could barely think.

I really need my vision to come back.

"Is that why you groped me?" he asked.

"'Grope' is such a harsh word. I just wanted to get your attention."

Well, she'd certainly achieved that. "You made a rather unusual first impression."

"An unusually awesome impression," she said, and he could hear the smile in her voice. Then she moaned softly, her hand moving to his shoulder. "I've wanted to run my tongue over these since I met you." Her breath was hot against the tip of his ear while she licked slowly, and he closed his eyes as hot pleasure shot straight through him, setting his nerve endings on fire. A new type of agony. Different. Intense. Hot as hell.

Fuck.

He was going to die here. Explode from anticipation.

Growling, he surged upwards, running his hands over her arms, and up her back until his fingers found the skin of her neck. Smooth, delicious. Her long hair was out, a cascade of silk around his hands, and he twisted his fist in it at the base of her head, holding her in place.

His voice was nothing more than a growl. "I'm going to kiss you."

"Do it."

It was a demand.

One he had every intention of indulging.

His mouth crashed against hers, hungry, challenging. Needing. Sabrina wrapped her arms around him, pulling their bodies closer. She dueled with him, her tongue clashing with his, accepting his passion, his lust, but desiring everything in return.

She nipped him, tugging on his bottom lip.

Kieran groaned against her mouth and his restraint snapped. His kiss turned ravenous, while he held her head in place. His free hand stroked down the side of her neck, to her shoulder, curving across her chest. Fuck, he wished he could see her expression; see what she looked like in this moment of passion. He found her breast, and he swept his palm over it, rubbing his thumb over her taut nipple, then down, under her sweater, and back up over the soft skin of her stomach.

Her belly tightened and she let out a shuddering sigh.

He pulled his mouth away from hers, tracing her jaw with feathery kisses, then licking a hot path to her ear. Taking her earlobe between his teeth, he gently bit, and pleasure lanced through his body. He let go of her hair and cupped her ass, pulling her higher so she was pressed against his hard length, his other hand closing on her breast.

He was going to die from the pleasure. The feel of her. The scent. The sounds she made.

Everything.

She wriggled, her fist twisting in his shirt. "Too many clothes," she muttered.

He shucked off his leather jacket and ripped his T-shirt over his head, but not before she'd tugged at his pants, unzipped his fly, and pulled his cock free. Her hand was cupped around it, pressing her palm into his shaft as she rubbed up and down. Holy fucking hell. He could barely breathe from the sensations coursing through him.

Must make her mine.

Claim her.

She leaned into him, her hot breath fanning his skin as she spoke. "Is that what you wanted when we were in the shower? My hand wrapped around your cock? Or was it something else?"

"Get rid of that damned sweater." He barely recognized his voice.

She laughed softly, the sound seductive and proud as she pulled her hand away, and he could hear fabric moving. The scent of her increased. His mouth watered, and his cock strained.

Her hands were on his chest, pushing him. "What are you—?"

"Lie down."

He wasn't used to commands. Didn't normally allow a lover to issue any. But Sabrina did things to him he had yet to understand. Everything about her turned him on. Her confidence. Her desire. The very sound of her voice. If this was anyone other than Sabrina, he never would have surrendered. But for her?

He'd do anything.

They were already connected; a sense of security and mutual trust pulsed between them, begging for the final acceptance that would fully tie them together.

He lay back, the grass cool and prickly against the naked skin of his back. Her hands stroked down over his chest, down past his abs, then cupped his erection. His hips bucked, and he started trying to think of something, anything other than what she was doing, or he was going to come all over her hands.

And he had no intention of doing that. Not right now.

Sabrina slid her palm over the sensitive tip, producing a bead of excitement. She licked the head of his cock and murmured, "You taste delicious." Swirling her tongue around, he felt the heat of her mouth close over his cock before sucking, opening her throat, and taking him all in, right to the base.

"Fuck." Kieran groaned, tilting his head back into the ground.

His hips arched forward, pushing him further into her warm, hot mouth. She slid back slightly and bobbed, then grabbed the shaft in one hand, stroking it, while running her fingernails lightly over his balls. Ecstasy beat a sharp rhythm in his blood.

I don't know how much more I can take.

He hadn't had sex in forever, and her wicked touch was driving him insane. Every suck was mind shattering, and he could feel the need to come burning through him.

"Not that I want this to stop," he gritted as he thrust between her lips. "But didn't you say you wanted to ride me until you couldn't think straight?" Gods, he wished he had his vision back. He would give his right hand to see what she looked like with her mouth wrapped around him. What it looked like when she took his entire cock down her throat.

She pulled away slowly. "That I did," she breathed out.

Kieran grabbed her hips, pulling her forward in a swift motion. She settled over his groin with a sigh, her slick sex ready and rubbing over him. He heard her hands rest on the ground on either side of his face. Leaning up, he kissed her, then cupped his hands over the curve of her breasts while rolling her nipples between his fingers.

Releasing the kiss, he brought her breast to his mouth and flicked his tongue out, grazing one of the hard peaks, before wrapping his lips around it and sucking. She tasted like berries and frost and honeysuckle—her own flavor, unique and utterly delicious. He worshipped the other breast, but it wasn't enough. Steadily she slid over his cock, wriggling her body into position, but he wasn't in her, not yet.

"You didn't specify how you wanted to ride me," he said.

"What—"

His hands were on her waist now, lifting her up, dragging her across his chest, so that she straddled his face. Her sex was swollen and hot in front of him. He pushed her down a little as he swiped his tongue across her, featherlight, teasing. Then he licked her properly, tongue lingering on her clit. Her moan filled the air, and her pleasure flooded through their bond, increasing his own. She tasted even better than he could have imagined. With each flick, the taste of her inundated him; made him crave more.

He opened his eyes, and his vision came back with force. There Sabrina was, head tilted back, lush mouth partly open, a soft keening sound emerging as she arched back, her pussy rubbing over his mouth as he licked. Her skin was glowing with light, and the clearing around them appeared like it was daytime, despite being the middle of the night.

Worth waiting for, he thought, as his tongue circled her clit, edging her toward her climax. She bucked against him, her hands coming down to hold his head in place. His fingers clenched on her hips, and he encouraged her to ride his face. He latched onto her clit and sucked as she thrashed wildly, bucking against his mouth.

"I'm going to come," she moaned.

He pulled away and she reached down, grabbing his hair in her fists. "No!"

Licking his lips, he savored the essence of her. "Come around my cock."

Cheeks flushed, dazed by her denied orgasm, she slid back down his body, his hands lightly grazing her sides. He had to touch her slickness with his fingers, had to see her come as he stroked her clit while she rode the length of him. But she distracted him by thrusting down, taking him in a long, slow slide to heaven. Her inner muscles gripped him possessively.

Fuck.

His head fell back; it was like she'd been made to take every inch of him. Each glide along his length had him clenching his hands, fighting an aching need to come.

Want to feel her come around me first.

She rocked her hips against him and increased the tempo, and he thrust upward to meet her, their bodies in sync. She slid one hand down her flat belly, settling at her center, and stroking her clit. His eyes locked on the feminine power of her, completely in control as she ground on his cock, seeking her pleasure.

"Bite me," she ground out. He paused mid-stroke and she growled, the sound dark and menacing and sexy as hell. "Keep going…"

He flipped their bodies, positioning himself on top and ignoring the pain in his back, focusing entirely on her. "What did you say?"

"I said keep going!" She tried to arch her hips, but he held her in place, his cock pulsing within her.

"Before that."

Her blue eyes glowed, her face wild. "I said, 'bite me'."

"Do you mean it?" It wasn't a love bite, and he wanted to be sure she wanted it.

"I wouldn't have said it otherwise. Bite me and fuck me. *Now*."

He leaned down and licked the side of her neck, slowly, sucking on a patch of flesh. Thrusting his hips against her, she moaned, and he kept going just enough to cause pleasure to rise between them again. He licked her neck again, feeling her pulse pound against his tongue. She tilted her head to the side, giving him more access, and he threaded his fingers through her hair, holding her in place. He drove into her again, kissing a spot on her neck with tenderness.

Then he bit.

Her blood poured into his mouth, and it was everything. The taste was electric, better than the blood he had re-animated. And just as good as the taste of her pussy. It flooded his senses, and his head roared as ecstasy flowed through his body, pleasure being drawn from each stroke of his cock, and each mouthful of blood he took.

She jerked, as if struck by lightning. "Kieran!" His name came out in a strangled cry.

Her inner walls clamped down as she came. Bliss threatened to devastate him as he thrust; she was part of him now, her pleasure his, her blood in him, his body in hers. Her orgasm screamed through his mind, and tingles spread from his feet, up to his spine and then burst out of control when it hit his groin. He gasped her name as he came, his body shuddering as he exploded deep inside her.

Holy. Mother. Fucking. Hell.

His heart thundered, and he panted like he'd run a marathon. He quickly rolled them over, and Sabrina collapsed against his chest, her body trembling through the aftermath. Raising a hand, he wiped away a few strands of hair that clung to her forehead. He licked the wound on her neck, but it had already healed. Pressing his lips to the spot, he left a gentle kiss.

"You do know what this means, right?" he murmured against her neck.

She raised her head, her eyes glazed with pleasure. "That that was better than I'd imagined? And I imagined a lot of things."

He chuckled and played with her hair, the strands glowing like rubies. He ran his tongue over his teeth, the taste of her blood lingering. His pain was gone, and he felt energized. "That it will be like that every time."

"Every time?"

"For the rest of our lives."

"Now that's jumping the gun a little—"

"Sabrina…you understand what just happened here. Right?" Trepidation began to snake through him. What if phantoms didn't feel the mate bond the same? Even if they didn't, surely she felt *something*? Even when she was dead, they'd wanted each other. If they could overcome that, they could overcome this.

"You're panicking. Why are you panicking?" She rubbed her head. "Wait." Sabrina sat up, her aquamarine eyes serious as she stared down at him. "You think we're mates? Like the fated kind?"

She didn't know.

Sabrina had inadvertently accepted him without knowing the rules.

"I don't think. I know." He grabbed her hand and kissed each knuckle.

"Okay," she swallowed and nodded. "Mates. What exactly does that mean? I know all about wanting to jump each other's bones, but is there more to it?" Inside, the dread started to thicken, threatening to trap him. Drown him. But they'd already done the impossible. He reminded himself they could do this.

"You have to accept or reject each other," he said. "To solidify the bond."

It was the truth, but only a partial one. Accepting and rejecting were all well and good unless you consummated it. At that point it was a done deal.

They'd done this backwards because Kieran assumed his lovely mate knew how it worked. He hadn't realized that her understanding of magic was still severely limited in some ways.

It didn't matter.

The important part was choice, and he chose her when he took her right here beneath the night sky. He'd choose her again, albeit after explaining things.

Now he just needed to help her choose him, because even if Sabrina could move on, Kieran couldn't. He wouldn't.

"Sabrina Fhearchair, I accept you."

CHAPTER 39

SABRINA

Sabrina had a mate—and she'd found him, even in death.

It explained why she'd been so drawn to Kieran in the first place; from the moment she'd laid eyes on him. And how he'd been able to see her when no one else had—and how she could see him when he was wearing an invisibility charm.

They were destined to always see each other.

To find one another.

Her mate was the step-nephew of the king of Blood and Beryl. If they stayed together, she would have to leave her family if the clan chose a different House, because long term, she wouldn't be able to tolerate being separated from him.

But I don't want to leave my family.

Not when she would finally be able to interact with the people around her. And get her justice. But she didn't want to stay, either, and give up her chance of love and happiness.

"…I accept you."

She had never thought three words would have such an impact on her life. They had changed her, fundamentally—shifted things in her soul that she hadn't realized needed shifting. But...she hadn't said them back.

She didn't know why.

Why couldn't she just agree? She could feel the pull of the mating bond—and Kieran was already linked to her mind. And she absolutely wanted him to be her mate.

But she didn't want him to want her because he *had* to.

She wanted him to want her because he *wanted* to.

Not because fate had decided they belonged together. But because they *wanted* to be together.

You're an idiot.

Yeah, she was. She should just say that she accepted him back, sign on that sexy dotted line, and be done with it. He'd be hers forever. They were already linked. He was a Master vampire and half-death fae; she would never find a more powerful—or hot as hell—mate.

But...she hadn't been able to do it.

Kieran hadn't seemed to worry—he could no doubt sense the turmoil in her mind, her heart. He probably thought she just needed time to adjust to being alive again. And to come to terms with having her mind blown by the most earth-shattering orgasm she'd ever had.

In fact, she had never felt so amazing in her entire life *or* death.

She lay with her cheek on Kieran's chest, the sound of his heartbeat strong and steady. He was hers. She didn't doubt that. But...she needed time. That was it. Just time.

Sweat slicked over his stomach, and she was tempted to lick it off, follow the trail of dark hair down further. But they had other things to do. Important tasks that couldn't wait. She traced a circle over his chest.

Everything has changed.

Her body felt different, too.

Before she'd died, she'd been weak, shaky. Now, she felt like she could run miles and miles without breaking a sweat. She was strong, she knew it. Even Kieran drinking from her—and gods, had that been amazing, her thighs clenched just thinking about the pleasure she'd gotten from his bite—didn't seem to have even left her the slightest bit lightheaded.

Lifting up a hand, she stared at the solid flesh, the skin; her lack of transparency.

She really wasn't dead anymore.

And it was all thanks to Tamsin and Kieran. Together, they had done what she never would've been able to.

Kieran's fingers gently combed through her hair, the offered comfort settling deep in her bones. "What do we do now?" he asked, voice quiet.

The glade around them held lingering bits of captured light, leftovers from the magic eruption. The night lilies also shone brighter, and even the blades of grass had picked up a teal glow.

"We should get back to the castle," Sabrina said, excited and reluctant simultaneously.

Kieran's hands slid down her back, cupping her ass. "Are you sure we don't have time for another round?"

She laughed, and playfully hit him on the chest. "So romantic."

"Hey, if you wanted romance, you mated the wrong guy." He grabbed her hand and kissed the inside of her wrist, his eyes staring at her with a level of possession that should have been scary.

Instead, it melted something inside her, made her feel like she was the most important thing in the universe. That she was *his* universe.

Fuck traditional romance.

She'd take this over that any day.

"Hurry up and get out here!" Tamsin shouted. "Clock's ticking!"

Kieran rolled his eyes and sat up in one smooth movement, cradling Sabrina as he did so. "Guess we'd better get dressed."

She grinned conspiratorially, then reached for her discarded sweater. Gods, how she hated that thing.

Kieran put a hand on her forearm. "I brought some clothes with me. They're way too big for you, but they might be better than what you were wearing."

Sabrina looked at him. "You brought clothes for me?"

"I figured you had to be sick of that sweater."

"You thought right."

That was the sweetest thing anyone had ever done for her. And sure, it probably said a ton about her shitty love life before she'd died, but this…it showed how much he'd cared enough about her *before* he'd known she was his mate.

Kieran reached into his small backpack and withdrew a black T-shirt, and a pair of gray sweats. He was right—they were way too big, with the T-shirt going down to mid-thigh. She had to tighten the waistband of the sweats as much as she possibly could, so they wouldn't fall down to her knees. But they were better than nothing, even if she looked like a child wearing her parent's clothing.

As for shoes, she figured her old sneakers would do. They had some blood splatter, but she doubted anyone was going to quibble about that, when she had literally risen from the dead.

Tamsin stumbled into the clearing, one hand covering her eyes as she wove her way through the draping branches of willow leaves. "You guys dressed yet?"

"Why would you assume we weren't dressed?" Kieran asked, voice dry. He picked up a shirt, and he'd somehow managed to get his pants on in the meantime.

Fuck.

She wanted to lick his chest, claw it—

"Because I have ears." Tamsin still held a hand in front of her eyes. Bangles and beads clinked on her wrist as she walked.

Sabrina's blush was instant. Wow. She sure didn't miss that sensation. Funny, how when she was a ghost, she hadn't had to worry about those embarrassing bodily tells. Now, she was sure she was as red as a tomato.

"We're dressed," Sabrina replied.

Kieran, unfortunately, had managed to get his shirt on over his head, and shrug on his leather jacket. It was a tad unsettling how quick he moved, but it was more disappointing he'd covered up all those glorious muscles.

At least he can go slow when it's important.

"*I can take things as slow as you want,*" Kieran said telepathically, a smug grin on his face as he slid on his backpack.

Her cheeks burned with heat. "*So, when can you hear my thoughts, and when can't you hear my thoughts?*"

"Sometimes I can, sometimes I can't. I'm sure we'll get the hang of it."

"Hello! It's rude to telepathically talk when someone else is standing *right here*." Tamsin lowered her hand.

"How can you—" Sabrina began, but stopped and shook her head. Tamsin was a woman of many secrets, and she'd been able to sense Sabrina when she had been a ghost. She had powers Sabrina could only dream about.

Tamsin let out a whistle as she took in both Sabrina and Kieran. "You look different than what I remember." The witch came forward, the grass dimming slightly as she stepped on it, as if the magic dissipated with her contact.

"Let me guess, you thought I'd be taller." Sabrina laughed.

Kieran stepped closer to her, as if drawn to the sound. She reached out a hand and he took it, threading his fingers through hers. It felt right, the connection.

Mates.

"No, I remembered you as being shorter. And your hair wasn't quite as red."

Sabrina frowned. She pulled some of her loose hair over a shoulder and stared. She'd always had red hair, but this was different. It was now the color of a dark red ruby, with purple highlights gleaming through.

"The color of life's blood," Kieran said into her mind.

"It's gotten darker," was all Sabrina said, even if her pulse skidded with uncertainty. What else had changed? *Had* she actually gotten taller? Was she still...*her*?

She let go of her hair.

At the end of the day, did it really matter, if she had come back...different?

She was alive. She wasn't dead, and if there had been some price to pay, then she'd paid it and the cost be damned. She had bigger things to worry about than her appearance.

She met Tamsin's wolf-eyes. "Thank you." She didn't like owing people, and she owed Tamsin her life. "This wouldn't have been possible without you."

"Oh, you didn't really need *me*, you just needed some guidance." The witch waved a hand dismissively. "Ultimately, what you needed was your body to get to this glade. Magic calls to magic."

Sabrina frowned. What did that mean, exactly? She had a feeling it was more complicated than it sounded.

"Can you change form?" Tamsin asked, voice urgent.

"I don't know?" She hadn't meant that to be a question.

"Try," the witch insisted.

Sabrina held up her free hand and stared. *Become invisible.*

Nothing happened.

"Maybe channel how you felt as a ghost," Kieran suggested. He was a wall of calm confidence next to her, and it made her feel invincible. Like she could do anything.

She remembered how she'd felt; insubstantial, untethered…free.

Her hand vanished.

"You did it." Kieran's hand tightened on hers, and she could feel his pride in her through their bond.

"Now I just have to learn to do that quicker."

"You probably want to do that sooner rather than later," Tamsin said. She rummaged around in the pockets of her layered dress.

"Why would that be?" Kieran asked. He leaned down—still holding Sabrina's hand, like he didn't want to let her go, *ever*—and picked up the machete.

Tamsin turned to face them. "We're not alone in the forest."

CHAPTER 40

KIERAN

"Come again?" Sabrina asked. Her eyes went wide as she searched the surrounding area. "Who else is here?"

"It's a forest. You're never alone in a forest," Kieran said as he watched Sabrina, still somewhat shellshocked from the confirmation that Sabrina was his. It explained the irresistible pull he'd felt toward her from the moment he'd smelled her blood, made stronger when he'd seen her the first time. She made him laugh—and he never laughed—and she made him actually want to try and be a good person for her. It didn't make him want to be better in general or to please anyone else; everyone could kick bricks for all he cared. But Sabrina, he'd do anything for her. He knew it.

She was his one weakness.

But she was also his strength.

"I don't know. I can only sense it. The magic storm generated from your resurrection packed a punch," Tamsin said. "Something is out there."

"Any idea what the 'something' could be?" Kieran asked.

"I would assume it's water monsters," she answered.

Colin and Angus had mentioned monsters after Kieran and Sabrina had stolen the amulet. Had the Portal Watch learned anything more since then?

"Kelpies?" he suggested. Sabrina had mentioned them once before, but even as he said it, he didn't truly believe it.

Human-world kelpies were horses that had been transformed by the portal magic. People only tended to talk about the effects of the magical gateways on humans, but some animals were affected, too. They went bad. Warped. Lost their original forms to even more beastly shapes.

The true kelpies had come from the fae world, but they didn't tend to cross the border to Earth—different magic, and a very different world system. Kieran had learned about them when he'd been held by his biological father; he'd learned a lot about the fae home world then. Enough that he had decided he never wanted to go there himself. He was far more vampire than he was fae, anyway. At least in how he identified.

But even though the human-world kelpies weren't true kelpies, both had horse forms and a hunger for flesh. Nothing he had scented so far suggested them, though.

Tamsin started walking toward the loch.

"They tried to overthrow us for decades, but we drove them out years ago," Sabrina said, following the witch. They came to a stop about two hundred yards from the willow and its hidden entrance into the glade.

What the fuck?

Gravity seemed to have stopped working. Pebbles, boulders, leaves, and even droplets of water from the loch hung suspended in the air. An electrical hum reverberated from the ground up, almost drowned out by a dull booming sound, like drums being rhythmically beaten.

"Can anyone hear that?" Kieran asked.

"No, I can't hear anything," Sabrina said.

Tamsin shook her head.

That was not a good sign. *Really wish I had Ysabeau's hearing right about now.* Sure, his was better than a phantom's or a witch's, but he really could do with knowing what was making that noise.

Before them, Loch Muick spread out beneath the moonless night. It reflected the sky above, a darkened mirror showcasing a star-studded expanse. It was enclosed by a ridgeline of treed mountains, and the scent of fresh water, vegetation and woodsmoke permeated the air. It felt...primitive. Untouched. He'd run past abandoned cabins on his patrols with Clint—people had once lived here, before the world changed. It had been a tourist spot, according to the faded signage. Now it was the territory of the phantoms, who no longer shared their land with outsiders.

Lights from the castle weren't visible from here, but you could see the telltale glow of civilization to the north and west.

It was kind of beautiful.

Except for the gravity-defying rocks and leaf litter.

Sabrina was also staring at the loch, but her expression was distant. What was she thinking? Their bond was patchy, never seeming to give him insights when he most wanted them.

"This land…if we leave it, we become extinct," Sabrina murmured.

He wasn't used to touch, but he wanted to hold her, so he wrapped an arm around her shoulders and over her chest, pulling her back against his body. Her scent swamped his senses, mixed with the earthy aroma of sex. He grew hard the moment her ass pressed against his groin.

"Well, not exactly," he said, ever practical. "The phantoms already transformed will survive."

"But there will be no more. We'd be forced to watch as our children grow old and die, with no chance of transitioning."

A large *crack* shattered the night, causing Kieran's arm to tighten reflexively around Sabrina. "What the fuck was that?"

Tamsin turned to them, magical light bleeding from her eyes. "They're here."

Kieran wasn't sure what he had expected from the monsters, but seeing an entire tree, complete with soil-encrusted roots being thrown over their heads—dirt raining down on them as it did so—and sailing into the loch, was not it. It landed with an enormous splash, the water shooting high, some falling back to the loch, some not.

Weird.

Too weird.

And he'd seen some pretty bizarre shit in his time.

A long tentacle erupted from the loch's surface and dragged the tree below. He paused, surprise holding him immobile. The scales on the tentacle were a purple so dark it glimmered black, and he swore it had pearlescent hooks along the length of it.

He stared.

And took a step further back from the water.

There was a monster in the lake? Was this the monster the Portal Watchmen had been referring to, or was it *another* one?

"Uh, did the Loch Ness Monster have a baby with a bloody kraken?" Kieran asked. "This is so beyond my fucking paygrade."

"They are not compatible species," Tamsin answered, like she'd considered the possibility before.

Sabrina swallowed. "Right."

Kieran turned to the tree line; he couldn't *see* any creature, but the tops of the trees were shivering, as if being brushed by something large.

Something is out there.

A roar blasted from behind them, the sound ending on a high-pitched note. He gritted his teeth in pain, his sensitive ears hurting.

I don't think the Portal Watch meant the loch monster.

No. Now they had *two* creatures to deal with.

Let's hope neither of them are hungry…

CHAPTER 41

SABRINA

They had a beastie living here?

How many times had Sabrina swam in the loch, not knowing another Nessie occupied it?

She shuddered.

Energy shot into Sabrina, streaming from the ground up, flooding her with power. Her fingertips tingled, and she felt like she could channel lightning. *What the fuck is happening?* Was she becoming a super-charged phantom?

It didn't matter. Whatever was coming from the trees, she would fight it, with or without newfound energy or powers.

No one, no one was going to take her new life away. But most importantly, no one was going to harm a single hair on Kieran's too-sexy head. The possessive urge to protect him overwhelmed her. Sure, he was faster than her, and probably stronger, too. But Kieran wasn't a true immortal, and she couldn't die.

Not again.

Never again.

She would be killed and regenerate a thousand times over to prevent him from leaving her.

Movement.

Crack.

Another tree exploded from the ground, this one on the edge of the woods. It hovered in the air, held by unseen hands, before it too was flung in the loch.

This time, however, the tentacled thing threw it back.

The three of them dropped to the ground, to avoid being hit. The trunk landed about ten yards in front of them and exploded into fragments, the lack of gravity causing the chips to float in midair, rotating slightly.

Holy hell.

Gravel tore at the skin of her hands and grazed the side of her face. Pain. Physical pain. It was surprising, how sharp and sweet it felt, after a year of feeling nothing at all. It was nowhere as good as the pleasure she had felt with Kieran, but it surprised her how she didn't mind it.

It meant she was alive, here.

It soon faded.

She pulled herself to her knees, as rocks bit through the gray sweats. She wasn't wearing the right clothes for a monster hunt. Or for any kind of outdoor activity, for that matter.

Just turn ghost and back again, duh. That will heal you.
Right.

She focused on her ghost state and felt the instant loss of her body. She fought the moment of panic that overwhelmed her with the sensation. She was not a proper ghost. She could get back. She reformed a bare second later, before her clothes had time to drop to the ground.

Kieran was already standing again, staring at the tree line, like he could see past the shuddering, darkened canopy and into the secrets hiding beneath.

A roar burst from the trees, and the ground thudded. A creature shimmered into view, like nothing she had ever seen before or could have possibly imagined, even in her worst nightmares. The creature was huge; its bulk reminded her of an elephant, but larger. It had long hind legs but moved bent forward as it walked. Overlong arms gouged the earth as it moved, long claws shooting sparks when they encountered rock, and its head was enormous. It was mottled in color, a mixture of grays and greens, and it had at least four eyes she could see. A large sail-like structure lined the ridge of its back, and dangling, rotting kelp clung to the small horns on top of its head.

The scent of pungent salt water and decay hit her.

It was monstrous.

Hideous.

But she couldn't take her eyes off it; primal fear had the hairs rising on the backs of her arms and neck.

It was a predator.

She was prey.

"Was this what you heard?" Sabrina asked Kieran, trying to step around him, but he kept edging in front of her, trying to keep her out of sight of the monster.

"I sure as hell hope so, or there's another one of these things out there." He shook his head and muttered, "Why do I keep coming across dinosaur-sized animals?"

This had happened to him *before*?

No, thank you. Once is more than enough.

The beast roared again, and Sabrina winced. Kieran lifted both hands—one still holding his stolen machete—to try and block his ears. Fae hearing was meant to be even more sensitive than a vampire's; if the noise hurt her ears, it would have been agony for him. He dropped his hands when it stopped, blood trickling out of one ear.

He looked at her and must have seen the concern on her face—felt it in the line that tethered them. "Burst my eardrums, but don't worry. It will heal in a moment. And it will stop me from hearing it as loudly again until it does."

Tamsin stood, blood smeared on her chin from a small cut. She must have hit her face when they dropped to avoid the tree. She held a glowing crystal ball in her hands. It must have been a weapon of some sort; Sabrina somewhat doubted she was going to use it to read the future.

The monster reared on his hind legs and roared again, and the air rippled at its feet in response. At least a dozen small creatures appeared as they reached the edge of the loch's shores, each one looking a little bit like how she imagined a velociraptor would appear: about as big as a turkey, but with more claws and teeth.

Invisible, she realized. They could turn invisible.

These critters didn't have feathers; their skin appeared smooth as a pebble, except for their heads, which were covered in short, white quills. They chittered amongst themselves, then looked at the large monster, as if waiting for direction.

Great. They can communicate.

A handful of velociraptor critters turned back to the tree line and vanished from sight. A moment later, the air shimmered again, and another small group emerged from the woodland. Wonderful. They'd gone and got friends.

"Why is their invisibility failing?" she asked.

"The magic eruption?" Kieran guessed.

It was a better explanation than any she had.

The group of small creatures turned to face them. The large monster let out a strange trilling sound.

"What the fuck do they want with us?" Kieran held his machete out in front.

"They probably don't want us, they just want the node," Tamsin said.

"Then why are they running straight for us?" Kieran asked, shoving Sabrina behind him again.

She wasn't a helpless damsel in distress. Yeah, she'd been murdered once. But she wasn't going to let it happen again.

The large monster hadn't moved. Instead, the tiny hoard surrounding it had sprung forward. They were *fast*. The scent of rotting fish and sea water increased. Within seconds, they had reached them, one jumping and trying to latch onto Kieran's sword arm. Another swiped a claw, raking it across his thigh.

No.

Sabrina darted around Kieran, turning incorporeal as she did so. Her oversized clothes dropped to the ground. She reformed her hand, grabbing one of the closer dinosaur-type creatures, before spinning and using the momentum to heft it into the loch. The splash was accompanied by a squeal as a hook-covered tentacle appeared, dragging it down.

Okay, so they are not friends.

"These are the water creatures? Not the loch kraken?" she asked.

"Worry about what they are later. Kill them first."

"Do we really need to kill them?" Sabrina had hoped there was another option—despite her having fed one to the krakenessie.

Kieran began tearing through the hoard of little creatures, slicing off arms, heads and tails with surgical precision. *Why are they staying visible?* she wondered. They were being slaughtered. Surely, they would use their camouflage to their advantage?

She turned to Tamsin, but the witch was protected within a sphere of sparkling light. A group of the creatures scratched at the magic, their claws glowing blue when they made contact with the temporary ward.

Sabrina floated closer to the giant monster, and it lifted its oversized head, nostrils flaring as it wetly sniffed the air.

"What are you doing?" Kieran shouted.

"Going to see if I can reason with it."

Kieran picked up a velociraptor-thing by the scruff and snapped its neck with one hand. He dropped it to the ground. He pointed at it with his machete. "Kill first, ask questions later."

"That's not exactly how that works."

You couldn't ask questions of the dead.

Or maybe he could. He *was* part death fae. But could these creatures even turn into ghosts?

Sabrina swept toward the large monster and reformed her head. The scent of rotting sea things was like a slap to the face. She began breathing through her mouth—which didn't help much, since she could now *taste* it.

Gag.

The beast blinked at her and growled low in its throat. She swallowed.

It can't eat you. It can't eat you.

"Dead thing. Leave. Our place now."

The words punched into her mind, sending her reeling back through the air. That *hurt.* Her ghostly hands rubbed ineffectually against her fleshed temples.

It was telepathic.

"Sabrina!" Kieran shouted as he slashed his way toward her.

"I'm okay!" She threw a hand out, indicating for him to wait.

Her vampire-fae against twenty beasties—they were apparently even odds. But her mate against a T-rex mutant sea creature? She wasn't willing to place that bet.

"This place is mine," she said aloud. "You must leave."

The beast snapped its jaws in response. *"Magic ours. Leave, or we eat."* The words were accompanied by a series of mental snarls and sounds she couldn't decipher. And it didn't hurt any less than the first time it had spoken to her.

"I don't negotiate with murderers," Sabrina muttered.

It tilted its head at her in response.

From her vantage point, she saw the leaves of trees moving in the distance, and a faint drumbeat sounded.

There are more of them.

The beast blinked three of its eyes, and then opened its maw. She retched on the stench of rotting flesh. *"We will eat."*

We are so fucked.

CHAPTER 42

KIERAN

Sabrina floated right up to that giant monstrosity of a *thing* and *talked* to it.

She had not listened to his advice.

But she'd told Kieran to wait, so he would. For now. Because he trusted that she would not put herself at unnecessary risk—not when she had just gotten her body back. Not after they had just found each other.

She turned completely incorporeal, then vanished, reappearing over the creature's back. She reformed a moment later, astride the thing's back—naked as the day she was born except for her amulet—hands grabbing at its horns. She hissed at the contact.

What the fuck was she doing?

He revised his opinion about her taking unnecessary risks.

Sure, phantoms were supposedly immortal. But what if this creature was her kryptonite?

He decapitated the last of the smaller critters. "Sabrina!"

A snarling jaguar dropped down from one of the nearby trees, landing behind her on the creature's back. The giant cat sunk its teeth into the monster's spine, just above the sail, grinding down with powerful jaws. The lizard thing roared in pain, bursting Kieran's just-healed eardrums. Pain lanced through his head, and he wiped new blood from his earlobe.

Great.

Now he wasn't going to hear much of anything for the next few minutes.

The animal reared, and swiped its freakishly long arms back, swiping at Sabrina and the jaguar. Sabrina turned incorporeal, the claws raking nothing but air where she had once been. But one of the dagger-like claws managed to slash the jaguar, sending the large feline to the ground. The snapping of bones as the big cat landed had Kieran wincing, just as the jaguar's scent reached him.

It was Clint.

Kieran cursed.

A blade spun through the air, emerging from the darkness of the trees, to impale one of the creature's eyes. Sky ran out from the shadows, her pink hair plastered to her sweat-covered face. She skidded to a halt, not fifteen feet from the creature.

"You! Scary monster thing! Come get me."

Even his damaged ears picked up her scream.

Sky waved her arms around, trying to draw the animal's attention.

What the fuck is she doing?

Did she want to get eaten?

Because that was how you got eaten.

Tamsin's voice began to register, and Kieran spun toward the witch just as a fireball emerged from the protective ward around her. The witch was clutching what looked like an angel feather, and her face was sheet-white. Sabrina grabbed the knife that was embedded in the creature's eye and pulled it out, stabbing it straight into another orb.

The fireball roared past Kieran and engulfed the monster.

"*Sabrina!*" His shout pierced the night.

She appeared above the fire-covered creature, incorporeal and unharmed.

Thank you, gods.

She can't die, remember?

Yeah, that was going to take some getting used to, he realized.

We have to decapitate it, Kieran thought.

He sprinted toward the creature, the magical fire already beginning to falter. He veered left, then leaped, landing on its back. His leather boots burned at the contact with the cooked skin, but he gripped the sail-like appendage on its back for balance. Then he began hacking downwards. Over and over he cut, the machete's edges already partially dulled from massacring the other reptilian creatures.

The creature thrashed, slashing its long arms back, trying to get him as he dodged out of the way. He avoided most, but one long claw slashed his side. The wound burned—poison?—but within seconds, the ache receded, healing.

That was quick, even for him. Had Sabrina's blood done something to him? Empowered him?

He didn't think Danni's blood made Elias heal quicker—but maybe it was a mate thing? Or a phantom thing? He should ask. Presuming he survived this whole shebang.

He lifted the blade and cut down with a huge surge of power, severing the thick vertebrae and cutting through the spinal cord. The beast collapsed to the ground, its limbs twitching, and its breathing labored.

He didn't stop.

The head *had* to come off.

It was the one surefire way to kill any immortal species, except—apparently—for the phantoms. By the time he was done, he was covered in gore, the blood and bits and pieces stinking like mildew and mold.

I need a shower. And a decontamination spell.

What the hell was on his skin?

Part of him wanted to run and dunk himself in the loch, but the owner of the tentacles may mistake him for lunch.

Thank the gods he'd never decided to go for a dip before now.

Never going to trust water again.

Sky ran up to them, panting. The blade she'd thrown at the creature—and that Sabrina had also used—was already in her hand. He could have sworn she hadn't even gone near the beast's head to retrieve it.

Sky slid past him, dropping to her knees when she reached the jaguar's side. Sabrina was already there, still nude. A possessive snarl rolled through his mind—he didn't like that others were able to see his mate naked.

Not the time, he told himself, but his knuckles turned white as he gripped his borrowed machete.

Sabrina's fingers were pressed to the cat's neck, and her expression was grim.

"Is he okay?" Sky asked, breathless.

"I don't know." Sabrina's voice was soft.

Kieran approached the shifter. Clint was still breathing, but it was labored. The fae in him knew the telltale signs of imminent death, and it wasn't looking good. But the Spirit and Sapphire ambassador had thrown himself on the creature's back, helping Kieran's mate.

He owed Clint a debt.

Kieran sliced his wrist as he closed the distance between them. He dropped to one knee and dribbled his blood into the shifter's mouth.

"What are you doing?" Sabrina asked.

Sky tried to slap his hand away. "Shifters don't survive being turned into vampires."

She was wrong.

Well, technically she was mostly correct, but he knew one particular shifter who had made the transition, and they had turned out to be scary as fuck as a result.

He ignored Sky's attempts to move his arm, instead massaging Clint's throat, encouraging him to swallow. The jaguar's lips barely moved, but the blood disappeared. "I'm not trying to change him. I'm not biting him."

"Vampire blood has healing properties," Tamsin said, her footfalls crunching against the gravel ground. "It might not be enough."

"Then heal him!" Sky demanded, staring at the spell-caster.

Tamsin sighed. "I'm not a healer. If he makes it, he makes it."

Callous, but true. None of them had the power—or the required ingredients on them—to heal damage as extensive as Clint's.

"We can't leave him here," Sky said.

"We can't risk moving him much, either," Kieran replied. Hauling the jaguar's body back to the castle would probably result in more internal injuries.

"Put him in the glade," Sabrina said, "if it won't hurt him too badly. It will hide him, while he heals."

Or doesn't.

She didn't say the latter out loud. None of them did, although they all knew the probable outcome.

Kieran picked Clint's body up; he was fucking *heavy*. Grunting a little, he strode back past the scattered remains of the dinosaur-like monsters, globules of their blood and innards now floating alongside the pebbles and exploded tree.

It was gorier than the night Elias had finally gotten revenge for his sister's death.

And that had been carnage.

He carefully lowered Clint onto the glowing grass just inside the stone circle, the blades dimming as the shifter's body made contact. "You'd better heal."

Kieran scanned the area, and couldn't see, hear or sense any other creature nearby. It was safe—for now, anyway. He headed back to the loch.

When he arrived, Sabrina was dragging the huge T-rex-like head toward the pebble beach. It had to weigh at least as much as two full grown adults. *How strong is she?*

Tamsin and Sky watched her, faces wearing expressions that varied between nausea and amusement.

"What are you doing?" Kieran demanded.

Her cheeks were tinted pink from the effort, her skin covered in bits of gooey green blood. Instead of answering, she grunted, "Help me."

Kieran sighed, grabbed the creature by a huge nostril—gross, so gross—and helped her drag it to the loch's edge. He then hurried the fuck back from the black water.

"Why did you…" His words died as two huge tentacles—easily as thick as the tree trunk they'd thrown back—emerged, slithering toward the head. They patted it, almost gently, before wrapping it in a stranglehold and dragging it into the dark waters, leaving barely a ripple after.

Sabrina threw two of the smaller corpses in after it. "Here you go!"

He might have a link to her mind, but he had no idea what she was doing.

"And here's some dessert!" She threw in a severed head. Sky joined her and began piling up the mutated sea-turkey bodies near where the giant skull had been taken.

Kieran's imagination was *surely* playing tricks on him. They weren't…feeding it, were they?

"Thank you for helping before!" Sabrina shouted. "If you see any more of these beasties, feel free to eat them for me—I mean, us."

Helping?

The thing had thrown a *tree* at them.

"Uh, Sabrina—"

His mate turned to him, wiping her hands together, as if that would actually make them clean. "Haven't you ever seen *Jurassic World*?"

He had no idea what was going on. "No."

"Spoiler alert: at the end, the giant water dinosaur eats the genetically mutated T-rex. We want Krakenessie to be our friend. To eat the mutated T-rexes out there." She pointed at the headless body of the long-armed monster.

He crossed his arms over his chest. He still had no idea what she was talking about—aside from the fact she wanted the kraken thing to eat the dinosaur-sized thing. "You *named* it?"

She frowned, and then flicked her ruby hair over a shoulder. "You *didn't*?"

A burst of surprised laughter made him snort.

It was sexy, damnit.

Both of them, covered in gore and gods-knew-what-else, grinned at each other like loons.

"So, uh…hate to break the moment." Sky twirled her dagger through her fingers, playing with it, then pointed the blade at Sabrina, in all her naked, grime-encrusted glory. "But who the hell are you?"

CHAPTER 43

SABRINA

R ight.

Sabrina hadn't met Sky before, in person or ever, actually.

I've spied on you a lot.

Yeah, she didn't think that was the line to lead with.

"My name is Sabrina Fhearchair, I'm one of the phantoms." She tilted her chin, daring the conjurer to argue.

She did. "I've never seen you in the castle." Sky flipped the knife.

"You wouldn't have." Sabrina didn't really want to elaborate further. Not until she was able to see her family, to explain her reborn existence. "But I've seen you. You're Sky Serpell, Spirit and Sapphire ambassador." *And you might be on a secret mission.* But she didn't add that. Not out loud.

"She is?" Kieran asked her through their bond.

"I'll explain later."

Sky's eyes narrowed.

"We need to go back to the castle and warn them about these creatures," Kieran said. He handed Sabrina her discarded sweats and shirt.

"Does anyone know what the hell they are?" Sky asked as Sabrina got dressed.

Sabrina winced as she put the clothes on, the fabric sticking to the disgusting gore that was splattered over her body. *I need a bath* and *a shower so bad.* Even though she'd sort of made friends with Krakenessie, she wasn't willing to test the waters. Pun intended.

"They have to come from the other side of a portal," Kieran replied. "I've never seen anything camouflage like they do. Thank fuck that whatever they were using to make themselves invisible failed when they reached the loch."

"Do you think they camouflage like a chameleon or squid; except they use magic to do it?" Sabrina asked.

"Chameleons change color for thermoregulation or due to their emotions," Tamsin said. "Squids change color to blend into their backgrounds. These creatures can meld into their surroundings so well you wouldn't even know they were there. They are truly invisible, like they can shift out of phase from our world. Kind of like the phantoms when they take on their ghost form."

"I don't know what 'out of phase' means, but if they can do that, how do we find them?" Sabrina asked.

Kieran flicked some gore off the machete. "Wait, if the phantoms are out of phase, could we—I mean, they—see these monsters if the phantoms were in their spirit forms?"

"It would depend on if they're out of phase in the same dimension," Tamsin said. "But none of them have commented on seeing the monsters before, and they're often in their spirit form."

"I thought witches had specializations. How come you know so much about all of these various different topics?" Kieran's eyes narrowed in suspicion.

Sabrina thought witches were meant to specialize in *one* thing. She didn't understand how Tamsin could open portals *and* make containment spells *and* raise the dead.

"My specialization is time. Not just fortune telling, but time itself. I can freeze it, hence the stasis spell. I can tell the future and read the past. Time is just another dimension."

"But you're able to make portals," Kieran protested.

"Portals warp space and time. There's overlap."

And that was all the answer they were going to get, she realized. And it was probably more than she admitted to most people.

"So why would these creatures come *here*?" Sabrina asked.

"The node," Tamsin said, waving a hand to encompass the loch and its surroundings, like it was obvious. And maybe it was, to a witch.

Kieran frowned. "There are nodes all over the planet."

"Yes, but not all are as powerful as this one. And the magic that generates here, it seeps out into the world. Can't you feel it?" Her pale eyes began to glow.

"I can feel it," Sabrina admitted. "I always have."

And she could see magic.

Maybe she wasn't *just* phantom. It was something she would have to ask her family about, later.

"Some creatures feed off magic. And your kind," the witch met Sabrina's gaze, her stare unearthly, "are transformed by it. A lot of magical beings would want access to this place."

Kieran frowned and she could *feel* the pieces clicking together for him. "It's not about the clan, is it? Take the phantoms from here, and there are no new phantoms. And whoever gets this place...then they may be able to make something new themselves. Or become stronger."

"Make us suspect that one of the Houses killed Sammy," Sabrina said slowly, following his line of thought. "And we get so angry, we refuse to align with a House."

"Normally, that would mean the phantoms would be wiped from existence," Tamsin agreed. "When the Houses decide someone has to join, they must do that or die."

Sabrina paled. "But phantoms are true immortals. That can't happen. We can't *be* wiped out."

She was the perfect example. She had been dead, and look at her now—the picture of health. She'd never felt better.

"But the monsters probably don't know that," Kieran said. "It's specialized intel. This means they were planning this. That they're intelligent. And that they have a contact in this world, who knows about the node and the phantoms."

"But—why would they even care about us if they want the node?" Sabrina asked.

"The House system—that is unique to Earth. The portal worlds, well, they each have their own rules. So, if these creatures recently snuck through from a portal, how would they know what to do to destroy the introductory talks?" Kieran's hand tightened on the machete's handle.

Tamsin walked toward the tree line. "They killed Sammy in a way they thought couldn't be traced back to them."

Sabrina swallowed; her throat tight at the mention of her cousin. "How do we know they came through a portal recently?"

"This is the first I've ever heard about them," Kieran replied. Sky and Tamsin nodded their agreement. He was high up in Blood and Beryl, Sabrina thought. His king would have no reason to keep something like this from him.

"We should call and see if they need help at the castle," Sabrina suggested, worry suddenly clawing at her. Her family, they didn't know that these creatures could turn invisible; they just thought there was *one* water monster loose on their lands.

Kieran pulled his cell from his jacket pocket. He jabbed a finger at the screen. "It's dead. It won't even turn on."

Sky did the same and shook her head. "Nothing."

"The magic explosion must have fried them," Tamsin muttered.

"Is that what that was?" Sky asked. The pink-haired woman turned to look back in the direction of the castle. "Clint thought he smelled Kieran sneak out, but he couldn't see him. We were tracking him when we got sidetracked by the monsters' scent. He said it had never been so obvious before, like it went from one or two intruders to a group. So, we followed them. There are a lot out there. More than before. Many more."

Interesting.

And scary.

"Are you sure?" Sabrina asked.

"Most of the scents when we went out the other day were a week or so old," Kieran said. "Some were fresh. But they belonged to only a handful of individuals. *Small* individuals; not like *that*." He nodded at the headless corpse.

So, while the creatures were invisible to the eye, they couldn't hide their sound, or their scent. A bit like Kieran and his necklace.

Invisibility has its flaws.

Like with phantoms—they could hide from outsiders, generally, but not each other. And when they reformed, well, they came back naked and vulnerable. It's why her family kept stashes of clothing all over the castle. *Both* castles.

"Let's go back to Braemar. And try and avoid being eaten on the way." Kieran clasped Sabrina's hand and walked to the trees. She tightened her fingers around his, enjoying the touch, the sense of belonging.

Sky started to jog, Tamsin following suit. "Let's go!"

Kieran released her hand, and they ran.

It was silent, except for the sound of their footfalls crunching on leaf litter and their breathing. Well, Tamsin and Sky's breathing; Kieran and Sabrina barely made a sound, which made her feel awesome and slightly worried. She was never this fit before—and phantoms weren't meant to come back physically stronger. Just harder to kill.

Worryingly, none of the night forest creatures stirred. Even the dull drumming sound had disappeared; she'd thought it was another one of those T-rex-like monsters out hunting. But why had it stopped?

Had it found prey?

Was it trying to find them?

Or was it looking for its dead comrades?

As long as it wasn't at the castle when they returned, she'd take it as a win.

The more they ran, the clearer it became that Kieran was struggling to keep from racing ahead of the others. She could practically hear his impatience with their speed, or lack of it. As for her, well, she still felt great. Like she could go faster, harder, run forever, which went against what she'd been taught to expect. If she'd been in her ghost form, well, she could have moved as fast as the wind. Charlotte was the exception to that rule; her cousin's father had been a shifter. Her speed was from that, not from her phantom blood. Although, as far as Sabrina could tell, Charlotte had never shifted, and didn't have an inner animal. It was a secret; and one that had only come out after Charlotte made the transition.

Kieran came up beside her, matching her speed. "You look like you're barely winded."

"I feel like I could run and run," Sabrina said.

"Interesting." He turned behind him. "Can you guys increase the pace?"

Sky nodded, and Tamsin rolled her eyes, but the two women sped up.

Kieran and Sabrina met the change easily.

What am I?

Did she have shifter blood, like Charlotte?

Sabrina's dad had never said who her mother was—she was dead, as far as Sabrina knew. Maybe one of her grandparents knew, or Uncle Max, but if they had, they'd never said anything when she had been alive.

The closer they got to Braemar Castle, the more her fingers tingled, like she had power there, ready and waiting to be unleashed. But she shouldn't have magic. Phantoms couldn't cast spells or manipulate energy, unless they had some telekinesis in their ghost form.

But she couldn't deny what she felt.

What kind of magic, though?

What if it were nothing but parlor tricks? What if it were something deadly?

"Do you feel safe if we run ahead?" Kieran asked the other two women.

Tamsin slowed to a walk, panting, cheeks red. Then she bent over at the waist. "Go ahead. I can ward us with magic if I have to."

Sky slowed to a stop. "I can keep going."

"I have a bad feeling," Kieran said. "With the noises we heard earlier, we should have come across more of the creatures. But we've been running an hour and nothing."

An hour? Had it been that long?

She wasn't even close to being tired.

Sky crossed her arms over her chest. "I can—"

"You won't be able to keep up, and I can only carry one of you," Kieran said.

"I don't know if I could carry either of you," Sabrina admitted. Sure, she'd dragged the giant head, which was a feat of strength she shouldn't have been able to do, but she didn't know if she could haul an adult around *and* run. Something to try another time, when her family wasn't at risk. "And I might have to turn ghost to keep up with Kieran."

Sky wiped the sweat from her forehead. "Fine. Go. We'll follow."

But the Spirit and Sapphire ambassador didn't look happy.

Splitting up is a bad idea.

Normally, yes. But right now, she had to get back.

Kieran ran a hand over her cheek, and she leaned into the touch, craving it. Craving *him*. "You ready?"

She nodded.

He ran.

Holy fuck.

He was *fast.*

She sprinted to catch up to him, and for the first time, she felt like she was working hard. Her breath began to saw in and out of her chest as her legs and arms pumped, and she couldn't keep pace. He dropped back, matching her. He grinned then, his expression open. Joyous almost.

Her heart fluttered.

This was the true Kieran—wild, unfettered.

Free.

She loved it.

She loved *him.*

They crested the final rise before Braemar Castle and stopped. It seemed to glow in the darkness, a welcoming sight...but ahead of them, a horde of twenty or so velociraptor critters loitered in the paddocks. They turned almost as one, before releasing a shrieking chitter.

The creatures ran.

Toward the castle.

Then they vanished.

"Why were they visible?" Sabrina asked.

Kieran shook his head. "I have no idea. Maybe they only use it when hunting or fleeing?"

Kieran and Sabrina followed, and as they approached, she detected the scent of smoke in the night air. Burning.

Up close now, she could see that the welcoming glow on the horizon was fire. The northern tower was aflame, screams echoing from within.

"Shit."

Fear for her relatives left a hard lump in her throat. Sure, the phantoms weren't going to die, but burning to death until their ghost form took over was going to hurt like hell. But that wasn't her main concern—kids lived in the castle, as did their mortal relatives. Not as many as at Balmoral, but enough. If one of them got eaten by one of those creatures or burned alive, there wasn't any coming back.

She hoped their other home and the town weren't also under attack.

More shouts and screams made her heart pound in her chest. As they reached the curtain wall, they spotted Feyre standing in the doorway to the castle. She was flanked by Uncle Max and Charlotte, her hands spread in front of her as she manipulated air, using it to create gusts of wind in the courtyard. Dull thuds indicated something hitting the curtain wall, but she didn't see any bodies. Somewhere Feyre's siren lover screamed, and a horrible popping sound rent the air. Moments later, a handful of the velociraptor bodies turned visible in front of them, slumped near the wall, heads cracked open like rotten melons.

Sabrina retched.

So, they lose their invisibility when they die.

Magic tugged within her, but she didn't know what to do, how to use it.

"Goddamn it," Kieran muttered, rubbing his ear. "That's the third fucking time today."

Concern for him flooded her, just as he stumbled back. Blood bloomed on his leg, wetting his jeans. He cursed and swiped out with the machete, earning a dying shriek from another creature. This one, when it materialized, was different. It was larger than the velociraptor-sized creatures and looked like an angler fish that had somehow evolved legs. Kieran had sliced through its lantern, severing it, before taking off half its head.

She was going to have nightmares from this. For the rest of her life.

"Where the fuck have you been?" Feyre shouted at Kieran.

He glared back. "I was busy killing monsters in the forest."

"Would have been better if you killed them here." Feyre swept the courtyard again, but there were no more thuds.

"Where's Ysabeau?" Kieran asked.

Lady Oleander, stepping from the shadows, jerked her head. "Inside."

Uncle Max's face was ashen, his gaze locked on Sabrina's. "Sabrina? Lass?" He took a step forward, but Charlotte held out a hand, holding him back.

"It can't be her," her cousin said.

Sabina shook her head, her hair wild around her, a ruby nimbus. "It's me."

"You're dead," Charlotte said. "We buried you ourselves." She looked at Max. "Maybe it's one of the monsters. A shapeshifter."

"Oh, I died all right," Sabrina agreed. Then she reached out, taking Kieran's hand in hers. "It just didn't stick."

CHAPTER 44

KIERAN

The air smelled of burning flesh, decomposing sea creatures, and death.

It left Kieran feeling a little queasy, but he ignored the sensation.

Instead, he focused on Sabrina's fingers intertwined with his. It did things to his insides, things he would normally hate, but here, with her, he welcomed them. Reveled in the sensation of being whole, complete.

He hadn't even realized he'd been broken before. Feral, yes; untrusting, also yes. But not broken.

There was so much he wanted to explore with her, but first, they had a castle full of monsters to vanquish. *That is not a phrase I ever thought I'd need to say.* He usually *was* one of the monsters, not a hero come to rescue the innocent.

And the quickest way to do that was to find Ysabeau. Fast.

A cracking sound accompanied something heavy smashing into the curtain wall. He spun on his heel.

There. An invisible monster was trying to break into the castle grounds—you couldn't see the beast, but the dust plume from the impact, and the resulting fissures in the curtain wall were plain. Rather than go over the wall, it was trying to go through it, which meant it probably wasn't quite as tall as the monster that they had killed at the loch.

"We need to be able to see these things," Kieran said softly.

"No shit," Oleander snarled. Her green-tinted skin was flushed, and she looked tired.

No wonder, he thought. She'd been bursting open monster's heads with her siren's call—that amount of magic use would probably knock her on her ass for the next week.

"Tamsin said they're out of phase, does that mean anything to you?" Sabrina asked them.

Both the fae and the siren frowned.

"I've heard the term before, but I don't really know what it means. Something about other dimensions?" Feyre said.

"They cannae be in another dimension," the elder phantom—Max?—said. "Because they can attack us and we can smell them and hear them. They're in this world. They're part of it. They're just invisible.

"Their skin—and eyes—are either refracting or bending light. For all we know, it could do that for most electromagnetic wavelengths, including microwave and radio waves, but we know it cannae do it for soundwaves. So, there's limits."

They all stared at Max like he was talking a foreign language.

"In Plain English, please," Oleander growled.

Max shrugged. "I was a physics professor before magic changed the Earth. Try shining UV light on them and see if that changes anything."

UV light. Electromagnetic waves.

Ysabeau.

Her eyesight was extremely powerful, and Kieran had long suspected it was more acute than a normal vampire's. *Could she see them?*

She hadn't come out on patrol when he had gone with Clint earlier in the week, but she had never mentioned seeing anything around the castle, either. And these creatures had clearly been sneaking in and out while they had been there—and who knew for how long prior.

It was worth finding her to test their theory—if she hadn't already discovered the answer herself, that is.

"I have some UV lamps stored down in the cellar," Max said.

"You do?" Sabrina asked, eyebrows raised. "Why?"

"They're good for detecting things like blood, and I store them for the kids who like to keep reptiles as pets. They may work."

"Why would you need to check for blood?" Feyre asked.

Her uncle didn't answer.

"Uncle Max is in charge of security for the family," Sabrina replied. To Kieran, she said, *"I still don't trust the Air and Amethyst ambassadors, but they took the front door of the castle, and defended it against intruders."*

So that meant they were owed some truth?

Kieran strode forward, boots slipping slightly in the green blood splattered over the courtyard. At least it didn't float here; that seemed to be restricted to the loch. The smell of their blood didn't appeal to him, didn't smell like food, which was weird, because pretty much every creature he'd ever encountered did.

What the hell even are these things?

Another scream, this one full of terror, high-pitched and scratchy. A darkened figure leapt from the window of one of the castle's towers, their body backlit by surrounding flames. They hit the ground with a sickening thud.

Everyone stared.

Get up, get up.

But the figure didn't move, didn't morph into a phantom form.

They were dead.

Please don't be Ysabeau.

His uncle would eviscerate him if his second-in-command died here. But she was an old vampire, and if that had been her, she should have survived, even if she broke every bone in her body.

Sabrina ran past him and into the castle, turning into her phantom form as she slid past her uncle, Charlotte, Feyre and Oleander. Her clothes dropped to the ground.

"Sabrina!" Max shouted.

She flicked a glance back. "You get your lamps, I'm going in."

Kieran followed his mate.

Running headlong into danger. If she wasn't a phantom, I'd want to reevaluate her sense of self-preservation.

I wonder if she's always been this way?

He kept up with her as she darted down hallways. She was careful to stick to a path he could follow—no misting through walls or doors, for instance—and it made something in his chest ache. Even worried for her family, she thought of him, of what he needed.

Suddenly, she stopped, expression tense.

"I think I'm standing in one of them," Sabrina said, eyes scrunched up.

He stared at her insubstantial legs, but he couldn't see any hint she had stepped through a critter. "Steel doesn't hurt phantoms, right?" Kieran asked, twisting the machete in his hand.

"Not to my knowledge."

He slashed out with the dull blade, meeting resistance as it passed through Sabrina's legs. For a moment he panicked, and tried to pull the machete back, thinking he'd hurt her.

But she moved away, unharmed and unfazed.

A form slipped into view. Another creature. It twitched as it died from his blow, but he cut down again, severing what he thought was the head. This one—he didn't even know where to begin to describe what it looked like. Ugly. Warped. Fishlike.

"What did it feel like?" he asked.

"Getting attacked by a machete?"

He glared at her.

She grinned. "Like nothing. But when I passed through the creature, it felt like when I accidentally mist through a person. Uncomfortable. Itchy."

Kieran turned back, thinking he should tell Max and Charlotte this latest intel. But they were already behind him, a lamp in Charlotte's hand. And they weren't naked, so they hadn't taken on phantom form.

He blinked. "That was fast."

Max shrugged. "We know a few shortcuts."

"Secret tunnels, I bet it's secret tunnels," Kieran muttered.

"No comment," said Charlotte, awkwardly holding what appeared to be a heat lamp.

They were wasting time. "Your invisible forms, they can detect them," Kieran said. "At least, Sabrina's can. And the creatures don't seem to see your spirit forms, so they don't actively try to avoid them."

Charlotte didn't budge. "I'm not willing to give up my weapons; they don't come with me when I transform. Plus, the lamp might come in handy."

Kieran nodded. He wouldn't give up his only advantage, either. "You can work as a team. Max can sense them, you can kill."

Charlotte nodded. "I like that idea."

He had a feeling she would.

"We need to find Grandpa," Sabrina began.

"We need to save the mortal family members," Max said simultaneously.

Kieran twisted the machete handle in his hand. "You go do that; we will find Angus."

And Ysabeau.

Hopefully they were together.

"Go to the 'throne' room," Max said, making air quotes with his fingers. Which was kind of weird when you could see straight through the guy. "He'll be there."

Sabrina nodded. "Keep safe."

Then she sped away.

"Kick some monster ass!" Charlotte yelled, holding the lamp up high.

"Oh," Kieran said with a grin. "We will."

Then he followed his mate to whatever fresh new hell awaited them.

CHAPTER 45

SABRINA

S abrina made it to the throne room in record time. Kieran was close behind her; he had killed another half a dozen or so creatures on the way. He'd traded his machete for one of the long swords that had been used to decorate the walls of the castle. It had a sharper edge than the gardening equipment, he said, after all the work he'd put it to.

How many of these things were *there?*

Too many.

That was about the only answer she had, and probably the only one she needed right now.

Sabrina misted through the double doors into the large room, unable to wait a second longer. Kieran kicked the doors in after her, the wooden panels fracturing around the lock and slamming into the plaster walls behind.

There, in the middle of the room, a group huddled together, weapons at the ready. Around them were decapitated bodies and loose heads, the gore soaking into the once mahogany-colored carpet. In the middle of the group, the human doctor huddled, bent over a prone form.

Ysabeau stood behind him, her dark sunglasses perched on the top of her head as she surveyed the room.

"Angus, ten o'clock!" The vampire's voice was sharp, direct.

Sabrina's grandfather darted forward with a dagger, grunting when it contacted an unseen foe. The fae Portal Watchman to his left also slashed out, this time with a sword that glinted gunmetal gray.

Sabrina ignored the screams of the dying invader and scanned the room, her eyes falling on two prone figures near the back. They were human. Unmoving. She moved forward slightly, trying to see their faces. Biting the inside of her cheek, she held back a scream of anger.

Dead.

They were dead.

Two youngsters—they had been but children when she'd left five years ago.

Aunt Connie, Granny Kim, Grandpa Angus, and the two Portal Watchmen tightened their circle around the doctor and Ysabeau.

"Guard A, to your right!" the vampire shouted.

The Fire and Fluorite Portal Watchmen twirled his sword with smooth efficiency, making short work of the enemy. The creature flashed into view, and for a moment, it appeared to stand still, before half of its head slid sideways to the floor. It landed with a sickening plop.

Not helping my future nightmares.

But that monster...it had appeared less like a mish-mashed animal, and more human-shaped. Still not anywhere near homo sapiens, but closer.

"If the phantoms shift into their ghost forms, they can feel the intruders. Then you can kill them!" Kieran shouted.

Instantly, Aunt Connie shifted, as did her grandmother.

They moved through the room, in their ghost forms, shouting as they cleared sections. But there were no more creatures.

Colin swept into the room, shouting about intruders on their lands. *A little late to the party.* She knew the moment Colin spotted her…or, *should* have spotted her. His gaze swept right past her, like she wasn't there.

What?

"You can see me, right?" Sabrina asked Kieran, worried that she'd somehow slipped into the nether again.

"Yes. Clear as day."

That didn't make her feel better—he'd always been able to see her, anyway.

As she prepared to shift back to her human body, time seemed to slow.

Sabrina turned to the door, tingles down her back making her feel uneasy. From the corner of her eye, she saw Ysabeau's pale eyes widen, as she too stared at the broken doorway. Someone—some*thing*—had arrived. This creature, it was different; it had to be, for Elias' second to react in such a way.

For her own ghost form to tingle almost in pain.

"To your left, Kieran!" Ysabeau called.

Sabrina's mate swept forward with the sword, the weapon an extension of his arm, smooth and sure and deadly. He was magnificent to watch. Never had she thought the delivery of death would be sexy, but it was. *He* was.

But the blow didn't land. It was the first time he had failed to make contact. Kieran spun, smooth as silk, blade singing through the air as he cut and slashed. But again there was no impact. No green blood.

He hissed, the sound low and pained.

Sabrina's heart pounded.

A slash appeared in his jeans, blood welling on his thigh. Then another, this one on his cheek. Kieran couldn't land a blow on the monster, but it was hurting him.

Kieran was injured.

Her mate was in pain.

Rage burst to life inside her.

In that moment, it didn't matter that she hadn't accepted the bond yet, because her instincts were screaming he was *hers*. No one else would ever come close to what he meant to her. What he was.

Mine.

He's mine.

These *things*...they had come to *her* loch and attacked her and her mate. They had hurt Clint. Killed Sammy. They had assaulted her family. Her home. She had seen someone jump out of a window to escape. There were two dead family members on the ground in this very room.

And now one of them was making her mate bleed. Was *hurting* him.

It was too much.

Somebody has to pay.

She surged forward, arms stretched out, trying to mist through the beast.

"Five o'clock, Kieran!" Ysabeau continued to shout directions.

Sabrina also struck, her form moving faster than Kieran's.

"Ten o'clock!"

A shudder rippled through her body as her arms touched *something*. It wasn't like the others; they had been uncomfortable to contact. This, this was painful. Like bamboo under her fingernails. But she grabbed it with phantom hands, and the creature flickered into sight.

"Who?" A telepathic voice bore into her mind, sending shards of torment along the connection. Not as bad as with the giant monster by the lake, but still no fun.

The others swore.

Sabrina opened eyes she hadn't realized she'd closed.

It *almost* looked human.

Oh, it would never be able to pass as one, but it had all the right components: head, two legs, two arms, a torso. And it had the right proportions, if you ignored the fact it was almost seven feet tall.

That was where the similarities ended. Its face was reptilian, with no nose, just two slits for nostrils. Its lips were thin slashes of skin, exposing razor-sharp teeth. It didn't have hair, but there were tendrils of *something* erupting from its head where hair would generally be. It was wiry, muscular, and had daggers for claws.

It stared at her.

She finally met its gaze—it was unnerving, alien.

Its eyes had horizontally slit pupils, and it didn't blink, as if it could burrow into her mind with a look.

And that's what it's trying to do.

The telepathic link it had initiated with her—it was still there.

Sabrina shifted into her human form, dimly hearing gasps from behind her. She stepped back, breaking contact. "Leave here," Sabrina ground out.

Its head tilted to one side in a jarring movement. *"No. We claim this place."* The words were accented, but it didn't sound like any she had heard spoken on Earth. The shrill roars and shrieks that had accompanied the lake monster were absent, but there was a strange hissing in the back of her mind.

"Correction," she replied. "This is my home. I claim it. You don't come from here."

That reptilian gaze assessed her. This time, it spoke out loud; "This is new home. We take."

The tingling in her fingers—which had started back at the loch—turned into a burning sensation now. She wiggled them, trying to ease the discomfort.

"Sabrina, step away from it," Kieran ordered. He was a solid presence at her side, but she didn't look away, couldn't break this creature's almost hypnotic stare.

Without thinking, she slammed her hands up to either side of its head. The moment their skin touched, their minds linked properly. Shock made the creature lash out with its claws, slicing deep grooves in the flesh of her stomach.

It *hurt*, but the pain was a welcome sensation, grounding her, helping her keep her mind separate, from being absorbed into the creature's.

Kieran shouted, raising his sword, readying to strike.

"Stop," she said telepathically. Even though her mind was linked to the creature's, she could still communicate with Kieran. It was a different pathway, she realized. A unique one, just for them.

He paused.

"I will end this," she promised.

And the wound? It didn't matter. She'd die, but she would just come back.

She ignored the pain, ignored the blood.

Sabrina hammered on the creature's mind. It had strong shields which blocked her from accessing more than the surface level of its thoughts, and she needed to get through them. It attempted to do the same to her, but she was stronger; the power of the node and her rebirth burning through her veins.

"Stop, dead thing." There was fear in its voice.

She smashed through its shields, breaking past the natural protection.

There.

Its mind—no, *his* mind—shone like a magic node on a dark psychic field. It was connected to a series of other minds, each represented as a smaller node, all tied together by telepathic ley lines. The network appeared like a green-tinted web in her imagination, punctuated by glowing gemlike dots.

This creature had hundreds of telepathic connections, although many were severed, the cut ley lines floating, untethered.

They are the ones we killed, Sabrina realized. As she stared at the telepathic field, she understood what these creatures were.

A hive. A network of minds, all joined together, each group tied to an anchor, or...*a node.* It then joined onto another, and another.

The male in front of her, he wasn't the equivalent of a queen in a beehive or an ant colony. She could sense there was one, but they were far away, protected from her reach by distance—and possibly a portal.

No, he thought of himself as a lord; high ranking, and in control of a small army of drones, but only in charge of one group of the creatures, not all. No, that was for the queen or queens.

Whoever—or whatever—she was or they were.

"If you promise to leave," she said through gritted teeth, "I'll let you all go. You can return to wherever you came from."

She didn't mean it. At least, she didn't think she did.

"Was told magic was ours. We take. You go."

"Who told you?"

Silence.

She tried to search its mind, but the thoughts were so utterly alien it would take too long to find the truth. All she was able to find was an image of the sea.

Not helpful. Not when most of the creatures had clearly come from the ocean.

"Who told you?" she shouted.

"An ally from this world."

So, they were from a portal. They had to be. But which one?

"Last chance to leave," she warned.

"We learn how to kill dead thing. Then we eat. And we take magic."

This being feared her, but it also thought it was stronger, more powerful. It clawed at her again, and Sabrina half-shifted, so that only her hands and head were flesh. The pain that had been holding her to the world lifted, releasing her.

The power of their minds pressed in, and the creature sensed her wavering.

"You can do it," Kieran's voice in her mind. His belief in her, even though he had no idea what she was doing, poured through their bond. *"You came back from death. You can do anything."*

Hell yeah, she could.

She beat death.

Kicked it in its fucking face, and stomped on it while it was down.

These creatures didn't stand a chance.

Riding the high of her inner pep talk, Sabrina used the open telepathic connection to seize the other minds in the creature's network. The magic that burned at her fingertips punched into him, flooding through him and out onto the ley lines, turning the greenish fibers a brilliant diamond-white.

He screamed, the sound piercing her eardrums until blood trickled down her earlobes.

She kept going, shoving whatever this magic was she now possessed through their connection, into his mind, and then into the network of drones. Shrieks and pained chitters reached her, flooding back through the telepathic link.

And then she *pulled.*

She needed these creatures gone, to a place where they couldn't harm anyone. Where they couldn't touch the magic, and where they couldn't turn her family into food.

Pressure built along the network, tried to pull her with it.

I need more power.

With the thought, magic surged into her, the node answering her call.

With one final shove, she grabbed hold of every alien mind she could. The web's filaments seared with dazzling magic, diamond-white and burning.

She turned completely ghost, dragging them with her.

The head under her fingertips vanished.

And so did she.

CHAPTER 46

KIERAN

K ieran's heart sank down, down through his body, right into the bedrock underneath the castle. Sabrina had vanished. Since the first time since he'd spotted her in this very room, he wasn't able to see her. Sense her. Hear her.

You lost her. You had her, and you fucking lost her.

No, he'd *trusted* her. When she'd said she had it under control, he'd believed her. Because she'd already defied the odds and come back from the dead. Her dealing with these monsters, he'd believed her when she'd said she could do it.

Because there was no future for them if he couldn't trust her, if he undermined her abilities. She was a phantom, and he had no idea what they were truly capable of. He hadn't wanted to stifle her. True mates supported one another, they didn't cut each other down. He'd seen that firsthand with Elias, who had taken his mate into an uneven battle, trusting in her ability to stay alive.

If she's truly dead…

He couldn't even go there. Wouldn't.

"What the fuck happened?"

"What the hell was that?"

"Is it dead?"

The questions were fired from all directions around him, but Kieran remained focused on the place where Sabrina had been hovering in her ghost form mere seconds before. He should have done something more. Grabbed her. Killed the thing before it had done whatever it had to her.

You fucking useless asshole. She's gone.

No.

She couldn't be.

She said she couldn't goddamn die.

His free hand formed into a fist, fingernails biting into the flesh of his palm. The sensation barely registered. He had vowed to never be weak again—not after he'd been kidnapped and held hostage as a youth. He'd gotten free and murdered his father as thanks.

But right now, right this minute, he had never been weaker.

There was nothing he could do to save her this time, no way to bring her back.

And he hated it. Hated himself.

"What the hell happened?" That was from Ysabeau.

Kieran turned to the vampire, then looked back at the scene, registering what the others had seen. The creature had collapsed to the ground, its body limp in death.

"Did you see her?" he asked, voice flat, disconnected.

"The redhead?" Ysabeau frowned. "She appeared briefly, then vanished. Meanwhile, you stood there doing nothing, while it stared off into the distance, talking." Her tone was chastising, and he knew she was going to rip him a new one for not decapitating the creature when he'd the chance. But she'd wait till he was alone. She didn't like airing the House's dirty laundry in public.

You just equated yourself to soiled undergarments.

Yeah, well, he was going to call himself a lot worse than that if his mate didn't return.

Her expression changed, as she considered what she'd seen. "Or were you waiting for the redhead to do something?"

He scowled back. "It's dead, isn't it?"

Ysabeau did not look impressed. Her sunglasses were still perched atop her head, and he didn't think he'd ever seen her without them for so long.

"Can you see any more creatures?" Kieran asked.

She shook her head. "No."

Kieran stepped closer to the corpse, going down on one knee next to it. He poked at the creature with a finger. Definitely dead. And really fucking ugly.

But where was Sabrina?

Magic had burned through his mate, just before she'd vanished. He had felt it through their bond: the power racing through her, some of it siphoning off to him, accelerating his heart, making his head spin. And she'd been doing something with it—what, he'd had no idea.

What if she isn't really gone?

And how, exactly, had she managed to kill the creature just by touching it?

He reached for their mental bond. There. It wasn't severed—the connection still existed, which meant she was alive, and she hadn't rejected him. She just wasn't *here*.

He tugged, impatient, relieved, too many emotions to even order them. *She isn't dead.*

"*Come back!*"

Silence.

Heart in his throat, he waited, ignoring the chaos, the voices around him.

Flickers of tumultuous emotion reached him: weariness, pride, and relief. It was followed by an answering yank on the bond.

Then she appeared.

Not in the flesh, but in a ghost form. Back to wearing that damned bloodstained sweater and jeans.

No.

She said she couldn't die—

And then she was there, warm, solid, alive, pressed against his chest, arms wrapping around his shoulders to hug him as he kneeled by the dead creature.

"You came back," he said softly, face pressed against her hair. The scent of frost and honeysuckle soothed him, cracked open more of his frozen heart.

Her voice was breathy. "I came back."

His hands cupped her face, thumbs caressing her cheekbones. "You promised you wouldn't die again."

"I don't remember actually promising that. But I didn't die."

"Does anyone care to explain what the fuck just happened?" The chief, Angus, demanded. He strode forward and stumbled upon sighting Sabrina.

Who was naked, Kieran realized. He shucked off his jacket and shirt, handing them to her. She dressed quickly, his T-shirt going down to mid-thigh, before pulling on his jacket. She stood, and he followed suit.

"*Sabrina?*" her grandfather asked, voice edged with shock.

The asshole who murdered her, meanwhile, was staring at Sabrina like he'd seen a ghost.

You're so fucking funny.

Yeah, he wasn't going to win any awards with his comedy. But that didn't matter. Because his mate was alive and well, and most importantly, within arm's reach.

"What happened?" Kieran asked Sabrina. She leaned back against his chest, facing her family.

"Who the fuck are ye?" The chief—Angus—demanded. "Why do ye look like *her*?"

Sabrina straightened, pulling away. She tilted her chin up, challenging. "I'm your granddaughter."

The phantom's fingers tightened on the knife in his hand. "She's dead, buried in our graveyard. Try again."

Kieran ran a hand over his hair and shrugged. "So, uh, if you went to her grave right now, you'd find a nice big hole with an empty coffin in it."

Ysabeau's glare cut into him.

Yeah, he had a lot of explaining to do.

"What?" The chief's jaw went slack, and he looked around at his family, like they might have the answers. Kim—giver of cake—just solidified, as naked as Sabrina had been earlier.

The blue-eyed bastard, Colin, looked uneasy. And he'd maintained his phantom form. *Can't think why*, Kieran thought.

"In case it wasn't clear, I dug her body up from her grave." Kieran wrapped an arm around the front of Sabrina's shoulders, pulled her against his chest.

"Quite clearly, my death didn't take," Sabrina chimed in.

Her big moment, and she was being sassy. He loved it.

Kim moved forward, her steps faltering. She stopped in front of Sabrina, eyes roving over her face, as if she were trying to compare remembered features with reality. "What is yer father's name, lass?"

Sabrina sighed. "*They really don't believe me.*"

"*They will,*" Kieran assured her.

"Douglas Fhearchair," she replied.

"And yer mother's?" Kim continued.

"I don't know. Dad never told me."

"When is yer birthday?"

"July, two months before the Great Sacrifice."

"What was Sabrina's favorite color." This was from her aunt, Connie.

"Celadon."

Kieran had never even heard the word before, let alone known it was a color.

The blood drained from Kim's and her aunt's faces. Their skeptical glares fell away and their eyes filled with unshed tears.

"Ye cannae be—" Angus blustered.

Sabrina ignored him, attention focused on her other grandparent's. "Your name is Kim Badelt, you're my great-great-grandmother, I think. I might have missed a couple greats. You aren't married to Grandpa Angus, even though you give the impression you are to outsiders. You are not *his* grandmother, instead, you come from the other side of the family. You're some kind of fourth cousin to him. You're in charge of the domestic running of the castle, and you were born in the nineteenth century."

"Who was the first of our kind?" The new voice emerged from the doorway. Kieran turned to see Max and Charlotte, both in their corporeal forms, and dressed, thankfully.

Sabrina didn't turn to look back at her uncle. "I was always led to believe it was Great-grandpa Fergus, but I don't know for sure."

Kieran had never met a Fergus since he'd arrived. Had never even heard mention of someone of that name.

"He wears the purple suit," Sabrina said. *"Always in phantom form."*

Right. The eye-watering, obscenity-shouting ghost.

"Ye are some kind of shifter—" Angus began.

Ysabeau, clearly bored with the interrogation, said, "Shifters change into animals. I haven't heard of one that takes on another human's form."

The chief threw his arms up. "Then *how?*"

"Well, when I was murdered," she shot a look at Colin, "I reached for the magic under the city. It wasn't enough to transform me completely, so I turned into a ghost. I've been here ever since. Watching you all."

Colin's transparent face somehow managed to grow paler.

"We never saw ye. Phantoms can see each other—"

"You didn't see her before, when she attacked the creature." Kieran jabbed at the corpse with a boot.

"There was no one there—"

"I did see a flash of red—"

"I thought I saw *something*—"

"Exactly," Kieran said. "You didn't see her in her ghost form. Just her physical."

"But *you* can."

It was like bashing his head against a brick wall. "Clearly."

Ysabeau mouthed something at him. He thought it was 'be polite', or 'bees pollinate', he couldn't be sure. Then she scowled at the phantoms. "He's half-death fae. They can see ghosts."

"You can see—" Charlotte began.

"Ghosts. All ghosts. I can see them."

Colin rematerialized, also buck naked. Great. Now he was going to have to wash his eyes out with bleach. He so didn't need to see his mate's murderer's flaccid cock. "But you cannae see us when we turn into our phantom form."

Kieran raised an eyebrow. "Can't I?"

"Oh, that reminds me, I almost forgot." Sabrina clicked her fingers…

…and the room filled with ghosts.

What. The. Hell.

CHAPTER 47

SABRINA

Sabrina felt Kieran's shock, even though his facial expression remained unchanged. The only physical clue were his eyes—they swept the room as he took in the newly arrived ghosts.

"How?" he turned to her, admiration clear in his voice. Nobody else reacted.

"What is going on?" Grandpa Angus demanded.

His reaction to her return wasn't what she'd expected. Sure, Sabrina had assumed he might be skeptical that she was who she said she was, but the outright rejection had hurt. *He needs to protect the clan. He's just being cautious.*

Still, it didn't change how it had made her feel.

Unwanted. Spurned. Outcast.

She'd had enough of being on the outside—she wanted to be part of her family again. To be acknowledged by them, loved.

"She turned them into ghosts," Kieran said, slowly, as if talking to a child.

Her grandfather clearly didn't appreciate the tone, but he was distracted by the statement. "Turned what into ghosts? Where?"

"The creatures." She tossed her loose hair over a shoulder. Then waved a hand around the room, indicating the corpses littering the floor. "I brought them into the spirit realm."

She hadn't meant to disappear when she'd done it. But then, she hadn't really understood what she was doing at the time. She'd mainly relied on instinct and the urges of the magic coursing through her.

When she'd felt Kieran tugging on the bond between them, she realized she'd gone deep into the ether. It had been nothing but darkness and light; heat and cold; life and death. It was a dichotomy, but it worked. It was something primeval, and a place she probably should have never visited. She'd dragged the monsters' souls there with her.

She'd had to work her way back, but she'd done it. Drawn to Kieran's mind like the moon to the earth.

If I hadn't had that...

She might have been stuck there with the creatures forever.

Sabrina shuddered at the thought.

It didn't matter, because she had returned, and having done that, she knew how to bring them back with her. The ether...it wasn't a place for souls to stay. It would have been cruel to leave them there.

And I may be a murderer, but I am not without compassion.

A murderer. The word sat uneasy on her, but it was true. These beings had been sentient, if alien.

But they had come to her home and killed her family. And she'd known, after touching their minds, that they were not going to retreat, to return through the portal into their world. They had been promised a golden land full of magic—magic they needed to survive.

She'd had two choices: leave them be and risk losing everything, or kill them.

For her, it had been the lesser of two evils.

Because they were just the advance guard. More had been ready to come. Hopefully this would dissuade the next wave from finding their way through a portal to Earth.

Although I have no idea what to do with them now.

The room was packed, so full of ghosts they spilled out into the hallways and filled the adjacent rooms.

"I dinnae believe you." Colin's jaw clenched. "I dinnae see any ghosts."

She looked at him. He was taller than her, stockier, but even though they shared the same aquamarine eyes, the same nose, she hated everything about him. Wanted to carve his heart out and feed it to Krakenessie. Their similarities only made her loathe him more.

She buffed her fingernails. "Because I have no reason to lie. Unlike you, Cousin."

He glared.

Kieran stepped up next to her, the sword's hilt turning in his hands. "Can I kill him? Just a little?"

"Kieran!" Ysabeau growled. "Remember why we're here. You're an ambassador."

"And he's a gaping asshole, but you don't see me telling him off for it."

The vampire ran a hand over her face, then pulled her sunglasses down. Her voice was low, but Sabrina still heard her mutter, "I told Elias this was a bad idea."

So. They couldn't see the creatures, but she could, and Kieran could. It had to be something to do with her magic, why she was invisible to the other phantoms even though she could see them. She bit her lip and frowned. *Make them seen,* she thought, and drew on the residue of magic within her.

Gasps rippled through the room.

"How on Earth—"

"Ghosts. They're all ghosts..."

Grandpa Angus turned to her. "*Ye* did this?"

"Yes."

His eyebrows were almost touching his hairline. "*All* of this?"

"Yes." She saw the moment he realized that she was more powerful than him. That she had access to magic beyond their ken. And that it made him uncomfortable.

It made them all uncomfortable.

There's nothing you can do. I can't be killed now.

But she could be exiled.

Hopefully it doesn't come to that. He just needs time to adjust.

The human doctor cleared his throat. She had all but forgotten he was even in the room. "The girl—she'll live."

At the doctor's feet lay a child with hair almost as red as Sabrina's, cropped short. She lay on her side, curled in the fetal position, and her face...it was a combination of Charlotte's and Sabrina's own.

The world spun, and Sabrina stumbled forward. "Who—?"

Charlotte rushed past them, gathering the girl in her arms. Her cousin kneeled on the ground next to the doctor, the two Portal Watchmen on either side. They looked tired and pissed. "She's our sister."

Sabrina froze. "*What?*"

Aunt Connie placed a hesitant hand on Sabrina's arm. "Yer father—he and Charlotte's mother celebrated Beltane a bit too much five years ago. Ainsley was the result."

Sabrina staggered backward, until she came up against Kieran's chest. His presence, it stabilized her. His touch anchored her.

She had a *sister?*

She'd been here for a year, and no one had mentioned Douglas' second daughter. They barely even mentioned her father's name at all.

How could I have been back a year and not known?

Because you spent most of your time stalking Colin.

Four years old. She was only four years old.

Sabrina wanted to go over there, to hold her sister. But Charlotte's body language indicated that would not be a welcome move.

I'm a stranger to her.

If Ainsley woke up and Sabrina was there…she might panic, wondering who she was. It hurt, knowing she could be of no comfort to the child, but one day she would be. She'd ensure it.

"Your dad slept with his cousin?" Kieran's voice broke through her thoughts. "I mean, I know most of you are related, but that's not good for long-term genetic health."

"Charlotte's mom isn't actually blood related to Douglas," Grandpa Angus snapped. "But the kids all call each other cousins."

"Right. That's—"

Granny Kim leaned forward, the usually benevolent-acting grandmother flashing with irritation. "It happens. Beltane is a time for celebration."

Kieran shrugged. "I was going to say that's not the weirdest pairing I've ever heard about." His gaze flicked to Ysabeau. The vampire ignored him.

There was a story there, one she might care to ask about later.

But right now, she had a *sister*.

Her father hadn't been able to tell her, because she'd gone off the grid. She hadn't even left a cell number. *I shouldn't have gone 'no contact'.*

"I cannae see any of our mortal people among the ghosts," Granny Kim said softly.

Sabrina sighed, pressing back against Kieran. He wrapped an arm around her chest, pinning her to him. "In all the time I was here, I've never met another ghost. I was alone. So, if they didn't make the transition…"

Charlotte's voice was sad as she stroked a hand over her sister's—no, *their* sister's forehead. The girl didn't stir. "Then they're gone. Forever."

Silence.

"Can you make them go away?" Colin snapped, breaking the quiet. He was swiping at the air; ghosts had surrounded him, pushing at him, biting.

Sabrina flicked her fingers, and they vanished.

Nice, that was totally going to be her new party trick. At least until she worked out what to do with them.

"Are they gone?" Grandpa Angus demanded.

"No, you just can't see them now."

Tamsin and Sky burst into the room, gasping for air, Feyre and Oleander right on their heels. Tamsin's dress was torn and muddy, and Sky's pink hair was wild about her head. The fae and siren didn't look much better.

The witch skidded to a halt and stared. "What's with all the ghosts?"

CHAPTER 48

KIERAN

Tamsin stepped through a small magic-created portal, her expression grim in the weak morning light. "He's dead."

Kieran growled low in his throat. Damnit. He'd actually kind of liked Clint. And the shifter had helped Sabrina, taking on a giant monster with nothing but teeth and claws. It was a blow, hearing the news.

He didn't take it lightly.

I should have done more.

Maybe moving him to the grove had done irreparable damage.

But shifters can heal from extensive injuries. He'd seen it firsthand. Although, he'd also seen when the damage was too much.

The witch met their gazes. "Come. See for yourself."

He turned back to Sabrina, who nodded. She leaned against a stone wall, her uncle Max next to her, like she didn't have a care in the world and could wait all day. Inside…inside she was a seething mass of anxiety. His mate still had to deal with her traitor cousin and the family that enabled him.

Kieran, Sky and Ysabeau made their way from the castle's front doors to Tamsin's portal in the courtyard; it was aimed at the grove near the loch, the waving willow branches visible on the other side. It hadn't required a flesh sacrifice, since she'd already been there, but she'd had to use another angel feather to power it. He shuddered a little at the memory of the last portal he'd seen opened. Eyeballs. It had required eyeballs.

Kieran could have run to check on the shifter, rather than use precious magical resources, but they'd wanted to get Clint back to the castle without any extra damage, and as quickly as possible.

A portal had been the best way.

Kieran was last across, the magic almost biting in its intensity as he stepped through the magical doorway. There. Clint lay in human form—not jaguar—on the forest floor, surrounded by eerily glowing red and purple mushrooms.

Those hadn't been there earlier.

Sky strode toward the shifter, her expression grim, sad. She carefully kneeled next to him, avoiding the fluorescent fungi. Bright colors in the natural world often meant poison—she was smart to stay away from them.

Then she turned to face them. "His throat—"

"Has been slit," Tamsin finished.

Kieran stared, taking in the details. The prone form, the dark red blood on the shifter's hands—different to the green of the creature's—and the slice at his throat.

The mushrooms…

Kieran studied the pattern of their growth. They seemed to have rooted where an arterial spray would have arced.

He let out a low whistle.

Clint's blood must have seeded them.

He crouched down, holding a hand above one of the numerous polka dot-patterned fungi. If blood was involved in their creation, he would be able to tell. Using his magic, he gently touching the curved top. It glowed even brighter in response, and his finger burned.

Yes, they were blood-born, he could sense it.

And toxic as hell.

He wiped his finger on the grass, which had lost its preternatural glow from the night prior.

This place is still creepy as fuck.

Trust his mate to have been brought back to life here.

"Kieran—" Ysabeau began.

He held up his hands. *Pretend I didn't touch the plague-inducing mushroom.* "What?"

The vampire turned her sunglasses-covered gaze toward him. He could *feel* the condemnation in her stare. "I can smell you were here. And your...friend."

"What? It wasn't me. I didn't do this." He jabbed a finger toward Clint's body. "I put him here so he could heal. I gave him my *blood.* I did *not* slit his godsdamned throat."

Sure, he had a reputation, but he had owed the shifter a debt.

He didn't repay kindness with death.

To be fair, he repaid a lot of things with death, but not kindness.

"Sabrina and I were here before that. Ask Tamsin." He jutted his chin in the witch's direction.

Tamsin nodded. "They were."

Elias' second didn't look convinced.

"Can you scent anything else?" Kieran demanded.

Ysabeau's mouth pinched. "Do you need me to say that you had sex here?"

"No," he slashed a hand through the air. "I already know that part. Anything—any *one*—else."

She sniffed the air again and frowned.

Sky stood, playing with a dagger. He got the feeling she did that whenever she was unsettled or nervous. "I need to get Clint home. And I need to speak to my superiors."

The Spirit and Sapphire ambassador moved away, to give Kieran and Ysabeau room to grab the body and avoid the mushrooms. Sure, he'd touched one briefly, but he didn't think it would be a smart idea for anyone else to. He would be immune to the effects, courtesy of his blood magic.

He hoped.

Kieran picked up Clint's legs, and Ysabeau his shoulders. Her nostrils flared as her head neared his wound. "Do you smell it?" she asked quietly—too quietly for anyone but him to hear.

He inhaled deeply.

He blinked at the vampire in surprise.

Someone had been very bad.

Kieran was going to love punishing them.

CHAPTER 49

SABRINA

S abrina grinned wickedly as the door swung shut behind Kieran. He had just stepped out of the bathroom, and he wore nothing but water droplets and a white towel. *Fuck.* Her gaze trailed over his broad shoulders, lingering on his chest, before coming to rest on his defined six pack, and that delicious trail of hair that swept down to the edge of the towel. She bit her lip.

She should have joined him in the shower, finished off what they'd started back before she had a body. Too bad she'd only just snuck into his room.

His gray stare turned smokey. "Hey, my eyes are up here."

"But all the interesting things are hidden under the towel."

"*All* the interesting things?"

She flushed. "Well, at least two things…"

He gave a small chuckle and walked to the suitcase next to his bed. "You're a temptress, but we have to—"

Taking advantage of his proximity, Sabrina launched herself at him, knocking her fae onto the mattress. She wasn't sure who was more surprised she'd succeeded: Kieran or her.

Not wanting to waste her achievement, Sabrina quickly straddled him, laying her palms on his chest to pin him in place. He could have freed himself, she knew that; instead, he lay sprawled beneath her, the towel still unfortunately secured around his waist. But the rest of him, the rest of him was on display. All smooth skin and sexy muscles and sinful eyes.

Mine. He's all mine.

His hair was a dark halo around his head; he was a devious angel come to steal her soul. Or save it, in this case. She wriggled her hips as she leaned forward, and his cock grew hard, pushing against that damned towel, rubbing her right where she needed it.

She ran her tongue over her lower lip. Then she offered a wrist. "Drink."

His breath hitched, and strong hands clamped on her hips, pressing her down. "I'm not sure we have time for this."

"*Drink.*" It was a demand.

Gaze locked on hers, he gently took hold of her forearm, keeping her wrist in front of his mouth. His breath fanned the delicate skin there, and she shivered. His gray eyes turned molten, and he licked her, the sensation shooting pleasure straight to her core.

Damn. She wanted to give him everything she could, *feel* everything she could...

He bit, slowly, sensually, the pain fading almost instantly. The first draw of her blood; it had her melting, her body tightening, growing slick with need.

She'd thought he was at her mercy, that she could do anything she wanted to him—

But she was at his.

I need this.

Wanted it; wanted *him* so badly. This was their treat, their reward for having both survived. For having won.

Losing Clint and her family members...

Don't think about it. Focus on Kieran. Only him.

The suction ceased, taking the feeling of ecstasy with it.

Sabrina let out a whimper of protest. No, she didn't want it to stop—

He released her wrist and sat up in one smooth movement until their faces were level. His voice was rough. "You're sad."

"My family—"

"Don't deserve you," Kieran growled.

"Some of them do, but I'm thinking about the ones that died. And Clint. Knowing we couldn't save them."

His expression softened, and she had the feeling she was the only one who saw him like this. Kind, caring. He gently touched her cheek, and she pressed against his hand, taking what he offered, wanting more. Wanting everything.

She grabbed his free hand and pressed a kiss into his palm. "Kieran, I—"

The door shuddered as someone knocked.

They broke apart, like teens who'd been caught by an angry parent. Her cheeks flushed, Sabrina straightened her clothes as Kieran rapidly dressed. By the time he answered the door, her wrist had already healed.

She hadn't even needed to shift.

Someone cleared their throat and she looked up. It was her grandfather, who smiled as he stepped into the room. "It's hard to believe yer back, lass. We missed ye."

Funny how they never spoke of her, though, even though everyone had missed her *terribly*.

Don't be cynical.

Kieran stepped back into the room, standing between her and Grandpa Angus, who closed the door to the room with careful deliberation. In the quiet of the room, the click of the latch catching sounded like a gun shot.

"Trust me," Sabrina said with a smile, trying to ease the strange tension. "I know."

"A year. Ye were here a whole year, and we had no idea." He shook his head sadly.

"It felt like forever."

"I bet it did." He flicked a glance at Kieran. "Were ye able to hear and see us, even though we couldnae see or hear ye?"

She nodded. "Yes. But no one mentioned Ainsley was Dad's daughter. I had no idea I had a sister."

Her grandfather had the grace to look sheepish. "Ack, well, it wasnae something Charlotte's mother wanted bandied about."

"If they're not related, then what was there to keep quiet about?" Kieran asked.

Grandpa Angus glared at Kieran. "I'm here to talk to my granddaughter."

Who simply shrugged. "I'm not stopping you."

"Maybe it would be better if we spoke alone." Anger sparked in her grandfather's eyes. Gone was the jovial semi-retired-gentleman persona he'd presented when the ambassadors had first arrived. Here was the hardened chief she had been waiting for. He'd never appreciated a smart mouth.

Except for hers. He'd always had a soft spot for her 'sassiness'.

"Watch how you speak, vampire scum."

Sabrina spun. Colin stood behind her, blocking the bathroom door. Kieran and Sabrina were between him and her grandfather. Pinned.

He wasn't naked, she realized after a moment, which was odd. How had he gotten in without them seeing him? And when did he have time to get dressed? His fingers were clenched around the hilt of a sword. She'd never seen it before.

Kieran didn't seem fazed by the new arrival. "I am the King of Blood and Beryl's nephew. I'm a Master vampire in my own right. I've killed more people than you've probably ever met. I murdered my own father. You think I give two shits about what you want?"

He'd killed that many?

Sabrina figured he'd have a past...but maybe not one that dark.

He's in Blood and Beryl. And King Elias doesn't have a reputation for nothing.

Silly of her to have thought Kieran was different, just because of how he acted with her. It didn't change anything, though. She still wanted him, darkness and all.

Grandpa Angus' mouth tightened.

"Master vampire?" Colin scoffed. "Rumor has it you're nothing but the bastard of a death fae."

"I can't be both?" Kieran's eyebrows rose.

She fought a smirk.

Rage blanketed Colin's expression and he lunged forward, aiming for Sabrina's heart with his new sword. It wouldn't kill her, but it would *hurt*. Without thinking, she morphed into her ghost form, his arm simply sliding through her.

Kieran grunted.

Sabrina spun and gasped.

The blade was embedded in Kieran's chest.

"No!" Sabrina shouted.

But her death fae simply pulled it out, spinning the hilt in his palm as he took a step closer to Colin. Blood poured from the cut, but he didn't seem to notice, intent on getting to her cousin.

A heartbeat later, Grandpa Angus grabbed Kieran from behind, tackling him to the floor. The sword clattered to the ground and Colin lunged, picking it up and raising it high above his head.

Sabrina stepped between them. "Stop!"

But he didn't.

He swung down, aiming for Kieran's neck, the sword going straight through her.

She was still in her ghost form.

Her mate rolled, dodging the attack. The weapon thunked into the floorboards, chipping the timber near his cheek.

No.

They were trying to sever his head.

Her magic welled at her fingers, and she grabbed Colin's arm with one hand, shoving her power into him. But nothing happened. He merely flickered into his ghost form and back, so fast his clothing didn't have time to drop.

Grandpa Angus wrestled with Kieran on the floor, grunting as the vampire slammed the phantom's head into the solid bed frame.

The next part happened fast, too fast for her to react.

Colin slashed again, slicing along the back of Kieran's neck. Blood poured from the wound.

He collapsed.

She didn't watch his head come off. Couldn't.

No.

No.

No.

Rage ignited in Sabrina, her fury so raw she couldn't see past it. It overwhelmed everything. She couldn't think; couldn't hear. She shifted back to her corporeal form.

They wanted to take everything from her. Tried to kill her again. Had killed her mate.

She leapt on Colin's back, her body shoving him off balance. He slammed into the wall, and Sabrina clawed at his face, his neck. Anywhere she could reach.

"You fucking murderous pig!" Her fingers snagged on the amulet's chain.

"Why wouldnae you stay dead, you stupid bitch!" Colin roared, shoving her off him.

Sabrina dropped, the amulet's chain snapping with the force of her movement. She landed awkwardly, her hip slamming into the side of the Edwardian chair. She hit the ground hard, coming up on her hands and knees straight after. Anger poured through her with each beat of her heart, and her magic flared out.

The prongs of the amulet gouged her palm, the metal biting deep. She turned her hand over, noticing four deep cuts. It *hurt*. Like, a lot. More than she would have thought, for the wounds it had inflicted.

Her rage thinned.

We need the amulets to make our transition.

"I already killed you once," Colin sneered, standing over her.

Somehow, the metal acts like a conduit for the node.

He shook his head, like she was a half-wit. "And yet, you come back, asking for more."

Then the node does the rest.

"You should have run. Gone far." He held up the sword. "This blade has the blood of a god forged inside it. *This* blade will kill anything, *including you.*"

So that was his plan.

All his research had finally given him an answer…

But if you didn't have an amulet…if you didn't have a conduit…

She reached out, connecting to the node as if it had been waiting for her. Magic flooded her, making her skin shiver, her hair stand on end.

Colin rammed the sword through her chest.

The pain, it was staggering. The sword's blade burned in her flesh, but she stepped closer. And closer still. The blade slid further and further into her body, emerging out her back. The agony was nothing compared to what she'd already been through. What she'd already lost.

Kieran…

Colin frowned. "What are you doing? Why aren't you dead?"

She was close enough to touch him now.

"You always underestimated me, Colin. Didn't you?" She turned his amulet around in her palm, keeping her hand close to her side, so he couldn't see. She imbued her magic into the metal, the power glowing like chips of diamond in her mind.

"Just fucking die!" He twisted the blade.

Sabrina punched her arm out, misting her hand through his chest, reforming it once it was within his rib cage.

Once it was in his heart.

She then rotated her hand, using the claws of the amulet to slice the traitorous organ. To shred it.

He screamed, high pitched, desperate. His free hand scrabbled at her arm, but it barely registered. Colin's form flickered as he tried to shift, but he couldn't. His amulet didn't respond to his magic; she'd blocked his connection to it. Coated it in *her* power.

She ghosted her hand to his spine, using the amulet to slice through bone and severing his spinal cord.

He collapsed.

She pulled her hand from his torso, wincing as he hit the ground hard. Paralyzed. Heart shredded.

But still not dead.

Just incapacitated.

She pulled the sword out of her chest, the pain so intense she thought she might black out. When it reached its peak, she felt her form slip, her body disintegrate. The sword clattered to the floor next to Colin.

Sabrina died.

But only for a moment.

She reformed her flesh, power coursing through her now-healed body.

She squatted next to Colin's prone form and stabbed the amulet into his throat. His mouth opened, and his blue eyes bulged, but no sound emerged. The amulet cut through his skin and muscle like it was butter. But it wasn't long enough to go all the way through.

"Stop!" Her grandfather screamed, rushing at her.

The rapid sound of three gunshots filled the room.

Her grandfather froze, staring down in disbelief at the bullet holes in his chest. Sabrina turned to the door where Sky stood, gun held steady in two hands, her amber eyes wide.

A dark blur burst into the room and leaped on the phantom chief. Barely a heartbeat passed before Ysabeau kneeled on Angus' back, grinding his face against the floor. His wrists were bound in what appeared to be iron shackles.

His form turned semi-transparent, and fear made Sabrina stab down faster, cutting over and over again into Colin's neck with the amulet. Blood sprayed up, splashing her in the face, stinging her eyes. And the squelching, tearing sound…it made her gag. But she kept going, eyes darting between the tussle next to her and her gory task. When she reached his spine…the bone only put up a token resistance.

Her grandfather's form faded before turning back to flesh.

"What the fuck did ye do to me!" Angus shouted.

Ysabeau slammed his head onto the floor again with each word. "Trapped you."

Sabrina shoved down hard and jerked her arm back.

Colin's head rolled loose.

She slumped to the floor, staring in disbelief. Her bloodied hands clasped the amulet, hiding it behind her fingers.

Had it worked?

Was he really, truly dead?

She raised her eyes, tears blurring her vision as she picked up the sword Colin had used to hurt her.

To kill Kieran.

She stood, towering over her grandfather.

"Beware smiling men who knock on your door."

Her fingers tightened on the sword's hilt. "Ysabeau, you're in my way."

CHAPTER 50

KIERAN

F ucking hell.

Kieran wasn't dead. Although he had damned near lost his head. And he had the headache to end all headaches, proving the body part was still attached. Surreptitiously, he rubbed the back of his neck, feeling a raised and puckered wound stretching from one trapezius muscle to the next. That was fast healing, even for a Master vampire.

Now. Where the fuck am I?

He opened his eyes. Ceiling above. Bed left, wall right. Okay, he was on the floor, crammed in the space between the wall and bed. His face was sticky. He touched it. Blood.

Phantom blood, his magic said.

Great. So one of the assholes had bled all over him as well.

Embarrassing.

That's what it was.

Fucking embarrassing.

Almost dying because he got sliced up by some stupid sword. It wasn't fair that his opponents could dematerialize limbs and torsos. They cheated. He was going to have to practice. And get some magical instruments that could cut through phantom as well as living flesh.

Like a sword imbued with a god's blood.

There was a reason those kinds of weapons were few and far between. Because they caused nothing but problems.

And near decapitations.

He rolled onto his side, facing the room. Sabrina stood a few feet away, splattered in dark blood, her hands drenched in it, so she looked like she was wearing crimson gloves. Her hair was a wild corona around her head, and she was glaring at someone he couldn't see, one hand holding the stupid sword.

She'd never looked sexier.

Kieran pulled himself to his knees, wobbling a little as his body continued to heal the damage caused by the sword. *Poison.* It had to have an effect like poison, since he still felt sluggish. He half-crawled to the end of the bed frame.

Which god did they take the blood from?

Wait.

You idiot.

It was a god's *blood.*

He frowned.

Turning his magic inward, he focused on his own blood, on the poison attacking it. Surprise knocked him into the bed frame. *Not poison.* Transformation. The magic that had seeped from the blood blade was being consumed by his power, changed.

He was absorbing it.

Really could do with knowing what god it was…

"I'm not going to let you kill him," Ysabeau said, cool and calm as ever.

"I have no problem with you. Step. Aside." The last two words were a growl from his mate. Sabrina raised the sword.

Like Sabrina was going to be able to do anything with the weapon other than piss Ysabeau off. *Although the god's blood…*

"She's not going to move unless you move her," Kieran muttered.

Sabrina froze, her muscles locking up, her aquamarine eyes going wide. She shook her head, her hair flaring as she did. Through their connection, he heard, *"No, no, I'm just imagining it."*

"I don't think your imagination could do me justice," he replied with an inner leer.

Sabrina spun, the sword clattering to the ground as she raised bloodstained hands to her mouth. "You're…you're alive?"

"Yeah. Score one for me." He pumped a lazy fist into the air.

She leaped across the distance, wrapping her arms around his injured neck.

"Oof."

She pulled back; her expression serious. "Did I hurt you?"

"A little, but I can take it."

She laughed, surprised. Delighted. Relieved. Joyous.

He could feel it all.

"I need to stand up," Kieran said quietly. Sabrina nodded, and subtly helped him upright. They came around the edge of the bed, and he finally saw what the timber frame had been blocking from view.

Carnage.

Absolute carnage.

He looked at Sabrina, then back at Colin's body. Then back at Sabrina. Then at Ysabeau and the trapped Angus. The clan chief's face was a strange purple color that could not have been a good indicator for long-term health. He also had an epic lump on his forehead.

Kieran looked back at his mate before he nudged the headless corpse with a booted toe.

Sabrina had done it. At least, he thought she'd done it. "What the fuck did you do? Cut his head off with a damned spoon?"

A muffled snort came from the doorway. When he looked up, Sky was rubbing her face in a suspicious manner.

Sabrina bent down and picked up the sword in answer.

"Nope, I don't buy it. That was not done by a sword," he said into her mind. He'd done his fair share of beheadings. They didn't look like...this...when you used a sharp and *long* blade.

Colin's neck was like shredded meat.

Sabrina's expression turned grim. *"I...I don't want to talk about it."*

Her words were like a blow, worse than the beating he'd just humiliatingly suffered. She didn't trust him.

She grabbed his arm and met his stare, her blue eyes intense. "Later. I'll be ready to talk later."

He nodded and held out a hand, and she passed the sword to him, reluctantly.

The blade was mostly steel, but the dark color meant there were either impurities in the metal, or it was an alloy with something else. The hilt was leather-wrapped, and on the edge of the blade was a Latin inscription: *in morte veritas est.*

In death there is truth.

Time to put your skills to use.

He gave her back the sword. He didn't need it.

"Trust me," he said to her.

Kieran closed the distance to Angus, pausing to grab a dagger from his bags. He dropped to his knees next to the clan chief.

"Kieran," Ysabeau warned.

"I'm not going to kill him." He shrugged, ignoring the discomfort from the movement.

Ysabeau let go of Angus' hair, which she'd been apparently using as a grip for when she smacked the man's face into the floor.

Kieran ran the blade over the phantom's cheek. A line of blood beaded, and Kieran dipped his finger in it.

Angus hissed in response.

Kieran held up his hand, as if he was studying the blood. The light caught on it, making the liquid appear a purple-tinged crimson.

"It's interesting, don't you think?" Kieran asked, tone musing.

When no one replied, he whacked Angus on the head with the dagger's hilt.

The phantom got the message. "Is what 'interesting'?"

"I'm half-death fae and half-vampire. So, I have blood magic." He concentrated, and the blood on his finger rose, forming a tiny sphere that rotated above his finger. "And yet, no one ever really wonders what I can do with it."

"Parlor tricks," Agnus scoffed.

"Great. Here we go," Ysabeau muttered.

"I'm right here," Kieran said to Elias' second. He shook his head. Hard to come off as scary and menacing when someone was undermining you right in the middle of it all. "Anyway, as I was trying to say, I can boil the blood in your veins. And since you can't die…I guess I could just…keep doing it."

The purple-cheeked rage was beginning to fade from Angus' face.

"Ye wouldnae dare."

"See, that's where you're wrong. I would dare."

"This is my land, and that is my granddaughter—"

Kieran waved the dagger with his free hand. "Funny how you give a shit about Sabrina now, when before you were trying to kill her."

"She's an abomination—"

Kieran slammed Angus' head into the floor, and then stabbed him in the shoulder, his movements so fast Ysabeau couldn't stop him.

"Kieran—" The other vampire looked pissed.

"What? I didn't kill him."

"Oh, so that's the line, is it? No death." Ysabeau's eyebrows lowered into a partial frown. "This man is still the ruler of the phantoms."

"Yes. The line is 'no death'. And I don't think he's going to be ruling anything other than a cell for a long time."

"Why ye—"

Kieran popped the blood bubble with his magic.

Agnus screamed, his body arching as the blood boiled in his veins. Literally.

"Stop!" Sabrina yelled, grabbing Kieran's arm. "Stop!"

"Okay."

He stopped.

Angus went boneless.

Sabrina bit her lip. "Is he—?"

"No. He's a phantom. Since he can't shift fully with the cuffs on, it will take him a bit longer to recover as he partially shifts."

Sabrina stared at him.

"You were going to kill him before," Kieran pointed out.

She huffed. "I thought he'd murdered you."

That was the nicest thing anyone had ever said to him. "Thank you."

She gave him a small smile.

"Crazy. You're both fucking crazy." Ysabeau shook her head.

"Sky, can you shut the door and guard it, please?" Kieran asked.

The Spirit and Sapphire ambassador looked like she wanted to argue, but nodded, and stepped out the room. "You owe me."

Sabrina nodded. "We do."

The door shut behind her with a firm click.

"I don't want to watch him torture you—"

"Torture me?" Angus growled.

"But I will if you don't answer this. Why were you about to let Colin kill me?"

Blood is truth. And blood doesn't lie.

His uncle and stepfather had rare gifts when it came to reading blood and the truth. He hadn't inherited it, since he wasn't of their line. But his mother had, because she had been turned by a Laskaris. And he'd been in her womb shortly after.

He just assumed it had skipped him, because of the circumstances of his conception.

The sword's magic...
In death there is truth.
Like calls to like, wasn't that the saying?

He cut Angus' face again, pulling the blood from the wound with his power. It rose, shaped like a cobra in a striking pose.

Angus was technically dead. And phantom blood...it was reanimated using the node's magic. Kieran had some of Sabrina's blood in him. Right now, *he* was part-phantom, too. Sort of.

Kieran sent his magic into the blood he had pulled from the cut, and then shoved the snake-like stream back into the wound.

"How long have you known Colin was murdering your family members?" Kieran asked, hoping—praying—that this would work.

Where there is will, there is power.
And where there is death, there's truth.

"Since the beginning." Angus' mouth opened and closed after he spoke, shock and fury warring over his face as he was compelled. "I knew he killed Bertha, Bernard and Stewart; and that he pinned it on that witch. He even had her enchant us to overlook his misdeeds. But it didnae take on me."

"You *knew*?" Sabrina cursed. "Wait—"

"Of course, I bloody knew." The clan chief spat out a globule of bloodstained saliva. "Ye watched us for a year and ye didnae ken that I knew?"

"What about Penny and Peter?"

Agnus frowned. "They were accidents."

Sabrina shook her head. "No, they weren't."

Angus swore.

Kieran tapped the dagger against his knee; he didn't really care about the list of dead family members. They were dead. "Why did you get him to kill Clint?"

Ysabeau jerked ever-so-slightly.

"I didnae tell him to kill him exactly. But we wanted to cause distrust between the Houses. Buy ourselves more time. Yer scent was all over the glade. Even Colin could smell it. When he found the injured shifter, it was too good an opportunity to waste."

"Clint's body plus Kieran's scent…"

"Blood and Beryl would get the blame." Angus' body faded and reformed. "We hadn't counted on the creatures. Or Sabrina."

That brought Kieran to his next question. "When did you tell him to kill Sabrina?"

She spun to face him. "What—?"

"When they received the message saying she wanted to come home." He looked at his granddaughter then, with something almost like sadness. "Ye weren't meant to make the transition."

Her voice was a wail. "But—why? You gave me the amulet."

"Because of ye mother."

"But I don't know who she was!"

"*What* was she?" Kieran asked, pushing his magic into the healing wound.

"A goddess. She was a goddess. She was Douglas' mate, but she didnae want him, not to keep. Enough to bed him for a time, though." The words were bitter, formed from an old anger. An old hate.

"Why not kill her as a child then?"

"We dinnae kill bairns." Truth.

It surprised him.

"When Sabrina left, it made it easy for us. We thought she'd die out there in the world, without the protection of a House. Then we wouldn't have to worry about her transitioning."

"What is so wrong with me becoming a phantom like you?" Sabrina demanded. She hurt, oh, how she was hurt by this rejection. Kieran felt it in his very bones.

Angus sighed, the sound deep and wary, like it came from the soul. "Colin is dead. Truly dead. By your very hand. Do you know how many of us have died before today?"

Her answer was quick. "None."

"Exactly."

"I don't understand." Sabrina shook her head.

Her grandfather closed his eyes, defeat descending over his expression like a weary mask. "Ye will be the destruction of us all."

CHAPTER 51

SABRINA

Y e *will be the destruction of us all.*

The words haunted Sabrina.

Her grandfather had been sent via portal to King Elias at Blood and Beryl's headquarters back in America. Ysabeau had accompanied Angus, and Kieran said she'd told him they needed to have a 'chat' later. He said it was going to be way worse than it sounded.

Sabrina turned at the sound of gravel crunching under foot. Granny Kim and Aunt Connie stood on the other side of a large boulder on the cobble-strewn sand, peering back at her, uncertain. Shoulders squared; Sabrina's grand-mother stepped past the rock, coming to stop just before Sabrina. "We've just waved off Feyre and Lady Price."

"We passed Max on his way out with Sky," Aunt Connie added. "He said she had a message for ye."

"Did he say what?"

They shook their heads.

"He's not thrilled to be the interim chief," Sabrina said, sensing they were waiting for her to say *something*.

Her aunt snorted. "Well, he's better than Angus."

"Connie!"

"What?" Connie shrugged. "Angus always thought he knew best. I dinnae know how many suggestions I made to help our clan and he rejected every single one. And then there's all the stuff about Colin—"

"Colin. That disgusting waste of space," Granny Kim said, cutting her off. She looked over at Sabrina. "Had ye not—" her voice broke slightly, and she cleared her throat, "had ye not survived all this, we'd have never known. Sammy. Everyone. This was their fault. I'm so sorry this happened to ye."

Their words soothed something jagged and broken inside her. She wasn't sure it would ever heal, but this…it helped. She bit the inside of her cheek. "Can I ask you something?"

Connie nodded.

"I never saw you mourn me. Any of you. You didn't talk about me. Did you even care I was dead?" The words were out before she could stop them; and they came from the lonely broken girl she'd been.

Aunt Connie's stern features softened. "Lass, I always missed ye."

"*We* missed ye," Granny Kim interjected.

"Emotions can be silent. Just because I didnae say it, it doesn't mean I didnae *feel* it. Ye were the talk of the clan when ye left. And yer dad, well, he couldnae stop braggin' about how ye were going to be an artist. The kids—Sammy included—had all their requests ready for ye when ye came home. And when ye didnae…"

"I didnae know how many times I said I wished we'd let ye re-paint that damned Green Room when ye'd asked,"

Granny Kim said, rubbing her forearms. "I think I even said it last week."

"You did?" *Maybe I missed more than I realized. I was so focused on Colin.*

Connie nodded. "She did."

"With Sammy—" Sabrina began.

"We're going to do right by him. Not how Angus buried ye. He will be remembered, and he'll get more than a tombstone with a one-line mention on it. We have to do right by family, I think we've all learned that."

Sabrina let out a long breath. "*If* our family stays together. Uncle Max said we need to discuss joining a House."

Granny Kim sighed. "That's the big question, isn't it? It used to be 'can we die?', but ye've got that one figured out. We'll figure this one out, too."

Sabrina winced.

"I didnae mean it that way. Yes, it probably scares a few of them. They'll get over it. A good reminder of our mortality, right? That cannae be a bad thing."

The sound of someone awkwardly clearing their throat had the three women glancing toward the tree line. Kieran stood there, leaning against a thick trunk, hands in his pockets, looking far too sexy for his own good.

Or for her good.

Aunt Connie and Granny Kim gave her quick, firm hugs, before they hustled back toward the castle. On her way past him, Kim muttered something about Kieran looking starved.

"So, talking about joining a House finally?" Kieran asked as he closed the distance between them.

"Yeah. Wasn't that the whole point of the welcome talks?" The talks that had gone so far off track they'd landed at the bottom of the Grand Canyon.

Instead of saving the clan, they had ended up burying far too many of their own—their mortal kin. And now, well, now they knew phantoms could die. Proper dead. Not just phantom dead. They weren't the 'true' immortals they'd thought themselves to be.

As for Colin—the snake—they'd burned his body on a pyre the evening before. She'd wanted to feed him to Krakenessie, but that had been vetoed by Uncle Max.

"They missed me," Sabrina said quietly.

Kieran's arms wrapped around her middle, reassuring her, comforting her just the way she needed. It was going to take some getting used to, their bond, but she didn't regret it. Didn't regret him at all.

She stood near the edge of the loch, staring at the black water, and placed both hands on Kieran's forearms as they rested on her belly. This should have been a gory place, but she felt a strange kind of peace here; the rocks and leaf litter no longer acted like gravity was meaningless, and the loch had returned largely to normal.

The bodies of the creatures had vanished—and not through an act of camouflage. No, there were slithery tracks all over the loch's banks that attested to something dragging the bodies into the water.

Aunt Connie and Granny Kim had been very careful *not* to look at those.

"Even if they're happy I'm alive, I think they're afraid of me," Sabrina said softly.

"Fear isn't rational most of the time." He tightened his hold. "But in this case, it's a good thing. They *should* fear you."

"But I don't want them to." It was stupid, the complaint of a little girl, not a woman who had defeated death twice, and who had the blood of an unknown goddess running through her veins.

He shrugged. "People fear me. They fear Elias."

"But he's the King of Blood Rage. Son of the Slayer of Alexandria."

"And I'm the Slayer's Shadow."

She hadn't heard that term before. "Why 'shadow'?"

"When I was young, I attached myself to Elias and followed him everywhere. They nicknamed me his shadow. Then I became his information procurement specialist." She cocked a single eyebrow at him. "Okay, fine. I became a torturer. That's when they added the slayer part."

"Does it bother you?"

He rested his chin on her head. "The title or that I tortured people?"

"Both."

"No."

Did it bother *her*, that he had killed and maimed people? The answer was also easy: no.

He had a past. And she had a present.

Neither of their hands were clean.

Had Grandpa realized what Colin was going to do with that sword once he killed me? Colin had wanted to murder his way to the top of the family and control them through fear. He wouldn't have blinked at killing his only ally, or anyone else in his path. But she didn't want the clan to be afraid of her, and she hadn't told anyone—not even

Kieran yet—how she had managed to decapitate Colin and prevent him from reforming whole. Her entire race depended on her keeping it secret. And she would. She wasn't about to destroy her own people, no matter what her grandfather said.

And one day…one day she'd tell Kieran.

"Should we be standing this close to the shore?" Kieran asked, interrupting her thoughts.

Sabrina shrugged. "Krakenessie seems to like me."

As if in answer, a giant aubergine-colored tentacle broke from the surface of the lake, before slamming down near its edge. Cold water sprayed them both, and the resulting wave drenched their shoes.

"I don't know if that was a hello, or a fuck you," Kieran muttered, lifting one hand from her waist so he could wipe his face.

Something blue fluttered on the shore near their feet; a piece of fabric had floated in with the wave. Sabrina bent to pick it up, examined it, and asked, "Who do you think told the creatures to come here?"

Kieran stepped back and shook water off his boots. "It could have been anyone."

Sabrina held up the material, showing him what she'd seen.

It was torn, ragged, but there, in the middle, was a crest. Kieran swore.

Her hand closed around the fabric, crushing it.

She wasn't going to be the destruction of her people.

No.

She was going to be their savior.

CHAPTER 52

KIERAN

K ieran hung up the call, then placed his cell on the charging stone. He turned to look at Sabrina, who was so damned beautiful it hurt. She was dressed in a pair of leggings and a long-sleeved green dress, and he'd never seen anything so simple look so stunning.

He nodded. "They're coming."

His phantom nibbled on her lush lower lip, her eyes distant as she thought about something.

He tried reaching through their bond to gauge her emotions, but they were faint, bare echoes of what she must have been feeling. Was she blocking him? Was she even able to?

"When do you think they'll be here?" she finally asked.

"Three hours."

"That soon?"

"That soon."

They were in Kieran's new room. He'd been moved to Balmoral Castle—Sabrina's family had taken over its care after the Great Sacrifice, apparently. It had once belonged to England's monarchy, but they had disappeared, along with the concept of independent countries. Now England was in No Man's Land.

"How come your family hosted us at Braemar rather than here?" Kieran asked. It was a more architecturally elegant building, with turret towers, smooth gray stone, and a scattering of aesthetically pleasing climbing vines.

"Braemar is the traditional seat of the Baron of Inver-cauld and Omnalprie. It's where Grandpa grew up. And he knew it like the back of his hand."

"The secret passages."

She nodded.

It's how Colin had apparently managed to get into Kieran's room without being detected—or having to shift to his phantom form and lose his weapons in the process.

Braemar was certainly more defensible: the curtain wall, the yett, and minimal windows made it harder to attack, unless you were an invisible creature from another portal. But the original builders could have never predicted that enemy. Balmoral Castle was more like a giant manor house, designed for leisure and fun, rather than safety and security. And it was where the main part of the family lived now Braemar was at capacity.

After Max had relocated both Kieran and Sabrina—he'd given his niece her own room—he'd told Kieran to avoid getting blood on the carpet and departed in a huff. The man did not like his new position of power, that much was clear. Apparently, they were having trouble cleaning Colin's, uh, remnants, from Kieran's old room.

Kieran *could* have gotten rid of the blood for him, but he hadn't wanted to. No, he'd wanted them to remember that they *could* die. That they were not 'true immortals' as they had believed.

He wanted the phantoms to be afraid. To understand their life depended on Sabrina's kindness.

Nothing more.

And certainly nothing less.

His new room was bigger than the one he'd first had, but it was scantly furnished, giving it an unfinished feel. Like him and Sabrina.

The bed is right there…

"Do you think Grandpa Angus will forgive me?"

Well, that certainly put a damper on his wayward thoughts. "What's there to forgive?"

"He's currently rotting in the bottom of a Blood and Beryl dungeon."

He wasn't the only one—

"He's lucky that's all he's doing," Kieran muttered.

"Do you think they're torturing him?"

"Well, considering I'm here right now, probably not." Then again, Adora was at the Blood and Beryl main house so she didn't have to, quote, 'listen to them fuck all the time'; she may have decided to keep herself busy.

His response didn't appear to reassure her. "Uncle Max wants me to lead the clan. A lot of them do."

"You're a demigoddess, and you know how to kill a phantom. You're the *only* one who knows how to kill one of your kind."

"I was never meant to be chief," Sabrina shook her head, her eyes serious; sad, almost. "I wasn't meant to be a laird."

He shrugged. "So just be you."

She frowned. "What if it isn't enough?"

He stepped forward, closing the distance between them. "It will be."

CHAPTER 53

SABRINA

Sabrina thought there'd be more…ceremony.

They'd convened in one of Balmoral Castle's large sitting rooms, the couches shoved to the edges of the space, leaving an open area in the center. Sabrina stood in front of the empty fireplace, Kieran on her right-hand side, and Uncle Max on her left. She wore a dress crafted from flowing silks that varied in hue from pale cerulean blue to fog white. It draped above her knees at the front and cascaded to the ground at the back. It had a tight bodice, but it was cold—the fireplace was largely ornamental—so she had shucked on a leather jacket, donated by Charlotte.

The outfit didn't really go together, but she had decided not to care. It's not like she had access to her old clothes, and she hadn't really wanted to wear anyone else's.

Kieran was dressed in his classic ensemble of black jeans, black T-shirt, and leather jacket. When she'd asked if he was going to dress up for the event, he'd told her he already had. These were his *slightly blacker* jeans, his T-shirt was new, and he'd wiped the blood from his jacket.

Uncle Max, meanwhile, was wearing a gray business suit. He *did* look like a college professor in it, complete with red sweater vest underneath, which she found amusing. Great-grandpa Fergus had also made an appearance, before misting out the room. She wasn't sure if the House leaders would be able to see him, but they'd soon find out if he reappeared.

A large white trestle table had been erected in front of windows that looked out over manicured lawns. A computer tablet was set up at one end and a large amethyst stone was in the middle, with vacant space at the other end.

In the middle of the room lay a long box covered by a thin white sheet. Tamsin had placed a stasis spell over it. There was also a smaller wooden box they had placed in the corner of the room, out of sight.

King Elias arrived first with his queen, Dannika Kresley.

Elias clapped Kieran on the shoulder and nodded a greeting, before walking to the table and placing a deep blue sapphire skull at the free end: a communication crystal. He then took up position on the opposite side of the room. The Master vampire was darkly handsome, while the female shifter had silvery white hair and piercing blue eyes. She was beautiful, the kind of stunning that had Sabrina's artistic instincts screaming for a paintbrush and a canvas.

They were followed by Councilor Hekate, the leader of the House of Earth and Emerald, who wore a green gown that hugged her body like a second skin, with a long split down the side. When the witch's white gaze met Sabrina's, her eyebrows lifted slightly, as if in surprise. She greeted them with a nod, before going to stand with the Blood and Beryl monarchs.

Sabrina's fingers burned—but not with magic this time, no. She desperately wanted to paint her and Dannika together—starlight and darkness.

Another time.

The ruler of the House of Gold and Garnet arrived a bare minute later, King Vesperus entering the room as if he owned it. Another vampire, he, too, was handsome, but his beauty had an edge of cruelty to it. His gaze raked over the room and everyone in it with cool disdain.

Last, but certainly not least, came Empress Asbesta, the ruler of the oceans of the world—and leader of the House of Sea and Serpentine. Her body was draped in a damp blue Grecian-style gown, the silk threaded with strands of silver wire. Her dark hair hung in waves down her back, and her skin was so pale it was almost translucent. Her feet left wet prints on the carpet.

The ocean is fifty miles away.

But the River Dee was basically in their backyard.

She doesn't just rule the oceans, but all the water.

Sabrina swallowed at the realization.

She really didn't have much of a choice but to plow on with her plan.

Hopefully we all survive it.

"Where are the others?" the empress' voice was throaty, her accent unusual.

Sabrina's skin pricked in response. Could her magic be reacting to the empress? Her demi-god blood responding defensively to the presence of a true goddess?

Each of the leaders had a glow to them—Sabrina thought it hinted at their magic. The empress had a sea-green aura that sizzled, while Elias' was black-veined red, and Dannika's was a bright silvery hue.

Uncle Max hurried forward and fiddled with the stones and the device on the table. He was joined a moment later by Tamsin, and together they got the two scrying stones working, as well as the tablet. The rulers from Air and Amethyst appeared like a hologram in the air above the large purple stone. Volker, the king, was next to his new queen, Rowe, whose chaotic red hair framed an achingly pretty face. She looked comfortable in a white T-shirt and brown leather jacket; her style was more like Sabrina's own.

The acting Fire and Fluorite Alpha Supreme appeared on the tablet. He looked uneasy but determined. He was dressed in a business suit, with two large timber wolves lying on the floor behind him. An image of the two leaders of Spirit and Sapphire was projected into the air above the sapphire skull. Odin wore a dark eyepatch over one eye, and a raven perched on his shoulder. Beside him, Lady Gabriella swatted at the bird's beak, as it idly tried to preen her sleek chestnut hair. The archangel had high cheekbones, bronze skin and tilted eyes, reminding Sabrina of east Asia. White wings arched behind the angel.

Sabrina had never imagined she'd have an audience with the seven House leaders. Ever.

"We have been called here for an emergency meeting by Blood and Beryl." King Vesperus' voice was curt. "I'd like to know what this 'emergency' is. I have…House matters to attend to."

Uncle Max straightened near the trestle table. "Thank ye for coming at such short notice."

"You are not the leader I spoke with previously." The Moonlight Wraith narrowed gray eyes at the phantom.

"No," Uncle Max replied, voice calm and almost serene. "That was my father. He is currently sitting in one of Blood and Beryl's dungeons. We have had a...change of leadership recently."

Very recently.

The archangel's feathers rustled, as the other leaders turned to glance sharply at Elias. The vampire king shrugged. "I was just taking out the rubbish for them. A mere offer of help."

"You seem to be doing that a lot lately, Laskaris." The jab came from Odin.

"Come now," Elias said smoothly. "Sometimes the trash takes itself out."

Silence, which seemed to indicate amusement, irritation, and disbelief from the various leaders.

"Why have you called us here, Laskaris?" Councilor Hekate broke the strange quiet. She waved a hand in the air. "This is...unprecedented."

It was.

But then, what Sabrina was about to ask for was even more so.

Elias tapped his fingers against his leg and indicated Sabrina and Kieran. "I believe you will need to ask *them* for that answer."

They all focused on the vampire-fae next to her. On the threat he represented. Not even one of them paid Sabrina any mind. It was infuriating, but also kind of funny.

She'd always been underestimated.

And look what happened to the last person who did that…

Empress Asbesta spoke, "Kieran Aspen. The Slayer's Shadow. You do not bear your father's name."

Kieran shrugged. "I do not claim any male as my father."

"Your sire's remains have sunk to the bottom of the Mariana Trench," the empress said, her eyes cold, flat. "It was an…interesting choice of burial location."

Kieran smirked. "It was more like a dump site. But we aren't here to talk about me. We're here to talk about *that*." He pointed to the sheet-covered box.

Dannika frowned and leaned forward. "It has a strange smell to it."

Sabrina stepped up and tugged the sheet free, exposing the dead creature within. Sabrina and Kieran had debated which invader to pick and had decided on the Lord. He looked even more disturbing in death than he had in life. The body was under a stasis spell, crafted by Tamsin, so it hadn't decayed beyond recognition. It also tempered the odor, which was horrible. Much worse now than when it was alive.

"What the hell is *that*?" King Volker demanded, stepping forward.

"And what is that?" Hekate frowned, indicating the piece of fabric at its feet.

Sabrina dropped the sheet to the ground and ignored her question. "This is one of the creatures that attacked us a few days past. It was the commander of a small army. It, along with its soldiers, could become invisible at will."

"You are talking about camouflage," the Moonlight Wraith said.

"It was more than that. They were truly invisible," Uncle Max said. "They refracted light in such a way that you could not see them at all. Only those with eyesight that could detect UV light could make them out."

Her uncle—along with the human doctor, who had found the creatures fascinating—had been studying the properties of their skin. They had concluded the creatures' invisibility was something that could be controlled at will, hence it failed once they died. They *thought* the magic explosion had interfered with it by the loch, which is why it had failed shortly after Sabrina's rebirth.

"Even if you couldn't see them, surely you could smell them?" The Fire and Fluorite shifter asked.

"You could hear and smell them," Sabrina said. "But they move almost silently. Clint was able to scent them, as was Kieran, but we phantoms don't have the same acuity."

Regret and something like sadness was visible on Lady Gabriella's face at the mention of the shifter.

"What happened to this so-called 'small army'?" King Volker asked.

"I killed some, the phantoms slayed others," Kieran replied. "And the Air and Amethyst ambassadors disposed of as many as they could. Together, we killed about seventy, maybe a hundred individuals."

"That is hardly an 'army'," the archangel said, speaking for the first time.

"I took care of the rest," Sabrina said, voice confident and sure.

It was the first time they focused on her. Truly focused on her. She could see instant dismissal in Empress Asbesta's eyes, as well as skepticism from the Fire and Fluorite alpha, Odin, and the archangel. In contrast, King Vesperus and the Air and Amethyst rulers turned appraising eyes on her. Elias appeared bored, and Dannika couldn't stop looking at the creature in the box.

"And how many would that be?" Hekate asked.

Guilt lanced at her, but she tilted her chin up. "Three hundred or so."

It was technically true, but if the Lord hadn't been telepathically linked to his army, then her power would have been far more localized. No need to tell them that, though.

"You killed three hundred monsters?" Volker pointed at the humanoid form. "That looked like that?"

"About three hundred. We haven't collected all the bodies yet." Sabrina tapped her chin. "They didn't all look the same. This was probably the least scary of them, in appearance. One was like a mutated T-rex. Maybe not quite as big. I fed the head of it to Krakenessie."

She *technically* hadn't killed it. But she didn't need to say that.

"T-rex?"

"What is a 'Krakenessie'?"

"Size of a dinosaur?"

"This has not simplified things," Dannika muttered.

"Show them," Sabrina said.

Uncle Max handed out a series of photos, some of headless corpses, and others, of bodies that had simply dropped to the ground after Sabrina had dragged their spirits into the phantom realm. Her uncle nodded toward the trestle table. "Ysabeau will have forwarded you the pictures by now."

"They appear to be amphibious," Lady Gabriella murmured.

Rowe pointed at an image offscreen. "See? There is kelp."

"You are trying to tell me you killed *three hundred* of these…creatures?" Odin demanded after staring off camera while he'd studied the pictures.

Sabrina fought the urge to roll her eyes. "Yep. All at the same time."

The god's eye narrowed.

"I do not believe you." Empress Asbesta demanded. "You are human. You do not have the power to kill so many at once. Are you trying to claim credit for the vampire hybrid's kills?"

"No. Ysabeau St. Clare was there. Members of the Portal Watch were there. They saw it happen. Surely your representatives told you as much?" She looked toward Volker, then the Fire and Fluorite acting alpha.

They made noncommittal noises.

They don't believe me.

"And…I'm not exactly human." She clicked her fingers.

Between one heartbeat and the next, ghosts filled the room, creepy spirits of the dead creatures. Elias and Dannika remained in place, pre-warned this may happen. But the other leaders…even Councilor Hekate took a step to the side, unnerved, and she was a witch Sabrina was fairly sure could see the dead.

"What is…this?" The water goddess' mouth pinched as she took in the creatures milling around her feet. One even walked *through* her. Asbesta quickly moved to the side.

"These are the ghosts of the dead creatures. The ones I killed. *Only* the ones I killed."

The room was packed. She waved at the window, and more of the ghosts could be seen outside. There, at the forefront was the Lord. He came forward, as if he recognized some of the living. She clicked her fingers again.

They vanished.

King Volker's expression was serious. "*How*?"

Sabrina wiggled her fingers. "Magic."

A sound strangely like a snort came from Rowe, Air and Amethyst's Rebel Queen, but her expression was serene when Sabrina looked over at the mystical hologram.

The empress sighed, as if she was losing patience with the meeting. "If the threat has been conveniently extinguished, why did we need to come here?"

"Because they were the first wave," Sabrina said. "The scouts, if you will. They want access to the node of magic here. They came from the other side of a portal and were told the magic here was for the taking."

"And you know this how?" Odin asked.

Sabrina flashed him an evil smile. "Magic."

"Of course." But his mouth quirked slightly, as if he was growing amused by her antics.

"There are nodes everywhere." The Moonlight Wraith seemed contemplative.

"Yes, but this one is particularly powerful and strong. And it can...alter the people around it." Sabrina shifted one of her legs, until it was transparent, before shifting it back.

"You are saying it is responsible for the creation of your species?" Rowe asked.

"Partly."

"We need to vote on who can access this land, then," Odin said. "The portals' magic transforms humans, so we guard the portals. This should be no different."

King Vesperus frowned. "The British Isles are under my command."

"Loosely," Lady Gabriella said. "Your House's headquarters is in Scandinavia."

"It's mostly neutral territory." Hekate's voice was calm. "Courtesy of the portal at Giant's Causeway."

"The British Isles are an archipelago. They are surrounded by my waters." Empress Asbesta tilted her head to the side. "It would be nothing to ensure this node's protection."

Sabrina's mouth went dry, but she had predicted that this would happen, that the leaders would want to control her family's home, to take away their powerbase.

To stop the creation of more phantoms.

"The land should come with the phantoms," Elias interrupted smoothly. "Whichever House they choose to join will have the phantoms, and access to the node."

"What if they individually choose to go to different Houses?" the Wraith asked, rubbing his chin.

Elias smirked. "Then majority rules."

"Nonsense." The water goddess' expression was one of irritation. "You should not let a group of dead things rule such a powerful place."

Dead things.
Sabrina had heard that term before.

Elias shrugged one shoulder. "Let's put it to a vote. All in favor?"

Five hands rose—all but the empress and the King of Gold and Garnet voted yes. Kieran had warned her Vesperus would side against them on this, simply because it was his lands that were being forfeited.

"So, have your people made a decision yet?" the Fire and Fluorite Alpha asked.

"Yes," Sabrina said, trying to talk around the sudden lump in her throat. *Here goes nothing. Confident. Be confident.* "We aren't going to join any House."

CHAPTER 54

KIERAN

F uck. Sabrina was amazing.

Kieran's heart swelled with pride as he looked at his mate. She stood slightly in front of him, her shoulders back, chin tilted up, daring the House leaders to rebuff her. She was so beautiful it almost hurt, her ruby-red hair spilling over her shoulders, and her figure swathed in yards of the softest silk.

They had all thought he was the biggest threat in the room, other than themselves. They had been wrong.

He might be deadly, dangerous, but she was cunning, hiding it with irreverence.

That was much worse.

"You cannot refuse to join a House," Odin said smugly, as if he thought she were nothing but a simple child. "To do so is death for your kind."

"You'd have to be able to kill us first," Sabrina said, voice sure and even, despite being nervous as hell—he could feel it, even if it was just a faint glimmer.

The leaders glanced at each other, all except Blood and Beryl.

"These phantoms. Are they associated with the prisoner I sent you?" the empress asked Elias.

His uncle nodded. "Yes."

Kieran could feel Sabrina's emotions spike, her heartbeat speed up.

So could the other vampires.

Vesperus studied her, as if searching for what could have prompted the change in heartrate.

Kieran *probably* should have mentioned Douglas to her before now. There just hadn't really been the right time. *'Oh hey, your father? Yeah, I tortured him. Just a little. Adora—Queen Dannika's sister—cut his finger off. But it's all good. It regrew'.*

It was not a conversation he really wanted to have.

"All supernatural creatures *must* join a House. That is the law." The Moonlight Wraith glanced at his mate.

Sabrina nodded. "We *will* join a House. Just not one of yours."

"There are no other Houses, child." The empress laughed, the sound like crashing waves. "There have always been seven Houses, and there will continue to be seven Houses. All the leaders are here."

"We seek to create a new House." Sabrina met each of their gazes, her expression serious.

You could have heard a pin drop.

"That…cannot be done." The Fire and Fluorite leader's voice was uncertain.

"Technically, there's no rule that *says* there cannot be an eighth House." Elias appeared amused by the situation.

He had been shocked when Kieran had approached him about Sabrina's plan, but after they had showed him the creatures and their other evidence, he had agreed. Then he'd had Ysabeau look up the legality of the whole thing. The old vampire loved to play by the rules. It was how Elias had saved his mate's life the first time.

Lady Gabriella shook her head. "We cannot allow people to form Houses whenever they want. Even if this *could* be done."

"We would have to vote on their establishment," Elias agreed.

"They also have to offer something worthwhile. A new House must be strong, must provide members with security and safety," Councilor Hekate said. "And an affinity that is lacking. The current Houses are designed to cater to the elemental magic users, the blood drinkers, the shifters, those with esoteric leanings...and the mercenary." Her gaze lingered on the Gold and Garnet king at the end.

"The leader also must be powerful. One of the strongest of their kind. You do not have any suitable candidates." The empress shot them a pointed look.

Lady Gabriella looked thoughtful. "They appear to have won over the Shadow. See how he stands with her, rather than his uncle."

He didn't know whether to be flattered or insulted.

The water goddess flicked a hand dismissively. "I *said* 'suitable.'"

Ouch.

She wasn't wrong, but damn. Words could hurt.

"That is because they are mated," Vesperus said. "The scent is clear."

If only they knew the truth: that Kieran was one sentence away from being damned, or blessed.

Sabrina drew herself up to her full height. "Not Kieran. Me."

There were a few laughs, and certainly some scoffing. Kieran glared at any who dared make such a noise, and they quietened, seeing the murder in his stare. He might not be like Elias, or even Vesperus, but he was just as dangerous.

And he only had loyalty to a select few individuals.

Three of them stood here; and one of them was his mate.

He might have been Elias' shadow, but he had kept to the darkness because it suited him; because he loved Elias like the father he'd never had. But if he had to come forward to protect his mate, and if a few heads got taken in the process, it would be a fair price to pay.

So yeah, he was strong enough to rule, but he didn't want to.

"Even if you had killed three hundred monsters, that is nothing compared to the armies you might face as a leader of a House. Or the enemies within," the Wraith said.

"This girl was a ghost when I came here to meet their former leader," Hekate said slowly. "How did you gain a body? Steal one?"

"She was probably just in her spirit form," Lady Gabriella said.

The councilor shook her head. "No, she was a true ghost."

"People don't come back from the dead." That was Vesperus.

"I did." Sabrina shrugged. "Kieran dug up my corpse. I was long buried. Tamsin can attest to that."

"Tamsin." Hekate nodded at her subject, providing permission to speak.

"It's true. I told them how to do it," Tamsin said, coming forward.

"You do not have death magic," Lady Gabriella said. "Even necromancers have limitations when raising the dead. Aspen's sire could do it, but they didn't come back…right."

Kieran winced.

His father must have been even more unpopular than Kieran had realized, for them to be mentioning him years after Kieran had beheaded the asshole.

Tamsin shook her head, the beads and tiny bells in her hair clinking. "No, but I *can* see the future. I knew what to do from that."

"You know the future is subject to change; there are infinite possibilities." Odin frowned, the raven on his shoulder ruffling its feathers. "This is why I say seers should be regulated. They should not be able to act on their prophecies."

"Is it interfering if you see yourself doing something? And what happens if every future you saw had the same outcome?" Tamsin sounded contemplative, but Kieran had the feeling she was just talking in circles around the god.

"Dahlia has been muttering about houses and death for a few months now," Elias added. "We did not know what it meant."

The witch had also foretold Elias' mate—only it had been obscure enough that no one had realized what it meant, at the time.

The empress frowned and glared at Sabrina. "I think we need to rule that anyone who dies here needs to be cremated. The dead should not come back."

"I don't think that will be necessary. So far this seems restricted to my clan alone—a genetic quirk, if you will. And well, I was not as human as I assumed before I died." Sabrina opened her palm, and ghostly swirls of magic rose from her hand, tiny firefly-like dots circling the air above. A soft glow emanated from her skin, glimmering.

She was stunning.

She never ceased to amaze him. She'd managed to break through his shell as a mere spirit; had shattered and re-paired his heart as a flesh-and-blood woman. And now, now he reveled just being near her, watching her master abilities she hadn't even realized she possessed.

"God's spawn," the empress hissed.

"Goddess' spawn," Sabrina corrected. "Half-god, all phantom. I can pull people from the realm of the living into that of the dead. It is how I killed the creatures so quickly and efficiently."

She closed her palm with a snap.

The glow faded, slowly, her skin glistening, as if it had been sprinkled with diamond dust.

"I would like to see these abilities tested," Odin said.

"Are you offering yourself as a subject?" Sabrina smiled, the expression sly. The god sneered. "No, I do not care to take the life of anyone today. I have done enough killing for the week."

"The main issue I have with this plan is that your people cannot die." King Vesperus scowled. "Say you form a new House. If your people decide to attack mine, there is no balance. No justice."

"There is no such thing as true immortality." Sabrina waved her hand, and Kieran fetched the small box they'd stashed in the corner of the room. He lifted the lid, and presented it to the leaders, pass-the-parcel style.

Hekate glanced inside "This is a head."

Sabrina's asshole cousin had finally been put to good use.

"He was a phantom."

Empress Asbesta waved a hand, refusing her turn at taking the box. "We tried decapitating your kind. It doesn't work."

Sabrina frowned.

Yeah, he was going to have a lot of explaining to do later.

"You creatures killed one of your own?" Elias asked. He already knew the answer, but he was playing along.

Sabrina shook her head. "No, I did it. But to be fair, he killed me first."

The Fire and Fluorite representative pinched the bridge of his nose. "I am not following."

"Sabrina was murdered by her cousin on the eve of the commemoration over a year ago," Uncle Max said. "We didnae know. He brought her body home claiming thugs were responsible. We believed him. Then, after she returned and killed the creatures, he attacked her again."

"How exactly did you kill him?" Vesperus raised an eyebrow, cynical.

"Tsk. You think I will give up our secrets that easily?" Sabrina wagged a finger. "However, in order to keep the balance, I am willing to tell three of the House leaders how to kill my kind under a blood oath. That way, they—and only they—will know how to do the deed. Whether or not what I did works for them, I don't know."

Odin nodded. "Then do it."

"Only if we get to form a new House. We offer the information as a way of ensuring balance."

Asbesta shook her head. "Then you should tell all the leaders."

"No. Not yet. Once my House is fully established, then I would be willing to review the number of leaders who know the information. But now, when we are weak? That exposes us to too much threat. Especially when some of you have already shown a desire to control the node."

"It is only natural we would want to contain something that has the power to grant immortality." The Wraith leaned forward slightly. "Tell me. What could you offer as a new House?"

"A place for those with an affinity for death," Sabrina said, earnest. "Phantoms. Death fae. Vampires. Witches. Some powers run darker than others."

"Many of those find homes within Gold and Garnet," Odin said.

Vesperus tilted his head. "It can be an…uncomfortable fit. Some trade their wares for profit, but the death dealers struggle with our ways."

"One last thing," Sabrina said, and bent down to pick up the fabric at the creature's feet. She unraveled it, revealing the crest of Sea and Serpentine.

Each of the leaders stared.

"Where did that come from?" Vesperus' voice was sharp.

Sabrina let her arm drop slightly. "The creatures."

"They appear amphibious, and they come bearing your House's crest." Elias turned to Asbesta. "Were you planning on taking this land?"

The goddess smiled, serene. "I had nothing to do with it."

"Then where did they come from?" Vesperus asked smoothly.

"You said they came through a portal," the empress said to Sabrina. "It could have been any of them."

"Clearly, the most likely is the Pacific Ocean portal," the Fire and Fluorite leader said. "It is underwater."

"And guarded by members of the Portal Watch," Asbesta countered.

Lady Gabriella frowned. "Who are mostly aligned with your House."

"Are you accusing me of setting these creatures upon these people?" Asbesta appeared amused for the first time. "For what gain?"

"The node," Sabrina said.

"Child, there are plenty of nodes under the sea. I do not need yours." But something flashed in her dark gaze.

"This gets us nowhere," the Wraith interrupted. "Even if Asbesta *did* send these creatures, she would never admit it." The empress went to speak, but the Air and Amethyst leader ignored her. "*None* of us would admit it."

A pause before the leaders all nodded.

"So," the fae continued, "I say we stop with the nonsense and get to the point. All in favor of this woman—wait, what is your name?"

Sabrina's eyes flashed. "Sabrina Fhearchair, Baroness of Invercauld and Omnalprie, and Chief of the Fhearchair clan."

"—of the baroness forming a new House and taking the British Isles as their home seat, raise your hand?"

"What about the other territories?" Lady Gabriella asked.

The Wraith glared.

Elias spoke. "We can divide them up later. As a new House they will be given minimal territory as they would not be able to guard it all anyway. We can always decide how to redistribute things later. Some of us might welcome giving up troubled areas of land."

The answer was smooth and practiced, and Kieran could tell some of the rulers were unsettled by the idea of giving up territory. But borders changed, that was inevitable, even in peace.

"Shall we vote?" the Wraith demanded.

Elias was the first to raise his hand. That was no surprise, and none of the other leaders even batted an eyelid.

Hekate soon followed, her eyes on Tamsin, not Sabrina. *She must trust the other witch.*

Vesperus raised a single eyebrow, then also put his hand up.

Three.

They only needed one more for a majority.

No one shifted.

"It does not appear—" the empress began, her expression smug.

"Volker and I vote yes," Rowe interrupted.

Four.

Four out of seven.

She'd done it.

She'd created a new House.

"We will have to come up with a suitable name." Lady Gabriella shifted, her wings rustling. "It must be something momentous."

Kieran reached out, taking Sabrina's hand in his. He knew he shouldn't, that she wanted to stand in front of them, tall and proud. But he couldn't resist, drawn to her like a moth to a flame.

She accepted his touch, her fingers clenching around his.

"No need," Sabrina said, smiling, gaze flicking to Tamsin. "I've already picked one. Apparently, it was foretold."

"Do tell." Elias' words were dry.

"Death and Diamond. We shall be the House of Death and Diamond."

CHAPTER 55

SABRINA

Sabrina's back slammed into the wall of the hunting shack, the rickety timber creaking in protest. Kieran's body pressed against her, his hands skimming the curve of her waist and over her ribs, as he trailed hot kisses up her neck and along the line of her jaw. She wrapped her arms around his shoulders, pulling him closer.

"I thought that meeting would never end," he grumbled, his warm breath teasing over the shell of her ear, making her shiver.

"I was thinking about being alone with you the whole time they were arguing about territory rights," she breathed out. She shoved at his shoulders. "Why do you always wear too many clothes?"

He leaned back and grabbed his shirt, pulling it over his head before tossing it to the floor. "That better?"

She bit her lip. "A tiny bit."

"You can talk." Kieran leaned back, taking her sweater off and dumping it next to his shirt. "I could hear every dirty thought you had in that meeting. It was distracting."

"Good. I was thinking as loudly as I could." Sabrina raised an eyebrow, giving him a smile she knew would drive him wild.

"Get out of those pants," he growled, giving her space.

She shimmied out of them quickly while she watched him undress. Her gaze locked on his groin, on his already hard cock. She licked her lips, picturing taking it in her mouth, sucking him until he couldn't breathe. He was so incredibly sexy, and he was all hers.

The thought of belonging to each other set her nerves on fire.

Kieran stepped forward and grabbed the back of her thighs, lifting her up and pushing her back against the wall. Her core was pressed against his belly, and she wriggled in his grip, trying to inch lower, closer to his hard length. He kept her lifted, not giving her what she wanted just yet.

"Tease."

He grinned. "*You like it.*"

He wasn't wrong.

Throwing her hands around his neck, she pulled his face to hers. Their mouths met, hungry and demanding. Sabrina inhaled sharply as the tip of his fang sliced her lip, the sting welcome. He lowered her body against his as his cock twitched, brushing against her right where she needed it.

A deep rumble escaped Kieran's throat, and the possessiveness of it turned Sabrina on even more. Her blood did that to him. Hers. No one else's. The way that made her feel would never get old.

"Gods, you taste so good," he said against her mouth, his fingertips digging into her legs. "I want you to ride my face again. I want to taste every inch of you."

"Foreplay later. Fuck me now." She locked her ankles around his waist and rolled her hips, desperate to have him inside her. His tip touched her wetness, but it wasn't enough.

Kieran looked at her, his gaze burning with hunger. They held eye contact. And damn, it was hot. Her body grew slicker as his hunger turned feral. She felt powerful. Sexy. And turned on. So fucking turned on.

In a swift move, he lowered her body, shifting his at just the right time. He thrust upward, filling her completely in one long move. Sabrina's eyes rolled into the back of her head as she released a heavy sigh of satisfaction. "*Yes.*"

Kieran grunted, his grip on her thighs tightening. Her nails scraped across his shoulders, grazing his skin, and he pounded into her. *Yes.* He gave her exactly what she needed, knowing exactly how she wanted it. Rocking her hips to meet his thrusts, she moaned, throwing her head back against the timber wall, clinging to him as pleasure thundered through her with every stroke.

Then he stopped.

"What—?"

The world tilted and spun so fast she couldn't keep track. The next thing she knew, Kieran was lying on his back, and she was astride him. He was still deep inside her.

"We got interrupted earlier. And while the leaders squabbled after the meeting, you kept thinking about how much you wanted to ride me…"

She lifted her hips slowly, so slowly, until only the head of his cock was within her. He stared at her, mouth swollen and lips parted, waiting for her to move. To decide what was going to happen next. Did she want to take it slow? Or did she want to go fast?

She plunged downward, taking him in one quick movement.

"*Fuck.*" His voice was a strangled groan.

He surged up, cupping her face in his hands as he kissed her. He drove into her as she moved, finding a rhythm they could both keep. Her wetness coated the space between them. With each wild rock of her hips, she found friction against the sensitive nub at her center, rubbing it over and over again. Tingling spread through her legs as she sat on the edge of release. His teeth grazed her lip again, and she jerked, grinding hard against her clit. Her orgasm raced to the surface, catching her by surprise. "Kieran!"

Ecstasy poured through her as her inner walls clamped down on his cock. His thrusts grew frenzied until all she could do was hold onto him; the pleasure so intense she could do nothing else. He shouted her name as his body shuddered while he exploded deep inside her.

Sabrina collapsed against Kieran's chest as he lay back down, her heart pounding like she'd just run a marathon. Her skin was slick with sweat, and her body thrummed in pleasure. She'd ridden him how she'd imagined when she'd first seen him—hard, long, and somewhat desperately.

He was still inside her, still hard.

And she wanted more.

More of him.

More of this.

He arched his hips, sending shock waves through her. She moved her hands so she could push herself back up, but Kieran wrapped his arms around her, pinning her body to his.

His voice was gravelly, rough from shouting. "Not quite yet."

She tried to tilt her hips, but he moved one hand down, stopping the movement. "But—"

"We have a little situation here we need to sort out." He slapped her on the ass, hard enough to sting, but not hurt. Never hurt.

Sabrina reveled in the sensation.

She lifted her head, expecting to see a wicked smile. Instead, his gray eyes were serious, and she couldn't sense much through their bond; their connection had grown slightly weaker in the past day or so.

Have I waited too long to claim him?

"What is it?" Curiosity made her pause.

"If this is going to be our little private getaway," he used his free hand to indicate the ramshackle hunting lodge that was covered with more dust than her apartment had been, "We really need to talk about redecorating." He angled his hips, sliding deep within her, wrenching a moan from her. "The furnishings suck. I don't even know what's poking me in the back."

She let out a surprised laugh and then stilled; now it was her turn to be serious. "We *do* need to talk. There is something we have to address. I never accepted you...but you accepted me..." her voice trailed off.

Kieran closed his eyes briefly then he gave her a lopsided smile. "Well, uh, this is awkward."

She frowned.

He ran a gentle finger over her cheek. "You did accept me. I mean, you didn't say it out loud, but when we fucked on that resurrection stone? We both accepted the bond."

"We *did*?" She hadn't known that. She thought you had to say it out loud…

"I can show you how we did it—" His hips thrust and for a moment—a wonderful moment—Sabrina lost herself to the sensation, to the pleasure.

"Wait." She shoved him back again. "We should do it officially. Make it proper."

"Okay. Sure. Later—"

She growled. "Now."

Kieran glanced to the side, like he was nervous. "There is one thing you should know first."

"You don't have a vampire STI, do you?" she asked, teasing him. She was pretty sure that wasn't even a thing.

At least, she hoped not.

"What? No." He shook his head but smirked in amusement.

"Well?"

He took a deep breath. "Your father. He's alive. Blood and Beryl have him."

She blinked down at him.

Then she swatted his chest. "You tell me this, *now*?"

"Uh, yeah?" One dark eyebrow rose.

"In the middle of sex. You bring up my father."

His cheeks turned the faintest shade of pink. "You're the one who wanted to talk. To do it 'properly'. I just thought you should know that before."

"I already kind of suspected," she admitted. Who else could Sea and Serpentine have tried beheading?

"Then why didn't you ask about it?"

"Because we are having *sex*. And I really don't want to be discussing my parents in the middle of it."

"Fair call." He chuckled, the sound causing subtle movements in important places.

Sabrina nibbled her lip. "I just have one question."

He cupped the side of her face. "Ask."

"I don't want fate to make this decision for us. I want you to want me, for me."

His voice roughened. "That is not a question."

"If I hadn't accepted you through sex, would you still want me?" Gods, how stupid did she sound?

Kieran went still and closed his eyes. "I wanted you when you were dead. I didn't know you were my mate then, and I helped you come back to life." He exhaled and opened his eyes. Her heart ached. "You just managed to create a new House. You negotiated with the most powerful people in this world and won. How could I *not* want to be with you?"

"I—"

"I would want you if fate said you weren't mine. I would choose you."

The last tiny resistance within her faded. She'd wanted him from the moment she'd first seen him. Had laughed and been delighted in everything about him. Sure, he had homicidal tendencies, but so did she, she'd learned.

He was the midnight to her twilight.

She traced a finger over his lower lip. "I love you."

"Oh? Tell me more."

She laughed; the sound free. "That's a great 'I love you, too'."

Kieran flipped them, so her back was pressed into the lumpy camp bed. *What the hell is jabbing me in the back?*

They were still joined, still together. He kissed her nose, the touch light, affectionate. "I love you, from the freckles on your nose, to your snarky attitude, and to your crazy powers."

She pursed her lips. "I am not snarky. And I don't have freckles."

She reached up, running a hand over his jaw, the stubble rough against her fingers. She marveled in the sensations; that she could touch, could feel again. And that she was touching *him.* "I accept you."

There. She'd officially said it.

The bond between them, it flared white in her mind, glittering and as strong as a diamond.

Mates.

Together.

Always.

CHAPTER 56

KIERAN

Their mating ceremony was going to be ridiculous, Kieran thought. But now that Sabrina was leader of a new House, and he was her consort...

It had to be big.

The bigger the better, according to Elias.

Damned traitor.

His uncle had simply done the traditional ceremony when he'd mated Danni, but no, Kieran had to go through a pageant-worthy event. Even Elias' mother had gotten involved in the planning, and she rarely stirred from Italy. It humbled Kieran, to see he'd been truly adopted into the family, even if his stepfather still refused to accept him.

There was a reason why Kieran's mother and stepfather had been given a remote piece of Blood and Beryl to manage. Even Elias couldn't stand his brother.

They had invited all the leaders of the other Houses, most of whom had accepted. Empress Asbesta had politely declined, as had Fire and Fluorite. But the shifter had issues of his own to deal with, so no loss there. And the sea goddess? Also not surprising.

And no loss.

She was probably still pissed she'd missed out on taking control of the node. She also tended to avoid dealing with land dwellers in general.

The ceremony was set to start in a few hours, under the light of a full moon. They would officially mate under the glow of a Frost Moon—and a lunar eclipse. The orb would glow bloody and red above them in the night sky while they spoke their vows.

Fitting, he thought. Sabrina had been brought back through blood and magic. Killed under the light of an almost sacred moon.

He looked out the window of the study that had been assigned to him. He was back at Braemar Castle; they both preferred the defenses there, and it felt more like…home.

Despite the creatures' attack, and those damned secret passageways.

"My debt to you is paid."

Kieran turned toward the voice. King Vesperus. The vampire stood just inside the doorway, looking formidable in a tailored suit.

"Debt?" Kieran quirked an eyebrow.

"Your biological father. He was part of my House, and he dishonored you and your family not once, but twice."

"I figured you turning a blind eye to my killing him was enough."

"Not to clear the debt," the king said. "But my vote has restored the balance."

He had wondered at the Gold and Garnet king's motivation. Now it made sense. Vesperus followed the old ways, Elias had said. Now Kieran knew what his uncle had meant.

"Then I thank you for clearing the ledger," Kieran said. The vampire king nodded.

A moment later Elias strode through the doorway, pausing when he spotted the other monarch. "You two finished talking?"

"Yes."

"Good. Here." Elias waved a hand.

Douglas stepped into the room behind him. The man was thin and tired looking, but whole. "Here's your mating gift."

"That is a rather unusual mating gift," Vesperus murmured, his cruel mouth tilting into a semi-smile.

Elias nodded, the picture of amicability. "It's his father-in-law."

"You are giving him his father-in-law as a gift?"

Douglas' eyes narrowed. "Funny."

Yeah, Kieran could understand the other vampire's confusion.

"What did the empress have to say about it?" Kieran asked. Technically, Douglas was *her* prisoner.

"She said she wanted 'it' back," Elias said, "but I pointed out how this could strengthen the alliance between Death and Diamond and Sea and Serpentine after that unfortunate misunderstanding."

"There is no alliance." Kieran's voice was flat.

"For your sake, I'd pretend there is," Vesperus murmured. "These islands are surrounded by Serpentine's waters."

"Is that advice free, or will it cost me something?" Kieran asked.

The Gold and Garnet king's gaze flashed. "I had heard that Blood and Beryl have acquired a phantom for themselves."

Charlotte Muick, Sabrina's cousin. She'd been furious at the discovery Colin had been working with Angus; even more so when she'd learned Douglas had been used as bait. She didn't take the betrayal lightly, had been enraged at the dishonor.

It didn't mean a lot to Kieran, but it meant a lot to her.

She'd decided she couldn't stand looking at the faces of her family—family who had turned a blind eye to murder and mayhem. Now Sabrina was in charge, Charlotte had felt comfortable leaving their little sister in her hands, and she'd chosen to go to Blood and Beryl, living under a shifter queen.

It was a good fit for her, he thought. Ysabeau had certainly noticed her before and been impressed, which was saying a lot. He even kind of liked Charlotte, too. And it would be good to have allies in the other Houses.

"I can ask the clan if anyone would be interested in joining Gold and Garnet," Kieran said eventually.

Vesperus nodded. "Excellent."

Kieran turned to Douglas. The phantom had been waiting patiently, but his gaze narrowed when he focused on Kieran. "*Ye.*"

Kieran shoved his hands in his pockets and rocked back on his heels slightly. "Me!"

"I take it ye two know each other?" Max stood outside the room, peering in. He'd become Sabrina's second-in-command, along with Tamsin, and was well-suited to the role. He'd even managed to recruit the two Portal Watchmen who'd been sent here to track the creatures, as well as the doctor. Humans weren't normally part of a House structure, but the man had been hired as a 'consultant'.

Max somehow managed to squeeze into the room and approached his brother. He crushed Douglas in a tight hug, which the other man reciprocated before pulling away. "He tortured me," Douglas said flatly, looking at Kieran.

Kieran winced. "Just a teeny bit. Barely anything at all, really."

A death stare. "Ye cut off my finger."

"That wasn't me. That was Adora. *His* sister-in-law." He pointed at Elias.

"Why throw me under the bus?" the Blood and Beryl king asked.

"You ordered him tortured in the first place! I didn't even use the ouchie-maker." Kieran threw his hands up in the air.

Vesperus mouthed 'ouchie-maker' behind Elias.

"Right. Well, let's get you dressed properly," Max said and ushered his sibling from the room.

"For what?" Douglas asked.

Max patted the former prisoner on the back. "Sabrina's mating ceremony."

"Her *what*?" They were already in the hall. "*Him?!* I thought they were joking!"

Eh, Douglas would adjust.

Kieran nodded at Elias. "Thank you."

He'd deal with the fallout later.

It was time.

○ ◊ ○

Under the glow of the Frost Moon, Kieran clasped Sabrina's hands within his. The red-tinted moon reflected in the black waters of the loch, eerie and perfect. They stood on a treeless outcrop above the lake, nothing but moonlight and ghostly fireflies illuminating the scene.

Sabrina's skin glowed ethereally, while her face was artfully made up, accentuating her lips and aquamarine eyes. She was so beautiful.

And she was his.

Mine.

She's all mine.

They had an audience in the cool fall air, but the watchers faded into the background, almost as if they were apparitions—there *were* ghosts, too, you just couldn't see them. They were going to have to hire a death fae to ferry them to the otherworld. Later.

Hekate moved forward, until she stood behind them, drawing him back to reality. To the moment.

The witch's voice rose as if she held a microphone, but she used nothing other than magic. "We are here today to witness both the creation of a new House, and the establishment of an alliance between Blood and Beryl, and Death and Diamond."

Sabrina's hands tightened on his, her smile wicked.

"Together," he said to his mate.

Forever.

MORE BY AMANDA PILLAR

The Heaven's Heart Series
Deadly Passion
Benevolent Passion
Winged Passion
Ascending Passion
Secret Passion (coming soon)
The Graced Series
Graced
Captive
Survivor
Bitten
Ashes
Freedom
Chosen (coming soon)
The Moonlit Hills series
Winter's Curse

ACKNOWLEDGEMENTS

When I was asked by Kel Carpenter to participate in the Immortal Vices and Virtues world, I was super excited and said yes almost immediately. We began throwing ideas around and I stupidly said, "I want to write a ghost romance!"

Remind me never to do that again.

Haunt Me is a big book. As Kel and Aurelia would say, it's a *girthy* book. And it was equally fun and challenging to craft—how do I write a sexy romance when one of the characters is *dead*?

I don't know. You tell me how it worked out, LOL.

But this book was also written during a challenging time. One of my children has been chronically sick, and we have been in and out of emergency departments, endless doctor visits, and a hospitalization. I've also been working long hours at the day job around caring for my family. My husband has supported me through this journey, giving me time to write and not complaining when I've spent too many evenings ignoring him, bent over my keyboard.

Finishing this book was difficult. Really difficult. During edits, my only biological uncle passed away and his funeral happened the same week I lost my 19.5 year old fur baby. Diving back into a book so focused on death was challenging, but I had a lot of support from Kel and Aurelia, who held my hand at times to help me through to the end.

I want to extend a thank you to everyone who supported me through this period. Ultimately, I am proud of this book and the journey I went on while writing it. It was tough, there were a lot of tears, but also a bit of laughter as I whipped out—what I thought—were killer one-liners. Okay, there was more than a bit of laughter. My kids make me laugh every day, even if I have no idea what I'm amused about half the time.

So first and foremost, thank you Kel. Thank you for asking me to participate in this series, for listening to my crap, and reading the first draft and boosting my ego enough to cope with the edits. Thank you, Aurelia, for your patience and for helping me spice it up. And for reading scenes over and over until I was happy with them.

I also want to thank my wonderful proofreader Dominique Laura who read this so fast and who also spotted way too many typos, and my eagle-eyed editors Analisa Denny and Pete Kempshall, who, as always, picked up on things I wish they hadn't. I also want to thank Kaydence Snow, Amber Lynn Natusch, Lexi C. Foss, and Everly Frost for all those plotting chats.

And last, but certainly not least, my husband, Tom. Thank you.

ABOUT THE AUTHOR

Amanda Pillar is an USA Today Bestselling author and award-winning editor, who lives in Australia with her husband and two kids. She's the author of the unique Graced series and the paranormal romance adventure series, Heaven's Heart. She is busy working on her next book and has plans for many more to come, all with lots of snark. Because snark.

She has had over a dozen short stories published and has edited nine anthologies over the years. People say it's because she's an 'over-achiever' but, in reality, Amanda doesn't understand the concept of 'relaxation'. (Please feel free to explain it to her. Use small words.) Compounding this issue, Amanda also designs book covers and has commenced work on a PhD. Because she's crazy.

Oh, and in her day job, she's an archaeologist.

For more information and to join her mailing list, please visit:

http://www.amandapillar.com